Perfect Contradiction

Peggy Martinez

THIS book is a work of fiction. Names, characters, places and incidents are the product of the author's imagination or are used fictitiously. Any resemblance to actual persons, living or dead, business establishments, events or locales is entirely coincidental.

NO part of this book may be reproduced, scanned, or distributed in any printed or electronic form without permission. Please do not participate in or encourage piracy of copyrighted materials in violation of the author's rights. Purchase only authorized editions.

Perfect Contradiction
Copyright ©2015 Peggy Martinez
All rights reserved.

ISBN:978-1-63422-106-1
Cover Design by: Mae I Design
Typography by: Courtney Nuckels
Editing by: Kelly Risser

Life's a dance you learn as you go.

One

A Happy Occasion

Breathe. I knew this was coming. I knew I'd see him today. I'd been preparing myself for this for over a week now, but no amount of inner pep talks could have prepared me for the sharp pain beneath my breastbone when I finally saw him. *Just breathe*, I thought again. This was Beth's day, and it was going to be perfect if I had anything to say about it. There was no way I was going to let some jerk-faced, son-of-a-monkey's-uncle get me flustered because he decided to actually show his face back in Salem after four weeks without a single phone call. Never mind that he looked sexier than ever in a black tux that had been made to fit him, showing off his trim waist and broad chest, or that his dark brown eyes were staring directly at me as if he had only been gone for a day instead of a month. I narrowed my eyes at Hunter, and the bastard had the audacity to grin at me. Clenching my fist, I turned on my heel and stomped back into the house. Hunter's chuckle followed me inside, which only infuriated me more.

Beth glanced up from her seat in front of the vanity in my room as I entered, and her brows immediately drew together.

"What's wrong, Jen? Is it the flowers? The cake? Oh man, please tell me Matt's dad is going to be on time." Beth stood up from the vanity and wrung her hands. I felt like a donkey's behind for causing her distress on her wedding day.

"No, don't worry. It's nothing like that. Your day is going to be perfect." I walked over and smiled warmly at her. She looked so beautiful with her cheeks lightly flushed, her hair done up in a pretty, loose, twist, with baby's breath tucked into her hair.

"Are you ready to put your dress on?" I asked softly. Beth nodded and moved over to the bed. The dress was the very last thing we bought while shopping for everything for the wedding. Beth had begun to really freak out when we were only a week away from the wedding and still hadn't found the *perfect* dress for her. I'd even found my bridesmaid dress three weeks before.

I'd asked Beth earlier in the week to go with me to check out a little bakery that opened up in a neighboring town, and as a wedding gift, I took her to get a manicure and massage. Just a day to hang out and not stress about the wedding. We were walking around the historic district and laughing about a guy who'd flirted outrageously with Beth until he noticed her diamond ring, when Beth stopped mid-stride on the sidewalk with her mouth hanging open. In the window of a little boutique shop hung a dress that was meant for her. It was a beautiful gown that hung to floor with an overlay of antique lace. It was stunning in its simplicity. The gown had fit her to perfection. There were many tears shed and a whole lot of laughter on the way home.

Beth slid off her robe, and I smiled. She wore robin's egg blue lingerie, which suited her skin. I had the garter special made for her as a gift. The perfect touch was the tiny pair of silver cowboy boots added to the ribbon on the garter. Beth was going to wear her boots after all.

"So, everyone's starting to show up, huh?" Beth asked as I helped her step into the dress.

"Uh-huh," I answered. Beth fidgeted as I made sure her veil wouldn't get caught in the zipper of the dress as I closed it.

"Umm, anyone you want to talk about?" Beth asked as she caught my gaze in the mirror. I sighed deeply. She wasn't going to drop it.

"Hunter is already here and no, I don't want to talk about it," I huffed. Beth looked lost, like she should be trying to repair whatever had gone horribly wrong between Hunter and me, but how could she? How could *I* when I didn't have the tiniest clue what *had* gone wrong?

"Listen, there's nothing wrong. I just don't

want to let something so trivial ruin your big day." Beth turned to face me. "This is yours and Matt's wedding day, Beth. I couldn't be happier for you two, and I'm not going to worry about anything… except maybe making a fool of myself when I blubber like a baby later on." Beth laughed as I put my arms around her.

"I'm so glad I have you in my life, Jen," she said softly. I smiled and hugged her tightly.

"And I'm glad you're in mine," I whispered back. Pulling away abruptly, I ran a finger under my eyes. "Now don't get all mushy on me already; my mascara has to last at least until you walk down the aisle." Beth laughed and turned back to face the mirror.

"Looks like I'm ready to get hitched," she said nervously. Picking up our bouquets of daisies, whose stems had been wrapped in pale yellow ribbon, we walked over to the bedroom door. We could hear the wedding music from the backyard as it drifted up stairs. *This is it,* I thought. My best friend was about to get married, and then I'd be all alone again in my huge house. I shook my head to clear my thoughts.

"Well, let's get this done, I hear there's some mighty fine cooking waitin' for us at the end of this shindig," I said with a wink and an exaggerated drawl. Beth burst out laughing again, breaking through her nervousness. She nodded her head and without hesitation, we walked down the stairs of my family home side by side. I knew as we walked that things would change between us once she was married. At least a little. Maybe a lot. She wasn't the same person who only had one friend in the whole world. She wasn't the same little girl who was scared of her parents and of disappointing an all-seeing god. She had found her equal in Matt, though, and that was the only thing that cushioned the blow of losing my dearest friend so soon after she'd come home to me. Matt was a good man. He'd be a good husband and friend to Beth. Their happiness was almost a tangible thing, and you could almost feel the vibrations of their love in the air when they were together.

    They completed one another, and I… I envied them.

Two
An Intimate Affair

"Let's have a hug now that you're my sister," Hunter teased as he pulled Beth into a bear hug. She laughed loudly, and I could feel her happiness lifting my own spirits. Hunter had yet to speak to me beyond the expected, polite pleasantries since the wedding. He was most definitely avoiding me. Well, two could play at that game.

"How about it?" Matt asked. I turned away from my best friend as Hunter made her laugh again and faced Matt. "I think a hug from my bride's best friend is in order," he said as he pulled me roughly into his arms. Laughing, I hugged him back. I had gained a brother in this match and for that, I was grateful. He just better never hurt her or I'd make sure there'd be hell to pay.

"You better take care of her," I whispered fiercely into his ear.

Matt pulled back and tipped his imaginary hat at me with a twinkle in his eye. "Yes, ma'am."

I smiled broadly and stepped back as more hugs and a whole lot more laughing ensued. Matt's momma tried to keep her tears in check, but it was a fruitless endeavor for both of us.

The wedding had been an intimate affair, just the wedding party, which had consisted of the bride, the groom, myself as the maid of honor, Hunter as the best man, and Matt's cousin's little girl as the flower girl. Maybe forty other guests filled my backyard and garden to watch. It had been a simple ceremony, but it was so beautifully touching that I doubt there were many dry eyes by the time they kissed as husband and wife. Only a fool would've doubted how much love Matt and Beth had for each other.

I hurried off to the kitchen to see if everything was in order for reception. I wanted everything to be perfect for Beth and Matt.

My small kitchen was bustling and filled with several volunteers who'd agreed to help me serve the wedding guests. I slipped off my heels, glad to let my feet catch a break. I grabbed my apron off the hook on the wall and began micromanaging everyone, getting them ready to take the first wave of food out and set up the picnic-style luncheon before the guests headed to the huge tent. I was struggling with my apron strings as I ushered the helpers out the back door with their trays. Hands reached around and gently took the strings from my hands. I stilled immediately, my body thrumming from his nearness.

There was no doubt about who was standing behind me, his body heat enveloping my own.

"Let me help you with that," Hunter murmured near my ear. I stiffened as he tied my apron for me and stepped back. I turned slowly, my eyes traveling from the fine cut of his tuxedo up to find his eyes on me. He was soaking me in, for once not guarding his emotions as he devoured the sight of me standing there in my kitchen, barefoot with my momma's old apron covering my pretty dress.

"What are you doing, Hunter?" I asked wearily. The shutters came down once again, and he took another step back and loosened his stance into nonchalance. He shrugged.

"Just came to help you out. I'm not big on crowds." I raised a brow. So, he wanted to help me in the kitchen. That, I could deal with that. I could pretend like nothing had ever happened between us, that we hadn't spent the two most wonderful nights of my life in each other's arms. Pretend I hadn't suffered a broken heart because I thought we had something special between us. Yeah, I could do that. *Absolutely.*

"Alright," I said as I marched over to the overflowing counters and table. "Please make sure everyone sets everything up real nice out in the tent. The different assortments of finger sandwiches need to be arranged together, the potato salad, macaroni salad, and the marinated vegetable salad also need to be together," I snapped, my eyes on all the mini-cobblers I made for desert. I'd used my momma's recipe and baked them in individual, serving-sized, ceramic casserole dishes. They'd turned out so cute. I took out my shaker of confectioner's sugar and began dusting the top of each of the cherry cobblers liberally with the white powder.

"Look, Jen...." I held my hand up. He couldn't have it both ways. I waited for weeks for him to call me and let me know what happened. I was devastated when he didn't show up at my house the day I waited to hear from my doctor… the day I waited to find out if I had cancer or not. He hadn't even cared enough to call to ask me what the doctor said. I had to *assume* that Matt had told him I was cancer free.

"Don't worry about it, Hunter. I was naïve to think that what we shared meant as much to you as it did to me." I glanced up and held his gaze. "I'm done wracking my brain for a reason that would have made you leave me like that, waiting to see if you'd ever call me. I don't have it in me anymore to worry about having done something wrong," I finished softly as I dusted the next two cobblers.

"You didn't do anything, Jen." Hunter ran his hand roughly though his hair. "You could never...." The back door swung open, and the volunteers came in with smiles and laughter.

"Take all of those on the far counter this time and remember to keep everything together," I reminded them with a smile and thanks. They were gone as quickly as they'd arrived.

"Don't worry about it, Hunter. It's over and done with," I said quietly. He didn't look like he wanted to drop it. I pulled a huge tray of fruit off the table, pushed it into his arms, and gave him a shove toward the back door. "Make sure that gets to the tent, please," I said without waiting for an answer. The screen door shut behind him and I went back to work on my cobblers, making sure they were just right. By the time everyone was finished setting up the reception area, Hunter and I hadn't had a spare moment to ourselves. I was glad for it. Pulling my apron off, I dusted off my hands and slipped my heels back on. Time to eat and make sure the afternoon went as planned.

"I'd like to make a toast." Hunter's voice rose above the guests as he stood. Everyone quieted down, ready to hear what the best man, the groom's brother, had to say. "I'm no good at stuff like this, but I couldn't pass up the chance to give my brother a hard time in front of so many people," he said with a charming grin. Everyone laughed, and Matt just shook his head.

"I've made several promises to myself as I've grown older. For one thing, I promised myself not to worry about how charming my brothers got, because everyone in the Wright household knows that I got all the good looks." I smiled as the crowd busted out in laughter and jeers.

"I also promised myself a few serious things.

To always remember how important family is. To remember how much I look up to my father, my mother, and my brothers. To always strive to be the best man I can be and try to become even half the man that Matt is." Matt shook his head as Beth wound her fingers through his with misty eyes.

"I also promised myself to live my life never being envious of what anyone else has or has accomplished. I've stuck by that vow… until today." Hunter's voice lowered, and his eyes met mine as he continued his speech. "Today, I can see how finding that one person in life that you can't live without changes a person. They are good changes, changes that complement each other so perfectly that you realize the two people—the two souls—have in essence, become one. I envy what my brother has found with Beth, and I hope that one day, I'll have that. That one day, the person who completes me will give me a chance to make them as happy as Beth has made Matt." My eyes were wide; my heart thumping so hard I was sure it'd leap out of my chest. Hunter looked at Matt and put a hand on his shoulder. He raised his glass.

"To Beth and Matt and the hope they give us all," he said sincerely.

Beth wiped a tear away as everyone raised their glasses and chanted, "*To Beth and Matt.*"

The rest of the reception flew by in a flurry of dancing, laughing, and tons of well wishes for the new couple. The next thing I knew, we were all lined up in front of my house and throwing lavender buds at the couple as they headed to their truck to go to the airport. Hunter stood close by, and I made sure I kept my tears in check. Things were changing so quickly. Beth turned and waved over her shoulder at me. I smiled widely at her and waved back enthusiastically.

"Lord, I'm going to miss her," I said softly.

"She'll be back soon, and you two will be joined at the hip again before you know it," Hunter said from behind me. I kept smiling and waving.

"Everything will change now. She has Matt."

"Jennifer Collins, you seriously can't think you're being replaced," Hunter said, closer to me this time. I shrugged lightly, but he was right. I'd only had Beth to myself for two months, and now she was going to be gone again. Hunter bumped my shoulder with his. "You know a husband can never replace a best girlfriend, right?" I laughed out loud and turned my head to look at Hunter.

"What?" he asked with a little shrug. "It's a truth universally acknowledged," he said seriously. I nearly choked on my laughter. Hunter never ceased to surprise me.

I turned back around just in time to see something flying through the air straight at my face. Putting a hand out, I snatched Beth's bouquet out of the air just in the nick of time. Everyone was cheering around me, and Beth even winked at me before jumping up in the truck and taking off with a line of dented soda cans following in their wake.

    It figures I'd end up with the doggone bouquet.

Three

Suck It Up, Buttercup.

The next day came too early. I mumbled beneath my breath the entire time I was in the shower and all the way down the stairs. I looked longingly over at my coffee pot, but I had to resist. I needed to get some blood work done and check in with my doctor. I'd been putting it off too long already. I hadn't even told Beth I was going in today. I didn't need her worrying about me going by myself when she was on her honeymoon in the Bahamas. Sighing, I sat down at my kitchen table and sorted through the shoe box of bills. They were really beginning to pile up. I'd used a good portion of my momma's life insurance on the funeral and paying off medical bills. I wasn't exactly hurting for cash, but I didn't want to get to that point either. My momma had floated most of the bills when she was healthy by working two jobs when I was growing up. I was going to have to figure out what I wanted to do for income. I'd taken care of my momma for so long that I hadn't really put much thought into what I would do when she was gone.

I glanced around my kitchen and smiled to myself. My momma had been toying around with an idea several months before she got really bad. She'd thought about getting a small loan, then putting a bit of money into the house and renting out rooms. Turning our family home into a small, country bed-and-breakfast was one of her dreams. I thought about it as I stared out of the kitchen window with my chin in my hand. It would be a lot of work. It'd take some money. I did have five extra bedrooms and a ton of extra square footage. I could even do the baking, which I loved, for the boarders. Maybe even set up a small room in the house to sell baked goods. The more I thought about it, the more I liked the idea. Glancing up at the clock, I sighed. I'd have to think about it later; I didn't want to run late for my appointment.

Hurrying out of the house, I jumped in my little car and drove out of town, thoughts of the bed-and-breakfast spinning around in my mind as I went. When I got to the doctor's office, I had to remind myself several times that I wasn't here to hear any bad news—I was just here to run some simple blood tests and get a physical. I'd never been to the office by myself, and it was more difficult than I thought it would be. I took a deep breath and got out of my car. *I could do this.*

The staff all knew me by name, and I really did like every one of them, it was just hard seeing them, knowing I'd been there with Momma so many times when she was sick. The office was a difficult place for me to visit.

"Jennifer Collins?" I rose from my chair in the waiting room and followed the nurse to the back. She made small talk as she wrote a few notes down and weighed me. I'd gained four pounds since the last time I'd been to see them with Beth almost six weeks ago. She was happy to see me put on a few pounds. I hadn't even noticed, but I guess my clothes were starting to fit me again. They had started getting a bit loose when my momma died. She took my blood pressure, asked me how I was feeling, and then took a few vials of blood.

"Here ya go, Jennifer. There's a bathroom a few doors down. Just leave the cup inside when you're done, and I'll meet ya back in this room with the doctor when you're finished." I nodded and took my little cup to do my business. When I came back, I sat down in a chair and flipped through *Time* magazine. After twenty minutes passed, I glanced over at the door. The doctor was usually very prompt. I'd just begun to get concerned when the doctor and the nurse came back into the room.

"I was just about to go looking for y'all," I said.

The doctor smiled at me and asked me how I'd been since I last saw him. I told him that I was doing well, but I was still battling fatigue since the funeral.

"Jen, when was the last time you had a cycle?" he asked as he made some notes on my chart.

"Cycle?" I asked in confusion.

"Yes, your menstrual cycle, I mean." I blushed and glanced over at the nurse. She smiled at me in encouragement.

"Ah, let me think." I felt like such an idiot. Of course he meant menstrual cycle. I thought for a few seconds, trying to remember my last. So much had happened in the past two months, with my mom being so sick, the funeral, Beth coming home, her engagement, and the wedding. I frowned to myself as I thought. *When was the last time I had my period?* Then a flash of something lit in my brain. I hadn't had a period since right after the funeral. As a matter of fact, I was pretty sure my period had begun the day after the funeral, and that had been a little over eight weeks ago. I glanced up at the doctor.

"I'm not sure, but I think it had to have been right after my momma's funeral," I answered in a quavering voice. I wondered if I had stressed so much that I'd thrown my cycle off, or maybe something *was* wrong with me after all. My head felt fuzzy all of a sudden. I reached up to place a hand on my forehead.

"Whoa there, you okay?" the doctor asked as he sat his clipboard down. I nodded, but he was already kneeling in front of me and handing me a small cup of water the nurse had procured.

"This could be bad, right?" I asked after taking a sip. I glanced up into the doctor's eyes. He smiled.

"Well, that depends on your definition of *bad*, I guess," he answered after a slight pause. I looked over at the nurse, and she was smiling as well.

"What does that mean?" I asked softly.

"Jen, we'll need to send off for a blood test to confirm it, but according to the hormone levels in your urine, it is safe to say... you're pregnant." The doctor stood slowly, the smile never leaving his face. I blinked at him and then shook my head.

"I'm sorry, did you say...?"

"Pregnant. Yes, I did. Probably six weeks or so along, I'd wager. Congratulations." I smiled at him and sat there while he went through all the things I should do next. He gave me a list of obstetricians he recommended, told me to take it easy, he'd call with the blood test results, and to try out the prenatal vitamin samples he gave me, and so on. I just listened like I was actually paying attention, like my whole world hadn't been turned upside down.

I recall walking out to my car with a list of instructions and recommendations in my hand. When I sat in my car and put my seatbelt on, I knew my world had just been tilted on its axis. Still, I just drove home, in shock and disbelief. Pregnant? How could I be pregnant? I'd only been with one guy in the last two years and that was the two times I'd been with Hunter. Two times and we'd used protection. *Hunter*. What were the odds? My head started thrumming as I drove, and I had a full-blown headache by the time I pulled up to my house.

When I got inside, I headed straight upstairs to my momma's bedroom and curled up in her bed, covering my head with the handmade quilt my granny had made. Still, I didn't cry. I knew I was probably in shock. It would have probably been better if I had cried. Instead, I laid there for the rest of the day until night fell. And when night finally came, I took a shower and then crawled back into bed and... *slept*.

The phone was ringing again. I wondered idly how many times it had rang since that morning. Sighing, I rolled out of my bed. It was time to stop feeling sorry for myself and really think about what I was going to do. I hadn't eaten in a while, and now I had... a life inside of me to worry about. I placed a hand flat on my stomach. For the first time since I came home the day before... tears threatened. A hot shower and food were in order. As I washed my hair, the only thing I could think was how I didn't even know if coffee was bad for a pregnant woman. After that, the tears started flowing and I was powerless to stop them. I would've given anything for my momma's reassuring embrace right about then. Twenty minutes later, I wrapped myself in a large towel and trudged back into my bedroom. I pulled my most worn and comfortable maxi dress and cardigan out of my closet and slipped it on. After I combed all the tangles out of my hair, I walked slowly down the stairs to my kitchen.

I made myself a plate of leftover food from the wedding and slipped on an old pair of glasses as I sat down at the kitchen table to read over all the info the doctor gave me. There was no way I was putting my contacts in as red and swollen as my eyes were. *A baby.* I wasn't even in a relationship, and I was going to have a baby. I had no source of income, and I was going to be a momma. Dear lord, what was everyone going to say? I groaned and stared at the papers. What were my options? Should I tell Hunter? Should I consider adoption? So many questions. I didn't know anything, and what if I'd hurt the baby taking medicine I shouldn't have? Or drinking the champagne the day before yesterday at the wedding? My hand flew to my midsection, and I jumped out of my seat to grab the phone off the wall. I dialed the obstetrician's number and all but hyperventilated by the time someone picked up.

"I just found out I'm pregnant, and I had champagne two days ago. Will that harm the baby?" I blurted. The receptionist on the other end asked me to calm down and give her some of my info. Before I knew it, I had an appointment for the next week and

I was reassured that a little alcohol had never been proven to hurt a baby in utero. When I got off the phone, I was feeling a little less panicky, at least as far as harming the baby was concerned. I had so many decisions to make, and I knew none of them were going to be easy. A knock on the front door brought me out of my thoughts.

Pulling back the curtain sheers, I glanced out the window and found Hunter Wright standing on my porch, a hand running through his hair in agitation. I took a deep breath and ran a hand over the skirt of my dress before opening the door.

"Hunter, what can I do for you?" I asked, my heart pounding too loudly in my ears. His eyes widened, and I cursed myself for not realizing how I must look.

"What's wrong?" he asked as he pushed into the house. I stepped back with a sigh and stared at a spot over his shoulder.

"Nothing. Everything's okay," I answered.

"Like hell it is," he snapped. "Beth said she's been calling you all morning to let you know they made it okay like she promised she would, and she said you weren't answering. She got worried because you *always* answer." He put a finger on my chin and turned my face until I had no choice but to look at him. "Why have you been crying, sweetheart?" he murmured. I pulled my chin out of his grasp and breathed in deeply.

"It's nothing I can't handle," I said softly. I wondered if I should tell him. What would he say? Deny it was his? Worse, that he'd want to marry me because of the baby. I wouldn't be able to live with myself if I trapped him to me because of our baby. He was just the kind of man who would do something like that too. We might not have worked out as a couple, but he'd be a good daddy to his kid. A stupid tear escaped the corner of my eye, and I wiped it away furiously.

"Jen, talk to me. Tell me what it is you need." The way he looked at me nearly melted me. It made me want to throw myself into his arms like I had not so very long ago and let him share my burdens. But I couldn't. I wouldn't.

"I'm sorry I hurt you. I never meant to," he said gently. "I wish I had a *redo* button so I could make it right between us." I nodded and stepped back out of arm's reach. He dropped his arm back to his side with his hand clenched into a fist.

"I never should've run," he muttered. I frowned in confusion before shaking my head and stepping toward the door.

"I'll call Beth right now," I said, trying to summon a smile. "And, ya know, if you'd like to help me, perhaps you could recommend a handyman. Someone who can help me do a little remodeling in the house. I'm going to open up a business, and I'll have a lot of work to do," I said, proud of how steady

I sounded.

"A business?" he asked.

"A bed-and-breakfast." I watched him as he looked around the house, and then turned back to look at me with a small smile.

"Yeah, I can see it. And with your amazing baking, it's sure to be a huge success," he said sincerely.

"I hope so. I'm going to need the income," I answered. A little voice of doubt inside kept whispering how I'd never make it work. How was I going to open a brand-new business all on my own while I was pregnant? And what if I kept the baby? How would I be able to take care of it and run a business at the same time? Just the day before, I'd been only concerned about myself and what I was going to with the rest of my life and suddenly, I was responsible for another life, another tiny, helpless human. Someone who'd have to depend upon me for everything.

"Well, if you're sure you're alright, I'll make some calls for you and get back to you later today, if that's okay?" I glanced up at Hunter, but I didn't really see him. My mind was off in too many different directions.

"Sounds good," I managed. I shut the door behind Hunter after he left. I had no idea if he'd said anything else; I couldn't concentrate on anything other than the need to go out to my garden, my little sanctuary, the little place I went to when I wanted to feel closer to God and closer to my momma.

The moment I stepped outside and felt the breeze in my hair and the sun on my face I could breathe just a little easier. I walked slowly through my garden until I came to the huge, old oak tree where a wooden swing still hung from its ancient branches. Sitting down, I pushed myself back and forth gently as I thought. Another breeze rustled the leaves of the ancient tree above my head. I craned my neck back until I was looking up into the branches of the oak where spots of blue sky and white, fluffy clouds peeked through. Letting my eyes fall shut with my face still to the heavens, I spoke softly.

"Lord, I know I have no right to even ask anything of you right now. I know this… *situation* isn't ideal, and it wasn't exactly planned or asked for. But, I also know that sometimes good can come from our mess-ups, and I know beyond a shadow of doubt that this baby isn't a mistake. I ain't gonna lie and pretend I know what to do or how I'm going to make this work, but if you'll just help me out a little down here, I promise I'll give it my all. I guess I just wanted to let you know I'm still in shock and still processing all of this, but I'm going to deal and I'd much rather deal knowing you're watching out for me. My momma didn't raise no quitter, and she sure didn't raise me to wallow in self-pity when the going got tough. So, please kiss my momma for me, tell her she's going to be a grandma, and that I'm gonna do my darndest to make her proud."

I let my head drop forward as I opened my eyes. I wasn't sure how long I swung outside under that old tree, but when I went back inside later, my heart and my spirit were lighter. Now all I had to do was make those words truth. It was time for me to face the music and adjust my plans.

I was going to have a baby.

Four

Just Me & You, Kid.

A week later, I sat at my kitchen table after my doctor's appointment. I stared down at the picture the nurse had given me at my doctor's office. It was just a little blob, but I couldn't help but gaze at it in absolute awe. It was real… my own mini blob was now growing inside of me. Mini Blob, who was half me and half Hunter, had already stolen my heart. I popped a prenatal vitamin out of one of the five sample packages the doctor had given me and swallowed it down with a cool glass of iced tea. I stuck four of the packs deep into a drawer in the kitchen, and then put one pack inside of my purse. I was going to have to remember to take one every morning.

"Well, looks like it's just me and you kid," I muttered to Mini Blob. I tucked the picture inside of my purse with the pills and went upstairs to get ready to meet the contractor coming over in the next half hour. Dressed in a long, jean skirt and a striped, boat-neck shirt, I bounded down the stairs when the doorbell rang. I stopped long enough to make sure my hair was all contained in the claw I'd secured it with on the back of my head. Confident I looked halfway put together, I went to answer the door. When I swung it open, my mouth fell open in shock.

"Surprise!" Beth shouted over the voices on my front porch. I stood there, unable to understand what was going on. Beth laughed and wrapped her arms around my neck. "You might wanna close your mouth," she whispered in my ear.

"I thought you guys weren't due back until tonight," I said breathlessly. Beth shrugged.

"We didn't want to have to drive back from the airport at night, so we moved our flight up a bit." She smiled again and chuckled under her breath. "The look on your face was worth it," she said, suppressing a smirk. It wasn't easy for her.

"I'm so sorry, y'all. Please, come in. My manners disappeared there for a sec." I waved Matt, Hunter, and Mr. and Mrs. Wright in. "I was expecting someone else, or I wouldn't have stared like an idiot for so long," I said by way of explanation. Mrs. Wright walked over and air kissed my cheek.

"My dear, there's no way anyone in their right mind would think you were an idiot," Mrs. Wright said with a smile. I glanced over and realized the guys were all carrying casserole dishes. What in the world?

Mrs. Wright tutted beneath her breath. "I can

also see by the look on your face that my son wasn't exactly truthful with us when he said you knew we'd be coming." Her glare at her youngest son was the kind that would have made a lesser man shrink back, but Hunter just grinned hugely and winked at his momma.

"Now, Momma, I said she knew she was going to have company and that she'd be meeting with a contractor," he explained. "I just didn't mention she didn't know *we* were the company *and* the contractors." He shrugged. My mouth fell open. Son of a… I couldn't let this happen. I felt panic rising inside of me. Spend weeks on end with Hunter and his family in my house, all the time, while being knocked up with his baby? *Impossible*. I tamped down my horror and called on my years of deep-rooted southern hospitality, pasting a smile on my face.

"Let's get these dishes to the kitchen, and I'll make y'all some drinks." Hunter flinched, and Beth frowned. Maybe I needed to work on my acting skills. I led the group to the kitchen, helping Beth and Mrs. Wright set out all the food on the counter and put the banana pudding away in the fridge. The guys went to take a look around the house while we set up lunch and drinks.

"I'm sorry about this, hun. If I'd known that boy wasn't being straight with me, I'd never have let him do something so boneheaded," Mrs. Wright said with a shake of her head.

I took a breath and smiled. "Oh, don't worry about it. I'm glad to have y'all here. Really." My smile was genuine this time, and Mrs. Wright smiled back. It wasn't her fault, and I really enjoyed the company of the Wright family. No, Hunter was to blame and he was going to get a piece of my mind as soon as I could get him alone.

"So, how did your doctor's visit go?" Beth asked over her shoulder. My eyes widened, and I nearly dropped the ice trays I was taking out of the freezer.

"My doctor visit?" I squeaked. Beth caught my gaze and then rolled her eyes.

"Did you think for a second I didn't know you were going to see your doctor as soon as I went on my honeymoon?" she asked as she unwrapped a dish of steaming mashed potatoes. Right... my regular appointment. I cracked the ice trays and started filling glasses.

"It was fine. I told ya it was going to be nothing to worry about." Smiling, I turned to face the glasses I was filling. I hated lying to her, but skirtin' the truth was unavoidable. I was a horrible liar, though, and even worse at keeping secrets from my best friend. I was going to have to tell her soon. I just needed to figure out how to do it... and how to keep her from telling Hunter. I sighed and both Beth and Mrs. Wright glanced at me, their brows both quirking up in concern. *Dagnabbit!* I bit my lip and started pouring the sweet tea.

When we were all seated around the picnic table in my backyard, Pastor Wright gave thanks and then we all passed around the food dishes. Piling potatoes and fresh salad on my plate, I took a roll. When the BBQ rib platter came around, I nearly ran from the table. How awful was it that my absolute favorite food now turned my stomach? Instead, I tried not to breathe in as I quickly passed the plate to my right. Beth's mouth dropped open. She knew how I felt about BBQ. I could put it away like a dude on my worst days and out-eat most guys on my best.

"I'm staying away from meats for a little while." I shrugged and then bit into my roll, hoping she'd just chalk it up to me trying out some new low-protein diet or something.

"I hope you're not dieting, Jen. You look so much healthier than you did when I first got back to Salem," Beth said, her eyes watching me too closely.

"You look perfect, Jen," Hunter said in agreement. "You definitely don't need to lose weight." I snorted when I thought what they would think of my weight in a few months when I looked like a beached whale. Everyone at the table stared at me. Snorting was definitely *not* the correct response to their comments. I stuck my fork into my salad.

"Y'all let her alone. She knows herself more than anyone else here, and she knows what she's doing." Pastor Wright winked at me, and I smiled back in thanks. I popped a sliced of radish in my mouth and nearly moaned. Were radishes always so tasty?

"So, Jen, what are you thinking as far as changes in the house? A bed-and-breakfast will be a welcome edition in Salem, I'm sure of it." Matt waited for me to answer.

"The wood floors need refinished. I'd also like to make the small sitting room that's near the dining room into a small bakery shop with a swinging door between it and the living room. All three bathrooms need to be completely redone, and all five of the bedrooms will need fresh paint, beds, linens, and such. I also have some changes I want made in my room." I glanced over at Beth.

"I hoped you and Mrs. Wright would help me find all the right stuff to decorate the rooms. I'm thinking each room needs a special, handmade quilt, and then we can decorate the rooms to match." Beth grinned, and Mrs. Wright seemed surprised and pleased that I'd ask her to help me with the decorating. Truth was, I didn't like to shop, but I did love my home, and I believed the little, special touches would make a big difference.

"I'd be glad to help," Beth answered.

"Good. I already applied for a business license, insurance, and all that other boring stuff, so we have a green light to begin whenever. You guys are standing on the property of the brand-new *Countryside Inn and Bakery*," I said with a huge smile. Everyone just stared at me, seeming shell shocked.

"What?" I asked after a sip of tea.

"I didn't realize you'd done so much while we were gone," Beth said breathlessly. "Wow, you don't waste any time when you make up your mind," she said with a laugh.

"Congratulations, Jen," Matt said, smiling ear to ear. Everyone else congratulated me and peppered me with questions and suggestions. The day was perfect, and I was actually sad to see everyone prepare to leave later that afternoon. When everyone started heading to their vehicles and after Beth had promised to come over for a visit the next day, I noticed Hunter hanging back. I waved to everyone as they pulled away, leaving Hunter and me alone on the front porch.

"Hunter Wright, I should wring your neck for pulling this," I said with a sigh. I glanced over at Hunter, who in didn't look sorry. Not one little bit.

"Come on over here and sit with me, sweetheart," he said as he took my hand and led me over to the porch swing. I sat next to him reluctantly. I was bone tired. Every afternoon, I got super tired… and now I knew why. Growing a baby took a lot of work.

"I'm not sure this is such a great idea, Hunter," I said softly. I glanced up into his eyes and found him studying me. "I mean, I love your family and I enjoy having them over, but I don't know that us being thrown together will be a good thing."

"You love my family?" he asked. I blinked. *Did he not hear anything else?*

"Of course I do. Your family is great," I snapped.

"Just my family?" he asked softly, watching my lips. I gulped and suppressed the need to lick my lips nervously.

"Don't ask questions like that, Hunter," I murmured, my eyes drawn to his lips against my will.

"Why not, sweetheart?" he asked, his lids lowered and his voice becoming husky with desire.

"It's not fair to ask me things like that now," I answered on a whisper. His hand raised and gently swiped a stray hair back, tucking it behind my ear. He cupped his hand behind my head, angling my face toward his.

"No one ever said love was fair, babe," he murmured as his lips brushed mine softly. My treacherous eyes fluttered closed and my hands came up to rest on his chest as his lips pressed fully into mine, his lips coaxing a small moan from me. My head kept screaming for me to stop the foolishness. I was kissing a guy who'd left me high and dry when I'd needed him the most. My heart tried to shut out my head. I had fallen in love with Hunter a long time ago, and I felt like everything was right when I was in his arms. Eventually, though, my mind won the battle. Pushing myself out of Hunter's arms, I stood up from the swing. I didn't have just myself to worry about anymore. I needed to keep a clear head so I could make the correct choices for myself, but more importantly… for Mini Blob.

"No, I guess they didn't," I said after I had a moment to gather myself together. Hunter stood and shoved his hand in his pockets.

"Jen… please give me another chance. I'm a moron, and I screwed up. I should have been here for you when you thought you had cancer. I should have been here holding your hand."

I turned to face him. *No. Don't.*

"I freaked out after you told me you might be sick… finding out that I might lose you." His eyes begged me to understand.

I died a little inside.

"I won't bother you with the *whys* of my freak out, but I realize now that I hurt you deeply when I left. I just didn't realize until I came back just why *I* was hurting so bad when I left." He captured my hand in his as he continued. "Only one thing has the ability to make you feel like heaven has landed in your lap even though you don't deserve it, and a split second later hurt you so bad that you'd rather rip out your heart than to feel such pain ever again."

I began shaking my head. *Please don't.*

"Only love has that ability, Jen. I love you. I have probably since that first day at the fair when Beth came into town."

I pulled my hand out of his and wrapped my

arms around my midsection. He'd said everything I'd wanted him to. The words I'd longed to hear since we'd made love so many weeks ago. The apology I'd prayed for even up to the day of the wedding. But it was all too late. What if I took a chance on him and he decided he didn't want an instant family? What if I took a chance on him and he decided to bail on me once again after I had the baby? Whatever issues Hunter had, I would have been more than willing to deal with if it had only affected me. But it *didn't* just affect me now… it would affect the baby. I'd lost a parent when I was a little girl, and I'd lost a parent when I was an adult. Both were devastating, and I never wanted Mini Blob to have to deal with that. I would rather do it all on my own than to put anyone through the same thing. Stepping back, I met Hunter's pleading gaze.

"I'm sorry, Hunter," I whispered. "I don't think I can take that chance." His eyes widened and then shuttered. I was screaming on the inside.

"Can you tell me why?" he clipped out.

I lowered my head and stared at the floor. "I have reasons I don't want to talk about just now," I answered. I glanced up after he didn't say anything for a few moments. His jaw was clenched tightly, and his hands were balled into fists.

"I guess I deserve that," he said finally. He sounded defeated. My arm lifted to cup his face before I stopped myself and let it fall to my side. He walked over to the steps of my porch and went down them. It took everything I had to stay standing still and not run after him. He turned his head to the side, but he didn't look at me.

"I hope you have a beautiful life, Jen. You deserve happiness and love." And with that, he loped across the yard and got into his truck. I still stood on the porch long after his taillights faded down the street. When I had the strength, I walked into the house to take a much-needed nap.

By the grace of God, I didn't fall apart.

At least, not on the outside.

Five

Baby? What baby?

Beth came over as promised the next day, full of energy and excitement over the renovation plans and opening my business. I felt like such an old lady in comparison. I'd read on the internet the night before that my energy would start to return after the first trimester. I prayed that it would. I had so much to accomplish before I opened the inn for business.

"So what are you thinking as far as the quilts?" Beth asked as she browsed through one of the fifty copies of *Southern Living* and *Southern Décor* that she'd rounded up and brought over for us to get ideas from.

"I was thinking of doing one whole room in blue and cream like that set of plates hanging in the hallway," I said as I flipped through my own magazine. "And maybe a spring green and cream in another room." I glanced up. "I have no idea for the other three rooms though. Maybe one in a country rose color?" Beth nodded and wrote those on her list.

"You could do one to match a multicolored rag quilt. Kind of eclectic, but country and homey at the same time." I smiled broadly. I liked that.

"I have just the thing for inspiration too," I said as I stood. "I'll be right back." I darted up the stairs. Opening the linen closet, I rifled around until I found what I was looking for. I petted the handmade lap blanket and sank my face into it for a second, remembering all the love my momma had put into it when I was little. It still looked good... loved, but in good condition. Maybe it could find a place in a room, hanging over a chest or a chair. I smiled, making my way down the stairs and back to the kitchen.

"Do you remember this?" I said loudly as I came through the dining room. I stopped abruptly in the doorway to the kitchen, my heart stuttering in my chest. Beth stood at the table with my purse perched on top of it and opened. My prenatal vitamins, the pamphlets the doctor had given me, and my ultrasound picture were out on the table. Beth's eyes were wide as she stared down at everything.

"Your cell phone was vibrating," she murmured distractedly. I walked the rest of the way into the room and sat down heavily in my chair. Beth's gaze met mine. I smiled crookedly.

"Surprise?" I said half-heartedly.

"Jen? What? When? How? Who?" Beth rambled before collapsing into her own chair.

"Pregnant? Yes. Eight weeks ago. The old-fashioned way. As for who… I think you can figure it out." Gathering up the pamphlets and pills, I shoved them back into my bag. I picked up the picture of Mini Blob and sat it on the table in front of me. Beth still hadn't said anything, but I watched as a myriad of emotions crossed her face. I knew the moment she figured out that her new brother-in-law was my *baby's daddy*.

"Hunter!" She slammed her hand on the top of the table, fuming. I flinched. She jumped from her seat and began pacing across the kitchen. "Does he know?" she asked. I shook my head.

"And I don't want him to know either," I said vehemently. Beth groaned and continued her trek across the linoleum.

"When are you due?" she asked after a few minutes.

"Next March," I answered immediately. Beth stopped her pacing and glanced over at the picture on the table.

"I'm going to be an aunt," she murmured beneath her breath. I smiled at that. She grinned back and then came over to sit down next to me. "How long have you known?" she asked softly.

"Since the day after the wedding, when I went to the doctor." I shook my head ruefully. "I hadn't even realized I'd missed my period." Beth picked up the ultrasound picture and ran a finger over it.

"You're going to be a mommy," she said, her eyes going misty. My own eyes widened as I tried unsuccessfully not to cry. "And that means I'm going to be an aunt," she said once again. I hiccupped a laugh through my tears.

"What if I mess this up? What if I'm a horrible mom and I ruin Mini Blob's life?" I wailed.

Beth laughed through her tears and sniffed. "You will be an *amazing* mom," she said so sincerely that I started crying the ugly kind of tears. She came around the table and wrapped her arms around me. "You will do the mom thing better than any mom in the history of Mom-dom." I snorted and then sniffled. "I'll help you and we'll figure this all out together, Jen."

I nodded and took the paper towel she handed me. After I'd wiped my eyes and blown my nose, I tucked my picture back into my purse.

"And please tell me you didn't refer to my niece as *Mini Blob*."

"Hunter asked me to give him another chance yesterday," I said softly. Beth's eyes grew round. "He said he loved me and had made a mistake."

"Isn't that what you wanted?" Beth asked gently. I smiled sadly and wondered if everyone knew how I really felt about Hunter.

"It was… but now that I have Mini Blob to think about," I began, "I just don't know if I can take the chance that he'd leave once he found out about the baby, or worse, leave after the baby got here. You know… if things got tough."

"You know he's going to find out sooner or later, right? About the baby, I mean?"

I nodded. It wasn't like I'd be able to hide it for long. "I know, but I just can't tell him right now. I want to wait for the right moment."

"There may never be a perfect moment to tell him he's gonna be a daddy. But, you better just be sure you tell him before he finds out on his own."

I nodded and picked up the ultrasound picture. Tucking everything back inside of my purse, I sighed. "What will Pastor and Mrs. Wright think of me?" I whispered. "What will everyone at church say when I start showing?"

It was the first time I voiced my shallow concerns out loud. I hated the thought of people talking about me, maybe even thinking poorly of Hunter. I could weather the dirty looks and the wagging tongues, but I wouldn't stand for anybody bad mouthin' the Wrights or the baby. I put a hand on my stomach protectively. Beth put a hand on my shoulder.

"Don't you worry about that, Jenifer Collins. The Wrights are good people and if anyone has anything to say about you or the baby, they can come and talk to me," she said fiercely.

I smiled through my tears. I had no idea what I'd ever do without my best friend. Reaching out, I put my arms around her neck. "Thank you," I whispered.

"What are best friends for?" she answered. "What are favorite aunts for?" she added in for good measure.

I laughed and hugged her even tighter.

"Don't you worry one little bit, Jen. You don't have to do this alone. You have me, and I'll always be here for you."

For a moment, I truly believed everything was going to turn out okay.

Six

Renovations

The house renovations had been underway for a week before I thought I was going to lose my ever-lovin' mind. Everywhere I turned, there was a Wright in my house. Even Beth was technically a Wright. All three bathrooms were finished quickly, and the men were already working on refinishing the hardwood floors and hanging a swinging door between the sitting room and the formal dining room that was soon to be my little bakery. I didn't realize how tightly strung I'd become with Hunter and his family in the house every day until I finally snapped.

"Jen, all the upstairs and downstairs room have been painted. All we're waiting on is what color you'd like us to paint your room and what changes you want made to that small, adjoining room."

"I was thinking a pale yellow paint. Something really subtle," I answered over my shoulder as I chopped lemons and mint for the lemonade. Mrs. Wright and Beth were sitting at the table shuckin' corn for the evening meal.

"And I'd like to have the entire wall between my room and the adjoining room knocked down to enlarge my room," I answered, my eyes on my task. I tried to avoid talking to Hunter as much as possible, and I'd even tried not to look at him if I could help it without seeming rude.

"That seems like a big change," he said in a bit of a surprised voice. I glanced quickly over at Beth, who was trying very hard not to listen to our conversation.

"I need more space in my room," I answered softly. I glanced up quickly into Hunter's questioning gaze. He shrugged.

"You could use it when your business opens. If not as a small, extra guest room, then maybe for storing some of your momma's things you won't want anyone to use when the inn is open for business," he suggested in a perfectly reasonable voice. My reasonability must have fled days earlier. I swung around to face him.

"I don't need it as an extra room or as storage, *Hunter Wright*," I shouted. "I need my room to be larger. Is that such a horrible thing?" I asked, seething, my knife, still in my hand, dripping lemon juice as I pointed it at him. The entire room went silent, and I suddenly realized exactly how much I'd overreacted. I turned and found Beth's eyes wide, her mouth hanging open. Even Mrs. Wright seemed shocked.

"I'm sorry. I didn't mean to holler, y'all," I muttered as I threw the knife on the counter, wiped my hands on my apron, and pushed through the back screen door. A soon as I hit the fresh air, I began running. I ran out past the garden and clothesline until I reached the old oak tree in my backyard. Rounding it, I hid behind it as tears began streaming down my face. I couldn't do it. I couldn't have him in the house and not go insane. Wiping my eyes on the hem of my apron, I then wrapped my arms around my waist. I was barely two months along, and I was already feeling like everything was going to be too much for me to bear. What if I couldn't do it?

"Jen?" Hunter's voice was close. I whimpered and drew further into myself. My tears had at least stopped.

"Jen, what's wrong?" he asked softly. Concern radiated from his body. All I wanted to do was throw myself into his arms, tell him everything, and ask him to make it all better. Instead, I tightened my grip on my waist and shook my head.

"That's a load of crap, Jennifer Collins. I know something is wrong. I've never seen you so emotional. You're upset about something," he insisted.

I laughed, but the sound came out brittle. It wasn't a happy sound. "It's nothing I can't handle, Hunter," I said after a moment.

"Let me help you. Talk to me, sweetheart," he murmured, his hands coming up to caress my arms.

I flinched and pulled away quickly. I knew the instant I did it that I'd hurt him. "I want you to leave," I said softly as I stared at my feet.

"Jen… you don't mean that," he said roughly, his voice letting me know he couldn't believe what I'd just said.

I swallowed and took a deep breath before meeting his hurt gaze. "I do. I need you to leave, Hunter. I can't have you here." My voice sounded more assured than I felt. It sounded steady even though my heart was cracking on the inside.

He reached out a hand. "Jen, please."

I moved back a step and stiffened my back even though that single word *please* nearly undid me. "I'm sorry, Hunter. I can't. It hurts too much, and this is the way it has to be for now."

He stared at me for so long I thought he meant to protest again, but something even worse happened. Taking a step back, his eyes suddenly went cold and distant. He nodded once before turning on his heel and leaving me alone behind the old oak tree.

As soon as I heard the back porch door shut behind him, I sank down to the soft grass and cried. When I made my way back to the house a long while later, everyone was gone for the evening… everyone except for Beth.

"You okay?" she asked.

I walked over and sat down next to her at the kitchen table. "I told Hunter I didn't want him to come to the house anymore," I answered. Beth raised her brow, but she didn't seem shocked.

"I kind of figured. He lit out of here in some kind of a hurry with an impressive scowl on his forehead."

I groaned. "The Wrights are going to hate me," I said. Beth laughed as she handed me a tall glass of lemonade she must have finished for me.

"What?" I asked before taking a long drink.

"Jen, hun, the Wrights love you like a daughter. I guarantee they left here wondering what Hunter had done to you and how they could get him to make it up to you."

I shook my head. "I've made such a mess of things," I muttered.

Beth put a hand over mine on the table. "Don't fret over this, Jen. It isn't healthy for the baby, and the baby is top priority right now. Everything else will work itself out. Just you wait and see," she said with a smile.

I smiled back. She was right of course. I needed to focus on the baby and getting the inn up and running. I'd worry about everything else—like the Wrights finding out they were going to be grandparents, about Hunter finding out he was going to be a daddy, and about how ill equipped I was to raise a child—after things settled down. This was going to be the easy part. I just had to make sure I told Hunter before anyone else found out. And I had to make sure I did it before I was as big as a house.

I just needed a little more time to figure out how to break it to him.

"I can't believe you'll be opening in two weeks," Beth said as she pulled down the attic stairs. She was right. Weeks had flown by and yet, when I was at home alone at night, thinking about Hunter and the last time we spoke, it seemed to me that time was crawling by intolerably slow. I hadn't seen him since that afternoon when I'd asked him to leave and even though I knew it was for the best, I still missed him terribly. Not only that, but I was nearly out of my first trimester already, and I still hadn't gotten up the nerve to tell him about the baby.

"Earth to Jen." Beth waved a hand in front of my face. She was already halfway up the attic stairs. "You coming?" she asked.

"Yeah. Sorry, just wool gatherin' I guess." I climbed the stairs behind Beth. She had already begun sneezing. The attic was super dusty. Maybe I'd give it a good spring cleaning when I got a chance. *If I ever got a chance.*

"You've been doing that a lot lately," she said over her shoulder as she moved a few boxes out of her way.

I sighed and shrugged. "I know. I'm sorry," I answered.

"No need to be sorry, Jen. I just wish you'd let me in," she said gently. "I want to help you, but I can't if you don't tell me what's going on in that busy head of yours," she said, smiling.

"Mostly how quickly my stomach is expanding and how much longer I'll be able to keep it a secret," I confessed, joining her to move a couple of old coats and piles of quilts that had seen better days.

"You thought any more about how or when you're going to break it to Hunter?" Beth asked.

"Are you certain I should tell him at all?" I asked. "I mean, I could move to another state or join the circus."

Beth snorted. "Seriously, though, it's only going to get harder the longer you wait."

She was right, but that didn't make it any easier.

"I'll tell him soon. I was thinking of taking a little day trip into St. Louis to do some shopping for the inn in a couple of days. I'll go by and talk to Hunter then."

Beth stopped and looked at me. "Really?" she asked in a surprise.

I took the last box out of her hand and nodded. We both looked down at what we'd uncovered. I ran a hand along the side of the bassinet that had once been mine and smiled softly.

"Yeah. It's time, don't you think?" I asked.

Beth nodded. "It is," she agreed.

And just like that, I'd made a plan to head to St. Louis to visit Hunter in two days.

"Well, let's get this downstairs and cleaned up so we can stow it in your room," Beth suggested.

I smiled and got started. Beth knew it was better if I stayed busy. If I thought about it too much, I'd likely change my mind.

The bassinet cleaned up beautifully. I ran my hand over the carvings in the white wood. The cow jumping over the moon and the dish running away with the spoon. I rocked the bassinet with a large grin on my face.

"It's perfect," Beth said with a happy sigh.

I nodded and blinked furiously, refusing to let the water works begin *again*. Pregnancy hormones were hell on my mascara. "I think momma would've loved the thought of me using this basinet for the baby," I said after a moment.

"She really would have," Beth agreed.

"Now it just needs a fresh coat of paint, a new mattress, and a quilt."

"It'll look just like new." Beth began looking around my newly renovated room. The guys had done a great job. New paint, a new throw rug, and a part of the wall that led into the extra room knocked down, and my room was a lot more spacious... spacious enough to add a bassinet, a chest of drawers, and a rocking chair for the baby. It was perfect. We already had the bassinet and the chest of drawers. All I needed was to find the perfect rocking chair and finishing touches and I'd be somewhat prepared to add a little human into my life.

Now to tell Hunter.

Seven

Mud Pies & Fireflies

"Are you looking for anything in particular, hun?" I turned to the sound of the voice behind me and met the gaze of an elderly lady. Caressing the pink blanket in my hand, I smiled. I couldn't get the pink, of course, but it had been so pretty, with all kinds of intricate embroidery, that I almost considered it there for a second. I let go of the blanket and turned to the shop owner.

"I'm looking for a baby blanket. Something neutral for a boy or a girl and some bassinet sheets," I replied. I glanced around the store again. It had a lot of great things for decent prices. I spotted an old, large basket across the room and perked up.

"You know, I'm also looking for some things for my new bed-and-breakfast…." I said as I started walking. "Maybe I can find some good deals here." I said it with a questioning voice, hoping the shop owner might be willing to negotiate on some of the prices.

"Well, you just tell me what you have your eye on and we'll see what we can do," the older woman answered with her own knowing smile. I flashed a grin and headed in the direction of the beautiful basket. It would be perfect to display some of my homemade muffins in for the bakery.

After sitting a few items on the counter, I followed behind the woman to see the baby blankets she said she had. Most of them weren't exactly what I was looking for. Too fluffy, to girly, or just too new. But then I found a gem. I pulled out the little quilt and held it against my chest as I ran a hand along the edge. A simple edge finished in hand-stitched binding. It wasn't what I'd originally pictured for the baby, with several colors, including pink, country blue, sea green, and a pale yellow all in different prints, but as soon as I held the quilt in my hand, I knew it had to be mine. It was old, but well taken care of. It had that worn, buttery feeling that quilts tended to get when they'd been loved and used. No stiff, scratchy fabric there. I ran my hand along the stitching once more and sighed. Such love and detail.

"It's beautiful, isn't it?" the older lady asked me.

I smiled at her and nodded. "It's perfect," I agreed. I folded the blanket back up, along with the two little bassinet sheets that I'd found. They would match well and were just as soft as the quilt.

"Is this going to be a gift or are you expecting?"

the little lady asked as she began ringing me up at the front counter. I was the only customer in the shop, which was a shame. There should have been people beating on the doors of such an amazing little place. I put a hand on my stomach. I wondered if she could tell. When I raised my head to answer, I found the lady smiling at me as she put the blanket into a bag.

"No, I can't tell by your tiny little stomach," she answered my unasked question. "It's just you have a little glow about you and the way you touched that blanket… well, I just kind of figured." I smiled tightly. This wouldn't do. If I couldn't hide it from a complete stranger, how much longer did I think I was going to be able to do so in my own hometown? My own very small and *nosy* hometown.

The woman in front of me tutted. "Don't worry about it, Hun. You'll do great." She shrugged and put the last of my purchases in the last bag. "And if you mess up something, you'll figure it out easily enough and make sure you do better the next time. Motherhood is a wonderful experience. Terrifying and wonderful," she said with a chuckle.

"Thank you," I answered after a moment of silence. "I needed to hear that today."

She smiled gently. "You're welcome. Just remember to enjoy everything and to let go of those stupid little things that parents seem to worry themselves over. In the end, children grow quickly and years fly by… don't waste them fretting over the unimportant things like ruined dresses and fancy preschools and whatever else parents put too much importance on nowadays, when you could be making mud pies and catching fireflies." She shrugged as I stood there, soaking in everything this wise old woman had to say and I was lucky enough to hear.

"When it's all said and done, grownups don't remember the expensive clothes they wore as children or if their preschool was the best in the state… they remember the mud pies, the camping out in the backyard, and all the little things they did with their family that probably cost no money at all. Enjoy life, cherish your little one, even the pregnancy part. You were given that little miracle for a reason."

I sniffled once and blinked quickly, taking the bags she handed out to me to set at my feet so I could pay her. She told me my total, and I frowned. It was a lot less than I'd calculated in my head while I was shopping.

"You sure you rang everything up, ma'am?" I asked, reaching for my bags.

"I'm sure," she said with a smile. "I took a little off for the baby quilt," she added. I started shaking my head. She'd already given me some price breaks; I didn't want to rob the poor woman. Before I could open my mouth, she started talking again.

"Besides, I made that blanket some thirty years ago, so I think I can sell it for as much as I like," she answered with a smirk. "I'm just happy it is going to be loved by a little one again after all these years."

"You don't have to take anything off. I'd be glad to pay the full price for the quilt... it is worth every penny," I said softly.

She looked at me over the top of her bifocals. "Consider it a baby shower gift," she said with a smile.

I would have argued more, but I could tell by the set of her jaw that she wasn't going to take no for an answer. Two stubborn Missouri women buttin' heads wasn't something likely to end well. Plus, I imagined her being able to give away that blanket was somehow as much of a blessing to her as it was to me. I handed over my credit card with a nod.

"Thank you for... *everything*," I said with my bags in hand.

"Anytime, dear. Anytime."

I left the shop with a smile on my face and the perfect quilt for the baby. All the other things I bought there were just an added bonus. From the shop, I went to the printers to pick up my new business cards and brochures. And from there, I ran a few other errands before I had gathered up enough courage to drive to my main destination—to tell Hunter about the baby. I was nervous as all get out as I drove when my cell phone rang, scaring the bejesus out of me.

"Beth, you nearly made me wet myself," I accused in the place of my usual greeting.

"What are you doing?" she asked after she finished laughing at me.

"Driving. But I was in the middle of some intense focusing when you called."

"Uh-huh. And what exactly are you trying to focus on?" she asked.

"Oh, you know, the usual. The words I'm going to use when I tell Hunter he's going to be a daddy. The different ways he could react. The different ways I could react to him reactin'." I groaned. It did sound a little crazy when I actually said it out loud.

"Uh-huh," Beth replied. "And you're sure you want to do this alone? I could be there in a hurry… for moral support," she offered.

I smiled. Beth was the best best-friend a girl could ask for. "No. I think I need to do this alone," I said.

"Okay, if you're sure."

"I am," I said. "But thank you for the offer."

"No problem. That's what I'm here for," Beth said. "By the way, the reason for my call. Matt said that Hunter will be at lunch about the time you get there. He said he usually goes to a small, local place near the office called *Hot Diggity Dogs* on Fridays, so he should be there."

Hot Diggity Dogs, huh? I thought. Guess it was as good of a place as any other to find out you were having a baby.

"What does Matt think I'm doing in St. Louis?" I asked.

Beth cleared her throat. "Only the truth… you

have some errands to run and then wanted to drop in and surprise Hunter."

I felt a twinge of guilt. Now I had Beth keeping things from her new husband. The sooner I told Hunter, the better. "Thanks, Beth," I said into my phone.

"No problem. Call me after," she commanded.

"Will do. Tell Matt I said hi and thanks."

"I will. Now, go get 'em, momma tiger!"

I smiled after disconnecting. Momma tiger, indeed.

Eight

Meet Me in St. Louis

I grabbed the small gift bag out of the passenger seat of my car along with my small purse. Standing outside of my car for several minutes, I willed my feet to move forward and take me into the restaurant. If Matt was right, Hunter would just be sitting down to lunch and he'd be there for a good forty or so minutes, giving him plenty of time to process everything I had to tell him. At least, I hoped so. I just couldn't make myself move. There was this horrible rock of uncertainty sitting in the pit of my stomach. Yes, he told me he loved me several weeks ago and it was before he'd known anything about the baby, but that didn't mean he wanted to settle down with me… that he wanted a family. People said they loved each other all the time. Loving someone and being there for them didn't always go hand in hand and Hunter, despite his declaration of love, had proven that.

I knew I had to tell him. I knew I didn't want him hearing from gossips that I was pregnant, but I still had doubts. I was human. I was emotional. I was pregnant, *damn it*. I took a deep breath and closed my eyes, gathering my nerve up for the last time. I was going to do this. No matter what, Hunter deserved to know. It would be a load off my mind no matter what happened. Even if we didn't end up together, Hunter needed to know he had a child on the way. Well, my mind said that, but my heart felt otherwise. I knew it would kill me to see him with the baby if we weren't together. But if it wasn't meant to be, I was sure I would eventually find the strength to move past the hurt that would cause me... for the sake of the baby. I would have to. With a new resolve and purpose, I gripped the gift bag in my hand and made my way to the door of the little restaurant.

Hot Diggity Dogs was a busy little place. People spoke loudly, ESPN was playing on several flat-screen televisions, and everyone seemed to be enjoying themselves. I stood in line behind two groups that were being seated, stretching up on my tippy toes to see if I could spot Hunter. He had no idea I was coming. Maybe I should have called him ahead of time... met him somewhere more private. So many doubts and thoughts. Finally, back in the corner of the room, sitting at the bar area, I found him. He was drinking a coke and watching the big screen up on the wall. I watched as he held up his arm and glanced at his watch to check the time. I wondered for a second if Matt had told him I was coming after all.

Peggy Martinez

When his head swung toward the front entrance, just a few feet from where I stood, partially hidden by the last group in front of me, I was sure he was expecting me. I started to raise my hand in greeting, to draw his gaze to me, when he smiled widely and stood up. He wasn't looking at me. I turned, somewhat in a daze, and watched as a bombshell-gorgeous blonde passed by. My stomach fell just a little, just enough to make me feel queasy. Just enough for prickles of awareness to dance across my scalp. I watched as she strode across the restaurant toward Hunter. She slipped easily into his embrace, leaning up to kiss him on the cheek like she'd done it many times before. When she whispered something into his ear, he laughed, the carefree sound reaching me easily across the rambunctious room of people. He sat down and motioned for the bartender to bring the woman a drink. Her body leaned into his, and it caused the knife in my chest to twist in even deeper.

"Ma'am? Ma'am?" I pulled my tear-filled gaze away from the scene at the bar. "You ready to be seated? Is it just you?" The hostess stood there with a menu in her hand.

I took a step back. "It's just me, but I don't need a seat," I mumbled as I hurried out of the restaurant.

The drive home from St. Louis wasn't a long one, but if felt to me like it took ages. When I finally pulled up in front of the house, I was tired and hungry.

Two things a pregnant woman should never be at the same time. I put my packages on my bed and changed into soft pajama bottoms and a T-shirt. Putting the baby quilt in a drawer, I took the rest of my purchases downstairs with me.

Besides the beautiful, old basket I'd purchased, I had also found several hand-embroidered table linens, a beautiful glass cake stand with a glass lid, some new baking dishes, and another vintage apron to add to my ever-growing collection that hung on an eclectic set of antique knobs on my kitchen wall. Instead of hanging the apron up on the wall with the others, though, I tied it around my waist and got to work. Nothing could get my mind off my troubles quite like baking. I preheated the oven, cranked up the sound on my iPod dock, and started pulling ingredients out of the cabinets. One peach cobbler, four dozen cookies, and three batches of jumbo muffins later, I sat down to call Beth.

"Well, you took your sweet time to call. I hope this means you guys had a good, long talk," she started out. I blew out a breath and rubbed the white flour splotch on my hand until it was gone.

"Jen?" she asked after a moment. "What happened?"

"I didn't tell him, Beth," I said softly.

"What do you mean? I thought you were going to," she said gently.

"I was. At least, I wanted to. But then...." The

picture of Hunter with the blonde at the restaurant flashed in my memory, and I cringed.

"Then, what?" Beth asked.

"Then I saw him with someone," I said softly.

Beth hissed in a breath through her teeth. "You mean…."

I nodded and closed my eyes. "Yeah. A woman."

"Oh, hun, that doesn't mean anything. He told you he loved you a few weeks ago. A guy like Hunter doesn't get over something that quickly."

"You didn't see him," I accused. "You didn't see the way they acted together." I blew out a breath. Beth waited on the line.

"He looked happy, Beth," I said. "They looked like they belonged together. Both beautiful, successful people living in the city. No strings. No huge commitments. No baby to hold them back… not like me."

As I said it, I knew it was what had been on my mind the whole time since leaving the restaurant. It was what hurt the most. Not that he had moved on so quickly after I told him I didn't want him around, even though I guess I hadn't expected him to get over me *quite* that quickly. No, that wasn't what had slapped me in the face and stung so bad.

What it all boiled down to was the fact that Hunter was free. Free to do anything. Go anywhere. Be with anyone. He had no strings holding him down…

not like me. I'd said it to Beth. I kind of felt trapped. I was already in love with the baby and I wouldn't trade being pregnant right then for anything in the world, but I still had that small, dark thought that it wasn't something I'd have chosen to happen to me. Yet, I had no choice but to accept it and own it. I knew those feeling were natural, but it didn't make me feel even the slightest bit better when I had them. I just didn't want Hunter to have them too. I didn't want to be the one to attach those strings. He'd grow to resent me for it. Worse, he might grow to resent the baby for it, and I never wanted that to happen.

"That isn't fair, Jen. It isn't fair to you or to the baby. You should still tell him."

I knew she would say that. But I had already made up my mind. "I've already decided that I'm not going to tell him," I said.

"Jen…."

"And I don't want the Wrights, including Matt, to know the truth either," I told her.

"I don't know, Jen… I mean, do you realize what this will mean for you?"

I swallowed. I already thought that through as well, about the time the second batch of muffins were baking. "I know, Beth," I answered. "I'll be completely and utterly alone. Pregnant in a small town with no one even knowing who knocked me up. People will gossip either way, but they would have gossiped just a little less loudly if they knew I was pregnant with a

Wright baby."

"Hunter would do the right thing by you, Jen."

I clenched my jaw. "Hunter would do what is expected of him, and that doesn't mean it is right by me," I said a little more harshly than I intended.

"I didn't mean…"

"I know, Beth. I'm sorry. I didn't mean to snap at ya."

"It's okay, Jen, I just hate it that you're hurting," Beth said.

"I don't think that can be helped right now," I answered softly. "But it will get better in time, don't you think?"

"I'm sure it will," she said immediately. "And I'll be here to help you in any way I can, you know that."

I smiled. I did indeed know that. One person I'd always be able to count on was Beth. "Thanks, Beth."

"What are best friends for?" she asked softly.

"Well, one thing you can be good for is coming over here tomorrow to see all the new stuff I bought," I said quickly.

"Ohh, I can't wait. I do love seeing your antique store finds."

"Well, I do find some great stuff," I said with a chuckle. "Plus, I kind of, umm, have a lot of stuff to send home with you," I added. There was a pause on the other end of the phone.

"Oh, Jen. You baked all afternoon, didn't you?"

I tried not to sound too miffed. "Well, I did want to try out a new muffin recipe," I countered.

"What else did you make?" she asked. I could hear the smile in her voice.

"Just a cobbler… and a few dozen cookies… and a couple batches of muffins," I admitted. Beth was giggling on the other end.

"Hey, well, at least you're productive when you're upset," she said with a laugh.

"You're just happy you get to reap the benefits," I accused.

"Dang right!"

I was laughing now. Beth was no stranger to my emotionally charged baking.

"Beth…." She stopped laughing and waited. "I don't want anyone to know that Hunter is the baby's father. And I mean, like, *ever*." Silence.

"Beth?"

"Okay, Jen. I'll keep it a secret for you, but I'm letting you know now I don't like it," she answered. "This is gonna come back to bite you in the hiney; you mark my words."

I grinned at her use of the word "hiney". She was trying to watch her language. "Thank you, Jen," I said sincerely. "I knew I could count on you."

"Yeah, well, don't think for a second that I don't expect a lot of those muffins and cookies to be coming home with me tomorrow," she said.

"Done," I answered quickly.

"And you know, Elizabeth is an *awfully* nice name if you happen to have a girl…"

I laughed. I thanked God every day for putting Beth in my life. "Noted."

"I'll see you tomorrow, Jen," Beth said. "And don't worry, everything's gonna turn out alright."

"Okay, I'll see ya tomorrow," I answered before hanging up the phone. I spent the rest of the evening cleaning my kitchen and reorganizing the cabinets and drawers.

I sat on the edge of my bed a few hours later, tired, but in a good way. The gift bag I was going to give Hunter was sitting there. I opened it up and pulled out the things I'd bought to announce the pregnancy to him. A card, a DVD of *Nine Months*, a DVD of *What to Expect When You're Expecting*, a DVD of the first show we watched on a date… *Braveheart,* a cigar, and the tiniest pair of cowboy boots I'd ever seen. I sighed, put everything back in the bag, and then shoved it under the baby quilt in my chest of drawers. When I finally made it to bed, I was exhausted. Exhausted enough to fall into a deep, carefree sleep.

Nine

Countryside Inn & Bakery

"Jen, everything looks amazing!" Beth gushed. I was grinning from ear to ear. The whole place did look great. We were standing in the living room. There were two sofas, two armchairs, the piano, and a small window seat in the room. It all fit together perfectly, and some of it was furniture I'd already had that just felt wrong to get rid of. I'd taken down most of the personal pictures of me growing up, but I did leave two pictures of my momma and me on the piano. One of us when I was a baby and one of us when I was grown. Those weren't going anywhere.

"Let's take a tour," I suggested excitedly. Beth hadn't been by in a week, and a lot of the finishing touches were done in that time.

"Ohh, look at the swinging door!" Beth squealed. I pushed through it lightly and held it open for her. That swinging door had once hung in a saloon from the late 1800s, but I wasn't going to advertise that interesting little tidbit. The guys had sanded it down and painted it to fit the rest of the house. The door led right into the bakery portion of the house, which used to be my formal dining area. Now it held two small, round tea tables and chairs. It also had a long, glass counter display box that took up most of one wall with just enough room for someone to step behind it and sell the baked good. A tiny cash register sat on the far corner of the counter. An eclectic collection of baskets and cake stands that I'd collected for the past few weeks lined the top of the rest of the counter. The window near the small tables had white lace curtains pulled back so guests could see out into the front yard. The front porch swing was right outside the window.

"It's perfect," Beth said after walking around the room.

"Let me show you the rooms," I said after a moment. I showed her the few finishing touches upstairs that she hadn't seen. A throw blanket here, an old vase there, even an antique toy truck I'd picked up for the multicolored room. It went perfectly.

"Ladies… we're ready for you." Matt's voice reached us from downstairs. My eyes widened. Pastor Wright and Matthew were out in the yard working on last two things I needed done before the grand opening in a few days.

"They're ready," Beth said excitedly. "Are you?" she asked.

"I am," I said, nodding my head. And I thought

Perfect Contradiction

I was. We headed down the stairs, refraining from rushing down them like a couple of schoolgirls, but it was a very near thing. When we got outside, I walked quickly with Beth to the front lawn. I stopped, my eyes welling up as I took it all in. Matt and Pastor Wright stood there with huge grins on their faces. The sign stood proudly in my front yard, close to the road. It hailed my home proudly as the Countryside Inn and Bakery. The sign was wooden and distressed purposely to look a little old fashioned, just like my house. Beth wound her arm through mine as we turned to look at the house itself. A sign hung there too. From two chains, a smaller, identical sign to the one in the yard hung from the porch just above the stairs. It looked like it was meant to hang there, that it had always been a part of the house. It was *perfect*.

"Your momma would've been so proud," Beth whispered.

I smiled and hugged her arm tightly. "Yes, she would have been," I answered.

"Thank you so much, Pastor Wright, Matt," I said after a moment.

"It was our pleasure," Pastor Wright answered with a smile. They began getting all their tools together and loading up their truck while Beth and I just stood there staring at the house.

"So, you're going to do this," Beth said softly. I knew she wasn't just talking about the inn.

"I am. It's for the best," I said. I could feel her

eyes on me, watching me as I stood there with my chin tilted defiantly.

"Okay," she answered after a moment and a sigh.

"Okay," I agreed. Now to stick with my plan and everything would turn out hunky-dory.

"Well, this time next week, you're going to be a busy lady with the inn opening up."

I was grateful that Beth had decided to change the subject. "Yeah, getting up that early to bake each morning is gonna be hell," I said with a groan.

Beth smiled widely. "My niece, little *Elizabeth*, doesn't like early mornings?' she asked in baby talk. She reached out a hand, but I slapped it away.

"Don't you even dare, Elizabeth Michaels Wright!" I huffed. Beth chuckled, but smartly let her hand fall away before getting too close to my stomach. "And besides... it *could* be a boy." Beth snorted in derision as I grinned.

"Beth! We're ready to head out." Beth waved over to Matt.

"Well, I gotta get going. I'll be over the day before the grand opening to stay the night and lend a hand like I promised," Beth said.

"Sounds good. We'll see how much your taste testing comes in handy," I said with a grin.

Beth put both her hand on her hips. "Quality control is an important part of any growing business," she said matter-of-factly.

I laughed. "And you are definitely highly qualified in that department," I joked.

Beth beamed. "I'm gonna take that as a compliment."

"You should," I agreed. "I'll see you in six days then. Please thank Pastor Wright and Matt for me again." Beth nodded as she left me standing in my yard to leave with the Wrights.

I walked slowly to the house and curled my legs up beneath me as I sat in my porch swing. *This time next week, I am going to be a business owner*, I thought. I laid a hand on my not-so-flat-any-longer stomach. *In a few short months, I am going to be a mommy*, I added.

Everything was about to change.

"I can't believe today is the day," Beth said *again*. I was rearranging the cookies and muffins in the case *again*. I couldn't stand still. I'd been up since before the butt crack of dawn, baking and making sure everything was going to go perfectly that day. I hadn't stopped for a second to even catch my breath. Breathing could wait until after the grand opening was over.

"Oh, God," I muttered beneath my breath.

"What? What is it?" Beth asked in panic.

"What if no one shows up? What if they think

the inn isn't nice enough? What if they think my prices are too high or my new muffins suck?" Words poured out, and my head suddenly felt like it was going to explode from the pressure there.

"Whoa, Jen," Beth said, coming over to pull me down into one of the small chairs in the bakery. "People are going to show up, I promise. Nothing this big has happened in Salem in so long time, they'll show up just for something to do."

I snorted. Leave it to Beth to say something so entirely ridiculous and… true.

"Your house was beautiful to begin with. Now… now it is truly a sight to see," she added. Her words were heartfelt, and I knew she meant each one of them. I smiled at her in thanks. "And don't get me started on your prices. You wanna be robbed blind, then that's your business. But, I'm just sayin' that if it were me, I'd raise 'em… your banana nut muffins are good enough to make a grown man weep."

"Thank you, Beth. I'm just freaking out a little here, I guess."

"You're entitled to. Just get over it quick, 'cause it's about that time," she said quickly, standing up.

I glanced over at the clock… ten minutes 'til opening time. *Sweet baby Jesus.* Standing up, I pulled my apron off. I was wearing a stretchy, black pencil skirt that hit just below my knees and a cream-colored, blouse with black polka dots and a scooped neckline.

Perfect Contradiction

Using my apron to wipe off the white sprinkles of flour on my pumps, I then straightened up. It was time.

Beth looked me over, eyeballing my tummy area hard. "You ain't got much more time to hide your baby bump," she whispered.

I rolled my eyes. "I'm fully aware of that fact," I said, smoothing a hand over my slightly bulging midsection. Mini Blob needed more room. Beth opened her mouth to say something else when the sound of vehicles drew our attention to the bakery window. Cars and trucks were pulling in. *People were actually showing up.* I turned to Beth with a huge grin on my face. Her face mirrored my excitement.

"Let's go welcome your customers," Beth said proudly.

I took a deep breath. "Yes, let's," I answered sounding more confident than I felt. We left the bakery area through the swinging door and opened up the front door to welcome people to the inn.

I was officially open for business.

"You know, I think I'll take your final dozen chocolate chip cookies, after all," Mrs. McGregor said with a devious grin. "I think the grandkids will enjoy them when they come to visit this evening."

"Yes, ma'am," I answered with a smile. "I'll package them up for you. Did you get enough sweet tea? I think there's still a little left if you'd like a fresh glass," I added as I pulled out the nearly empty cookie tray from the display case.

"No, no, dear. I'll be floatin' away if I drink anymore." I laughed lightly and handed her the box of cookies over the counter. She handed me cash and waited while I made change for her.

"The inn looks lovely, Jennifer," she said sweetly. "Your momma would've been so proud of what you've done here."

I smiled and handed her the change. "Thank you, Mrs. McGregor. I truly appreciate you sayin' so."

She patted my hand and then reached over to grab a business card. "You know, I've got someone coming to town in a few weeks or so who might need a place to stay. I'll be sure to send him your way." I smiled at the elderly lady. Old Mrs. McGregor had to be nearing eighty years old. I wasn't sure how she got around so well, but I was sure that if she remembered, she'd send him my way.

"We'd love to have him here at the Countryside Inn," I said politely.

"Alright, dear, well, I better be getting' on. The old man will be wondering where I got off to if I don't get home soon. Men are a helpless lot naturally, but one that's been married to the same woman for over fifty years can't do anything on his own, you know."

I laughed lightly. "I wouldn't know," I admitted.

"Well, you will one day, dear. Don't you doubt it, what with your pretty face and eye for business and bakin'… men'll be lined up here at your door in two shakes of a lamb's tail, just you take my word for it."

Perfect Contradiction

I was grinning widely when I walked out the front door and to her car as she prattled on. Her daughter was there to drive her home. I was still smiling when I walked back into the house. The day was almost over, and I'd been going nonstop for hours. It seemed like the entire town and a few others had shown up to check out the inn, buy cookies, muffins and other goodies, tour the house, and sip on a free glass of sweet tea. I handed out more than twice as many brochures and business cards than I'd anticipated. I had two rooms booked for the next week, and my bakery case looked like a small tornado had blown through and cleaned it out. I was overwhelmed by the turnout.

When the final customer had bought what I had left in muffins and headed out of the house at exactly five minute past closing time, I was exhausted and giddy. Beth strolled up to me with a smile that said it all.

"What was that this morning about no one showing up?" she asked, scratching her head. "And something about no one liking your muffins…"

I rolled my eyes and sat down the empty muffin tray and basket. "Alright, I admit I was worrying over nothin'," I said, taking the high road.

"Jennifer Collins, you were very near a freak out," she said with a wicked gleam in her eyes.

I opened my mouth to object, but no one won an argument with Beth. She was a master; she should've been a criminal defense attorney.

"Well, I'd say the day was a smashing success," I answered instead.

"You're dang right it was!" Beth gushed. "Now, get your shoes on," she commanded. "I'm taking you out to dinner."

I was so tired and happy, I didn't even argue. I just ran to pick up my pumps and slip them on. I was starving.

In hindsight, I should have seen what came next a mile away.

Ten

Congratulations & All That Jazz

Even as we walked into the Italian restaurant, I had no clue. I was just happy to be out with my best friend and getting some pasta and breadsticks. I was still floating on a cloud of happiness from the successful opening day of the inn. I'd completely ignored all the warning signs until it was too late. And then there they were… shouting their congratulations and all that jazz while I stood in the doorway of the private dining room with my jaw hanging open. Not only had Beth managed to shock the crap out of me, but it looked like the entire Wright family had been in on it as well. Of course they had… Beth was a Wright now and they were her family.

"Congratulation, Jen," Mrs. Wright said as she hugged me. "Everything looked perfect today, and the entire county is all abuzz about the Countryside Inn and the amazing bakery."

"Thank you so much, Mrs. Wright. I'm sorry I didn't get to chat with you while you were there, I was completely overwhelmed by the turnout."

"Don't you worry a second about that; I was just fine with Beth showing me around and hinting to the ladies from the church at how wonderful your muffins would be for tomorrow's women's meeting," she said with a wink.

Ah-ha! "Well, I hope everyone enjoys them tomorrow," I said with a grin.

"Oh, I have no doubt that we will... I've had your wonderful muffins before, you know."

I laughed. "That you have. I hope Beth didn't make y'all try all those trial muffins I baked the past few weeks," I said. "I kinda went overboard in my quest for the perfect recipe," I admitted.

Mrs. and Pastor Wright exchanged a glance.

"Jen, every single one of those muffins were delicious and they never lasted in Beth's or our house for more than twenty-four hours."

I smiled widely. I did love to hear that my muffins tasted good.

"You must be exhausted and hungry. Let's order some food and drinks," Pastor Wright said, moving our group further into the private room. A figure I hadn't noticed over by Matt brought me up short. *Hunter.* With a hammering heart, I kept moving forward, hoping my face didn't betray the emotions I was feeling. I glanced around the room to see if he brought a date. It seemed he didn't though. At least there was that.

I walked around the table where everyone else had already begun to take their seats. I found the only empty one, and it happened to be right next to Hunter. I twisted around once I was seated to find Beth, scowling over in her direction. She was mouthing the words *I didn't know he'd be here* at me. I sighed. It wasn't her fault. I just wanted food. Hunter came over a few minutes later after talking to his oldest brother and his partner and sat down next to me. I was hyperaware of the small space between us.

"Congratulations, Jen. I heard the grand opening was a big success," Hunter said softly from beside me.

I turned and smiled at him as naturally as I could. "Thank you, Hunter. That means a lot to me," I answered. Hunter searched my gaze and opened his mouth to say something else just as the waiter entered, ready to take everyone's order. I ordered a plate of garlic aioli pasta to go with my unlimited salad and breadsticks.

"And bring us two bottles of a good, red wine," Pastor Wright said from the other side of the table. "We're celebrating, after all," he said. Everyone was looking at me. Beth's eyes were wide and apologetic. She hadn't thought this through, had she?

"Thank you, everyone," I said. "I truly appreciate y'all coming out to congratulate and celebrate with me. The Countryside Inn and Bakery wouldn't be what it is without your hard work the past few weeks. I'm grateful for each and every one of you," I finished softly, fightin' tears. Beth was smiling widely, and Mrs. Wright was dabbing her eyes.

"Should've saved that for the toast," Matt interjected. Everyone laughed. That was exactly what I wanted to avoid.

"I'm sorry I wasn't there today," Hunter said a few minutes later once all of our salads and drinks were served.

I was adding extra oil and vinegar to my salad. "It's okay, Hunter," I answered without looking at him. "I know you must be busy in St. Louis."

"I am," he acknowledged. "But I still should've made my way down earlier. It's just that I wasn't... I wasn't sure you wanted me there after the last time we spoke."

"I've been meaning to talk to you about that," I said after finishing my bite of salad. "I wanted to apologize. I didn't mean to be so harsh. I was... I *am* going through some things right now, and I took them out on you." I met his gaze and wished immediately that there was a lot more room between us. There was something between Hunter and me that I couldn't quite understand. Something that made the rest of the world fall away when he was near me and looking into my eyes like he was now. Something that made everything else seem absolutely insignificant in comparison to what I was feeling for him in that moment. I swallowed and pulled my gaze away from his.

"Jen... you know I'm here for you, right?" he said after a moment. "I mean, if you ever need someone to talk to." I turned away from him to spear a poor, helpless cherry tomato with my fork. "Or if you need someone to come around and left that heavy ass sofa of yours," he added with a shrug and a chuckle. I smiled. He had helped take that sofa up to my bedroom once they had finished knocking down the wall and expanding it.

"Hey, I like that couch," I said, chagrined. He smiled a small, crooked smile. One of those panty-melting smiles he was so very good at.

"Oh, I like it too," he said, his eyes twinkling. "We made some good memories on that couch," he murmured huskily near my ear.

I swallowed and turned away from his lips. They were very enticing lips. *We made a lot more than memories on that sofa*, I thought with a small snort. I was saved from having to explain myself when the waiter began bringing out the food and serving the wine. I pushed my wineglass out of reach and asked for a refill on my ice water.

"Don't like the wine?" Hunter asked several minutes later.

I took a sip of my water and shrugged. "I have a slight headache and wine tends to just make them worse," I said, not really lying. I did have the beginning of a headache, but it was more from the strain of having to hold myself so rigid and watch everything I said and did next to Hunter, rather than anything else. Hunter was staring at me. I could feel it. I just didn't understand why I was under his scrutiny. I mean, he had a girlfriend, I wasn't showing enough for anyone to be suspicious, and I'd been nothing but polite to him all night. Oy vey, I *did* have a headache after all.

"Huh. Beth has a migraine too. I wonder if it's from how late you guys stayed up working last night for the grand opening," he said.

I glanced over at Beth, who was looking a little pale and in pain. I scrunched up my brow in concern.

"She's fine. Matt gave her something when you guys got here," he said, reading my mind in the annoying way he did sometimes.

"She didn't tell me," I said.

Hunter snorted. "She's kind of stubborn."

I smiled at him. Indeed she was. "Still, I hope she's okay. Do you think she needs to go home? I don't want her to stay just because she wants to be here for me," I said.

"I can tell her you're worried about her and you command her to go home if she's hurting," Hunter offered. His eyes were searching mine, ripping away the barriers I'd placed there one by one.

I cleared my throat. "If you don't mind…." I said. My voice was husky. *Damn these pregnancy hormones!* Hunter's grin should've been illegal.

"Not at all, sweetheart," he said.

Perfect Contradiction

He was across the room and whispering into Beth's ear before I could even remember that he shouldn't be calling me *sweetheart* anymore. From where I sat, I saw Beth argue, then nod, then argue, then shoot daggers in my direction as I did a little finger wave back to her, and then nod in obvious defeat before Hunter came back to sit next to me once again.

"She loves you," he said seriously.

I snorted. I very seriously doubted the earful he'd just gotten had anything about *love* included, but I appreciated the little white lie. A few minutes later, Beth and Matt excused themselves from the group and said they were headed home early because Beth needed to lie down. I hugged them both and told Beth to take it easy. She scowled, but she hugged me anyway. Since she didn't even argue, I knew she must have really been hurting. It wasn't until dessert was over that I realized I didn't have a ride home.

"Oh, Jen, I forgot you rode here with Beth," Mrs. Wright said as we left the restaurant.

"I'm sure we…" Pastor Wright began.

"I'll make sure she gets home," Hunter said, surprising me. I searched his gaze for a moment and before I realized it, the Wrights were on their way to their vehicle, waving goodbye and telling me congrats for the last time as I was being pulled along by the hand toward Hunter's truck.

"Hunter…" I began.

"Don't worry, sweetheart. I won't molest you between here and your house," he promised with a small, tight smile and a Boy Scout salute.

"It isn't that," I started to explain.

"Oh, it isn't?" he asked, a grin spreading across his face, promising mischief and a very, very good time. I swallowed and backed up until my back hit his truck door. One hand came up to the side of the truck near my head. The other came to rest on my waist. I was surrounded by him. His scent, the warmth of his body. I couldn't think straight with him this close. I closed my eyes and turned my mouth away from his gaze, from the warmth of his breath as it whispered across my cheek.

"Hunter, please," I begged. Just a whisper.

"Please yes or please no?" he murmured near my ear. He rubbed his lips along the edge of my earlobe and then down the side of my neck. A small kiss along my collarbone. Madness. I had to stop the madness.

"Please… no," I forced out. A breathless plea. Hunter immediately stopped. His finger caressed my jaw and then tucked a wayward strand of hair behind my ear.

"Okay, sweetheart," he answered softly before stepping away. My very wobbly legs barely supported me when Hunter opened the truck door for me and I had to climb in.

We drove in silence most of the way to my

house. The awkwardness in the small space was suffocating. I didn't know what to say to make it better. *Hey, let's make out* didn't seem appropriate. *How's your gorgeous girlfriend?* And *you're my baby's daddy* didn't make the cut either. We pulled into the driveway, and Hunter came around to open my door for me.

"The sign looks great," he said, smiling as we passed it.

I smiled back. "Thanks. I think it does too. Your dad and brothers did a great job," I said as we walked up the steps to the porch.

"Yes they did," Hunter said, his voice serious.

I unlocked the front door and waved for him to follow behind me. "C'mon in, Hunter. I'd like to send a few things with you. I have some mini loaves of pumpkin bread I'd like you to have. I know they're your favorite," I said as I walked through the swinging door and through the bakery on into the kitchen. Slipping off my pumps, I grabbed a large container out from under the counter. I was already putting two mini loaves in the container and about a dozen pieces of peanut butter fudge when Hunter finally strolled into the kitchen.

I froze when Hunter stepped up behind me, wrapping his arms around my waist and burying his face into my hair. My heart began pounding. Surely, he'd notice….

"Jen… I miss you," he murmured against my

neck.

I breathed a little easier, but I was in the one place I couldn't be. The place I wanted to be, but couldn't allow. "I've missed you too, Hunter," I confessed.

Hunter groaned and swung me around to face him. I had nowhere to go. Nowhere to hide from him or from my feelings. He tipped my head back until I had no choice but to meet his eyes.

"Tell me why, Jen," he muttered as his lips touched my cheek. My eyes fluttered. "Tell me why this isn't right." He kissed my ear, just a tiny caress. My head dropped back. "Explain to me why you keep fighting what we have between us," he said gruffly. His lips came down gently at first. Just testing, touching, and becoming familiar with mine again. But it didn't last long. It never did. We didn't need to become familiar with one another. My lips would always recognize his. My body would never forget his touch. My spirit recognized his spirit, and it was the missing piece that that made me whole.

"Remind me of all the reasons why we won't work out," he said softly.

I couldn't. The same reason that said we wouldn't work out was the exact same one that told me we had a fighting chance. The baby could break us or the baby could bond us. It was all a confusing jumble of contradictions. His kisses scattered what wits I had left to the four corners of the earth, and I melted into him. Too many fevered kisses and several buttons of my top undone later, Hunter's cell phone rang, effectively snapping me out of the madness I was quickly slipping into. I put a hand up and gently pushed Hunter back. He took a step back, his eyes hooded in desire, his lips still perfectly kissable. I shook my head and grasped ahold of the only thing I could think of at the moment.

"Was that your girlfriend?" I asked, trying to put more space between myself and the man I wanted desperately. Hunter's head whipped back like I'd struck him.

"Girlfriend?" he asked in a low, calm voice.

I turned and put a lid on the container of goodies I had been preparing for Hunter. "Blonde, long legs… *beautiful*?" I reminded him harshly. Still he stared at me like I'd grown two heads. "The woman you were with at *Hot Diggity Dogs* a few weeks back," I prompted, my head starting to pound.

"You were in St. Louis?" Hunter accused instead, effectively dodging my question.

Uh-huh. "Yeah. I had some things to pick up for the inn, so I swung by to see you," I said, not looking at him as I began straightening up my already immaculate kitchen.

"Why didn't you tell me?" he asked, oblivious. *Just like a dude*.

"Umm, hello? The blonde bombshell you were kissing wasn't enough of a clue?" I asked.

Hunter blinked. He looked angry and hurt.

I felt confused. "Can you tell me you aren't seeing her? That I made a mistake?" I asked. Dear God, my voice had sounded hopeful. I hated myself for that.

"No, I can't say that," Hunter answered evenly.

I nodded, unable to trust myself to speak. "That's what I figured," I muttered a few seconds later.

"You should have come up to me, Jen," Hunter said again.

I rolled my eyes.

"Sometimes life has a way of making me think that God is just playing one big, cosmic joke on me," he said. He sounded as tired and emotionally drained as I felt.

"Listen, Hunter, I've had a long day and I have to get up really early to bake," I started. I held out the container of sweets I made for him. Reaching out, he took it from me. He turned and took a step toward the kitchen door. My heart felt even heavier if that was at all possible. I felt like we were on a precipice and whatever we said and did in this moment was going to change everything between us. Hunter spoke first.

"I've decided to take a more permanent position in the family business," he said. Hunter's family not only owned farmland, but they also owned a thriving movie theater business that spanned several cities in Missouri. "I'm almost finished with my business degree, and I guess I should just go ahead and put it to good use."

"That's… great, Hunter," I said. *What did that mean exactly?* I wondered.

"Yeah. I'll be moving to St. Louis permanently tomorrow and doing a lot of traveling," he said with his back to me.

"Wait. What?" I asked.

"I'll be taking over most of the business. My dad wants to phase himself out of the movie theater business. He's busy enough with the farm and the church as it is. He asked me tonight if I would consider taking over."

My mind was spinning. Hunter would be gone from Salem on a permanent basis. I sucked in a sharp breath. It hurt even more when things worked out like I hoped they would. With Hunter gone, it would make things easier on me when people found out I was pregnant, easier to keep it from him, and easier to pretend I knew what I was doing. Still, to hear him say he was going to be gone permanently hurt me on a level I didn't realize was possible.

"I don't know what to say," I answered truthfully. "I never thought you'd leave Salem."

Hunter turned and smiled sadly. "Neither did I."

"So, this is goodbye for now then?" I asked, suddenly unsure of everything I'd been so sure of a few hours before.

"This is goodbye," he confirmed.

I walked over to him and put a hand on his shoulder. His eyes closed as I reached up to kiss him on the cheek. "I wish you the best, Hunter," I whispered.

He took a deep, shuddering breath and pulled me to him in an embrace. "And I wish the same for you too, Jen," he whispered back. He pulled back and walked away from me without looking back. I locked up behind him and got everything ready for the rest of my week at the inn.

Planning and organizing kept my busy.

Keeping busy kept my mind off everything I didn't want to think about.

And that was all I could handle right then.

Eleven

Baby Bump

"To be honest, I have no idea how you've kept *that* a secret as long as you have," Beth said, motioning to my rounded tummy.

I turned this way and that, looking at myself in the mirror. "Well, it's cold out now, so I've gotten away with it by layering, wearing a sweater over my clothing, and avoiding going out of the house unless it's absolutely necessary," I said, running a hand over my stomach and the long-sleeved dress I wore. It was soft, comfortable, and it accentuated the one thing I'd been hiding for the past three months—my big, 'ole baby bump. I was just sick and tired of it. Here I was a few weeks away from my final trimester and I hadn't had any tummy pictures taken, I hadn't bought any pretty maternity clothing, and I hadn't enjoyed a single moment of my pregnancy journey… all because I didn't want people to start talking.

"Well, they ain't gonna misunderstand what that dress is trying to display," she said with a wide smile. "Are you sure you're ready to just let it all hang out there though?" Beth asked, eyeing me up and down.

I looked over at the stack of clothes we'd already tried on and the things I'd fallen in love with and was planning to buy. I put a hand out on my tummy when I felt a little kick. Baby Jedi was happy with the dress. I'd been working my rear end off for over three months since opening the Countryside Inn and Bakery, all while keeping my pregnancy a secret. It was exhausting and by god, I wanted to be able to waltz into the Piggly Wiggly in my pajama bottoms and maternity tee and purchase a jar of pickles and a container of ice cream without giving a hoot who saw me. *Yeah, I was over it.*

"Oh yeah, I'm ready," I answered. "I'm ready to really begin enjoying this pregnancy before it's all over, and I realize that I was so busy worrying about people's opinions that I missed the entire experience." I set my jaw and watched Beth in the mirror.

"Well, it's about friggin' time!" she squealed. "Get that dress. You look fabulously pregnant in it." She jumped out of the chair she was sitting in and left.

"Where are you going?" I shouted.

"I'm going shopping for my niece finally!" she shouted back.

I went into the dressing room to change with a huge smile on my face. We were about to do some major damage in this mall.

Perfect Contradiction

"Beth, seriously, what are you going to do if it's a boy?" I asked, eyeing the pile of pink baby clothes piled up on my bed. Beth snorted and held up another little outfit for me to fall in love with.

"Only a little girl would be so stubborn as to not even let us get a good look-see and keep us in suspense all this time," she shot out.

Okay, I had to admit that was pretty good reasoning, but I suspected it was really just a lot of hot air so she could buy what she wanted. Auntie Beth had her heart set on a little girl to spoil rotten. Beth began folding the onesies and blankets and every other little thing she'd bought the baby, putting it all in the tall chest of drawers we'd bought a few weeks back. I sat on the sofa and glanced over at the bassinet. It still needed a fresh coat of paint. I guess I needed to carry it downstairs soon and get that done.

"So, what are you going to tell Matt when he asks you if you knew I was pregnant this whole time and if you know who the father is?" I asked after a moment. It had been on my mind since I'd made the decision to stop trying to hide my pregnancy.

Beth shrugged. "The truth," she said simply. "That of course I knew the whole time, but that I made you a promise not to tell anyone who the father is."

I sighed. "I'm really sorry about this, Beth," I

said again.

"There's nothing to be sorry about, Jen," Beth answered immediately. "You have the right to keep it to yourself. I may not like it and think you're gonna regret it, but that doesn't mean I can't support you and your decision."

I smiled at my best friend, nearly buried in a pile of tiny, pink clothes. "Well, after tomorrow, we won't have to worry about keeping it all a secret any longer. Everyone in Salem, hell, probably half the *state* will know I'm pregnant," I answered wryly.

"Yeah, about that…." Beth began. "You think this is the best idea you've ever had? I mean, deciding to let the cat out of the bag is one thing… but letting the cat out at *church*?" Beth raised a brow.

I huffed and rearranged myself on the sofa to get more comfortable. "I want it all out there and quickly, with no way I'll be able to doubt that everyone knows," I answered. "You know of any other place as good as a church for spreading gossip that quickly and effectively?" I asked.

Beth shrugged. "I suppose you're right," she admitted.

I smiled. "I know I'm right."

"Okay, if the is how you want to announce to the world that you're expecting then… I'm in," Beth said.

Perfect Contradiction

"You ready?" Beth asked me as we sat in the parking lot of New Hope Community Church. I'd been attending Pastor Wright's church since Beth started going on occasion with Matt. I taught Sunday school every other Sunday and helped with a lot of the children's ministries. This Sunday, I wasn't teaching my little kindergarteners; it was my week off in the rotation. I took a deep breath and nodded. It was now or never, and I was ready to put this behind me already.

"Ready as I'll ever be," I said with a shrug. We got out of my car and headed for the church together. When we entered, we both took of our jackets. Taking a deep, fortifying breath, I hung my jacket over my arm that carried my Bible. I followed Beth into the church where most of the adult congregation was gathered and fellowshipping before services would start a few minutes later.

"Jen!" I heard a familiar voice call from a few feet away. "I was just telling..." McKenna's voice trailed off when she saw *all* of me. My dress was a knee length, wine-colored sweater dress with a pretty, draping neckline. It also had little pleats stitched in just above my baby bump, meant to really highlight a pregnant tummy. And man, *did it*. It was adorable, soft, and comfortable though, so I'd chosen to wear it to church that morning for the exact effect it was having on several ladies as their eyes rounded when they realized what they were looking at. *And boom goes the dynamite.* McKenna Jacobs… the biggest gossip in three counties, possibly more. Just the person I needed to see. I clenched my jaw and stepped forward.

"McKenna," I gushed, reaching in for a little hugs as usual, like nothing was different. I placed a hand on the top of my stomach as I spoke. "I was hopin' I'd get a chance to talk to you before services." Her eyes hadn't left my stomach.

"Jen… when did…?"

I cut her off immediately. "I have those classroom cutouts for you that I promised to bring with me." I put a hand out and patted her arm. "Don't forget to get them from my car after church, hun," I said quickly with a huge smile.

"Beth." Matt waved as he walked up to us. His smile faltered once he realized there was some tension in the room.

"What's going…?" His voice trailed off as he reached Beth's side. His eyes widened as he saw my hand resting on my belly and all the women standing around gaping like he was just then. Beth elbowed him in the side, never breaking her smile. An *oomph* left his mouth as he rubbed his side, looking completely flabbergasted.

"Well, we better take our seats," Beth said with a huge, sugary-sweet voice. She tucked her arm in mine and turned me away from the group.

"She just doesn't know how to take it easy, ya know?" Beth whispered over her shoulder. "I keep telling her she's got to sit down and rest every once in a while. It takes a lot out of you, growing a baby and all that… Or so I've heard," Beth said with a grin.

"Just think, Matt," Beth said loudly as we headed toward the pew where the Wright family usually sat. "We'll be able to spoil this baby like it is our own… maybe we can hold off trying for one after all," she added in a mock-whisper. Matt looked so lost that I actually felt bad for the poor guy. Beth had just confirmed I was pregnant in front of the whole church, showed her support and Matt's, and managed to start another small thread of gossip that she was anxious for her own baby. That was going to take a teensy bit of the spotlight off my own scandal. Beth was freaking *amazing*!

"We're going to be talking about this later, right?" Matt whispered into Beth's ear as we sat.

I cringed. Poor Beth. Beth just patted his hand in answer and snuggled into his side until the class started. I had no doubt that by the time church was over that Salem would be abuzz with the news. Shrinking down into my seat, I frowned. A tiny little nudge from Mini Jedi brought a smile to my lips though. For the first time, I was able to lay a hand on my stomach without worrying about anyone seeing me. By the time Sunday school was over, I was grinning ear to ear. It didn't take long for that to change though.

In between Sunday school and church services, I decided to hurry to the restroom. The baby seemed to press on my bladder in the worst way when I was seated. Eyes followed me as I walked, whispers did too, but I didn't care… not too much, anyway. I was washing my hands when a voice broke up the happy thoughts I was having.

"Jennifer Collins."

I cringed and turned to the sound of the most annoying voice on the face of the planet. Jill Mason and her super nasally, southern drawl scraped against my eardrums.

I grabbed a few paper towels and began drying off my hands. "Jill," I acknowledged. Jill had been the bane of my existence in school. Not even Beth knew of the lengths Jill had gone to in order to make my life miserable. I thought she might have changed once we were all adults, but if anything, she became worse. No, she didn't bully me anymore, but she didn't waste an opportunity to be nasty either. Looked like today wasn't going to be any different.

"Look who done went and got herself knocked up," Jill said as she turned on the water in the sink next to me. "Goody-two-shoes Jen Collins." She sneered at me. A few other ladies were in the restroom, some clearly finished, but they were hanging back to hear the gossip, to hear what I might have to say. I wasn't going to give any of them the satisfaction though. I smiled as wide as I could without pulling a muscle in my cheek.

"Well, bless your little heart for noticing, hun," I gushed, rubbing a hand over my baby bump. "Everyone keeps sayin' I'm so tiny that they hardly realized I was pregnant." Jill had never been pregnant before *that anyone knew of,* but it was a known fact that people regularly asked her if she was expecting, only to find out *quite embarrassingly* that she just had added quite a bit of pudge around her middle section since high school. Her face turned a mottled red sort of color as I continued on as if I were oblivious.

"I keep thinkin' I need to wear a sign or somethin' to announce I'm carrying this precious cargo around every day," I said sweetly. "Thank you so much for making me feel better about my tiny baby bump," I added in for good measure. By then, Jill looked like she was ready to blow a gasket. I took a step back, ready to make my exit and let my face cool off before the main church service started.

"Why, Jen, look at you!" came a sweet voice from behind us all. I twirled around in mortification. Mrs. Wright, the pastor's wife and Hunter's mother, stood there. She must have been in one of the stalls. She had to have heard everything. I could feel a blush working its way up my neck and across my cheekbones. Jill Mason grinned like she was the cat who ate the canary—smug and self-satisfied.

"Mrs. Wright…" I began.

"How did I not know you were expectin' a little blessing?" she asked with a bright smile as she washed her hands.

I tried to find words, but they just wouldn't come out.

She dried her hands off quickly and came over to me. "May I?" she asked.

I nodded, unable to even think straight. She placed a hand on my stomach and smiled at everyone in the ladies room.

"Babies are such a joy in a woman's life, don't y'all agree?" she asked, her voice dripping honey. All the women smiled and nodded. The baby decided just at that moment to bump into Mrs. Wright's hand. She smiled even wider and rubbed her hand lightly over my stomach.

"That's right, sweetie, Mrs. Wright is here to spoil you rotten to the core," she cooed at my stomach. The baby rewarded her with another small kick and Mrs. Wright laughed, encouraging them to feel the baby moving all about in there. By the time we walked out of the ladies room, Jill had slunk off somewhere and I had been promised by a couple of women that they'd go through their old baby stuff and bring by all the things they had for me to see if I wanted any of it. Mrs. Wright never left my side, gushing over my "cute little baby bump" and the "precious little angel" I was expecting to everyone as we made our way back to our seats. Mrs. Wright had a way with people. They loved her, they looked up to her, and a lot of them wouldn't have dared disrespect her enough to say anything against me or the baby when she was singin' our praises. At least, not to her face.

"Jennifer Collins, you're lucky I don't tan your hide for not letting me know you're expectin'," she whispered fiercely as we took our seats on the pew.

I swallowed and nodded. "Yes, ma'am," I murmured. "I'm sorry... I just didn't know how to tell everyone. I wasn't ashamed... just overwhelmed and confused," I answered.

"All this time, you've been working all hours of the day at your new inn and all that baking you've been doin'..." *Uh-oh... she wasn't happy.* "I could've been helping you."

"I've been doing okay," I said softly.

She snorted. "You've been doin' better than okay... I know you've been running out of baked good halfway through the day and havin' to bake a whole second batch just to keep up with demand. I know you've been gettin' requests for catering jobs as far out as Dent County."

My mouth popped open in a little *O*. "How did you...?" Beth. Of course, Beth had told her how well I'd been doing... and how much work I'd been puttin' in. Truth was, I was exhausted. Between the baking, the catering orders, and the inn itself, I was wearing myself thin.

"The point is, young lady, you've got a lot on

your plate. You need some help whether you want to admit it or not. That baby will be here sooner than you think. And just imagine trying to do all you've been doing lately when you're as big as a house and can't even bend over to pick up something you've dropped." Mrs. Wright harrumphed when she saw the look on my face.

She patted my knee and smiled. "Don't worry. We'll talk after church," she said.

Pastor Wright walked up to the podium just then, asking us all to stand and join him in song. Mrs. Wright handed me a hymnal and carried on like any other Sunday morning.

Twelve

Cowboy Take Me Away

"So, what do you think?" I asked, eyeing the girl as she glanced around the tiny room. We'd already toured the house and the kitchen. We were sitting at the small table in the bakery talking. I fingered the application she'd filled out. She smiled shyly.

"Are you sure you want me?" she asked. "Outside of babysitting and cleaning my own house, I don't have a lot of experience. I mean, I'm not tryin' to talk you out of hiring me or anything, but I don't want to disappoint you either, Miss Collins," she said.

I smiled at her. If I had any doubts at all, she'd just have obliterated them. Out of the handful of applicants that answered the part-time ad job I'd placed, Rachael was by far the best choice. She was shy and didn't have a whole lot of self-confidence, but she was sweet, well-mannered, and I could tell we'd get along just fine. Plus, she did have babysitting experience, and I'd already told her that would eventually come in handy.

"I'm sure, Rachael," I said with a small smile. "And please, call me Jen."

Rachael smiled, took the hand I offered, and shook it.

"So, after school each day?" I asked.

"Yes, ma'am," she answered. "I'll be here just as quick as I can each day and whenever you need me on weekends, I'll be available," she offered with a grin. I smiled and stood. She followed me over to the counter where I put a jumbo chocolate chip muffin in a bag and handed it to her. She looked surprised.

"There's a lot of perks to working here," I said with a grin and a wink.

"Thank you," she said again. "I'll be here tomorrow then?"

I nodded. "Can't wait," I said honestly. She slung her messenger bag across her back and left with a small wave over her shoulder as she pushed through the swingin' door. I heard her tell someone where they could find "the owner" just before the front door squeaked shut. *I need to get those hinges oiled*, I thought, adding it to my mental to-do list. I had a lot of things to get done. Christmas was right around the corner. I was gearing up for several different holiday catering gigs, and I hadn't even had time to put up a tree in the front room of the inn.

"You need the hinges on your front door oiled," a deep, masculine voice said.

Perfect Contradiction

"I was just thinking that…" I murmured without looking up from my notebook. I was scribbling as fast as I could. I had just thought of a new recipe and wanted to write down what I'd thought before I forgot. "I'll be with you in just one sec, hun," I said to the male voice in the room.

"Take your time, ma'am," he said, his deep voice hinting at a grin.

I finished writing down the inspiration I'd had for a brand-new dump cake, snapping my notebook shut and slipping it into the pocket of my apron before turning a smile up to my guest.

"I'm sorry about that…." I started. The rest of my words stuck in my throat. A pair of the sexiest eyes I'd ever seen stared twinkling back at me. Blue eyes, the color of a crystal-clear sky set in a tan face with tiny laugh lines at the corner of full lips. The man's hair was a bit shaggier than I was normally attracted to, but the dark brown waves looked… right on him. He held a black cowboy hat in his hand. I looked him up and down. A cowboy through and through it seemed. Tight fittin' Levis, a button-up shirt you couldn't find anywhere but in a western store, and a well-worn pair of black boots. *Yee-haw!*

"Can I help you?" I finally blurted out. His smile was slow, sensuous, and just a little crooked. *Oh my.*

"I'm hopin' you can," he said, his deep voice thrumming through the entire room. "I was told you might have a room available."

I nodded and quickly looked away. What was wrong with me? Danged extra hormones flowing through my body. "I do. Would you like to take a look to see if it's to your likin'?" I asked, meeting his gaze once again. I moved out from behind the case, and his eyes traveled over me from head to foot. A blush had begun. I looked like a house in my maternity jean skirt and plaid, long-sleeved blouse.

"I'm sure if it's even half as charmin' as everything else I've seen up to this point, it'll do me just fine," he said with a wicked gleam in his eye.

I knew beyond a shadow of a doubt that I was blushing bright red by then. I decided to blame it on the pregnancy. "Just the same, I'd like to take you up real quick like. I don't want you to be disappointed."

"Yes, ma'am," he said, following me out of the room.

"I'm sorry, I didn't get your name," I said as we stepped onto the second floor.

"Jackson Sharp," he said as I opened the door that led into my biggest guest room. Jackson was a big man, and I figured he'd need all the room he could get. He walked into the room and looked around.

"This is the largest room I have," I explained as he walked over to touch the homemade blue quilt on the bed. He glanced over at the small shelf and picked up a picture there.

"This room would suit me well," he murmured. "Plenty of room and very homey," he said, setting the picture down. "Family?" he asked, referring to the black-and-white photograph he'd been looking at.

I walked over and picked it up gently. It was a picture of a woman smiling and kneading dough on a floured tabletop. It was an old picture, but not that old. I just loved it in black and white.

"That was my mother," I said softly. She looked so happy in the picture, so carefree and peaceful. No one would've known how much she had gone through. She was my hero.

"I see where you got your beautiful smile," Jackson said from beside me, pulling me out of my thoughts.

I laughed lightly. "Why, thank you, Mr. Sharp," I said with a wink. "She was a beautiful woman inside and out." I put a hand on my stomach as I walked to the door with a smile on my face.

"When is the little one due?" he asked casually.

"March," I answered over my shoulder. "Not too much longer now." Jackson smiled and followed me out into the hallway. He sure did take up a lot of room. I glanced over at the bassinet I'd pulled out into the hallway an hour ago, meaning to get someone to carry it down for me. I'd forgotten all about it. I didn't have anyone else staying in the inn that week. Jackson Sharp would be the only one.

"I'm sorry about that; the inn is usually pretty clutter free. I meant to drag that downstairs to work on this weekend," I said with a frown.

"You're not going to lift that yourself though, are you?" he asked with a frown. "Your husband will do it surely," he said.

I stiffened and looked away from his searching and concerned gaze. "I'm not married, Mr. Sharp," I said shortly.

The poor man shuffled next to me, moving his hat from one hand to the other.

"I'm sorry, I didn't mean to offend you. I'm a big idiot and tend to stick my very large, booted foot down my throat on occasion," he said gruffly. "Please accept my apology."

I waved my hand in his direction. "Don't worry about it at all. I'm just a little touchy lately," I offered up weakly. "I know you didn't mean anything. Would you like to book the room then?" I asked with a smile. Jackson grinned and stuck a hand out. I put my much smaller one in his and shook it.

"I'd love the room," he said.

"Good," I said with a release of breath. "I've got homemade chili for dinner and some cobbler for dessert tonight. Sound good?" I asked from the second stair down. I turned back and found Jackson with his arms full of the baby's bassinet.

"Sounds delicious, ma'am," he said with a grin.

"Mr. Sharp..."

He shook his head. "It weighs nothin' and I won't rest easy thinking you'll be lifting it down these stairs, so might as well not argue." His eyes never left mine. There was no argument to be made there.

"Alrighty then, but you can stop calling me ma'am and start calling me Jen," I said in a huff as I kept moving down the stairs. "And you be sure to knock your boots off before you enter the house," I threw in for good measure.

"Yes ma'… will do, Jen," he said. "I'd appreciate it if you'd call me Jackson as well," he countered.

I nodded my agreement. "That only seems fair," I said. Jackson took the bassinet out to the back porch for me and then paid for his room. I got him a key and a fresh set of towels for his room.

"Dinner will be at six. I didn't make anything fancy seeing as how the inn is mostly empty this week, but if you need anything, feel free to ask or leave me a note downstairs. I'm usually here, though, so I doubt you'll have a hard time findin' me if ya need anything."

"Thank you, Jen. I'll see you at dinner," he said before heading out of the bakery with a smile playing on his lips.

I used a bill on the counter to fan my face. It must have been a little warm in the house.

Thirteen

Comfort Zone

Jackson Sharp had been stayin' at the inn for almost a week when I realized how much I was enjoying his company. It was nice to have a guy around. We ate breakfast with each other each morning and dinner with each other each night. Each afternoon, he'd show up just about the time my second wave of bakin' was finished and carry all my trays out to the bakery case for me. It was useless for me to argue with him. He would just grab a cherry hand pie when he was finished and say *the fringe benefits are well worth it* with a cocky grin and a wink.

"I don't know," I said as I rubbed my hands together to keep them warm.

"It's pretty big," Rachael said.

I nodded. It was *huge*.

"You said to get a nice tree." Jackson waved a hand to the ginormous tree with a grin. "So, I got a nice tree."

"I don't think it'll fit," I said seriously.

Jackson scoffed and motioned for Rachael and me to get out of the way.

"Watch and learn, darlin'," he answered. I shook my head. Men were so stubborn. Jackson got the tree inside, situating near the piano and the front window. Rachael helped him hold it steady as he got it secured in place. Both of them wouldn't let me even think about helping. I rolled my eyes and stood back, itching to do something.

Once the tree was just perfect, according to Jackson and Rachael, we all went over to the other side of the room to see how it looked. I turned my head just enough to catch a glimpse of Jackson's smile. Oh lordy, I was going to have to say it. I sighed and crossed my arms over my stomach.

"Alright. You were right, Jackson Sharp. It's perfect," I admitted. Rachael was giggling, and Jackson had the good sense not to rub it in.

"So, can we start decorating it?" Rachael asked. I smiled over at her and nodded. She squealed and ran to get the boxes we'd brought out of storage earlier in the day.

"She is very excited to decorate that tree," Jackson commented.

I snorted.

He glanced over with a questioning look. "What?" he asked. "What did I miss?"

I smiled and walked over to sit down on the sofa where we'd put a huge container of popcorn to be strung for the tree. Jackson followed me and sat down. I shrugged.

"If you think Rachael is excited about stringin' popcorn and decorating that tree, you've got no clue," I said as I began pushing popcorn kernels onto my needle and thread. Jackson picked up his own threaded needle and set to work as well. Stringing popcorn for that big a tree was going to take some time.

"So, clue me in," Jackson said near my shoulder. I stiffened just a little at his nearness. Jackson Sharp was all man and completely overwhelming sometimes. Sad truth was that he had no idea.

"You," I answered with a tiny shrug, not meeting his eyes.

"Me?" he asked. "You gotta give me more than that, darlin'," he said gruffly.

I sighed. "She's got a crush on you," I said plainly. Jackson didn't say anything for a few seconds. I stopped what I was doing and glanced over at him. He looked astonished. I laughed and slapped his knee.

"She's a kid," he said in horror.

I rolled my eyes. Truly clueless. She's a *teenager*. Too young for you, but just old enough to wish she wasn't," I said softly. "And don't you dare act weird around her. She's a good kid and she'll be a good woman one day, best not to crush her hopes," I said seriously, but with a hint of mischief. Jackson had made himself an easy target.

"Oh, I wouldn't dare," he said quickly. "I wouldn't want to fall out of favor with the lady of the inn," he added softly.

Heat rose to my cheeks but I batted his words away. He was playing around. No one could be serious about a woman huge and pregnant with another man's baby. At least, I didn't *think* they could. Rachael came bouncing back into the room before I could give it much more thought. For that, I was grateful.

"So, how about we watch a Christmas movie while we decorate the tree?" I suggested. "I have a stack of movies we can choose from." Jackson and Rachael both seemed to think it was a great idea, so I got out my holiday movie collection and sat it on the table for them to choose from. I kept stringing popcorn while they laughed over each other's choices and reenacted scenes from the ones they each had dubbed the "best Christmas movie ever". I brought out egg nog and the special Christmas cookies I'd made for everyone, and we all settled on *A Christmas Story* as the movie of the night.

After a lovely evening of decorating, movies, and good conversation with friends, I sat back with a mug of hot cocoa and *another* gingerbread cookie. I sighed happily as I looked at the tree. It was trimmed in colored lights, silver bells with bows, strung with popcorn, and had a variety of bulbs and ornaments my mother had gathered over a lot of years. Tons of that messy, silver tinsel hung from the tree as well. A tree wasn't complete without that stuff. A pretty, twinkling white star topped it. I smiled when I remembered Rachael trying to tell Jackson where to move it to make it "perfect". I'd laughed so hard I'd almost wet myself. It had been a wonderful time. Now Rachael had gone home, Jackson went to pick up some stuff he needed in town, and I was there just enjoying the view of my Christmas tree.

Rachael was going to be an amazing young woman when she realized how beautiful and smart she was and how much she had to offer the world.

Jackson was going to make some woman very lucky one day.

And I... I was content.

Fourteen

Midnight Muffins

It only took about three weeks after I showed up at church in my most baby bump-revealing maternity dress before something I'd been dreading actually happened. I knew it was just a matter of time, but once nothing happened after the first two weeks, I kinda got my hopes up. But sure enough, after three weeks post-church reveal and about ten days after Jackson Sharp had been stayin' at the inn… it happened.

"I hope I'm not upsetting you," McKenna said, biting her lip. The picture of innocence. "I just thought you should know. *I'd* want to know if it pertained to me," she added in for good measure. I clenched my jaw and then took a second before I answered. I was putting away all my classroom supplies right after Sunday school class. The kids had been making macaroni art to take home with them. Ironically enough, they covered a large "P" for patience.

"Of course, McKenna," I said after a moment.

"Thanks for telling me. I appreciate it." Pasting a huge smile on my face, I continued cleaning up the room. I glanced back over to where I left her standing. She hadn't gone anywhere. She was hoping I had something to say out of anger or spite or whatever, but I wasn't about to give her more gossip and hatefulness to spread around.

"You should head on over to the main building," I said sweetly. "I'd hate for you to be late. I still have some cleaning up to do here before I can join you." Without waiting for a reply, I strode off into the supply closet with my elbow macaroni, glitter, and glue bottles. When I came back out, McKenna was gone. *Thank God.*

I sank down into a kiddie chair and took my time getting a hold of my emotions. So, some of the mothers were talking about how they didn't think it was right or moral that an unmarried, pregnant woman was teaching their children's Sunday school class? That someone who was a *godly* and good *example* for their children should be doing the job. *Ouch.* It hurt a little more than I expected it to, even though I *had* expected it. I wasn't sure even Beth had thought something like this would happen… but I had. I'd prepared for it even. Still… it stung.

I heaved myself out of the kiddie chair—that had been a mistake—and grabbed my bag and purse off the desk near the door. Turning out the lights, I turned to look over the classroom. I loved my time with the class twice a month, but I'd already planned how I'd react weeks back. Walking slowly back to the main building, I sat in the back pew of the church. The mom of one of my kids sat two rows ahead of me. She saw me sit down and turned around quickly to whisper something in her sister's ear. Both of them had kids in my class. I snorted under my breath. *As if*. Shelly Yancey had her little boy five months after her own shotgun wedding, but you didn't see me refusing to teach her kid or gossiping about that during services. I had no doubt they were some of the pot-stirrers, but it didn't matter one bit. If parents at the church didn't think I was fit to teach their kids, then that was that. Who was I to argue?

The services seemed to drag by intolerably slow. When they were over, I hung around until most of the church had emptied out before asking to speak with Pastor Wright.

"What can I do for you, Jennifer?" Pastor Wright asked from behind his large desk. I smiled at him. He was a good man and a great pastor.

"I'm afraid I'm going to have to give up my Sunday school class," I said.

Pastor Wright sat forward, seemingly shocked. His eyes widened though, and I knew what he was thinking immediately. He would have let me step down if he thought I was being bullied or because people were gossiping. He was a very good man. I didn't give him a chance to ask me any questions though.

"It's just that with the inn, I've got a lot on my plate," I started. "I've been working almost every day, including Sunday evenings, just to keep caught up. Even with hiring part-time help, I've got a lot going on."

Pastor Wright sat back in his chair. "Are you sure that's it?" he asked, watching me closely. "I know you love teaching those kids, and I must say... you're one of our best teachers. The kids adore you, and they learn a lot when they love a teacher like that."

I smiled. I did love those little terrors. "I'm sure... well, besides the obvious, I mean," I said, patting my stomach.

"Yes, I imagine that keeps you even more tired," he said carefully. "You know you can talk to me about anything, right?"

I nodded. I actually did know that.

"And if it's something you don't feel comfortable talking to me about, Mrs. Wright is always available. Night or day."

I nodded again, feeling a little more emotional than I was comfortable with right then. "Thank you, Pastor," I mumbled softly.

"We feel as though you're a member of our family, Jen," he said gently. "Take advantage whenever you feel the need, just like all our other kids," he said with a smile.

I snorted. "I'll remember that," I said with a

sniffle as I stood.

"See that you do," he answered.

I left the church sad that I wouldn't be teaching twice a month any longer, but kind of glad to get it over with. There was nothing else anyone could take from me, nothing else anyone could do or say to make me feel bad about who I was or my baby. I kind of felt... relief. It didn't last long though.

By the time I got home, I was seething again.

Freaking jerks had no right to judge me! I thought. Where was their Christmas spirit? Evidently nowhere in sight even with Christmas only ten days away. I hoped they all got coal in their stockings.

I guess I didn't realize exactly how upset I was until I found myself baking dozens of mini pies and muffins at midnight that evening. I huffed. It wasn't like I had anything else to do, might as well get a jump on the Monday mornin' baking. I set to work, oblivious to everything around me, just wanting to quiet my thoughts and emotions.

"Everything okay down here?"

I was so in the zone and deep in thought as I searched through my cabinets for the last dozen or so mini pie tins I knew I had somewhere, that I hadn't heard Jackson enter the kitchen. I squealed like a little girl half scared out of her wits.

"Holy crap, Jackson, give a girl a heart attack why dontcha?" I said, narrowing my eyes in his direction.

"Sorry about that," he answered with a slow grin.

My eyes widened when I realized what he was wearing… or rather *not* wearing. Low-riding pajama bottoms and no shirt. My mouth suddenly became dry. I shook my head and turned back to my cabinet.

"What are you doin' down here anyway?" I asked. Jackson had been staying at the inn for almost a week now, and he was due to check out in a day or two. I had to admit I was gonna miss having him around. He was kind and funny, and we'd shared dinner and breakfast together every morning and evening. He was easy to talk to and a very steady sort of man. I liked that about him.

Jackson laughed.

I snapped out of my thoughts and glanced back over at him, trying with all my might not to stare at his very nice chest instead of his face.

"You're kidding, right?" he asked. I frowned, not following. "You've been taking a lot of frustration out on those pans and cabinet doors for a few hours now," he said with a smile.

"Oh my lord. What time is it?" I asked softly. Jackson walked over to me slowly. I stood from my kneeling position in front of my cabinets.

"Nearly five AM, I'd wager," Jackson said, his

eyes never leaving mine.

"Sweet baby Jesus," I whispered out a breath. "I am so sorry, Jackson. I did not mean to keep you awake all night."

He reached out toward me, and I stiffened. His smile widened, but my breath caught in my throat.

"It's no big deal, darlin'," he said softly. "Let me just get some coffee in me," he said, his deep voice vibrating along my nerve endings. His arm snaked around me as he pushed the power button on my coffee machine. I blushed and stepped out of his reach. It'd gotten too warm near the coffee pot suddenly. Jackson's eyes crinkled at the corners, and he smiled widely.

"I can't believe I baked straight through the night like that," I said, glancing around the kitchen. Apparently, I'd decided in my haze of anger to fight to control it and get a jump on the day's baking and then some. Hand pies, mini pies, cookies, muffins, fudge, and tons of other goodies lined every surface in my kitchen.

Jackson began laughing. I whipped around to face him, my cheeks aflame.

"Jackson Sharp, don't you dare laugh!" I reprimanded. "Now what am I supposed to do with all this food?" I asked, a hand on my hip.

"Darlin', you won't have a bit of trouble selling off every last pie, you take my word for it," he said as he walked slowly over to me. "You just flash everyone that beautiful smile of yours, let 'em catch a whiff of the magic you make in your kitchen, and they'll be eatin' out of the palm of your hand."

My eyes widened when his hand came out to touch my face. His thumb caressed my cheek, and a small dimple appeared along with his lady-killer grin.

"You've got some flour on you here," he whispered huskily. I blinked once and then twice before my thoughts were coherent enough to understand what he said.

"What's wrong, darlin'," he asked gently, still cupping my cheek.

"I'm pregnant," I blurted, blinking back tears.

"That you are," he agreed.

"I gave up my Sunday school class so I wouldn't cause any trouble for the pastor of my church after some people began talkin'," I admitted, turning my face and eyes away from him.

Jackson turned my face back around gently and tipped my head back to meet his gaze. "They're all just jealous," he murmured.

I snorted and rolled my eyes. "Jealous of what?" I asked seriously. I put a hand on my stomach. "Of this?" I whispered.

Jackson placed his free hand on top of mine on my stomach. "Of course," he answered immediately. "Jealous that you're pregnant with a baby bound to be as beautiful as his or her momma, jealous that you're smart, strong, and a successful business owner. And jealous because they know you're the type of woman who doesn't get beat down when life throws her a curve ball. Instead, you readjust your game plan and become the best one-man team in the US."

I blinked up at him. "That was a very good sports analogy," I said with a grin.

"Why, thank you, ma'am," he answered with a chuckle.

And suddenly, I was aware that I was in the warmth of Jackson's embrace. I was in my pajamas, and he was barely dressed. He must have realized the same thing at about precisely the same moment. He leaned in slowly, cautiously. I didn't stop him. I knew I should, but I just didn't want to. His mouth caressed mine gently, exploring. It was… *nice*. It was eye opening. I pulled back gently in a daze.

"I'm pregnant," I whispered.

Jackson loosened his grip on me and put a little space between us. "I thought we'd already verified that," he said after a moment. He searched my face before taking a step back, raking a hand through his disheveled hair.

I cleared my throat in an effort to clear my mind. "I'm going to grab a shower and get dressed for the day," I said softly. Jackson nodded. "Grab one of those cherry hand pies I know you love to go with your coffee if you'd like," I said with a small smile.

"A woman after my own heart," Jackson said gruffly.

"Jackson…." I began, feeling like I had to say something. *Anything*. I didn't want things to be weird between us. Not when it was his last few days at the Inn.

"You don't have to say anything, Jen," Jackson said gently. "Not a single word that wouldn't tell me what I already figured out."

I smiled shyly over at him before heading toward the kitchen door. "Thank you, Jackson," I said. "For everything you said, I mean." I was blushing ferociously by then. Jackson was back to grinning in his usual, devilish way.

He took two hand pies, set them on his plate, and picked up his cup of black coffee. "No, darlin, thank *you*," he said.

Wicked, wickedly tempting man, I thought with a laugh.

I was still grinning when I stepped into the shower.

Fifteen

Ghost of Christmas Past

"You know, you don't have to do this," I said for the fourth or fifth time. My words fell on deaf ears. "You're supposed to be a guest here, for cryin' out loud," I added in.

"Oh, I am," Jackson said with a grin thrown over his shoulder. He was putting the second coat of white, baby-safe paint on the bassinet. "And believe me, I'm getting the better deal here."

"How do you figure?" I asked, a brow raised in skepticism.

"Well, the room is a great price as is, but add in the cherry hand pies, the free coffee, the best breakfast and dinners in all of Missouri, and I figure I should really be paying a whole lot more for my stay."

I harrumphed.

"Matter of fact, this doesn't even make us even. I should probably start taking up odd jobs around the inn just to even out the scales."

"Jackson Sharp, you are full of it," I said with

a laugh.

"Yes, I am, but let's not discuss exactly what that might mean." He stood up from his job and looked it over.

I joined him. "It looks beautiful," I said softly.

"Looks ready for a baby," he agreed.

I blew in my hands and rubbed them together. "Now, let's get inside and grab a hot cup of coffee for you and cocoa for me in the kitchen."

"Yes, ma'am. You don't have to tell me twice," Jackson said, following me back into the warmth of the kitchen.

Once we were seated and had hot, steaming cups in front of us, I glanced over at Jackson. "So, you finally talk some sense into old Farmer McGregor?" I asked after I'd thawed out a little.

"That man is the most stubborn old jackass in the entire state of Missouri," Jackson said gruffly. "I swear, he has just been messin' with me for the past week. There for a while, I didn't think he even really intended on selling his farm equipment."

I smiled. Sounded like old man McGregor. "But he is?" I asked, curious.

"Yup. We finally came to an agreement this morning. Old coot had the papers already drawn up and ready to be signed, sittin' right there, pretty as you please," he said with a laugh and a shake of his head.

"I'm glad. I'd hate you have to go home empty-handed with nothing to show for all your time and trouble," I answered.

Jackson sat his drink down and smiled at me. "The trip would've been well worth it either way," he murmured.

I blushed and hurriedly glanced away from his intense gaze. "So, you're leave in the morning after all?" I asked gently.

"Looks like I am," he answered carefully.

"I've enjoyed having you here, Jackson. I hope you know you'll always have a room here if you ever happen to blow back through Salem again," I offered.

"I appreciate that, Jen." He was quiet a moment. "If I had another reason to visit, I'd visit often…" he said softly.

I knew what he was asking me. I wasn't stupid. I also wasn't heartless. I liked Jackson a whole lot. Any woman who had half a brain could see he would've been an amazing catch. But… not for me. Sighing, I met his eyes. I put a hand out and laid it on top of his, squeezing it gently.

"I can't give you any other reason." My voice was soft, gentle, and yes… almost apologetic. Jackson looked a little pained and disappointed, but he was too good a man to say so.

"He's a lucky man," he said after a moment.

My mouth popped open to answer, but I clapped it shut quickly. He was right after all. I wasn't over Hunter. I didn't think I ever would be.

"And there's a very lucky lady out there waiting for you, Jackson Sharp." Jackson just shook his head and then continued sipping his coffee. Life was so surreal sometimes.

"I tell you what. You've been working like crazy lately. How about I take you out for a drive tonight to look at Christmas lights?" Jackson asked a few minutes later.

"Jackson...." I began.

He held a hand up. "Just as friends, I promise, Jen. I'm not going to pressure you. I just want to do something nice for you before I leave tomorrow morning." I hesitated. "Consider it a Christmas gift," he said sweetly.

I laughed. "Alright, I'll go. But no funny business, Jackson Sharp, or I'll take back that box of goodies I was plannin' on wrapping up for your trip home," I warned. Jackson threw his head back and laughed, a warm and pleasant sound. *Some lucky woman, indeed*, I thought.

"I wouldn't dream of endangering that box of goodies by getting' fresh, ma'am," he said seriously.

I snorted and then eyed him over the rim of my mug of hot cocoa. "Alright. Later this evening then?" I asked.

"Sounds like a plan," he answered.

I was sitting back, pretty relaxed as Jackson and I drove slowly down the snowy streets. George Jones was playing softly in the background.

"Thank you for tonight, Jackson," I said. "I really did need a night out, and the lights were beautiful in the light snowfall."

"My pleasure. I had a good time too. These little things remind me how much we take for granted, how many simple joys we let pass us by because we're too busy trying to go places and get things in our lives." Jackson shook his head.

"Mud pies and fire flies," I murmured. Jackson smiled like he understood exactly what I meant.

"Mud pies and fire flies," he agreed.

"Is there anywhere you'd like to stop before we head back to the inn?" Jackson asked.

"I don't think so," I answered. "Well… can we stop at the Piggly Wiggly?" I asked.

"Sure. Anything in particular you need? I can go in and grab it for you so you won't have to get out of the truck," he said as we pulled into the parking lot.

"Nah, I need to go in myself and see what it'll be," I answered.

Jackson raised a brow.

"I'm craving ice cream," I admitted shyly.

Jackson glanced out the window at the falling snow and the twenty-something degree weather.

I shrugged. "I can't help what I crave."

Jackson smiled. "What kind of ice cream?"

I blushed again. "No clue, guess I'll find out once I get inside and stare at the cooler," I said with a grin before opening up my passenger side door. Jackson was chuckling under his breath as we made our way into the Piggly Wiggly with only a few minutes left before closing time.

"Vanilla?" Jackson asked.

I shook my head and scrunched up my nose. What a waste of calories... *vanilla*.

He smiled. "Okay, definitely not vanilla. Rocky Road?"

"No."

"Cookies and Cream?"

"Nah.".

"Strawberry?"

"Nope."

"What about butter pecan?"

Ohhh, butter pecan. I grinned and grabbed the ice cream.

"Butter pecan for the win," Jackson said as we headed to pay for our purchase. We walked outside, laughing, with the bag containing my ice cream. I stood in front of the Piggly Wiggly, staring out at the beautiful, snowy evening.

"It's such a peaceful night," I murmured next to Jackson.

"Yes it is. A perfect night."

The baby picked that very moment to make its presence known with soft little kicks and wiggle. I rubbed my stomach through my heavy sweater and smiled up at Jackson. "I think the baby is saying it can't wait for that butter pecan," I said laughingly.

"Can I...?" Jackson asked softly.

"Of course." Jackson put his hand gently on my stomach. I took his hand and moved it across my belly, just in the right place. The baby was showing off its Jedi moves for him. His eyes lit up, and he put a second hand on my stomach. He was smiling widely, seemingly in awe over what he was feeling. I bet he'd never felt a pregnant woman's stomach before.

"That's amazing, Jen," he whispered. I was smiling when suddenly I heard someone say my name from a few feet away. It was a strangled sound, half disbelief, half anger.

"*Jen?*"

Jackson straightened up and took his hands off my stomach. We were both still smiling when I realized who it was that had called my name. *Hunter*.

"Hunter?" I questioned softly. It had been months seen the last time we'd seen each other, and I realized with a jolt that he wasn't even looking at me, not really. He was staring at my stomach. I placed both my hands there out of habit. His eyes roamed over my face then, questioning, trying to comprehend everything. Then he looked over at Jackson, and fury flashed behind his eyes. He took two steps forward before Jackson moved to step halfway in front of me. Hunter stopped. His anger was a palpable thing hanging in the air between us. I was frozen in horror, unable to think of a single thing to say to diffuse the situation. Hunter looked ready to tear Jackson limb from limb, and Jackson looked ready to take up the challenge even if he had no idea what Hunter's problem with him was. Oh man, this was a fine mess.

"Please," I said after a moment. "Let's just go, Jackson." Jackson stiffened in front of me, but as I moved to walk around a patch of ice, he was instantly there, taking my arm so I wouldn't fall before we reached the truck. Hunter had already turned on his heel and strode away back across the parking lot.

"So, that was the guy, huh?" Jackson asked as we walked into the house. I sighed. Jackson Sharp wasn't one to miss a thing or mince words.

"That was the guy," I answered, not even bothering to pretend I didn't know what he was talking about. He followed me into the kitchen where I plopped down in a chair and removed my scarf and hat. Jackson grabbed a spoon out of the silverware drawer and handed it to me as he sank into a chair next to mine. He popped the lid off my ice cream for me. I sighed. *Why couldn't I be in love with Jackson?* I took several self-loathing bites of ice cream before he spoke up again.

"He didn't seem to know anything about the baby," he murmured.

I sank lower into my chair and spoke around a mouthful of cold, creamy goodness. "How do you know the baby's his?" I asked. Jackson snorted.

"I'm not even going to bother replying to such a ridiculous question," Jackson scoffed.

"He hurt me," I replied softly a moment later.

Jackson stiffened.

"Not physically," I put in hastily. "He wasn't there when I needed him the most. Something scared him, I'm not even sure what, but the fact of the matter is he ran and left me to face everything alone." I scraped my spoon across the top of my ice cream and sighed. "Because of that, I decided I didn't want to take the chance that he'd bail on the baby at some point if things got tough. That the baby would love him and then lose him."

"Everyone gets scared of stuff sometimes," Jackson said.

"I know. And I know I should've given Hunter a second chance all those months back when he asked for it. But, the truth of the matter is… it was my turn to be scared." I glanced up at Jackson. He searched my gaze, seeing my heart there. The pain and the uncertainty. I didn't let many people see all of what I was feeling. Not even Beth.

"And now?" he asked.

I sighed and took another bite of ice cream before answering.

"Now I'm pregnant with my pastor's son's baby, and I haven't told anyone but my best friend and you. I wish I had pushed past all my fears and insecurities and given us a real chance. Now Hunter is seeing someone else and is a *bigwig* in his father's company." I set my chin in my hand and propped my elbow up on the table. "Now it's too late to take it all back."

"It might be too late to take it all back, but it's never too late to try and set everything to rights," he said.

"I don't know," I answered.

"What's the worst thing that you think could happen if you told him?" Jackson asked.

"That he won't want anything to do with the baby," I answered.

"He won't have anything to do with the baby if you never tell him anyway," he said in a reasonable voice.

"I know. But what if I tell him and he feels trapped into taking responsibility? Trapped into doing things he doesn't want to do?" I asked.

"If he sees that baby you're carrying as just a trap, then you're better off without him anyway."

I searched Jackson's face. What was this? Tough love or something? "And if he decides to give us a chance and it doesn't work out? Even if I don't let it destroy me… how can I keep it from hurting our child?"

Jackson sat back in his chair and took my ice cream from me. He took a few bites before handing the container back over. "It seems to me you're suffering from the delusion that you can control the future if you just avoid anything that *might* end up hurting you or your baby," Jackson said gently.

My mouth flew open, but he didn't give me the chance to defend myself.

"Life is about taking chances, darlin'. Some of them are small and some of them are big ones. The question you gotta ask yourself is whether or not the risk is worth the end reward."

I sat back, my mind racing with Jackson's words.

"You can't know for sure that this guy will never hurt you again. That he'll never disappoint your little one. But, what you can know for sure is how you feel right now and how you'll feel years down the road knowing you never even gave him the chance. Are you willing to feel this way for the rest of your life and possibly miss out on the love of your life to spare yourself and your child pain and suffering that might not have even happened?"

I stuck my spoon in my ice cream and sat back, crossing my arms across my protruding tummy. "Damn you, Jackson Sharp, for being such an optimist and romantic," I growled.

Jackson grinned at me before stealing my ice cream once again. "If I'm going to be damned, it might as well come from the lips off a pretty woman calling me a romantic," he said with a crooked grin.

I snorted. Of course he was pleased with

himself. He did just turn my entire way of thinking about the baby and the pregnancy around with a few well-spoken and true words, after all.

"And if you ever just need me to open a can of old-fashioned whoop ass on your man for you to get him to see the light… well, I'm just a phone call away and happy to oblige," he said with a wink.

"I appreciate that," I answered with a huge grin.

"Anytime, darlin'," he said. "Well, I better be heading to bed. Got to get all packed up and ready to head out tomorrow morning."

"Alright, Jackson. Thank you for a lovely evening."

"Goodnight, Jen," he said softly as he left the kitchen.

"Night, Jackson," I whispered into the silence. I sat at the kitchen table for a long time before turning out the lights and heading to bed. The inn was going to be closed for the week of Christmas, but I still had baking to do for some catering jobs and for the holidays.

And Hunter Wright was back in Salem for Christmas.

Sixteen

Christmas with the Wrights

"So, your *lodger* left this morning?" Beth asked with a sideway glance.

I continued putting the sheet on the new bassinet mattress, ignoring her tone. "Jackson? Yeah, he left bright and early for Flat River," I answered, shoving the mattress into place inside the bassinet.

"And you heard who is back in town, right?" Beth asked. "I mean, you're beatin' up that poor mattress, so I figure you might've heard."

I stopped shoving the mattress in place and sat down on my bed, deflated. "I did more than *hear* he was in town," I said after a moment.

Beth's eyes widened.

"I kinda-sorta ran into him last night," I confessed.

"Oh my lord!" Beth whispered. "And he noticed all of…." She waved her hand around indicating my stomach.

I rolled my eyes. "It was worse than that," I

admitted.

"Worse how?" Beth asked, setting aside the baby's quilt.

"Well, Jackson and I had been out looking at Christmas lights," I began.

"Holy sh—" Beth barely stopped herself.

"We stopped in at the Piggly Wiggly for some ice cream and when we came out, the baby started kickin', so Jackson asked if he could feel it." Beth groaned loudly. "He walked up while we were laughing and Jackson was cradling my stomach with both hands."

"What did he say?" Beth asked, her eyes wide.

I shrugged as I played with the edge of my pillowcase. "Nothin'. He just walked away," I said softly. "He looked angry and… hurt."

Beth whistled between her teeth and shook her head slowly. "Well this is a fine mess."

"I don't see how it matters," I said softly. "It's not like he doesn't have a girlfriend back in St. Louis or that we haven't really been together for the past six months."

"I told you, Jen. Men like Hunter Wright don't tell women they love them if they don't mean it."

I started to reply when Beth held up a hand and cut me off.

"I'm not sayin' he ain't an idiot for leavin' you high and dry, for not standin' by your side when you needed him there for you, but everyone gets scared sometimes and everyone deserves a second chance. Hunter deserves to know that baby is his."

"He bailed on me at the first sign of trouble," I murmured.

"He did," Beth said.

"He didn't even call me or come see me until after your wedding," I added.

"No he didn't," Beth agreed.

"He did tell me he was sorry and that he loved me, but that doesn't excuse any of it," I growled.

"No it doesn't."

"He deserves a swift kick in the pants," I muttered.

Beth chuckled. "Don't they all?" she asked.

"He may bail on me… on the baby later on down the road," I voiced.

Beth came over and sat on the bed next to me. Taking my hand in hers, she squeezed it. "He may," she answered.

"But he should be told he's gonna be a daddy," I huffed.

"Yes he should."

I smiled wearily and squeezed Beth's hand back. "I guess I know what Hunter will be getting for Christmas," I said weakly.

Beth smiled and patted my hand. "I'll be here for you no matter what, but I think you're making the right choice," she said softly.

Glancing up, I searched her face. I sighed

deeply and sat back into my pillows. "I still love him," I confessed softly.

"Yes you do," Beth agreed with a tiny smile.

"Life is so complicated."

"It is," Beth said. "But it is also unbearably beautiful despite the complications at times." She reached over and laid a hand on my tummy. "This is one of those times."

"Thank you, Beth," I said after a moment.

"Pshaw! That's what I'm here for. Now, get up. Let's get some food and go shop for an outfit for the Christmas Eve party."

I groaned. The annual Wright Family Christmas Party.

Well, this was gonna be fun.

"I don't know, Beth," I said once again. Beth grabbed my arm and pulled me along the walkway that led up to the Wright's front door. I clutched my bag tightly on my shoulder. I was second-guessing even more than Beth imagined. I'd re-wrapped the "*Surprise, we're pregnant!*" gift I'd put together months before in Christmas wrap and planned to give it to him if we got a chance to talk alone.

"You look beautiful. Everyone knows you're pregnant and you *were* invited, Jen," Beth said. "You can't skip out on this. Plus, you provided most of the desserts, so you should be able to enjoy a few of them," Beth added in with a smirk. I rolled my eyes as we made it to the front door. It swung open just as we stepped onto the porch.

"Beth, Jen, we're glad you're finally here. Everyone's been asking for you two," Mrs. Wright said.

"Jen takes forever to do anything now," Beth said with a wink.

I gasped. "Beth!"

"Now, now, I'd watch out what you say, Elizabeth," Mrs. Wright said with a smile. "One day, you'll be the one on the other end of all the pregnant lady jokes and then you'll wish you'd been nicer."

Beth laughed. "Yes ma'am," she said with a grin.

"Now y'all come on in. Everyone else is here already and you know the guys... they'll be actin' like they're starving if we don't feed them soon."

I grinned and followed them into the large farmhouse. I did love the Wright family and when they were all together under one roof, I felt my heart fill up. I'd always wished I had a large family. I had no family now except for Beth, but by extension of her marrying Matt, I'd been adopted into all the Wright family shenanigans. And I loved it.

"The girls are finally here," Mrs. Wright announced as we entered the family room. Hugs and laughter surrounded me.

"Merry Christmas, Jen," Matt said as he kissed

me on the cheek and then put an arm around his wife. "You both look beautiful tonight."

I grinned at Beth, who was beaming at her husband. They were so happy, and I was happy for them. And then Hunter was standing right in front of me, his eyes searching mine. He wore loose-fitting blue jeans and a black, long-sleeved shirt. He looked tired.

"Merry Christmas, Jen," he murmured as he kissed me on the cheek softly.

"Merry Christmas," I whispered. The words barely left my lips before Hunter had turned and walked away. I glanced over my shoulder and caught a glimpse of Beth's look. I ignored her and let myself be pulled into the dining room by Mrs. Wright.

"Let's eat before the men begin to get grumpy," she said cheerfully. "Afterwards, we'll open gifts."

"Thank you for inviting me this evening, Mrs. Wright," I said as we walked into the dining room arm in arm. Mrs. Wright made a sound of dismissal in the back of her throat.

"You're a part of this family, Jennifer Collins," she said softly. She leaned closer and lowered her voice. "And if I'm not mistaken, so is that little one you're carrying," she added gently.

My heart thumped so hard I was sure the entire house heard it. My head felt fuzzy, and I was sure my mouth was hanging open unattractively. "How did you…?"

Mrs. Wright patted me on the arm and led me to my place at the table. I could hear everyone else as they began to enter the room. I met Hunter's questioning gaze from across the room. He had to be wondering what his momma and I were discussing off by ourselves.

"It didn't take a brain surgeon," she whispered. "Once I realized how far along you were, how you were acting when Hunter was at your house during the beginning of the renovations, and how you're normally such a cautious young woman... well, it was an easy conclusion."

"Mrs. Wright, I..."

She then shocked me by pulling me into a hug to whisper into my ear. "No apologizing, Jen. Just know I'll love that grandbaby of mine no matter what and no matter how bullheaded that son of mine becomes." She pulled away and patted me on the back softly as everyone joined us at the table.

Hunter approached us cautiously, eyeing me and his momma curiously as she went about organizing everyone around the table the way she wanted them and laughing with Pastor Wright. I didn't dare meet Hunter's gaze until I'd gotten my own emotions under control.

"What was that all about?" Hunter asked as he took a seat next to me. I was spared having to answer when Pastor Wright called for everyone to bow their heads as he blessed the food. What came next was one of the things I loved most about the Wright family. Noise. Chaos. Love. Usually, I wasn't one for all the craziness, I like everything orderly and in its place, but there was something about loud laughter, joking, and passing food around the table haphazardly that all added up to the perfect family dinner. *Joy*… that was what it was. I could feel the joy in the room as I ate and soaked it all in. There was nothing else like it in the world.

"Hunter… about last night," I said softly halfway into the dinner, while everyone else was talking amongst themselves.

"Yeah, about that." Hunter sat his fork down and turned to me. "I'm sorry I overreacted and just took off like that." I looked up from the little bit of food left on my plate. Hunter looked uncomfortable talking about it. I knew how he felt.

"I was just shocked to see you…" He motioned to my stomach. "And with someone else," he added, his jaw clenched. A muscle twitched in his cheek. Evidently, he was still a little angry about it.

"I know. And I'm sorry you had to find out like that. I'd hoped to seen you sooner so it wouldn't have come as quite as much of a shock as it did," I said.

"And he treats you well?" Hunter asked through gritted teeth.

I searched his face, confused.

"The guy you were with, the baby's father. He's good to you? Makes you happy?" he questioned.

My eyes widened, and I took a deep breath. "He's not the baby's father," I whispered. Hunter's head swung around, his eyes widening as he let what I said sink in. "We weren't *together-together* last night either," I offered. "Jackson was just a friend who took me out to see Christmas lights."

Hunter shook his head. "I saw the way he looked at you," he accused.

I shrugged, not knowing what else I could say. "He wanted there to be more between us, but I didn't," I said. "He was staying at the inn, but he left this morning."

Hunter's mouth popped open, but he quickly closed it. I could see all the emotions he was sorting through as they crossed his face. Anger, relief, hurt, and confusion.

"If he isn't the father…" Hunter began. I tensed up. This was the question I'd been dreading from the beginning. The one that could cause so much pain, so much damage, or so much… joy. "…then who is?"

I sighed and turned to him to answer just as Pastor Wright stood and announced that we were all moving into the family room for eggnog and to open presents. The noise tripled as everyone stood from the table. Hunter's oldest brother, Daniel, had his arm around me and was leading me out of the room before I could reply. We followed everyone else to sit around the Christmas tree.

Besides making the desserts and individual

goody tins for everyone to take home, I also wrapped a small, personal gift for everyone. I guess I just hadn't thought I was going to receive one from everyone in return. Soon covered in lovely gifts from Beth, Mrs. Wright, and everyone else in the Wright household, I had let my mind drift away from my problems and what I was going to say to Hunter once we were finally alone and able to talk. Instead, I let myself enjoy the evening, laughing with everyone and soaking in the best Christmas Eve I could've wished for. If my momma had been there, everything would have been absolutely perfect, but with my hand on my tummy and a joy in my heart, I knew she had to be looking over me right about then. When a second gift from Beth and Matt landed on my lap, I glanced up into her grinning face, confused.

"I already got a gift from you guys, Beth," I warned.

"I know," she said quickly, moving to sit back down between Matt and Keith on the large sofa. "This one isn't for *you*." Beth was positively beaming.

The entire room was watching me, including Hunter from his seat across the room, so I sucked it up and opened up the pretty wrapping. I sucked in a breath and blinked back tears. I ran a finger along the edge of the beautiful, large frame. Beth had taken copies of the baby's ultrasound, the photos we'd taken the previous week of my pregnant belly, and a gorgeous poem about motherhood and had them placed in a keepsake frame.

"Thank you, Beth, Matt, it's beautiful," I said softly.

"Well, might as well open this one too then," Daniel said with a wide smile, placing a large gift bag on my lap. "Keith and I couldn't help ourselves," he said with a wink over at his partner. The bag was filled with lotions, socks, onesies, and tons of other helpful baby stuff. It also included one of those baby books you could fill up with all the baby's "firsts".

"And while you're at it, here's a gift for the baby from Pastor Wright and me," Mrs. Wright said.

I was shaking my head. "You guys, this is all too much... I don't know what to say." I fingered the wrapping paper on the stack of gifts Mrs. Wright had piled near my feet.

Daniel snorted. "You don't have to say anything, sweetie. Don't let anyone fool you," he said with a crooked grin. "We all just used your pregnancy as an excuse to buy all the tiny things we never get a chance to and we wish we could more often. Believe me, it's more about us than you," he explained. Everyone laughed and nodded in agreement. His eyes were twinkling and I knew he was playing it off... wanted to give me an out from becoming a blubbering, emotional mess.

"Well, I don't know," Pastor Wright said after a moment. "It has a little to do with you. We all love you, Jen, and we wish you and that precious little bundle the best," he said. Mrs. Wright nodded, wrapping her arm around her husband's waist.

"Now open the presents!" Beth commanded. Everyone laughed and added in their own commands. I was smiling like an idiot when I began to open the rest of the baby's presents. Diapers, toys, clothes, and more. The Wrights had truly gone overboard. But when I opened the final gift, my eyes swam with tears. I lifted the beautifully hand-knit blanket, hat, and booties out of the gift bag and sat them on my lap. A pretty, gender neutral sea green, I knew they would match the baby's quilt and bed just perfectly. They were absolutely breathtaking, and I knew Mrs. Wright must have taken a lot of time working on them for the baby. The details were exquisite.

"You shouldn't have," I murmured with a sniffle.

"Of course I should have," Mrs. Wright said gently, her eyes saying everything she couldn't. *Anything for her grandbaby.*

"Thank you so much, everyone," I said through my tears.

Beth wiped away her own tears and then shook her head. "How about some of that eggnog?" she broke in. "Just make sure it's the non-alcoholic for the preggo lady." Everyone laughed, and I was glad to have a moment to get my emotions under control.

The rest of the evening went by quickly and before I knew it, I was headed back home to spend

Christmas Eve all by myself.

It was after ten when I finally made it home and changed into my nightgown.

It was approximately fifteen after ten when I realized the gift I'd wrapped up for Hunter wasn't in my bag where I'd placed it.

It was about seventeen after ten when I realized the gift must've fallen out of my bag in the Wrights' living room while unwrapping gifts… and that I'd left it behind.

It was exactly eighteen after ten when I realized that Hunter Wright was about to find out he was my baby's daddy. And it was at exactly that same moment I muttered a few choice words that I'll never *ever* admit to actually saying so long as I live.

Seventeen

Baby, It's Cold Outside

It was Christmas morning, and someone was knocking on the front door. Scratch that, they were most definitely *banging*. I debated pretending I wasn't home for a moment, but I quickly discarded that idea. My car was out front, and it was Christmas morning after all. I glanced over at the back door in the kitchen. Make a run for it? I looked down at my fuzzy, white house slippers and protruding tummy. *Nope.* I took a deep breath and headed for the front of the house, where the banging had gotten louder and more frantic.

"Jennifer Collins, come open this door."

I cringed. Hunter sounded angry. I got to the door and pulled the sheer curtain away from the glass window. Hunter's eyes met mine. They were as wild as his hair, which looked like he'd ran his hands through it no less than a hundred times that morning. He was wearing jeans and a gray T-shirt in twenty degree weather. I unlocked the door and pulled it open.

"Come in and get out of the cold, Hunter," I said. I stepped back to let him enter and shut the door behind him.

"I need to talk to you," he said gruffly.

"So I gathered," I answered with a sigh as I headed back into the kitchen. I poured a large cup of coffee, adding two spoons of sugar and a splash of milk before handing it over to him.

"You should've been wearing a jacket," I admonished. "You're gonna get sick running around in the snow in short sleeves."

"I don't care about that," Hunter said angrily. I sat down at the table and waited for Hunter to do the same. A growl accompanied by mutterings I chose not to understand accompanied him as he sat roughly into a chair across from mine.

"You got my gift?" I asked. Hunter's eyes met mine; he was still processing, still kind of in denial and shock. I glanced down at my hot tea. "I didn't mean to leave it there. I'd planned to give it to you myself when we got a moment alone to talk." Hunter ran a hand roughly through his hair, his arm muscles flexing from the force.

"You're sure?" Hunter asked.

Jackass. I narrowed my eyes. "That I'm pregnant?" I asked, a hand on my enlarged belly. "Pretty freaking sure," I snapped.

Hunter's gaze softened.

"And if you meant if I'm sure it's yours, I'll

kick your behind right back out in the snow without a second thought, Hunter Wright," I promised with a glare. Another angry swipe through his hair. Looked painful.

"I'm sorry, Jen. I didn't mean that. I have no clue what I meant; it's just a lot to take in. I'm trying' to understand," he said quickly. "Why didn't you tell me before?"

My heart clenched painfully. *Before he had a girlfriend and a great job traveling around, he meant,* I thought.

"I had a lot of reasons. Some were good reasons, I thought," I said. "Others maybe not so much, but I did what I thought I had to do at the time."

Hunter stared at my stomach for a while. "How long have you known?" he asked softly.

Putting a hand on my stomach, I rubbed it back and forth. I stood slowly, and Hunter jumped out of his seat as if he suddenly realized I might need help. I rolled my eyes.

"Come on. Let me show you something," I said as I left the kitchen. Hunter followed me up the stairs and into my room without saying a word. Walking over to the baby's bassinet, I laid a hand on the soft blanket Mrs. Wright had knitted that hung over the side. I turned around toward Hunter. He was looking around my room, his eyes taking everything in. We'd argued over this room the last day he'd been helping with the renovations. Well, I'd argued—Hunter had just taken the brunt of my anger and confusion.

"The room expansions... they were for the baby," Hunter murmured. He walked over and ran a hand along the tall chest of drawers, which had tons of baby products laid out on the top and was filled with newborn necessities. He moved across the room to stand next to me and stare down at the bassinet, newly painted with a fresh mattress inside, a beautiful old quilt, and Mrs. Wright's gifts inside. His eyes met mine, and I couldn't read them. There was too much going on in his mind, too much to sort through. I sat down on the edge of my bed and waited for Hunter.

"I knew the day after Beth and Matt's wedding," I whispered.

Hunter's eyes widened as he remembered back. "When Beth had me come check on you and you'd been crying...."

I nodded, looking down at my lap. Hunter was starting to piece everything together on his own.

"The way you were acting when I was here during renovations." He clenched his jaw, hurt, and then anger flashed. He stood there, thinking back, probably doing what I'd done countless times—replaying all those times we'd spoken, all the times we'd been together since the wedding.

"And St. Louis?" he asked softly after a few moments.

I sighed and leaned back into my pillows. My back was killing me.

"I'd gone to get a few things for the inn, like I said," I answered. "And then I was planning on seeing you... to tell you about the baby. I'd bought the gift you found last night that day and was going to give it to you, but then..."

Hunter sighed deeply and shifted on his feet. "But then you saw me with Tabatha," he filled in.

Tabatha. So, that was her name. I tightened my lips and turned my face away from his searching gaze. I nodded. And then Hunter... *chuckled.* I whipped my head back around, not sure if I should be angry or worried.

"Hunter Wright. You stop laughing right this instant," I commanded.

"We weren't together then," he said.

"What?" I asked, confused.

"Tabatha and me. We weren't together. She had been hinting around that she wanted to date, but we weren't at that time." He shook his head and picked up the baby's knit blanket.

I replayed everything I'd seen that day in St. Louis. Had I overreacted? Been so blind by my own hurt and disappointment that I'd read more into the situation than was truly there? I swallowed down the thick knot that had formed in my throat.

"That doesn't matter now. You guys were dating when I saw you on grand opening day of the inn," I said softly.

Hunter nodded. "We were then, yes," he

answered.

"So it doesn't really matter at this point, does it?" I asked thickly.

Hunter smiled and sat the baby's blanket back in the bassinet. "I said *were*," he whispered.

"Were?" I asked. "What does that mean?"

"It means exactly what you think it does. We *were* dating. Past tense. As in, not presently."

His eyes watched mine, waiting for me to say something. I had no idea what he expected me to say. I had no idea what I should say, so I didn't say anything. My mind was having a hard time keeping up with everything I was feeling.

"And you and this Jackson?" Hunter asked after a moment. His gaze was intense.

I licked my lips. I needed a drink… of water. Yeah, a drink of water. "Jackson?" I asked with a raised brow. "Jackson is just a friend like I said. Just a good man who stayed at the inn as a guest."

"He wanted more," Hunter said.

"He did," I confirmed, watching Hunter from my spot on the edge of the bed.

He walked over to me. "But you didn't?" Hunter asked softly. I fidgeted, smoothing out the fabric of my T-shirt over my baby bump.

"No, I didn't," I answered finally.

Hunter knelt down in front of me, just inches away from me. "Why didn't you?" he asked seriously. A muscle ticked in his cheek. "He seemed like the type of man who would've taken care of you… of the baby." His eyes flashed dangerously and I suddenly felt surrounded by him, caught up in the turbulence of his intensity and of my own emotions.

"He was that type of man. A good, honest man who wouldn't have blinked twice about taking care of another man's baby as his own," I answered softly. Hunter turned his face away from me, but not before I saw the anger there.

"So, why didn't you let him?" he asked harshly. "Love you. Take care of the baby."

I reached out a shaking hand and caressed the side of Hunter's face, moving it until his eyes met mine. "Because he wasn't you," I whispered. "And I didn't love him, couldn't love him, because I'm still in love with you." I leaned forward and let my forehead rest gently on his.

"I'm sorry, Hunter," I said. "I should have told you before now."

Hunter shook his head gently and brought a hand up to cup behind my head. "Jennifer Collins, I've loved you for a long time now," he murmured against my cheek. His lips skimmed across mine and then he kissed me gently, showing me without words how much he missed me, how much he loved me.

My heart was pounding in my chest. *This*. This felt so right. Hunter pulled away. He was smiling. His eyes widened, and he sat back on his haunches. Holding a hand out slowly toward my stomach, his eyes asked for permission. I nodded. He rested his hand lightly on my belly and then added his other hand a second later. He still looked flabbergasted, kind of like his entire world had been rocked off its axis. *Welcome to my world*, I thought with a tiny smile.

"Is it a boy or a girl?" Hunter asked, his voice thick with emotion.

"It is a little surprise," I answered. "The baby wouldn't let us catch a glimpse to find out what we are having," I added.

Hunter raised a brow and glanced back down at his hands resting on my huge stomach.

"Of course, Beth is convinced it's a girl."

Hunter chuckled softly.

"She's already bought a truckload of pink clothes and has been referring to the baby as *Little Elizabeth*."

"Sounds like Beth," Hunter muttered.

I grinned. Sure did.

Suddenly, the baby kicked gently against Hunter's hand. His eyes widened into saucers and a smile spread across his face. "Did you feel that?" he asked in awe.

I nodded, not having the heart to voice the *duh* that immediately sprung to mind. Hunter rubbed his hand back and forth until the baby kicked again. He laughed and bent forward to place a small kiss on my stomach. I blinked away the tears that formed in my eyes. Such a gentle touch, a kiss for his unborn child, such reverence. I'd been wrong to keep the pregnancy from him.

"Let's get married," Hunter blurted.

Maybe I hadn't been wrong after all.

Eighteen

Oh No You Didn't

"Jen, calm down," Hunter said, which, of course, only infuriated me all the more.

Calm down. As if.

"Hunter Wright, you're lucky I didn't clunk you over the head with something hard. Of all the idiotic, boneheaded ideas," I yelled. I slammed a pan down on the stove, adding a pad of butter and a little oil.

"What are you doing?" Hunter asked as he paced back and forth in the kitchen behind me.

"What does it look like I'm doin'?" I asked sharply. "I'm making breakfast. I'm hungry. And I'm angry. And when I'm angry, I cook, okay?" I asked, miffed.

"Okay," Hunter said, his hands raised in surrender.

"You'd know that if you *really* knew me at all," I shot out.

"I do know you," Hunter countered. "I know that I love you. I know you love me, and I know you're havin' my baby."

I groaned and cracked several eggs into the sizzling pan. "That's not enough," I answered, popping bread into the toaster.

"Of course it is and once were married, you'll see how right I was," he offered up.

Oh, wrong thing to say buddy, I thought. I swung around with my spatula in my hand and pointed it at him.

"You think for one second that's enough and that I'm actually gonna marry your sorry behind just because *you love me* and *I love you* and *we're havin' a baby*, then you've got cotton between your ears, Hunter Wright!" I shouted. Hunter looked more confused than ever, and I had to turn around and flip the eggs before I threw my spatula at him. I'd never been angrier at him than I was right then. Hurt? Yes. Angry? Not even close.

"Sweetheart, once you calm down, you'll see that what I'm sayin' is right," Hunter said with a nod of his head. "Once your pregnancy hormones stop making you crazy and you get some food in you, you'll realize what I'm telling you is what has to happen."

"Hunter, I swear on all that is holy, if you don't stop your yammerin' right this instant and sit down, you're gonna regret ever getting' out of bed this morning," I promised through clenched teeth.

Hunter wisely decided to do as I suggested. I let my thoughts and emotions swim around my head as I continued making breakfast. I knew Hunter would try something like this, and yet it still took me by surprise. Surprise that any man in his right mind would propose like he had. Hunter was about to get a dose of reality. Even if I wanted to marry him, even if I loved him with all my heart, even if he felt the same way about me, marriage wasn't the answer to all our problems. And I refused to use marriage like a big 'ole Band-Aid to cover up the ugly problems and the old wounds that still festered.

A few minutes later, I sat a plate of eggs, corned beef hash, and toast, along with a glass of orange juice, in front of Hunter. I sat down across from him with my own plate and glass. Hunter clenched his jaw in frustration when he realized I wasn't going to talk just then. I couldn't. Not yet. I had to let myself cool down a bit, and I was starvin'. Hunter shook his head and began eating too.

Once we were both done, I got up to clean off the table and do the dishes. Hunter stood with a sound of frustration and took the plates from my hands. I cleaned off the table as he did the dishes in silence. I grabbed two saucers, served some fresh apple cobbler onto them, and headed into the living room. Hunter followed, his eyes telling me he was clearly not pleased with being put off. We both ate in the living room where the Christmas tree sat. It *was* Christmas morning after all.

"I'm not going to marry you, Hunter," I said

calmly a few minutes later.

But—" Hunter began.

I cut him off. "Almost everything you said is right," I said. "I do love you, and I believe you love me too. And we are having a baby together." I took his hand and placed it on my stomach.

"Then what's the problem?" he asked in confusion.

"First of all, did you even wonder why I decided not to tell you about the baby straight out?" I asked. Hunter frowned. "It wasn't because I thought you wouldn't be a good daddy or that you wouldn't want anything to do with our baby," I assured him.

"Then why?" he asked.

"Because you hurt me, Hunter," I said truthfully. "You hurt me more deeply than you know. When you left without saying a word right when I was at my lowest and most terrifying point in life, I was shattered. I felt abandoned and alone."

Hunter flinched away from my words.

"I don't even know why you did it," I confessed. "But then I found out I was pregnant, and suddenly you were in my life again at the exact moment everything had been turned upside down. And the only thing I could think was that I never wanted the baby to feel alone. To feel unwanted if things got tough. I didn't want to be left to face life's most difficult moments alone when I counted on you. I wasn't sure if whatever caused you to bolt could happen again after the baby came, and I didn't want to take the chance that it would devastate our baby like it had me." I swallowed and looked up into Hunter's eyes. He looked pained, sick even, but he needed to hear all the truth. He needed to understand everything.

"We don't know everything about each other, Hunter. And I'm not sayin' we have to, but we *do* need to get to know each other a bit more before we even talk about something as important as marriage," I suggested softly.

Hunter was very quiet, letting everything I said soak in. After a few minutes, he sat back and met my gaze. "Alison Carter," he said softly.

I scrunched up my forehead. Alison Carter sound familiar somehow, but I wasn't sure why or why Hunter was mentioning her right then. Hunter ran a hand over his face, clearly worn out.

"Her brother, Logan, and I were friends. Alison was a year younger than us and a *girl*, but that didn't keep her from hanging out with us any chance she got. She hated everything girls were into, and so she didn't fit in. She enjoyed boy stuff way too much," he said with a sad smile. "Our families got together often to cook out, go swimming, you know, the usual stuff. Soon, I realized I'd fallen in love with Alison. My first real, honest-to-God crush."

I swallowed slowly and relaxed beneath Hunter's hand as he rubbed it back and forth gently in soothing circles. "How old were you?" I asked.

"Oh, I don't know. I guess about sixteen. Still a boy, but growing into a man," he answered sheepishly.

"What happened?" I asked softly.

"One summer, we were all hanging out at the river. Most of our family was there barbequing. We were all having a good time, laughing and listening to music. Several of us kids were out in the water. I was watching Alison's brother showin' off on the bank, getting' ready to jump in, when I turned to Alison, who had been swimming close to me." Hunter swallowed. "I don't even remember what it was I was going to say… but it didn't matter. She wasn't there. I called out her name, looked all around, and then I began to panic. I screamed for her, hollered for help. I dove under the water looking for her until I could barely breathe myself. I couldn't find her anywhere. None of us could. My dad and Daniel had to drag me out of the water."

I put a hand to my mouth, horrified for him, for what he'd gone through.

"They found her body down river that evening. Something about her having a seizure; some kind of medical condition caused it that they never even knew she had," Hunter murmured. "I was never the same after that," he confessed.

I lifted the edge of the arm of his T-shirt, revealing the only tattoo he had. A rose being squeezed by thorns with drops of blood dripping down. The initial A.C. and H. W. were on either side.

Hunter Wright and Alison Carter.

"I got that after I turned eighteen, about nineteen months after Alison died," Hunter said.

"I'm sorry, Hunter," I whispered. Hunter sat back once again and pulled me with him. I let my head fall on his chest. I remembered hearing about the drowning now that Hunter brought it up. It happened only a county over, and I was pretty sure my momma had sent flowers and food to the family. I'd had no idea Hunter had known, *had loved*, the girl who died.

"It's not an excuse," Hunter promised. "But, that's why I left. I got scared. Plain and simple. I was terrified I'd lose the only woman I'd ever truly loved. That history was bound to repeat itself. I'm sorry for that, Jen."

"It's okay, Hunter. I get it, I do. But you see now what I mean, right?" I asked. "About us not knowing all that much about each other? And that rushing into marriage, no matter how much we love each other, no matter how much I want to, could be disastrous?"

Hunter pulled me closer and sighed deeply. "I know I don't want to hurt this baby and that I want to be a part of yours and the baby's life in whatever capacity I can," he answered slowly. "Don't get me wrong, I plan to marry you, Jen, so you might as well just get used to the idea, because I plan to work very hard from here on out to make you see just how good we will be together."

I couldn't help myself. I was grinning. "I can

live with that," I answered softly.

"So, what happens now?" Hunter asked.

I melted into him, suddenly tired from staying up all night worrying about that stupid present. "Now we have a baby," I answered easily.

"And what happens between us?" Hunter murmured as he kissed the top of my head. "Where do we go from here, since everything is all out of order?"

Man, was he ever right about that. I thought for a moment. "Well, there's a nice little movie theater downtown," I said with a small smile. "I hear the owner may be able to hook us up with some free tickets and all the boxes of *Whoppers* this pregnant girl can eat. I also heard it's a good spot for first dates and makin' out." I peeked up into Hunter's face.

He looked half amused and half surprised. "Jennifer Collins, mother of my unborn child, are you asking me out on a date?"

I grinned impishly. "Yes, I think I am," I answered with a laugh.

Hunter watched me for a while before answering. "I think a date would be perfect," he answered softly. He nuzzled my ear, making me squirm and giggle. "Especially the making out part," he murmured.

I swatted his chest.

The curtains in the living room were pulled back, revealing the snow-covered front yard. We sat there watching the snow as it fell, blanketing the world outside in a fresh layer of beauty. It reminded me of new beginnings and of fresh starts. Something Hunter and I were lucky enough to have together.

"Merry Christmas, Hunter," I said.

"Merry Christmas, sweetheart."

Nineteen

A New Year, A New Start

"So, dating, huh?" Beth mentioned.

"Yup. Dating."

"This is good, right?" Beth asked, eyeing me over the apples I'd tasked her to core and peel.

"I think so," I agreed. "Time to really get to know each other before the baby gets here and see if we can work everything out together.

"Makes sense," she said. "And Hunter was good with the idea?"

I snorted as I continued peeling my own pile of apples. "Once I got it through his thick skull that I wouldn't be marrying him, yeah, he was good with it."

Beth's eyes were round. "He asked you to marry him?"

"Demanded, more like it. Me in my pajamas, him just back in town and speaking to me after months, and he decided marriage was the answer," I huffed, peeling the apple in my hand a little too harshly.

"Men can be such knuckleheads sometimes," Beth muttered.

"Preachin' to the choir," I said with a sigh.

"But everything is good between you guys now, right?" Beth prodded.

I smiled. "It's very good," I confided.

"I'm so glad, Jen," Beth said.

"Yeah, he went home on Christmas afternoon and told his family, except for Matt, of course," I said. Matt had been home with Beth, and Beth had let him in on the family gossip.

Beth was grinning. "Matt was so shocked that he didn't say anything for an hour," Beth said with a shake of her head. "I have no idea if the biggest shock was that you were pregnant by his baby brother or that he was old enough to be an uncle." Beth and I both laughed.

"Hunter said his father had the same reaction. He said Daniel just laughed and congratulated him, Mrs. Wright cried, and his father was just shocked he was going to be called grandpa soon," I said with a chuckle. "Of course, Mrs. Wright knew even before Hunter. I swear I will never try to keep something from that woman again."

Beth clucked her tongue. "A fruitless endeavor. Mrs. Wright is a sharp woman. She had to be while raising three boys… She's the only woman in that family." Beth and I both shuddered.

"I'm just glad everything is out in the open

now." I sat my peeler down and cut few pieces of apple to nibble on. "It took entirely too much energy keeping all those secrets." Beth swiped a few pieces of apple for herself.

"And what about Hunter's job with the company?" Beth asked.

"He's going to keep running it in St. Louis for now. But he's going to cut back on trips until the baby is born, and then try to work mostly from their home office here and commute when he needs to." I shrugged. Hunter said he hated the traveling and was glad he was going to have an excuse to work more closely to home. He was a homebody. He'd only agreed to the traveling because he thought we were over.

"And the business here seems to be doing great," Beth said with a wide smile.

"It's doing real good. The inn is super slow right now, but that's to be expected. The bakery is doing enough to make up for it."

"You seem happy with how everything has turned out," Beth said softly.

I smiled. "I am. I guess I should be all stressed out or freaked out or whatever, but I think that time has passed. I feel good about where I am right now and where mine and Hunter's relationship is," I answered with a shrug. "That will probably change just as soon as I'm headed into the delivery room."

"Don't worry, I'll remind you of this very

moment when you said you were all calm and whatnot," she said.

I laughed and nodded my head. "And you would too."

"So, when will you be seeing Hunter again?" she asked.

"He's going to be in St. Louis for a day or two, and then we're going to go out for lunch and do some shopping for the baby together this weekend."

"Wow. He must *really* love you if he's letting you drag him out shopping," Beth said with a romantic sigh and a dramatic flutter of her lashes. I rolled my eyes and tossed an apple peel at her.

"And after that?" she asked.

"And after that, we'll see," I said. "Though I happen to know Hunter has a pair of Super Bowl tickets burning a hole in his pocket, so we might take an overnight trip for that."

Beth raised a brow. "Ooh la la," she murmured.

I rolled my eyes at her again. "I don't want to rush this. I want us both to really get to know each other and to realize what we're getting into here," I explained. "And I never want to be proposed to again in my pajamas, looking like a tired, beached whale all because that is what we think is expected. I want it to be right."

Beth blinked a few times and then turned her face back to her job. "I should kick Hunter's rear end *for* you for that messed up proposal," Beth muttered darkly.

"Awe, don't go givin' him a hard time. He was dealing with everything the best way he knew how," I said. "And I gotta say... he took a lot in in a short amount of time and handled it pretty well. I could've done without the impromptu proposal, but it could've been worse."

"That's very true," Beth agreed. "Still, I thought the guy had more game than that."

I laughed. "Well, he loves me, I love him, and we're both dedicated to being there for the baby," I said. "What more can I ask for?"

"What more could any of us ask for?" Beth said with a small smile.

I started chopping the apples for hand pies and apple crumble.

It was a beautiful day for baking.

Twenty
Just a Love Story

I look like a freaking blimp, I thought as I stared at my reflection. I was wearing a red halter-topped, baby doll dress with a flirty hemline that hit just above my knees and a little, pink sweater. I didn't know in that moment if I'd kiss Hunter or hit him if he brought me a box of chocolates for Valentine's Day. I ran my hand over the top of my stomach and turned to the side. *Not much longer now, little one*, I whispered. Only four weeks left before my due date.

"Jen?" I heard the door shut behind Hunter as he entered the house downstairs. I grabbed my small purse off the bed and gave myself an once-over in the mirror. I huffed. Well, I was as good as I was going to get.

"Coming," I yelled down. I came down the stairs, excited for our big night out and our first Valentine's together. We'd gone out together twice a week since Christmas—to the movies, out to eat, shopping, sometimes just out for long walks and to talk. Things had been going well, and I was starting to feel like we were on the right path. When I made it to the bottom of the stairs, Hunter came up to me with a look of absolute love and longing on his face. I could feel myself blushing. It never ceased to amaze me that as huge and unattractive as I sometimes felt, Hunter could wipe all that away with a single glance.

"You look beautiful," Hunter murmured. He held out a hand filled with pink roses and baby's breath. I grinned, reaching out and bringing them to my face to breath in the intoxicating scent. Hunter brought his other arm from behind his back and held out a small, plush puppy with floppy ears and a large, heart-shaped box of chocolates.

"Happy Valentine's Day, sweetheart," Hunter said softly. I smiled up into his eyes and closed the space between us. Hunter took his time showing me exactly how much he'd missed me. And how much he loved me.

"You keep kissing me like that, and I'll be wanting to stay here instead of going out," I murmured against his lips. Hunter pulled back and grinned wickedly.

"Oh no you don't, Jennifer Collins. I get to be seen out on the town tonight with the prettiest girl in all the world. You can't take away braggin' rights from a guy on Valentine's," he said with a wink.

I slapped a hand on his chest. "We're just

going to have dinner and see a quick movie then," I said. "Because this baby insists on sitting right on my bladder lately and doesn't give Mommy a rest." Hunter bent down in front of me and put his hands around my stomach. I rolled my eyes as he spoke to the baby. He'd been doing it a lot lately, saying he was determined that the baby's first word was going to be Daddy.

"You hear that?" he said with his lips near my stomach. "Mommy says you're not letting her rest, but Daddy says when you come out that you can play, kick, and wiggle as much as you want and he'll be right beside you, not bothered in the least."

I glanced down at the top of his head. My heart swelled each time I saw him like this, bonding with his baby. I knew without a shadow of a doubt that the highlight of his day, of his week, was when he was with the baby and me, and that knowledge kept me going day after day despite my comfort and despite being well over the pregnancy honeymoon phase. Hunter continued on his little banter with the baby for another minute or so before standing. He had a black dress shirt on with the sleeves rolled back and pair of black slacks. He came straight from his office in St. Louis to pick me up.

"Suck up," I muttered.

Hunter threw his head back and laughed. "I have to get my time in when I can. You get her to yourself twenty-four hours a day," he said.

I raised a brow. "Don't I know it," I answered. "And… her?" I asked, teasing.

Hunter shrugged. "Beth has finally gotten to you," I said with a tsk.

Hunter reached over and gave me another breath-stealing kiss. "The only person that has ever gotten to me is you, Jennifer Collins," he said huskily. He stepped back and took my goodies from me. "Now let's go before I let you talk me into stayin'," he said with a wink.

We had dinner at our favorite Italian restaurant just outside of town before we headed for the movie theater. We went in through the front without tickets and stocked up on all kinds of goodies before heading to our theater. There were a lot of perks to loving Hunter, but owning movie theaters was high on the awesomeness list.

"There's no one in here," I whispered as we found the best seats in the whole room. Front and center, midway back. Close enough to see everything, but far enough away we didn't get a kink in our necks. I settled back into my super comfortable chair while Hunter settled beside me. He was fidgeting with the goodies we bought, turning off his phone and wiping his hands on his pants. What the heck? Twitchy much?

"You need to go to the bathroom?" I asked with a crooked grin. Hunter rolled his eyes at me. "And where is everyone?" I glanced around the theater. It was Valentine's night, surely other people in Salem thought a movie date was a good idea that night.

"I reserved this specific theater just for us," Hunter said. He laughed at the expression on my face.

"You reserved us an entire theater?" I asked, gobsmacked. Hunter reached over and pushed my jaw up. I took the hint and closed my pie-hole.

"It pays to be the owner," he said by way of answer.

"I guess so. And by extension, to be the sweetheart of the owner," I said.

"You'd be right about that, sweetheart," he murmured.

The lights begin to dim, and the regular movie theater commercials began playing. I leaned over, resting my head on Hunter's arm. I was a lucky lady.

Once the normal, *buy your goodies in the lobby and don't be a jerk, turn off your phones commercials* were over, the good previews would begin. I relaxed into Hunter. Previews were one of my favorite parts of going to the movies. But instead of a normal preview popping up, something else caught my attention.

On the screen, a few simple words, set in a scenery of black and white, appeared, making my mouth pop open and my heart hammer in my chest. I sat up in my seat, letting go of Hunter's arm.

"Once upon a time, a beautiful princess was born." A baby picture appeared then. One of me when I was a newborn, one that had been in my mother's room for as long as I could remember. I blinked in

confusion and glanced over at Hunter, who was smiling. He pointed back up at the big screen. *What the heck?*

"*Her mother named her Jennifer Collins.*" Another picture of me appeared, but this time, my mother was in the picture as well, smiling and holding me in her lap. I clasped a hand over my mouth, blinking back tears of surprise.

"*Jennifer grew in beauty and grace and everyone loved her, for she was a kind and generous little girl.*" More pictures now. Pictures of my mother and me when I was growing up. Pictures of Beth and me after we'd become friends in grade school. Pictures of me in school and at church.

"*One day, Jennifer grew up and became a lovely young woman. She was strong, smart, and a friend to everyone she met.*" Pictures of me helping out at church and of Beth and me at her wedding. Pictures of Hunter and me the past summer and even more recently.

"*When Jennifer became a mother, her grace and beauty multiplied tenfold. And so did everyone's admiration of her.*" Tears were running down my cheeks now. Pictures of me pregnant, ultrasound pictures, pictures of Beth patting my stomach, and of Hunter kissing it and kissing me.

"*Then one day, Hunter Wright (the handsome prince) came back into Jennifer's life after making the worst mistake of his life by running away.*" Pictures of

Hunter pouting and one of him obviously begging for forgiveness. Pictures of us together I hadn't even know someone had taken. I was laughing and crying at the same time. Hunter pressed a napkin into my hand as I watched the screen.

"The handsome prince, Hunter, became a father when Jennifer became a mother and he wanted nothing more in this world than to welcome their new baby into a family when she was born." Pictures of Pastor and Mrs. Wright holding up a sign that read: *"Welcome to the family, Grandma and Grandpa love you."* A picture of Daniel and Keith holding up a sign that read: *"Welcome to the family. We're your favorite uncles."* And finally, a picture of Matt holding up a sign that read: *"Welcome to the family, little Elizabeth,"* and Beth holding up one that read: *"Now put the man out of his misery, Jen!"*

I snorted. Leave it to Beth. The final picture faded away, and another screen popped up.

"You see, Hunter realized his life was incomplete without the lovely Princess Jennifer by his side. He wanted her to know that he loved her more than he had loved anyone his entire life and that his love for her and the baby she carried was stronger than his fears." A picture of Hunter on his knee, holding a dozen roses and a ring box.

And then a final screen.

"Will you marry me, Jen?" was all it read.

The lights started to come on slowly, and I

glanced over to Hunter beside me. He was kneeling on the floor next to me, holding out a ring in a small, black box. Tears were pouring down my face and I was sure I looked like a hot mess, but it didn't matter right then. All that mattered was Hunter.

"Jen, I'm not asking you to marry me tomorrow, or even six months from now. I know I hurt you, and that we have a lot of learnin' about each other left to do," he began. "But I want you to know that there's nothing on this earth that's going to pull me away from you and our baby again. I'm here for the long haul." Hunter smiled crookedly and pulled a pretty white diamond ring out of its box, holding it out to me.

"Say you'll marry me… *eventually*… Jen. Say you'll let me love you until the end of time," he said gently. "Say you'll make me the happiest man in the world."

I sniffled and wiped my eyes on another napkin. "I love you, Hunter Wright," I answered softly. I smiled crookedly. "And I guess you're really gonna be stuck with me now," I answered softly.

Pausing, I watched Hunter's eyes widen. He was terrified.

"Yes, Hunter, I'll marry you… eventually," I said with a wink.

Hunter *whooped* loudly, standing up and gathering me gently in his arms. My stomach took up a lot of space and he laughed, reaching down and enveloping my belly in his arms.

"You hear that? Mommy is going to marry your daddy," he whispered hoarsely to my tummy. "How lucky is Daddy, huh?"

Tears streamed down my face. Joy and love shown from Hunter, and I felt so very blessed. Soon, I was aware of a lot of banging from close by. Hunter grinned crookedly and nodded to the movie booth. I glanced behind us.

"Oh yeah, I forgot to mention that we have an audience," Hunter said offhandedly, with a small, roguish smile.

My eyes rounded. What in the world?

A few moments later, the theater was filled with everyone I loved. Beth and Matt, Pastor and Mrs. Wright, and Daniel and Keith. I gasped as I was surrounded by Hunter's family… and now *my* family. Mrs. Wright was crying and so was Beth, but everyone was congratulating us and clapping Hunter on the back.

It was chaos.

It was loud.

It was *perfect*.

Twenty-One

One Plus One Makes Three

"Are you sure you should be doing this as big as you are?" Hunter asked.

I turned to him and stared him down with a withering glare. "I'm sure I did not hear what I think I just heard," I gritted out.

Hunter winced. "What I meant was, can't this wait until after the baby is born, sweetheart?" he amended sweetly.

I blew out an exaggerated puff of air, moving the hair hanging in my eyes. "When am I gonna find time to get all this done after the baby arrives?" I asked. I looked around the kitchen. Pots and pans were everywhere, drawers and cabinets had been emptied out, the curtains had been taken down, and I had one hand full of newspapers and the other gripping a bottle of window cleaner.

"Jen, the baby is going to be here any day now. Your due date is tomorrow, and the doctor said your body is getting ready to deliver." Hunter looked around at the mess I'd made and shook his head. "I'm just not sure you should be doing all this work."

"Well, the spring cleaning ain't gonna do itself," I said, spraying the windows over my sink. "I mean, did you see the dirt come off that ceiling fan?" I asked, waving toward the once-dirty ceiling fan in the center of the room.

"Your kitchen was immaculate before, sweetheart," Hunter reasoned. "I could do all this for you. Why don't you go and put your feet up or somethin'?" Hunter suggested.

"I can't, Hunter," I answered. "I realize I'm acting kinda crazy… but I'm *feelin'* kinda crazy right now." I sat the bottle down on the counter and wiped the window with my newspapers.

"You ever feel like you're about to crawl out of your skin?" I asked. "Like something's about to happen and you have no control over it whatsoever, so you grasp onto all the things you *do* have control over?"

Hunter nodded and ran a frustrated hand through his hair.

"Well, this is the only thing I have control over right now, and I'm graspin' the hell out of it," I explained. "I just want everything perfect for the baby's arrival. I've got reservations for the inn every single week for the next three months and all the baking that will be waiting on me once I'm back from maternity leave… I just don't want to have to worry about cleanin' and such on top of everything else."

Hunter came over and stood in front of me. He pushed the hairs that had escaped my messy bun out of my eyes and grinned at me. "Okay. I get it. We'll get this done today then. I'll make sure of it," Hunter agreed. He leaned forward and kissed me on the tip of my nose. "But if you try climbing a ladder again today, I'm going to tie you to a bed until the baby decides to come," he threatened.

I swallowed and nodded my head. "It's a deal," I said with a tiny salute. Hunter gave me a small kiss and then turned on his heel to finish scrubbing out the drawers and cabinets. I returned to the windows.

"The baby's been awful calm in there today," I said, rubbing my tummy. "She's hardly kicked me at all."

"Well, the doctor said that would happen once we got closer to your due date since the baby's startin' to run out of space and all that," Hunter answered.

I sat my cleaning supplies down and started washing my hands off in the sink. "I'm going to go grab the curtains off the line," I said, heading for the back door.

"Okay."

I took a deep breath as I walked outside. My backyard was the epitome of spring. Flowers startin' to bloom, a nice, warm breeze blowing through. I closed my eyes when I reached the clothesline. I loved this time of year. I loved spending time out here in my garden and even hanging my linens to dry on the line. There was something serene and cleansing about the whole process. Maybe it was because my momma had loved it, and I had so many fond memories of us together hanging clothes and talking. Maybe it was the time alone and the fresh, country air I enjoyed most. Whatever it was, it made me smile. I reached up and took the clothes pins off the kitchen curtains. I held them to my face and inhaled. Clothes even smelled better when they were fresh off the line.

A dull ache in my lower back knocked the smile right off my face. I'd been feelin' that all day. I hadn't told Hunter. I didn't want to worry him. I was sure it wasn't anything anyway. Just random pregnancy pain, and man, had I had a lot of that the past few weeks. I began walking up to the house when another dull ache in my back, combined with a sharp pain shooting around my lower abdomen, took me by surprise. I gasped and laid a hand on my stomach. *Ouch.* I came back into the house a whole lot less cheerful than when I had went out.

"Can we hang these real quick?" I asked, pasting a smile on my face.

"Sure," Hunter said, coming over to help me put them on the curtain rod and then hanging them up for me.

"I'm almost done with these cabinets. I'll start putting everything back in the drawers as soon as I'm done," Hunter said with a smile.

I smiled back and then turned to get myself a glass of ice water. Maybe I did need to take it easy. After the kitchen was finished, I'd talk Hunter into a movie up in my room. I could relax on the bed for a few hours.

"How about a movie after this?" I said, voicing my idea as I walked across the room to sit down for a second.

"Sounds great," Hunter said, not looking up from his work. Another pain came, hurting enough to stop me in my tracks and pulling a small gasp from my lips. Hunter stilled, his head whipping around to find me standing in the middle of the kitchen, clutching a glass of water with one hand and my stomach with the other.

"Jen?" Hunter asked quickly. "What is it, sweetheart?" He dropped what he was doing immediately and rushed over to help me to the table. The pain was gone by the time I sat down. Hunter was kneeling next to me, his brow creased in worry. I laid a hand on his shoulder.

"It's over now. I guess I did overdo it," I said with a small, apologetic smile.

Hunter searched my face, clearly not even close to being satisfied with that answer. "How long have you been in pain?" he asked seriously.

I shrugged. "I just had some dull aching in my lower back today," I answered honestly. "The sharp pains didn't start until I went to get the curtains off the line."

"Okay. So, what do you need me to do?" he asked. "You need something to eat? A pillow for your back? We should get you upstairs to rest."

Smiling, I reached over to kiss him lightly on the lips. I felt like it'd been an eternity since I met Hunter Wright. I was sure I'd love him for at least that long. "I'll go upstairs if it will make you feel better," I said softly. I stood from my chair with his help and walked out of the kitchen.

"Maybe I'll watch some HGTV for a while or something," I said as we entered the living room.

"Sound like a plan," Hunter said distractedly.

I raised my foot to climb the first stair to go upstairs when another pain hit me with enough juice to take my breath away. *Son of a....*

"Jen?" Hunter grasped me around the waist and led me over to an armchair. "Jennifer Collins, speak to me, sweetheart," Hunter begged.

I realized I'd sucked in a breath and was concentrating so hard to get through the pain that I'd tuned Hunter's voice right out. "I'm fine," I gasped out. "I'm fine." I glanced up at Hunter, gave him a little smile, and shrugged.

"It looks like you better grab my overnight bag from upstairs," I said. Hunter's eyes widened into two saucers. "My phone and purse too." Hunter stood there staring at me, a deer in headlights. I clucked my tongue.

"Not to freak you out any more than necessary, but you'd better get a move on, babe," I nudged. Hunter snapped out of his frozen state and took the stairs two at a time. I heard doors slamming open and winced. I sure hoped he didn't break anything. He was back downstairs just about the time the next contraction hit me.

"Get the car, Hunter," I gasped. "And call Beth and your momma. We're about to have a baby!" Hunter had his phone in his hand and hit call before the words had completely left my mouth. He was on his way out the door when I heard his words to his brother Matt.

"It's time. Operation *I'm Gonna Be a Daddy* is a go!"

Even through the pain, I couldn't help but smile.

Twenty-Two

It's a... Baby!

"You can say it now," Beth whispered from her coveted spot on the edge of the bed. She was holding the baby, not even looking at me.

I rolled my eyes. I knew this was coming. "I don't know what you mean," I said.

Beth glanced up from the bundle in her arms and raised a brow before quickly looking back at the baby. "Don't play coy, Jennifer Collins. You know exactly what I mean," she answered back.

Mrs. Wright, the only other person in the room at the moment, snorted. "Better tell her what she wants to hear, Jen," she said. "She ain't gonna let you rest until she hears it."

I harrumphed as well as I could while wearing a hospital gown and reclining back in a bed. "Fine," I said finally. "You were right," I answered.

Beth grinned, but she still didn't look at me. She was mesmerized by the little one in her arms. We all were. Mrs. Wright had to threaten Hunter and the rest of the Wright guys out with things only a momma could threaten them with to make them go get some food and for Hunter to get a shower before coming back to the hospital.

"That's right," Beth cooed at the baby. "Your Auntie Beth knew all along you were a little princess."

I shared a glance and a small smile with Mrs. Wright. And Beth had been right, of course. Exactly six hours and twenty-two minutes after we made it to the hospital, little *Elizabeth Grace Wright* was born, weighing in at seven pounds and eleven ounces. Named Elizabeth for Beth, of course. And Grace for my mother, Evelyn Grace Collins. She was all of twenty inches long and the most beautiful baby in the entire universe. And she'd been told as much a hundred times in the past twenty-four hours since she'd made her debut into the world.

"When will they let you go home?" Mrs. Wright asked.

"As long as everything looks good with the baby and me, it looks like we'll be discharged tomorrow morning," I answered. And it wouldn't come a moment too soon. I was ready to get out of the hospital and get back to the comfort of my own home. I'd never been a fan of hospitals... too many bad memories.

"You guys did good, Jen," Beth murmured, holding a hand out to me.

I smiled and grasped her hand in mine.

"Thank you, Beth," I whispered, fighting the tears. There'd been enough of those the past few days.

"We should go and let Jen and the baby get some rest," Mrs. Wright suggested.

Beth sighed and placed a gentle kiss on the baby's tiny head. "Yeah, I guess I've kept them awake long enough, hogging up all the baby snuggles," Beth said. She handed the baby to me and stood next to Mrs. Wright.

"We'll see you back at the inn tomorrow," Mrs. Wright said softly. I nodded at her and Beth. The baby was snuggling into my chest and fighting her sleep. And I was helplessly under her spell.

Hunter just couldn't stay away. He was supposed to come and pick us up at the hospital the next morning, but here he was, entering the room behind a nurse later the same evening. At least he looked refreshed and showered. His eyes lit up when he entered the room and found me and the baby awake and sitting up in bed.

"Hey, sweetheart," Hunter murmured before placing a kiss on my lips and then one on the baby's forehead.

"You talkin' to me or your newest little sweetheart?" I asked.

Hunter flashed me a wide smile and then one at his daughter. "Both," he answered softly. "Can I take her?" he asked.

I nodded and helped him pick her up gently.

He sat down next to me in a rocking chair. "You know she's going to be spoiled rotten before we ever leave the hospital, don't you?" I asked with a happy sigh.

Hunter shrugged. "If this is spoiling her, then I'm a hundred percent for it," he answered. I smiled as I watched him with little Grace. It was clear to anyone with two good eyes, heck, even one would do the job—that Hunter Wright was head over heels in love with the little bundle in his arms.

"She's going to want to be held all the time," I warned.

"Well, then, I'll just quit my job, sell the business, and become a full-time baby holder," he answered seriously.

I snorted. "You just want to make her a daddy's girl," I accused with a smile.

"And what's wrong with that?" Hunter asked with a twinkle in his eye. "Then I'd have the two most beautiful girls in the world under my spell," he said with a wink.

"Oh really?" I asked with a raised brow. "You got me under your spell, huh?"

Hunter looked down into the face of our daughter and smiled, his face full of wonder and love. "You're right," he agreed. "I'm the one under the spell." He looked up at me as he held the most precious thing on the planet to either of us in his arms and smiled.

"And I never want to be anywhere else," he said softly.

Epilogue

Tutus & Cowboy Boots

"You guys look like you spent a lot of time in the sun!" Beth said. She only sounded a little jealous.

I grinned over at Hunter, who was talking with his dad and brothers as they stood around the barbeque grill. Hunter winked at me, and I blushed. We sure had. Our honeymoon had been beautiful and relaxing. It had lasted two weeks and had taken us forever to finally get around to. Six months after we'd married, in fact. Time flew when you were busy and had a two-year-old to care for. For our honeymoon, we had gone swimming, snorkeling, took surfing lessons, and even spent some quality *"alone time"* on our private beach one evening. *A lot of things checked off my bucket list*, I thought with a grin.

"Oh my, I don't even want to know what that smile is all about," Beth said with a smirk.

I cleared my throat and shook my head.

"Momma… Daddy say… Uncle Matt likes 'em,"

my little princess said as she patted my arm.

I glanced into the bucket and squealed. A frog. *Ick*.

"Okay, honey, well, how about you go and show Uncle Matt then?" I said with a gentle push. Grace was wearing a leopard print T-shirt, a pink tutu, and a pair of brown cowboy boots. All curtesy of Auntie Beth. I rolled my eyes. I had to admit, though, Grace reminded me a lot of her Aunt Beth. Same wild and restless spirit, same heart of gold, same inexplicable love for cowboy boots.

"So, when do you find out what you're having?" I asked. Beth laid a hand on her tiny stomach and growled. I was grinning.

"Not for another four weeks," she said. "Doggone kid. Now we have to wait until they can fit us in at the place that does those fancy ultrasounds." Beth frowned. She had been very displeased when the doctor couldn't tell for certain what she was having.

I grinned. "Well, you know what I think…" I said.

Beth held up her hand. "Don't you dare, Jennifer Wright. I'm warning you," she shrieked.

I just sat back and took a sip of my sweet iced tea, watching her from over the rim of my glass. She didn't want to hear my predictions. *She is so havin' a boy*, I thought to myself with an evil chuckle. Beth raised a warning finger, and I laughed.

Matt came over, kissing Beth on the cheek

and rubbing her stomach. He was beaming with love for his wife and their unborn child. In a few months, Grace would have a little cousin to play with.

Grace's giggles and screeches drew my attention to her. Her daddy was chasing her around the yard. When he caught her, he lifted her up over his head and blew on her exposed tummy. I smiled softly. Hunter then carried her over to her grandpa and uncles, where they all pretended to fight her big, bad daddy to win the hand of the fair princess. It was times like this that I was reminded just how much I had to be thankful for. And at times like this, I was sure I could feel my momma's presence all around me.

My life was beautiful.

Had the journey to get to where I now found myself been what I'd always thought it would be? A straight and perfect road, planned out in detail and followed exactly? No, it hadn't. But I wouldn't have traded my curved, unplanned, and imperfect journey with anyone else's.

Just like life… I found I actually preferred my journey with all its detours and glorious imperfections.

Perfection was overrated and imperfection was reality.

Life was imperfection.

Life was a… *perfect contradiction*.

The End

Read on for an exclusive look into the next Contradiction novel—Beautiful Contradiction.

Releasing via Crimson Tree Publishing in 2016

One

Charlie

"'mon, James, I don't want to let this jerk win," I said in exasperation. James put a hand on his hip, a sure sign he was agitated.

"It's not about winning or losing, Charlie. It's about keeping you safe," he snapped, his crystal blue eyes daring me to argue further with him. James MacAvoy, my agent and longtime friend, was quite a bit older than I was, but not so much so that people didn't have fun writing articles about what all we did or didn't do together behind closed doors. That would have been a decent story, except for the simple fact that James not only treated me like a younger sister, but he didn't exactly have a thing for the opposite sex of which I was a part of either. We shared a Chicago condo, which I was sure added fuel to the fire, but it worked for us since our schedules were so busy. He hated to let them think we were sexually involved, but I told him I didn't mind. After all, if they were so sure he and I were banging boots, then they wouldn't dig deeper into my personal life or his. In my eyes, that was a win-win.

"I know… it's just that I feel like getting away for a few weeks is the same thing as running from this." I slung an arm out toward my bedroom, where several policemen were still writing notes and taking pictures. I'd been getting weird messages lately on my phone and in my fan mail. I chalked it up to some weirdo trying to freak me out. When you were in the public eye, these things happened… I knew that. But when I got home from shopping that afternoon and found my apartment door ajar, things had escalated to a whole new level. James had also happened to be out of the apartment, and we were still trying to figure out how whoever had broken in had gotten into our building in the first place. We had tight security, and we were in an upscale neighborhood. But that didn't stop my stalker from getting into my home and then making his way back to my bedroom. The police officers had been at the scene for several hours when they finally began packing up to go home. James saw them to the door.

I walked over to my room and looked around at the mess. My room, my personal space, had been violated, and I wasn't even sure if I could ever sleep there again. All my lingerie had been artfully arranged on the bed, snapshots of me doing so many different things, regular everyday things, were spread on top of the satin and lace. At any other time, the photos would have been pretty, artistic even, but they were too intimate, the photographer catching my moods, the way I held my head when I was listening to someone, the way I chewed on my bottom lip while trying to make a decision. The photographer had been watching me for a very long time and knew my habits well. I shivered and rubbed my hands up and down my arms. At first, I had been angry. I'd seen red over the incident, but now… now I just felt violated and *scared*.

"Charlie?"

I sniffled and turned toward James. His face was scrunched up in concern and in anger. When he saw my face, his anger vanished.

"Come here, hun," he said softly. I put my head on his chest and let him wrap me into his embrace as I cried. "Don't worry, sweetheart. The police will find this creep, and you'll be back in Chicago and back in front of the camera before you know it."

I nodded my head as he kept telling me how everything was going to be okay and how I could use a nice trip to the country anyway. I went to sit down on the couch as James did what he does best and took control of the entire situation. Before I even knew what was happening, the mess in my room had been cleaned up, my bags had been packed, and I had a ticket in my hand for the first flight out of Chicago the next morning. I was going to be flying under an alias, which happened to be my birth name, a name that

Perfect Contradiction

not even the press knew—Charlotte West.

The high-profile, world-famous, real-sized runway model Chey Weston was about to disappear.

Two

Jackson

"That'll be fine," I said into the telephone. My good friend, whom I happened to owe a favor to, as he reminded me several times, had some rich kid from Chicago needing a place to lay low for a few days.

"My friend in Chicago says this kid, Charlie, is some kind of high-profile client of his. He's having trouble of some sort and wants to get out of the city until everything blows over," John said apologetically. "I would have him at my house, but I'm in the middle of ripping down half the kitchen for renovations."

I sighed. The truth was, I didn't like someone in my house all that much. I was a private sort of man. I did have plenty of room out here all to myself though, and the agent was willing to pay a nice little sum for a week, so I was tempted.

"How do you know this guy?" I asked.

"We met a long time back when I'd moved to Chicago thinking I could hack it livin' the city life,"

John said with a chuckle. "James wasn't such a big deal back then and when we met at a mutual friend's wedding, we found we had a lot more in common than an inner city kid and a boy from the country should've had. We had lunch weekly after that to talk and keep track of one another."

I shook my head. If John liked him, it meant James MacAvoy couldn't have been all that bad of a guy. I sighed again.

I did wonder why this guy, Charlie, didn't talk to me himself. A twenty-four-year-old man could surely make a call on his own. Aw, hell. I hoped he wasn't one of those uptight, rich city guys who wore all black and only listened to heavy metal, trying to defy his rich daddy at every turn.

"Not to offend you or anything, John, but this guy, Charlie… he ain't into drugs or anything bad, is he?"

"No, no. He ain't into drugs or anything like that," he answered.

So, maybe Charlie was just a spoiled rich kid. I could handle that for the extra money. "Good, then I don't see a problem. I'll have a room ready for him when he gets here, and I'd be glad to pick him up from the airport."

"That would be perfect. Thanks, Jackson! I appreciate this, man," John said in a rush. "Charlie will be there bright and early in the morning at seven-thirty via Astor Airlines, flight 202. I'll call you tomorrow to see how you and Charlie are gettin' on."

"Sounds good," I answered before ending the call. Rubbing the back of my neck, I went to put away the bills I'd spread across the table.

Looked like I was getting' a housemate in less than twenty-four hours and a little extra cash to take care of a few of these bills.

I sure hoped the guy wasn't a slob.

About the Author

Peggy Martinez is the author of The Sweet Contradiction Series, which was picked up by Crimson Tree Publishing in early 2014 and is scheduled to release under this new imprint in the Summer of 2014. Martinez's New Adult Contemporary Romance series will include Sweet Contradiction, Perfect Contradiction and Beautiful Contradiction.

www.ingramcontent.com/pod-product-compliance
Ingram Content Group UK Ltd.
Pitfield, Milton Keynes, MK11 3LW, UK
UKHW041301180426
11947UKWH00009B/602

9 781634 221061

PRAISE FOR THE BOOK

'I am sure readers, especially aspiring managers, sportspersons and those making a crucial career choice will benefit hugely and adopt certain aspects explained in the book in their day-to-day lives' SACHIN TENDULKAR

'A roadmap for all of us to help unlock our full potential and make the most of our talent' STEVE WAUGH

'This book gives a perspective that only Simon could share – showcasing his intellect, honesty, and attention to detail that made him a world class umpire. The messages and learnings apply to both sports and business people aspiring to be better. It's a fascinating read' JOHN WARN, Former CNSW Chairman & Westfield senior executive

'Simon belongs to that rare breed of leaders who epitomizes integrity and honesty. A gentleman of impeccable character. My interactions with him have been very enriching and it's no surprise that this book has hit all the right chords' RAVICHANDRAN ASHWIN

'A must-read for aspiring match officials, and for so many others who in business, leadership, and life are working towards being the best they can be' DARREN GOODGER, Executive Officer at NSWCU&SA, State Umpire Manager

FINDING THE GAPS

Simon Taufel is a five-time ICC Umpire of the Year and was a part of ICC's Elite Panel of Umpires, till he retired in 2012. He later, took over as ICC's Umpire Performance and Training Manager and remained in this role till September 2016. He now lives in his hometown in New South Wales and travels the world, to speak at business institutions and train executives in leadership, values and integrity.

FINDING THE GAPS

SIMON TAUFEL

IVL

Published by IVL
www.integrityvaluesleadership.com

ISBN 978-0-6487602-0-7

Copyright © Simon Taufel 2019

All rights reserved. No part of this publication may be reproduced, stored in or introduced into a retrieval system, or transmitted, in any form, or by any means (electronic, mechanical, photocopying, recording or otherwise) without the prior written permission of the publisher. Any person who does any unauthorized act in relation to this publication may be liable to criminal prosecution and civil claims for damages.

This book is sold subject to the condition that it shall not, by way of trade or otherwise, be lent, re-sold, hired out, or otherwise circulated without the publisher's prior consent in any form of binding or cover other than that in which it is published and without a similar condition including this condition being imposed on the subsequent purchaser.

*This book is dedicated to both of my families.
The one off the cricket field (Helen, Harry, Jack, Sophie,
Ella, Yolanda, John, Kiel, Tegan, Chris, Mamiko, Anna,
Josh, Roger, Robert, Michelle, Andre, Sylvia and Adrienne)
and the one on it (everyone at the NSWCU&SA,
Cricket Australia and ICC)*

CONTENTS

Foreword by Sachin Tendulkar — xi
Introduction — xiii

1. The hardest call I've had to make — 1
2. The game begins before the game begins — 19
3. Results through routines — 37
4. Adapt to advance — 56
5. Attitude determines your altitude — 64
6. Coachability — 73
7. We cannot be perfect — 91
8. Seven traits of a top team — 100
9. Leading with integrity and values — 122

Contents

10.	The 'C' word	139
11.	Pressure can create a diamond or burst a pipe	162
12.	Managing conflict	176
13.	Why focus beats concentration	190
14.	Bouncebackability	199
15.	Discipline is the difference	220
16.	Use by date	249
17.	Enjoy the journey	261

Acknowledgements   270

FOREWORD

AN EARLY STARTER TO being a celebrated international cricket umpire, then a mentor to budding adjudicators, and now a leadership and performance consultant, Simon Taufel has indeed come a long way.

It takes tremendous zeal and courage to take one's experiences and learnings as a cricket umpire and mentor to a different level and share the same with the future managers of the world. I am glad Simon has decided to pen all his interesting experiences in the form of a book, which takes us through an intriguing journey of life and how to encounter situations at large.

My two-decade long association with Simon has been fascinating and eventful; we share a warm and cordial relationship. He was one of the most genuine international umpires I have come across. Simon, as we all know, took to umpiring at a relatively young age, before going on to become one of the best in the business. Receiving the ICC Umpire of the Year title five times in a row bears ample testimony to his ability to reaching the top and staying there.

As Simon has rightly pointed out, success does not come on a platter. It involves a tremendous amount of hard work, dedication, and patience. For one to be at the top one must leave aside his ego, and one must remember that you have to be competing with yourself and keep bettering yourself. He has also stressed the need for coping with failures and not to lose focus.

As a sportsperson, I can relate to the contents of the book. Simon has put across the various aspects of experiencing and tackling different categories of situations in a very lucid manner.

Simon has left no stone unturned in making sure the readers get the ideal insights in tackling various situations and work towards becoming good leaders. I am sure readers, especially aspiring managers, sportspersons, and those who are making a crucial career choice, will benefit hugely and adopt certain aspects explained in the book in their day to day lives. The book will be handy for future leaders in shaping up their professional life and for the current ones in adding more value in their existing roles.

I wish Simon and his book all the success.

Sachin Tendulkar

INTRODUCTION

HAVING SPENT OVER TWO decades studying the world's best in different endeavours, to see what they did to attain world class, I don't believe the 'formula' or 'ingredients' have changed. My development as an umpire on the cricket field from grassroots to the international level, followed by several years in training, coaching, and administration, has taught me a lot about myself and what it takes to get to number one. And, thus, I wanted to share my successes, failures, and learnings with a broader audience. For those whom I cannot meet in person, I'd love to have a conversation via this book. I want to share some of the highs, the lows, and critical takeaways, about what it takes to get to world class, stay there, and exit on your own terms.

If you don't already have a coach or a mentor, get one. It was one of the best decisions I made early on in my career, and even today I have and use them. This book covers many transferrable skills and techniques that can be applied to just about any vocation or person. If you seek sustainable success and longevity at the top level, you need to be a good person. We are who we are every hour of every day and our personal qualities and values underpin whatever we choose to do with our lives. The door to personal growth and development opens inwards.

Most of us are good at something, but the challenge is to be great – I sincerely hope that the contents of the chapters help you identify the performance gaps (with your coach) that can be closed so that you too can be great.

We live in an age of increased self-gratification and self-interest. There are significant leadership challenges in many industries, political parties, religions, companies, and sports. We seem to be crying out for our leaders to do the right thing, to make the hard decisions, and to serve with humility, respect, and compassion. Just like the game of cricket, leaders can get themselves into trouble when they take something simple and overcomplicate it.

One of my dislikes is seeing things wasted. I dislike wasted opportunity, wasted talent, wasted food, and wasted money, for example. It is so disappointing to see people not explore opportunities, or to see people with talent not use it to their potential. It is similar to seeing food go into the bin when others go hungry. Have you ever reflected on how many people would give to have your talents or your opportunity or your health and abilities? Why would you not use them to their potential? Apart from asking you to think about your own 'game', whatever your 'game' may be – business, sports, charity, or contribution to society – I hope this book inspires you to reach for your potential and try something new.

Well done for deciding to pick up this book. And thank you. I hope you will get something valuable out of it that will make a difference if you choose to act on it. While knowledge is powerful, it is useless unless you do something with the information. My challenge to you is to take at least one thing from each chapter and make a positive shift in behaviour to be a better you – to be the best person you can be.

1
THE HARDEST CALL I'VE HAD TO MAKE

BEING A CRICKET UMPIRE and having given this chapter title, you may think I'm about to narrate the story behind answering a difficult appeal, but the 'call' is not about something that happened inside the boundary. Rather, it was an occurrence during one of my travels to the cricket ground.

1 March 2009. The second Test match between Pakistan and Sri Lanka was scheduled to be played in one of the largest cities of Pakistan – Lahore. I had officiated in Pakistan around six times already, and during those assignments I had found the people and environment very welcoming. Visiting and officiating in cities like Lahore, Karachi, Faisalabad, Islamabad, and Peshawar, all have their challenges; however,

in each of those cities, I found moments to enjoy and memories to cherish. This last trip to Lahore though was to produce something that I would prefer not to recount or ever see happen again. The events were to change not only my life, but the lives of many others and also the global game of cricket.

Facilities here are often basic, life for the locals is fairly simple, and structures and processes are less formal, but what unites the people is the love for cricket and their team. The surroundings are normally filled with smoke and pollution from burning rubbish, and the antique trucks, cars, and tuk-tuks pack the roads, the constant sound of horns reverberating around. The place has, in its own way, its natural charm and character.

We were staying at the Pearl Continental Hotel in Lahore, only a few kilometres from the Gaddafi Stadium, home also to the Pakistan Cricket Board (PCB). The hotel was a terrific place to spend time at, the staff always looked after us well, even though language was challenging at times – especially when ordering food. I was part of the umpiring team, with fellow members Steve Davis (on-field umpire), Chris Broad (ICC match referee), Nadeem Ghauri (third umpire), and Ahsan Raza (fourth umpire). We were ably supported by our ICC regional umpire manager, Peter Manuel, a Sri Lankan, and the local liaison offer provided by the PCB, Abdul Sami

Khan. Our liaison officers were critically important in these parts of the world, as they allowed us 'normality' on our off days by helping find and purchase essentials and visit places of interest to help keep the cabin fever of hotels at bay.

As I said, I'd been to these parts several times before and it was always good coming back to Lahore to see known faces like Abdul and our regular driver, Zaffir, plus several of the PCB umpires, who became part of my family away from home. You do develop some tremendous and close relationships with these people and their families, which is one of the greatest joys of what we do.

Before this series, Steve, Chris, and I had been quite aware of the potential security issues within Pakistan, and we went to extraordinary lengths to communicate with the ICC on these matters and we were given repeated assurance. The first Test in Karachi came and went without incident, but as we were finishing it, there were murmurs about possible issues in Lahore, and there were talks of holding the next Test match also in Karachi. The only people who were interested in staying on were the batsmen as during this Test several of them, like Younis Khan, who scored a triple century, had loved the pitch and conditions at the venue.

But the decision was made to play the next Test in Lahore, and we started preparing to head there, however that was where we hit the first hurdle. We boarded the plane on time, but sat for almost an hour. I was asleep and quite comfortable when an announcement to get off the aircraft, following a technical problem, was made. There was a fault with the landing gear and we were put on another flight a couple of hours later. I was glad the discovery was made before takeoff!

The couple of days leading up to the next Test in Lahore were quiet, but our activities were limited given that many streets in the city were closed due to political demonstrations and protests. The pre-match humour had come from my struggles at the hotel and several restaurants to get a simple iced coffee. They would arrive as iced chocolate, iced coffee made with water, iced coffee made with hot milk, etc.! I ended up making my own by just asking for the ingredients and preparing it in front of Steve at the table. Adaptability and perseverance are necessary traits to be a successful international cricket umpire.

Before long the first morning of the Test arrived. It's a day which always brings about a bundle of nerves, anxiety, and excitement. In umpiring for me, there is still this paradox – you cannot wait for the match to start and when it does you cannot wait for it to finish and 'survive' the experience, metaphorically speaking, without making too many mistakes. On this first morning, the large security convoy left the hotel sharp at 8.15 a.m., with lots of police, guns at the ready, and sirens going. I remember thinking we must not have been too popular making so much noise early on a Sunday morning with no one on the streets as we woke the locals from their Saturday night slumber. Our van nearly took out a police motorcycle through a roundabout, but he survived and so did his pillion police rider carrying a machine gun … but maybe a change of underwear was required for him!

We arrived at the ground which was bathed in sunlight, despite the photochemical smog. Pakistan won the toss after some confusion, it must be said, from the calling captain and the commentator in charge, so, just as well, the referee, Chris Broad, was also present. Apart from some political disturbance on the ground that day, the only other commotion worth noting came in the form of several blokes in orange T-shirts cheering and clapping for the umpires. Yes! The 'Taufel Fan Club Lahore'! I recall pulling out the radio off my belt and saying to my fellow on-field umpire, Steve Davis, 'Thank goodness, after at least five years of coming here, they finally spelt my name right on the banner!'

Soon enough we had reached day two. We took off again in a convoy and sped through the local streets of Lahore at a speed close to 100 kilometres per hour. Steve and I loved our driver, Zaffir, who seemed to excel at giving us whiplash and crunching the gears. Steve had named him 'Bobby brake hard' due to Zaffir only having two driving speeds they being stop and very fast! Our heads were either well out in front of our body or well behind our shoulders. The weather again was ideal for cricket, not too hot and the sun was 'shining'. Sri Lanka pushed on and amassed a massive total of over 600 runs.

The Sri Lankan batsmen weren't the only ones ducking bouncers. David Richardson, the then ICC general manager, was invited into the commentary box for around half an hour and he found a lot of tough questions bounced his way on topics such as the referral system, location of the Champions Trophy, how to play more cricket in Pakistan, and such others. All questions, no doubt, were played with a straight bat.

Day 3. 3 March 2009. A day that saw the cricketing world change forever. For some a life-changing experience, for others, unfortunately, tragedy.

Just like every other day, I followed my usual routine, but reached downstairs at the hotel lobby a little earlier at 8.15 a.m. Peter Manuel was always the first to reach and wait for us at the lobby. Being a creature of habit, I would typically sit in the same spot in the van, especially when the match was going well for me. I'm a little superstitious regarding some aspects of my game, and this was one of them. But that day, for some reason, I didn't go by my habit. I chose to sit towards the back with Peter. He got in first and went over to the back seat. I followed him in and took the seat in front of him. As I said, not my usual spot. A decision and event that would later prove to have made a significant difference.

As was customary for security, both the team buses and the match officials' van travelled together in a convoy with the armed police and an ambulance, that would be the last vehicle in the motorcade. We waited in the hotel driveway for the Pakistan players to board their bus. After a while, and not being able to depart at the agreed time, the security team decided to have the convoy leave for the stadium, minus the Pakistan team bus.

And so we set off, our van behind the Sri Lankan team bus. The upcoming days' play kept me occupied. We drove past the people on the roadside who were watching us keenly. We were travelling along the regular route and were about a kilometre away from the stadium, entering Liberty Square, when I heard something that sounded like firecrackers. Immediately, the Sri Lankan bus stopped and so did we. Then suddenly our van started to be hit by bullets. I later found out, after speaking with the Sri Lankan player Dilshan, who was sitting in the front of the Sri Lankan team bus, that two cars had pulled in front of their bus and three men got out with machine guns and started to shoot at their vehicle.

I was at the back with Peter, Steve Davis sat in front of us. Ahsan Raza, the fourth umpire, Chris Broad and Nadeem

Ghauri, the third umpires, were sitting behind Zaffir and Abdul. I think it was Nadeem who had shouted, 'Everybody get down!' We all crouched down and kept as low as we could. I grabbed Peter's arm pretty tight. For some strange reason, I was very protective of my umpiring hat and perhaps could have got lower down, but did not want to crush or damage it. Bloody stupid thought I know, but this was a first for me.

There were loud explosions all around – the gunfire was getting stronger, our van was being hit in the front and on the side where I was sitting. The front window and the window on my side had been blown out, and we were sprayed with shattered glass. As I crouched into a foetal position, Chris asked what was going on. The engine was revving so loud, but our van was not moving, and I certainly wasn't going to stick my head out to take a look.

It sounded like a grenade had gone off and some of the hits on our van seemed more substantial than others, which may have just been larger calibre bullets, I'm not sure.

A lot of thoughts were running through my head at this point. When would it stop? Would I get hit? When would help arrive? Who would be coming to help? I was never anxious about not seeing my family again. I believed we would get out of this – it just seemed too surreal to be that serious a situation. I expected to get hit, but I also expected to survive. I was thinking positive, optimistic, and realistic. My senses, without sight, were working overtime.

As the gunfire continued to crack through the air, I heard Chris shouting to get us out of there. What we didn't know at the time was that Zaffir had been shot in the head and was dead. He must have died with his foot planted on the accelerator. Zaffir, our Bobby brake hard, lost his life by simply driving a transport van for us. We were naturally very shocked and saddened. The back window was shattered, and I knew it was only a matter of time before I got hit. Soon, our van was jolted hard. We heard moaning and what seemed to be someone shouting out an Arabic prayer out aloud. I still wasn't going to put my head up to see who had been hurt, but it turned out to be Ahsan Raza.

Minutes later, the side door of the van opened up. I thought it was the police to help get us to safety, but it only a local policeman diving for cover. He tried to shut the door behind him, but Chris shouted at him to get out and drive us to safety, but he did not comply. After further remonstrations, the policeman got out, but, as we found out later, he took refuge under the van. When he did open the side door a second time, I could see that our ambulance had stopped on the left flank of our van. It was partly protecting the rear left side where I lay hidden.

At this point, I thought we were in serious trouble. The van was continuously being hit by bullets. The air was heavy with a thick smell of gunpowder. Chris demanded Abdul to drive us away from there, but he was shot in the shoulder and was trying to reach help on his mobile phone.

At around 8.50 a.m., the gunfire and the commotion seemed to have stopped. Another policeman turned up a few minutes later, telling Chris that he would have to drive the van. But Broadie would have none of that. Eventually, the policeman pulled Zaffir's corpse out from the front seat and we sped off. We still stayed where we were and did not look out of the windows at any point. The van stopped outside the stadium perimeter. We were not allowed to enter at first; my fear was that perhaps the security forces thought us to be part of the terrorist group. There was shouting and moaning inside the van, yet, there was a mood of controlled purpose.

We reached the stadium a couple of minutes later and tried to get the staff to open the door and get us inside the forecourt. However, they refused, and we ended up exiting outside the secured environment of the stadium compound. When I finally got up to leave the van, I saw Ahsan lying on his back. He was conscious, but his white shirt was bloody from waist to neck. He was taken out of the van and laid on the pavement, while the rest of us ran to the safety of the umpires' changing room. Safe at last!

However, it remains one of my deepest regrets that I did not stay behind and remain with him until he was safely under the care of medical staff. He deserved better, he deserved more compassion, and he was, and still is, a valued member of our team.

Abdul was fine despite the gunshot wound, and he left shortly after to get treated at the hospital.

When we reached the umpires' changing room, we checked each other to see if we were OK. Chris's shirt was stained with Ahsan's blood from trying to help stop his bleeding. Peter, Nadeem, and I were fine, and Steve only had ripped trousers from the shattered glass. Physically, we were relatively unscathed, but not our minds (even today).

With the room falling silent and the events starting to sink in, we quietly and spontaneously hugged each other. It was such a special moment, difficult to describe or put a value on it — the preciousness of human connection and the sense of togetherness, resilience, gratitude, and relief. Those who know me well, know that I'm not a great hugger when it comes to grown people, but this just felt like the right thing to do and be a part of.

We did not feel like leaving the safety of the room for some time and were trying to gather our thoughts around what had happened. I'm telling you, it must have been the longest five to ten minutes of my life. We were stranded there, like sitting ducks being hit by bullets. We did not know then that the Sri Lankan team's bus driver had narrowly missed being hit by a bullet and managed to drive off, and save the entire Sri Lankan team. He is a hero.

Later in the morning, I decided to use Chris's phone to call home. It would have been mid-afternoon back on the Southern Highlands of NSW.

My wife Helen answered. I immediately said, 'Hi, I'm calling to let you know I'm OK. There is probably something that will appear on the news shortly, but I'm fine.' It was the hardest call that I have had to make in my life, to date. So difficult that I started to cry when I told her about what had happened and how not all of our team got out alive. I rarely cry in front of others as it is just not the done thing for a bloke, but I couldn't help it and freely did so in front of my colleagues. Helen broke down as well. Not much made sense after that, but I reassured her as best as I could that I was safe. Somehow though, I could feel she didn't believe me and that was troubling me.

As I mentioned, I didn't sit on my usual seat that morning. It was occupied by Ahsan. Had he arrived at the van earlier than me, my fate would have been different – fighting for my life with bullet injuries to my lungs and spleen. I later reflected on these events and still sigh at the thought of it.

All this terror, loss of life, and carnage, and I was just going to umpire a game of cricket.

After about an hour in the umpires' room, I went across to the Sri Lankan team dressing room to enquire about them. Around six of their players and staff were injured, ranging from a bullet in the leg to shrapnel lacerations. They were lucky their driver got them out of there. More explosives – rocket launchers and grenades – were later found left behind at the scene and probably would have been used had the bus remained stuck there.

Before we left the ground, we had a look at the Sri Lankan team bus and ambulance that were hit. I could count up to 25 bullet holes on the bus. The ambulance's windows were shattered, it had two shot-out tires on either side, oil poured from the engine bay, and had many bullet holes, some so large that I could put my thumb into them. We did not get to see the damage to our van as it was not safe to go outside the gate. But I really wanted to see it, to gain an appreciation for how lucky I thought we were. I suppose I was starting my search for an understanding, an explanation, and some closure to what had happened.

At around 11.30 a.m. we were driven out of the grounds in civilian cars with armed escort despite our requests otherwise. We didn't want to draw any more attention on our journey back to the hotel. We had to quickly pack and leave for the airport to catch a 2.20 p.m. flight to Abu Dhabi. The phone rang as soon as I reached my room. Officials from the Australian High Commission had rung from Islamabad to check up on Steve and myself. The Australian foreign minister was seeking an update, and the staff in Islamabad were relieved to hear that we got out unhurt. To their credit, they kept in contact with me right up to boarding the flight to make sure we were safe and being looked after.

We were watching the news on TV while waiting at the airport lounge, silently realising what we had been through. So many thoughts, so many emotions. A sad day for Pakistan, the game of cricket, and lives of so many involved.

It's one of those things you really can't appreciate until you go through it. You never think it will happen and when it does, you don't believe it. Life is precious, life is short, and all we were trying to do was get to the ground to play a game of cricket. What is this world coming to?

Steve, Chris, Peter, and I flew to Abu Dhabi. Steve and I were seated next to each other, and we started to jot down notes and swap recollections. However, just out of the blue, something bizarre came about during this process. Steve and I were recounting when the van door opened for the first time during the attack while we were all down on the floor. I offered my thoughts: I assumed it was someone coming in to rescue us from the nightmare, while Steve's response was entirely the opposite. He thought the bad guys were coming in to finish us off. What amazed me was how the same event could be looked at by two people with a completely different mindset. Today, it's a great example to illustrate how 75 per cent of the world is not like you, and before we pass judgement it is wise to understand the others' point of view. There is no disputing the event was the same, but the interpretation based on how we think and our own experiences means that we can see it differently. That just means we need to be respectful of the views of others because they are not right or wrong – they are just different.

We landed in Abu Dhabi and were met by the Australian High Commission officials as we stepped off the plane. We were taken to a lounge for a quick chat and a debrief. They helped us get through customs and immigration smoothly and avoid most of the media interest. Outside, some staff from the ICC picked us up and drove us to our hotel in Dubai, which was about 90 minutes away.

We checked in and went downstairs to recount the day's events with the ICC media manager, Brian Murgatroyd, ICC general manager, David Richardson, plus Clive, Sarah, and Tariq from the office, who helped us get out of Lahore quickly. We chatted amongst ourselves for a couple of hours before the ICC people left, leaving Chris, Steve, and I to reflect on the events once again. We needed time together to ... just to be together. No one really wanted to go to sleep or part company, but we had to. One last goodbye hug to Chris, who was leaving before us early in the morning, back to the UK and his family.

That night I slept alright, but woke up early next morning. There was no point trying to go back to sleep with so many thoughts in my mind. Steve and I had breakfast before meeting with another Australian consular official, who was present to check on our well-being and ensure we reached the airport safely. As I put my travel uniform on, which included the same pair of trousers I wore to the stadium that fateful day, I found a piece of shrapnel wedged in the back just above the pocket.

Since that day, loud noises and sudden bangs make us jumpy, and at breakfast that morning, the sound of a spoon hitting the floor almost caused us to lie flat on the floor again. I thought it might take us some time to work through this disaster, and I wasn't sure if we would be able to put it entirely behind us. Even today, fireworks and the sound of any guns, or similar loud sounds, are somewhat uncomfortable.

I was finally bound for Sydney to reconnect with my family and as I settled into my business-class seat in Emirates, the flight attendant came up to me to personally offer her support regarding the incident. The feelings and emotions immediately flooded in. I explained to her that I intended to sleep, and I did not want any food or service, just privacy. I drew the pillow over my face and burst into tears as the plane roared up the runway for takeoff.

Two weeks later, and after spending time with my family, I was again travelling to umpire an international match, this time in New Zealand. For me, it was important to heal quickly and to talk about the events freely, openly, and honestly. I needed to debrief, unpack, and share with those around me. I learnt that trying to suppress or withdraw was not going to help me move forward. We are humans, after all, there were events that happened that I needed to grieve about, and opening up to others and speaking freely is a great way to reach the end of that grieving process faster. It would still hurt, but I'd rather rip off the Band-Aid quickly than have it pulled off slowly and suffer the pain longer.

I know it was hard for Helen and my kids, Harry, Jack, and Sophie, to see me walk out the door again to travel overseas and accept that this was my calling. I want to thank them publicly for the courage they showed in allowing me to do so. One never achieves anything worthwhile on their own, achievements celebrated by yourself are hollow. Both families are important to me, my blood one and my cricket one.

The Lahore tragedy also made me reflect on what I had been given. A second chance. I had literally dodged a bullet, and that was something to be extremely grateful for. I was grateful for the tremendous people around me. My friends and family who rallied around me got in touch, offered support, and helped each other deal with the ordeal. The staff at Cricket Australia and the ICC were fantastic. Cricket Australia went the extra mile in looking after Helen and the kids so that I had some time and access at Sydney airport before facing the media. My colleagues and friends at the NSW Cricket Umpires and Scorers Association were also very supportive.

All this support allowed me to process the events better and move on faster. I had something to look forward to and not remain stuck in the past.

My message here? Dance like no one is looking, make the most of the present, be grateful for what you have, don't be greedy or selfish, and enjoy the simple things in life, like a hug. So, go on! Hug the special people in your life at the next opportunity you get.

2

THE GAME BEGINS BEFORE THE GAME BEGINS

PREPARATION IS STRATEGY. IT involves thinking about your game before the game begins and working out what you are going to do to get the results you desire. We all want good outcomes, but through effective and strategic preparation along with hard work, we set ourselves up for the outcomes we deserve. Be alert, but not alarmed. Being able to remain composed and knowing how to respond when an event occurs, by being *there* before, through practice or scenario-based planning, to already have some options to draw upon.

Preparation is king; it is one of the foundation blocks from which we build our performance and reputation. There are a lot of clichés and great one-liners that could be used within this topic, and while they are all nice, they are somewhat meaningless without the detail and effort behind them. I believe no one knows you as you know yourself. No one knows your game better than you, and therefore, like routine, preparation is also very much a personal thing. You should know what works and what does not. It is essential to work out what elements and timings work best for you.

Most of us prepare or practice until we get it right. The best in the world, the real professionals, practice and prepare until they can't get it wrong. World-class preparation involves the six following elements, and we'll explore each one of these.

- Planning
- Knowledge
- Fitness and diet
- Relaxation
- Focus
- Skill development or self-evaluation

Planning

An appropriate place to start with preparation is writing out a plan. Why write? Because when you write something down, it provides clarity. Seeing something on paper allows the information to be processed more rationally and methodically. If we keep it in our head, the information is somewhat jumbled up and messy – we may have a general idea, some say a dream, but are not able to organise the content and structure very well. A plan is a roadmap to success. Have you ever tried to remember a roadmap and reach the destination on time without taking a wrong turn or being a little anxious? It is a challenge for most of us. Thank goodness for Google Maps and that little blue arrow telling you where to go. On reaching life's roundabout, you need to have the plan ready to be able to refer to, check again, and to make sure you choose the right exit.

What has struck me over my umpiring career is how many people lack skill around effective planning. Effective planning and preparation can take some serious think time – to consider what we need to do, why it is important, and how are we going to do it. Whenever I have looked at planning tasks myself or with my umpires, we need to obey some golden rules.

Firstly, be really clear and specific about what you want to achieve. It is essential to focus on the process and not the outcome. For example, I would often see umpires write down that they wanted to be appointed to the final or be ranked number one. My typical response is, let's go back a step and look at what our strengths and weaknesses are, and once we know that we can target preparation and training around consolidating our strengths and improving our weak areas, and if we do that very well, the appointment goal should look after itself in time.

Secondly, while long-term goals are useful and necessary, short-term goals are the key to making a meaningful improvement. Having a plan devoted to achieving the short-term goals is more desirable, and once you can clearly articulate these stepping-stone goals, you are able to plan out how you are going to achieve them.

When forming plans for a match, an event, a function, a project, or something similar, we should also have a Plan B. While our preparation should revolve around what is normal, we should also consider the external factors and develop strategies around what I call the 'what-if scenarios'. For example, while preparing our match officials for an ICC global event, my boss and I would take ask ourselves, 'What could go wrong with the officiating or event?' Also, 'What are the high-risk areas this time?' Often, issues like security, technology, the condition of the match ball, social unrest, and cultural differences would come up. We would then design our preparation workshop around the identified high-risk areas and include our Plan B within the content.

Some of my personal Plan Bs with preparation around an overseas event would look like the following:

- Know the hotel details in case no one turns up to collect me from the airport.

- Have local currency if I need to pay for transport.
- Take an extra month's worth of prescription medication in case ICC changes my appointments during the trip and I need to stay on.
- Keep a photocopy of my passport in a separate bag.
- Take my own pillow in case the hotel ones do not suit (in my early days).

Knowledge

When studying for an exam, knowledge is vital. You have to know your material. Every day at work is like a test, we need to know how things work, what needs to happen, what policies and rules say to stay within the framework provided.

It was no different for me when I was preparing for an event, match, or series. For match officials, the players will forgive the odd decision-making error, but no one will forgive us when we make a knowledge error. And there is so much to be across – the 42 *Laws of Cricket*, fifty-odd pages of playing conditions for the match, policies for Code of Conduct, Clothing and Equipment, Suspect Bowling Action, and Decision Review System or DRS guidelines!

With so much information to keep up to date with, it was essential to have it in the front of my mind and be able to draw on it quickly and with accuracy. I would prepare through constant daily revision of Laws and playing conditions. I would use a star statement map process for Laws (revising six Laws per day) and then summarise the playing conditions by hand – taking out the most critical and relevant sections that were different for the upcoming match. Doing a monthly online Laws exam was also a good way of practicing what I already knew and where I needed to brush up.

Together with my umpiring coach and partners, we would do a quiz exercise pre-game to test our knowledge and also double-check common understandings. The quiz was also based around the what-if scenarios, and we would also go over a wet-weather calculation if it were a limited overs match to practice the application of our knowledge of the process.

It's alright to get this knowledge wrong in the training environment – that's the best place to learn and find out where you lack. But it's not alright to get knowledge wrong in the match or during the exam! That's where the price of learning can be very high.

Fitness and diet

You cannot perform at your optimum if you are not healthy and feeling well, no matter what line of work you are in. You are no good to anyone if you are sick and not able to function. In another chapter on leadership, I talk about the servant-leader and how important it is to serve others. Here, we need to make sure we look after our health so that we can serve others.

Let me ask this, have you ever been on a flight? Do you remember the pre-flight safety briefing? What about the part when they show you how the oxygen mask will drop down when cabin pressure falls? Do you remember what they say? Yes, that's right, they instruct you to put your own mask on first before helping others! It's the same principle with your health.

Daily exercise and making the right food choices are fundamental to good health and foundation preparation for anything we have to do. Looking after twenty-two players and a cricket match (often a multimillion dollar event) is pretty important. Looking after yourself is fundamental and needs to be a priority. How you feel does impact those around you, so making an effort every day for your well-being underpins your performance.

Sometimes our attitude or self-discipline can get in the way. We find reasons not to exercise or to choose comfort foods if we are feeling a little stressed. I'm human too, and I needed the support of my fitness coach and dietician to help me choose the right programme for me, establish good habits, and keep me accountable and on track. With regards to my fitness, Jock Campbell worked out a regime that would support my on-field sedentary work and international travel. With my diet, Simon Austin reviewed my food diary and then made recommendations to help me make better choices. Cardio fitness went up, core strength and flexibility improved, and weight dropped. Small, daily improvements over time lead to great results.

Whatever you do here, the preparation for fitness and diet needs to fit in with your lifestyle and is all about making small steps to reach better outcomes. If it doesn't fit and you are struggling, it will not last. Fundamental to preparation is looking after yourself because chances are no one else will.

Relaxation

This part of the preparation does not get enough airtime. Planning rest, recovery, and relaxation is not something most of us are good at. When others expect a lot from us, if they see us resting, it is sometimes not looked upon favourably.

This aspect of preparation is targeted around getting sufficient sleep. With a lot of research around, the consensus is to get between seven and nine hours of quality sleep per night. As we know, everyone is different, but the fundamental remains – sleep and quality rest are essential. The odd late night is the exception, but once you are behind in terms of sleep, it *will* catch up with you and affect performance.

To know what the right sleep and relaxation timing was for me, I maintained a performance diary over a three Test match period. I would record my daily sleep timing and resting heart rate when I woke up and compared that with my match-day performance. What eventuated was my better umpiring days coincided with going to bed at 10.30 p.m. and waking up at 6.30 a.m. And, for the record, my resting heart rate was 54 beats per minute. Maintaining this record helped me prepare better for peak performance by getting the right amount of sleep and rest.

Being away from home can affect your sleeping patterns and routines. I often get asked about travel, jet lag, and sleep. How do you sleep on long flights? How do you handle jet lag? From a preparation perspective, it is ideal if you can stick to your normal sleeping pattern, but with travel that is sometimes not possible. For international travel, I would try to schedule night flights – have dinner at the airport, don't eat on the plane, put the shades on right after takeoff, and sleep for around seven hours. After arriving in a different time zone, I would try to fit in the new timings for meals and rest. Sleeping is not always easy if you are not tired. I used to force myself to try and sleep. I got angry if I woke up at 3 a.m. local time and could not get back to sleep. It would make me grumpy with myself and have an affect on those around me. The best thing for me, I worked out, was not to get stressed about falling into line with the new time zone straightaway – if I woke up early, I did some work or read. Then, in the afternoon if I was in the hotel and felt sleepy, I took a nap. The trick was to listen to my body and let nature take over as much as possible. This way you are allowing time to your body to adjust.

Focus

World-class preparation involves focus. The ability to stick to your plans through self-discipline and have the strength and courage to say 'no' to people or tasks that distract you from your goals.

One of the best ways to remain focused is to have regular reminders of your goals and why they are important through visualisation. Putting up your goals in prominent places around your home or workplace may seem awkward or embarrassing, but they act as a constant reminder of the 'what' and 'why' you are doing. If you don't have a coach, get one! I think everyone should have a coach to offer support by asking the right question at the right time. They can provide external accountability on matters like focus and completion of tasks when your own accountability slips.

I would share my preparation checklists, training activity spreadsheets, and goals with my coaches. That worked for me and helped me to stay on track. We can take shortcuts, but then we have to accept the outcomes that go with them. A book worth reading is Wayne Bennett's *Don't Die with the Music in You*. He talked about his training sessions with rugby league players when they were doing sprint work. The guys who were not committed to training and preparation by pulling up three steps short of the finish line were not only hurting themselves by taking a short cut, but also jeopardising team performance. See the finish line and run through it. Hard work, self-discipline, *focus*! You have to be able to clearly see the target to hit it, just like the archer. Aim for the bullseye and don't let anything else distract you.

When the effort appears to be slacking, focus on what you are doing, but, most importantly, why you are doing it. What will ultimately determine how successful you will be is what you do when no one else is watching, so keep the focus and don't get distracted.

Self-development and self-evaluation

After each performance or an appropriate period of time, it is important to review yourself and also to get some feedback. Most people often do a self-review, but in a way that might not deliver the best value. A self-review is always done in our head – sometimes even during a competition or an event. However, the best way to self-review is to write it down in a useable format. The fundamental areas for this brain dump can be categorised into are three basic areas: keep doing; stop doing; and start doing. Fundamentally, what went well (relative to your goals), what did not go well, and what should I try or do next. Self-assessment is a real opportunity if done well, to build self-confidence, identify areas for development, and then offer options to plan for a better match or experience next time. Honesty is, therefore, necessary for self-evaluations. Brutal honesty. Anything less is worthless.

I would prepare for every match by starting with a self-assessment from the last match. Looking to consolidate and build on what worked (keep doing), plan to address the processes and performances that didn't work (stop doing), and identify what I can try or do to increase performance (start doing). Areas in my game that I was continually working on included staying in the present (to make better decisions) through pre-delivery self-talk, reducing distractions by focusing on my game, and running through the finish line of the match. When I started to look at performance trends, using the combined information of my self-assessments, one trend stood out for all Test matches. The majority of my decision-making errors were occurring on the last day of the match. I would start well with much energy and focus, but by the last day I started to think about the return trip – while my body was still on the field, my mind was already on the plane. That evaluation process allowed me to better plan and prepare for tackling the fifth day with a better mental application, which then led to better Test match performances.

Along with self-assessment, feedback is another form of important information that can help with more productive preparation. Feedback leads to 'feedforward' and should be treated like gold. It would be best if you are always receptive to feedback and never be dismissive or argue. What do you think will happen when a person giving you feedback is faced with a counterargument? More than likely, the person offering it will feel sharing their thoughts was a waste of time.

Always thank the person for their feedback, however, this does not mean that you need to pay attention and act on all the information received. You should carefully consider the following elements:

- Was the source of the feedback credible?
- Was the feedback valid and relevant?
- Did the person giving the feedback have my best interests at heart?

If any of the answers to these questions is 'no', perhaps you should throw it away. You can decide what feedback to take further and consider more carefully and even double-check the information with your coach or trusted colleagues.

While focusing on your work skills is great, you also need to work on yourself. Where are you getting your new information to improve your skills from? What was the last book you read (besides this one)? What have you done in the previous six months to get better – personally and professionally? Pretty hard questions to answer? Within your planning and preparation, I would encourage you to look at the holistic development – developing your work skills (whatever they are), your physical skills (stamina, strength, energy), your mental skills (composure, relaxation, visualisation), and your personal skills (listening, handling pressure, conflict).

Here's how preparation fits into the continuous improvement cycle.

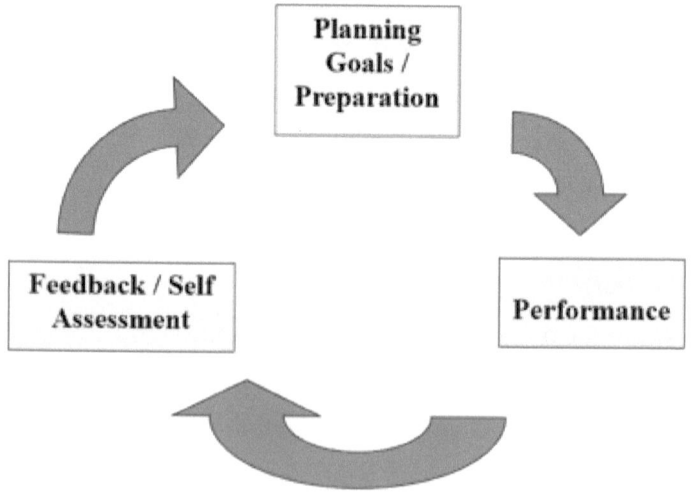

Another question often asked of me is, 'Do you prepare in the same manner for every match you umpire?' The answer is yes *and* no. There are so many fundamentals of my preparation that are the same – the packing, the knowledge, the fitness and diet, the goal setting, and self-assessments. Then there are the unique aspects of the match format (Test or limited overs), the venue, the players, the captains, my partners, and the environment, that all play a role in adding another layer to my normal preparation that helps me to deal with the 'what ifs' and 'Plan Bs' with these added variables. I hope the tips and tools provided here will assist you in improving what you do and help you be ready for the next opportunity because when it does come along, it is too late to prepare.

Preparation is king. Long live the king!

Chapter summary points

- The game begins before the game begins – it should start with a review of your last performance.
- Preparation is one of the foundation blocks to success.
  - Be prepared through strategy, training, and what ifs.
  - Be ready when the opportunity presents itself; if you're not ready, it's too late to prepare.
- Prepare and practice until you can't get it wrong.

- Preparation is individual. You need to do what works for you – to be ready, to build confidence, and give yourself the best chance of delivering high performance.
- World-class preparation involves these six key areas:
  - Planning
    - Make a plan – commit it to writing.
    - Identify strengths and weaknesses.
    - Use short-term process goals to improve your weaknesses.
    - Be very specific with your goals – the more specific, the better.
    - Always have a Plan B.
  - Knowledge
    - You need to know your stuff.
    - Practice and test yourself – make mistakes before the 'exam'.
    - People will forgive a decision error, but not a knowledge error.
  - Fitness and diet
    - Look after your health so that you can look after and serve others.
    - How you feel impacts on your work and other people in your life.
    - Prioritise exercise.

- Make good food choices every day consistent with your goals.
- Get a coach – get support.
- Health choices need to fit your lifestyle to make them sustainable habits.
- Relaxation
  - Actively plan your rest, relaxation, and recovery.
  - Don't feel guilty taking time out to rest and recover.
  - Adequate sleep is essential to performance – work out how much you need to be at your best.
  - Listen and be aware to what your body is telling you.
- Focus
  - Focus on your plan and goals – put them up so you can see and connect with them regularly.
  - Don't allow yourself to get distracted from your goals – have the courage to say 'no' to distractions not consistent with your plan.
  - Focus on the 'why'.
  - See the target and don't take shortcuts.
- Skill-development and self-evaluation
  - Self-evaluation of your last performance is the beginning of the preparation for your next one.

- Brain dump your 'keep doing', 'stop doing', and 'start doing'.
- Commit your self-evaluation to write for clarity and objectivity.
- Look for trends across a series of self-evaluations – this will help you narrow down and focus your preparation for success even further.
- Feedback is gold. Accept all feedback and then decide what to keep and what to throw away.
- Develop your holistic skills, not just your professional ones – develop your soft skills as part of your overall preparation and development. You are who you are all the time.

— Prepare with a base of consistency – do the basics to an excellent standard all the time.
— Top up your preparation with anything needed to allow for the variables of the match, event, or task (additional variables).

3

RESULTS THROUGH ROUTINES

THOSE WHO HAVE WORKED with me know that I'm big on routines. In my pursuit of high-performance umpiring, I have looked to develop and then strengthen many routines. This chapter will explain why routines are necessary, how they can serve your game or purpose, but also how they can compromise optimum performance if you are not careful.

We are by nature creatures of habit. We tend to have the same daily rituals that have developed over time because they generally work and serve a purpose. As we don't like change, when they seem to work, we are reluctant to alter them. However, routines should have more importance put on them, and they should be developed and refined like every other part of our game. They are a process, a set of steps that have the purpose of producing better and more predictable outcomes, and when those outcomes are not what we wanted, we go back to the process and review it.

Everyone craves consistency, especially in sport. I can't recall how many conversations I have had with captains and coaches over decisions on bad light, weather, player behaviour, and playing conditions interpretations – and the fundamental request is consistency. Put simply, consistency and routines go hand in hand, and keeping a routine was intrinsic to many parts of my game, especially in the areas outlined ahead. Some might call these processes rituals, others might call them superstitions. I call them routines, and they lead to results. The three segments of routines we will look at cover my normal match scenario, but they can also cover any other type of workplace or vocation. These are:

- Pre-match
- Match day
- Post-match

Routines, like preparation, are very much a personal part of your game. However, routines are only useful if they actually serve you and your game. Someone else's routines, like mine, may not work for you and they are only shared to provide an example. They are not here to impress you, they are here only to give you a framework of what a routine might look like and why it might help your game, whatever game, that is.

Pre-match

Part of preparing for the event is the training, the practice sessions that physically and/or mentally get you ready for the match. Throughout my career, I had several training routines for non-match days. At the peak of my career, the best routine that I followed looked like this.

- Wake up at 5.30 a.m.
- Gym or pool session with stretch and warm-down (60 minutes).
- Breakfast.
- 6 *Laws of Cricket* to summarise (40 minutes) – plus do one Laws exam in the month.
- Review playing conditions for next match (30 minutes).
- Online eye gym training (15 minutes).

By mid- to late morning the training routine was complete, which left time to either do some other work or other things around the house. If I was on tour, the routine was a little easier as I had no family responsibilities to compromise the process.

Preparation also meant travelling to matches and that wonderful process of packing. Yes, I really did spend many years living out of a suitcase, and whenever I did return home, I did not unpack, I just left it on the floor with the lid open. I did, though, develop a checklist and routine for packing. In my early days with the NSW Cricket Umpires and Scorers Association, they made several suggestions which were adopted and placed into the pre-match preparation routine. Things like:

- Contacting your umpiring partner a couple of days ahead of the match to introduce yourself (if new) or confirm location, match parameters, arrival time, and uniform.
- Revising playing conditions at least one night before.
- Packing my bag the night before (with its own checklist).
- Preparing my match goals for the day's play.
- Researching my partner, captains, ground, and playing teams.
- Putting everything in my car the night before (including my hat).

This last point of the routine was added after an incident. I was halfway to a match, and was mentally dressing in the car, when I realised that I had left my hat at home! I panicked and turned around to get it and reached the ground only several minutes before the start of the match. This oversight had a considerable impact on my match, and on my colleague, as it disrupted our normal pre-match routines.

The packing checklist and routine did vary for local, interstate, and overseas matches. I kept the checklist on the wall and would go through it meticulously while preparing to leave. It is important to note that the checklist not only had just the things that I needed to carry, like the usual clothes and umpiring kit, but also had review tasks such as preparing for any birthdays or anniversaries that I was going to miss during interstate and international matches. Presents and gifts were to be organised and handed over on the right day. Some upcoming bills had to be prepaid, the visa and passport to be checked and packed, local currency to be organised, research the hotel and local weather, packing the right power adaptors, and ensuring sufficient script medication was purchased.

The packing routine and checklist were updated with every mistake I made, although the errors were small personal ones as information was sought from the more experienced umpires before I went down this path.

My other significant pre-match routine involved ground inspection, and, you guessed it, I had a checklist for that too! The pre-match inspection routine is essential to prevent any little surprises sprung on the morning of the game when it usually is too late to fix. The routine involved checking the rooms, spare equipment, establishing the working protocols with the groundsman, meeting with the umpires to advance teamwork issues, and hopefully getting a net session or two with the teams to get your eye in and also to start mentally visualising for the match.

Our preparation routines have become so much more professional over the past ten years, and they needed to as the game has become more challenging off the field with modern technology, equipment, and design of the stadia. We also owe it to the game and ourselves to leave no stone unturned in preparing ourselves to give the best performance possible – this pre-match routine helps lay a solid platform for a good match.

We avoid or dismiss routines at our peril. For example, a couple of seasons ago in 2017 when I was a match referee for Cricket Australia, we nearly started a match with the wrong ball. It was a tour match between Cricket Australia XI and England. We were using a Dukes cricket ball, and the box the umpires were given contained two types of Dukes balls – the first class and a lower grade. The match officials did not check prior to the team selecting their ball, and you guessed it, the player was about to choose the lower grade ball when one of his teammates brought it to the attention of the umpires. We took out the wrong balls and then ensured the right ones were made available for selection. We dodged a bullet that day, and, as a result, the checking of the new (and replacement) balls has been incorporated into our routines and checklists to avoid the impact of this error in future.

Match day

As umpiring is a team sport, there are some routines we did as a team, and some were conducted on our own. With that comes one of the personal preparation routines that was required – find out from my teammates how they would like to prepare and how I fitted into their routines, or not.

For example, at one stage of my career, I was into a pre-game warm-up routine. This would involve getting into my training gear soon after arriving at the ground, jogging or walking a couple of laps, doing some stretches, and mentally switching on. Some of my partners at the time were prepared and wanted to join me, and there were some who did not – that was their call, and despite the odd interesting conversation around this, I respected this choice. Why did I choose this pre-match warm-up routine? Because it got me switched on and game ready. It helped me physically, but more so mentally. I was able to start soaking up the ground environment more, rather than just sitting in the umpires' room possibly with nervous thoughts and visualise what I wanted to do and make happen.

Apart from this warm-up routine, I/we had others. My partner and I would walk out to the centre, meet the groundsman, try and talk to the captains at some point, look at the pitch, and decide what ends to stand at. We developed a ritual of tossing the bail for the choice of ends. The cricket bail has a long spigot at one end and a shorter one at the other. The taller umpire would have the long spigot end and whatever end this spigot pointed to after the toss, was where they officiated at. So, if you happen to go to a match and the umpires are out in the middle doing their pre-game routine inspection before the start, and you see them standing side by side and up very straight, chances are they are trying to work out who is the taller one for the sake of the bail toss!

My routine of leaving the umpires' room and walking out on to the ground for the start of the match or session was always the same. It was my way of getting ready and respecting the opportunity. Before leaving the room, I would re-read my three or four match goals and recite my mandatory positive affirmation statement: '*I can* umpire well, *I will* umpire well, *I am* going to umpire well.' I would make sure I had all my umpiring tools in my hat (as per another checklist), I would make sure my umpiring partner had the ball (I never liked to carry it), and I would always make sure they would walk out first (this kept me humble by putting my colleague first). When stepping on to the field, my routine was to shake my partner's hand, wish them luck, and look up to the sky. I would think of past mentors who gave me so much help and opportunity, who had since left this world – Wykes, Marshall, Shepherd.

After the day's play, we had a group routine of conducting a debrief meeting. This looks slightly different if it is the last and only day of the game compared to a day with more to come in the match. However, the fundamentals of the process were to discuss what worked on the day, what did not, and what needs to be changed for the next match or day. It's a routine very important to the high-performance continuous improvement cycle and is also under ongoing refinement.

The last routine for the match following this was mine. After some time, I gave up the game-day routine of the warm-up and replaced it with the warm-down. In many ways, it was similar in content to the warm-up, but, obviously, it was done later. I tried this at the advice of my fitness coach, Jock Campbell. I had options of running or walking a few laps around the field followed by some stretching, or I could do it back at the hotel by using the gym bikes or pool. These routines were personal and were adopted merely to help my game – they were not for everyone.

I recall officiating a Test match in Multan between Pakistan and India with David Shepherd. The conditions were sweltering, and we both came off the ground sweaty and fatigued. As per my routine, I changed into my training gear and was headed out for my warm-down on the ground. As I left the room, I looked across at Shep, who was still slumped in his chair, sitting underneath the air conditioner, shirt half-open, bright rosy red cheeks with sweat still dripping. My mate looked up at me with a smirk and said, 'Hey Si, how about you do an extra lap for me?' and I replied, 'No worries, Shep, and you can have my scoop of ice cream!' Now that's teamwork, and that's individual routine!

Jokes aside, when I got as much as I could out of the pre-game routine and didn't need it anymore and took up the post-match warm-down routine instead, I found it really helped my recovery and made me feel fresher the next day, which helped the quality of my umpiring. Routines with results.

Post-match

Post-match routines are just as important as the other segments, but sometimes can be overlooked because you might think that the game is finished, so what's the point. Well, your next match actually starts with your post-match routines from the current match. A simple example will help you understand this better: if you are in an office environment, your Monday begins with your Friday review of how the week went and what you need to take out of it to apply to the week ahead.

Apart from the post-day and warm-down routines mentioned earlier, my post-match routine always consisted of a shower (preferably a combination hot and cold) to get the circulation going and wash away the 'scars of battle' and change into travel clothes. I stood with many umpires around the world who preferred not to shower at the ground and would do so only after returning to the hotel. Routines are for the individual.

Following that, I would complete my self-assessment review/report that night, while events and thoughts were still fresh in my mind. I would compare my performance to my designated match goals – what went well and what did not. I would acknowledge my errors and think strategically to be better at my next game. My coach would always receive my self-assessment report within a day of the end of the match.

Hopefully, you can see how routines lead to results from these examples. If used properly, they are very helpful and necessary for high performance.

However, there is always an exception to every rule, and the one here is complacency. It is the enemy of routines. We can have a routine that works, but if we execute with complacency, the routine may as well not even exist. Execution of the routine with purpose and focus is important – it's the same for checklists. We sometimes fall into the trap of having a routine (or checklist), and then get complacent by thinking if we just follow the routine everything will turn out alright. Unless you use the elements of the routine for their desired purpose *with* purpose, you are just going through the process of ticking a box.

So, how do you prevent complacency? Airline pilots appear to get around this common trap by executing their routines in pairs, thereby having another person to add accountability to the various routines and checklists.

You could try adding some variety to the routine by tweaking an element (as long as it is required), attaching more meaning to the routine (with a goal that has greater self-awareness around the quality of execution), or documenting the routine or checklist and striking it off when fulfilled. You can also add another layer of accountability by having to demonstrate to someone else (like your coach or colleague) that you have performed the routine correctly.

Improving self-belief and confidence is a by-product of having an appropriate routine that works for you. When the routine is complete, there is a sense of achievement and accomplishment before the next phase is about to start. You can tell yourself that you have put in the required work are now ready for what comes next, and this is where self-belief kicks in. Being mentally prepared to engage with what happens next helps you overcome one of the biggest hurdles that can possibly hold you back – the element of surprise. There is no such mental roadblock as you feel ready. This feeling cannot be measured, it does not have a number, but it is a vital feeling to have before you head into any challenge. That is why routines are so crucial, they help create the feeling of self-belief to move you closer towards being in a zone to deliver your best, so why would you not work on, improve, or even document your own routines? Go to it!

> **Chapter summary points**
> - Routines are essential and should be developed like every other part of our game.
> - Getting consistent results means that routines should be a focus in the process of performance.
> - Routines are personal and should be designed to serve you and your game. Applying someone else's routine or going through the motions may not work.
> - Checklists can be developed and incorporated into your routines to ensure all details are covered and no human errors occur.
> - When things go wrong, you should always go back to your routines and processes, so it is important to get the routines right and keep improving them.
> - Applying the routines that work for you provide an underlying feeling of confidence which plays a significant role in allowing yourself to deliver your best.
> - If you find that a current routine is not working or delivering the results you want, change it. Try a new one.

- There is always an exception to every rule, and the exception here is that routines can breed complacency if they are not executed with purpose. There has to be effort and purpose behind following your routine and not just going through the motions.
- Routines can be varied slightly to provide that little bit of variety that makes you take notice of what you are doing and most importantly, why.
- Documenting your routines and checklists may be an excellent way to precisely follow your processes that deliver your personal best.

Simon Taufel's sample checklists

Pre-series preparation checklist

Preparation

- Tour itinerary: check supplied flight schedules and accommodation details to ensure they match. Hotel rooms to be provided for lengthy stopovers
- Airline tickets: accuracy and timings to be checked
- Passport
- Valid visa for destination
- Pre-series medical check including immunisation check

- Research venues, airports, cities, and hotels
- Research players in series
- Copy of itinerary to family with relevant contact numbers
- Tour goals and objectives
- Review anniversaries, birthdays, and other important events that will occur while away; pre-plan for these
- Pre-recorded message on mobile phone

Items to take
- Contact lenses and glasses
- Computer, power cable, and USB stick
- Camera
- Mobile phone handset and charger
- Black valuables bag
- Umpiring kit and clothes (remove sharp items from carry-on luggage) – place in carry-on baggage
- Snack foods/drinks (Vegemite, muesli bars, etc.)
- Medication – enough for the trip
- Three changes of clothes (appropriate for climate of destination)
- Music: CD case
- Personal development work to do/reading material
- Uniform

- coat
  - pants
  - field shirts
  - training gear warm-up shorts and shirt
  - socks (field and training)
  - flight socks
  - field shoes
  - training shoes
  - undershirt vests
  - tie and travel jacket
- Gifts for the local liaison officer
- Hat case with hats
- Power adaptors for countries to be visited
- Sunglasses
- Sun cream
- Watch/heart-rate monitor
- Diary
- Leave cash for Helen
- Shaver/toiletries bag
- Electric toothbrush

Pre-match ground inspection checklist

- Sightscreens – big enough and in the right position
- Ground clock to be used

- Meet the groundsman and discuss:
  - watering and mowing protocols for the outfield during the match
  - choice of rollers available
  - method and timing of repairing foot holes
  - ability and process to use artificial lighting
  - markings for runners
  - remarking popping creases at drinks breaks
  - available covers and timing to get pitch/square covered
  - source and direction of bad weather
  - provision of bowling markers
  - staff location during the match
  - spare bail and stump to be provided
- Location and signalling methods of scorers/scoreboard
- Security of umpires' dressing room:
  - restricted access
  - where meals will be served
  - shower/hot water
  - right amount of space/tables
  - supply and location of a fridge
  - cleanliness and hygiene
- Location and notification method into players' dressing rooms.

- Location and signalling method for third umpire – video screen/lights
- Type of two-way communication devices to be used – charged/quality
- Location and appropriateness of spare balls – quality and range
- Catering: required types of food (served hot), fresh fruit (bananas), and various drinks; timing of food and what will be supplied at the end of the day's play
- Third umpire protocols/teamwork:
  - ability and teamwork issues associated with code of conduct reports
  - tells us if TV shows something we should know (no balls, player conflict, ball tampering)
  - tell us exactly what you see – not an abridged version or your summary
  - communicate 'boundary 4, boundary 6, runs as scored'
  - count balls per over yourself and overs per bowler for ODI as a backup
  - Try to refrain from radio conversation during an over unless important
  - Record time off field for fielders

- Fourth umpire:
  - what he is required to bring out at drinks:
    - type of drink
    - saline solution
    - bananas
  - restricted access to pitch
  - mowing/rolling supervision
  - his location during play
  - may need to give time wasting warnings to batting side if instructed
  - check on-fielder's condition if off the field for longer than advised or injured
- Supply of light metre and ball gauge

4

ADAPT TO ADVANCE

MOST PEOPLE UNDERSTAND THAT the only constant in life is change. If we don't get comfortable with being uncomfortable with change, we are limiting our prospects and opportunities for advancement. While not all change is good or for the better, we need to keep an open mind to change and the possibilities it can create. The game of cricket has seen more change over the past twenty years than it has over the past two hundred, and, therefore, the skill of adaptability has become increasingly relevant and essential.

We've seen the advent of the T20 format of the game, including the prominence of the franchise leagues and how that has brought the best talent from around the world together and combined it with music and theatre. The Indian Premier League (IPL) has driven much change,

Adapt to advance

both on and off the field, and in a packed international calendar it has now created its own event 'window' through sheer economic value. Those who have had the pleasure of umpiring or playing in it have had to adapt to starting a match at 8 in the evening. It has been something different to adjusting preparation routines to this unique start time, as well as getting used to alternative sleeping routines, all along focusing on performing at your best. I suppose it is like moving from the day shift to the night shift after a long time.

Still, on T20 and IPL we have had to adapt to the strategic timeout. A two-and-a-half-minute break that occurs twice in the innings at the discretion of one side and then the other. While the players have their coaching and support staff come out on the ground to offer instructions and feedback to help pass the time, what do the umpires do? It does break the routine and offers another challenge to avoid silly errors when play resumes. The music and atmosphere in the IPL must be fantastic for a spectator, but as an umpire, how do you adapt to an environment where you cannot hear the ball hitting the bat? How do you adjust your game to be able to rule on caught-behinds and LBWs when you cannot hear the ball touching the bat? You must adapt if you want to survive and advance. The best in the world develop strategies to combat these challenges, rather than sit back, play the victim, and make excuses.

In this last example, my strategy for adapting involved several elements. I had to keep telling myself that it was OK and reasonable not to hear an edge, that is, the ball hitting the bat. I had to take that element out of my normal decision-making process. Then, I had to trust my eyes entirely and focus harder on what I needed to see – a narrower focus on the ball around the batsman was required to pick up any slight deviation. Lastly, I had to follow my gut and umpiring instincts on appeals and decisions. Did everything 'look' right? Was there something else on the field to see, like the flight of the ball, the angle of how the ball left the batsman, the reaction of the fielders or the batsman that gave me a clue to the missing pieces of the decision 'jigsaw puzzle'? On many occasions, I had to use my experience and follow my gut. You make far more correct decisions when you trust your instincts than when you second guess them.

My 'office' on the field can be sweltering, freezing, noisy, windy, calm, or anywhere in between. It could be five minutes from home or more than fifteen thousand kilometres away, in a similar or different culture. If there is one thing I have learned in my career, it's how to adapt to the different work environments. Sometimes that learning happened the hard way, sometimes it was given a bit of a push by coaches and colleagues. In particular, I'm grateful to Daryl Harper, who toured with me several times. Daryl has this amazing ability to strike up a conversation with almost anyone at any time. He would possibly best describe me as 'humourless' and 'lacking personality', maybe because he is just the opposite. However, Daryl, in his way, taught me how to embrace the local culture through learning some of the different languages and exploring some of the cities we toured. We would spend time with the local people and see what the culture on the streets had to offer, which was a very enjoyable side to our work. Adapting in this sense meant understanding how things worked in other countries – for example, bartering. This bartering or negotiating became a real skill for us in places like Morocco, India, Pakistan and Sri Lanka. We also had to adapt to the food and hygiene challenges, and so tolerance and acceptance were just as important in order to feel comfortable and be able to deliver our best on the field.

Sometimes, adapting means 'finding a way' or 'having a go'. With food, at times, I failed to adapt to the spice metre or the meal time. For example, on the subcontinent, dinner time can be anywhere from 7.30 p.m. to 10 p.m., which don't suit me, but within a team, you have to learn to be flexible and adjust to the needs and preferences of others. Umpiring with subcontinent partners meant food and timings around team dinners were going to need a bit of give and take. We all had to adapt to the preferences and needs of each other

– anything that was one-way traffic was going to be selfish and unsustainable. If I could not adapt to the food, I would find a way to eat something that that didn't compromise my performance. Often, that meant having a banana wrapped in a roti or nan bread for lunch during a match. The flip side saw some great new varieties of cuisine opened up by being 'forced' to have a go and try new things.

Adapting to the local language is something I've always tried to embrace. I can count to six in seven languages that are used in cricket. Why six, because there are six balls in an over and one of the most common questions by the players is 'How many balls are left to go in the over?' If you can respond in the local language, the players are impressed and more connected with you as a person. For me, it was also about knowing when the crowd or a player was using derogatory words – I was able to deal with matters more effectively through knowing what names people were calling each other. Or me! I also felt that learning some of the basic words and phrases around the ground, hotel, airport and streets helped with adapting to life on the road and making the most of the experience. It tended to open doors and relationships faster through the respect I had for the local people and culture.

The introduction of the pink ball and day/night Test cricket has caused much debate around the future of this format of the game and what can be done to reinvigorate it. Why have so many players, so many teams, been apprehensive about the pink ball? Is it about how the type of leather behaves differently to the conventional red leather? Is it the change in playing times? Or is it something else? I suspect it is the adaptability to be able to play cricket well with this different colour coming at you at around 150 kilometres per hour under lights. This change needs to be managed in a way to debunk the myths that may exist, or at least test them, and build the confidence of the participants. What is hard for the batsmen is hard for the umpires. The umpires too need to be able to adjust and adapt to the different coloured ball. They need to have many practice net sessions and warm-up matches under different light conditions. They need to make mistakes and adjust their processes and judgement skills for this new coloured ball. If anyone approaches this challenge with scepticism or a defeatist attitude, success through adapting is severely undermined.

Perhaps the most significant area I had to learn to adapt to was that of TV officiating. Back in the mid-1990s when I commenced in this role, there was no training, no support, and no pathway. My first match as a third umpire was an international match. So, I had no domestic matches to practice this role on, make mistakes, and improve. Umpires continue to get appointed to this role on the basis that they are good on-field umpires. Therefore, they have to possess the skill to adapt and remain composed under pressure, be excellent communicators, be able to interpret the technology, and manage the overall process. While this is the hardest role in the officiating team for me, I cannot underestimate the challenge of adapting to this environment, the changing technology tools in video replay rates, hotspot, real-time snicko, and ball tracking, especially when you might only umpire a handful of these matches in a year. One of the best ways of adapting here is to learn and watch others in the room, prepare actively through simulated-based training sessions, and, most importantly, keep calm when something unusual happens.

The game of cricket will continue to change. Over the last thirty years, we have gone from two to four umpires and a match referee officiating an international match. Your work environment will keep changing. Do you have the skill of adaptability, trying something new, or having a go? Adapting your processes to the changed environment can be difficult at first, but it does help to have that positive growth mindset and acceptance. Resisting change of the non-controllables is a big red flag to advancement and progression. You need to find a way, take a shot, and keep a growth mindset.

Chapter summary points

- We need to get comfortable at being uncomfortable and keep an open mind to change.
- The best in the world develop strategies to combat the challenge of change, rather than sit back, play the victim, and make excuses.
- Sometimes adapting means 'finding a way' or 'having a go'.
- In a team environment, you have to adapt to the preferences and needs of each other – anything that is one-way is going to be selfish and unsustainable.
- Practicing with the variables can help you adjust and adapt faster, and as with all forms of practice, be patient with yourself.
- If anyone approaches adapting to something new with scepticism or a defeatist attitude, success is severely undermined.
- Adapting faster to something new can be fast-tracked by learning from or watching others.
- A positive mindset is fundamental to being able to adapt to new processes and environments.
- A resistance mentality is the enemy of advancement.

5

ATTITUDE DETERMINES YOUR ALTITUDE

OVER THE YEARS, I have seen many good umpires put in substandard performances, including myself, because we decided not to be positive. We let other emotions — fear, anxiety, negativity — take over our thought processes. It is here that I will emphasise that the role of 'self-talk' is very important. How we think and how we talk to ourselves can set us up for success or failure.

Why is this important to performance and success? Quite simply, our attitude and thoughts lead to our words, our words lead to our actions, and our actions determine the outcomes. If we want good outcomes, we need to go right back to the start of the process and look at how we think.

If we get our attitude and thoughts right, we are beginning on the right foot. In this skill area, a quote by Henry Ford comes to mind: 'Whether you think you can or whether you think you can't, you're right.'

Our attitude is a choice. We can choose to be open-minded, optimistic, positive, accepting, and welcoming, or the reverse. We can also choose not to make a choice and just let our default thinking pattern take over. Not to make a decision is to make a decision as the status quo will be the outcome, and sometimes we may not realise just how our thinking is affecting our ability to progress and perform. When our default response is not the right one, we need to make a conscious effort to turn the negative thought or attitude into a positive one. Some of us are naturally better in this area, while some are not, and these people need to work harder. Like all skills, this takes practice and patience to improve upon.

For cricket umpires, how many of us have thought, *I hope he doesn't bowl from my end*, or *I hope I don't make any mistakes today*, or *I don't like umpiring at this ground or umpiring that team*? This type of self-talk is negative and creates self-doubt that affects performance – it sets you up for failure.

For the rest of us, an example of poor attitude and self-talk might look like *I'm not sure I can do this*, or *What if they laugh at me*, or *This is not one of my strengths, what if this goes pear-shaped*? Again, this attitude of insecurity, negative talk, and self-doubt will make it significantly harder to deliver your best.

Self-awareness is an important skill that needs to be highlighted. The goal is to be connected to how you think and be aware of your thoughts and self-talk and if it needs to shift, to do so. Let's see if we can create some self-awareness and put you in touch with how you think through a quick exercise.

Do you think positively or negatively? Please read the following statements and just answer 'yes' or 'no' if you agree that they apply to you.

- I have a 'can-do' attitude.
- I display good body language.
- I enjoy my work.
- I don't blame others for what happens to me.
- I can stay calm when things go wrong.
- I can focus on what needs to be done.
- I don't need to try and impress others.
- I am accepting of others' strengths and weaknesses.

How did you go? If you answered 'no' to any of the above, you have some work to do in improving your pattern of thinking and self-confidence. We are often our own worst critic, and when things get tough, you might be subconsciously destroying yourself.

Let's look at some ways to build self-confidence and self-belief.

It is essential to realise that you have control over your thoughts and you can decide to be positive and confident. There are often many external negatives surrounding us, and I hope to give you some tips and advice on how we can keep our thoughts positive to 'protect' yourself from those negatives.

Building a positive attitude and confidence
Leverage off experience
As we do what we do, we build experience on what works for us and what doesn't. We get more knowledge of what to expect in varying situations. It is vital that we take the good things out of our performances and write them down to demonstrate our abilities: then we have something to refer back to when times are tough. It's a good exercise to write down all of your successes, achievements, positive comments received, and highlights.

It is also just as vital to learn from our experience and mistakes. The more mistakes we make, the more we learn! Former Queensland and West Indies cricket coach Bennett King's philosophy is that it is alright for one of his players to make a mistake, but terrible if he makes the same mistake twice. It is essential to remain positive after making a mistake by seeing it as an opportunity to learn from it and get better. An attitude of growth mindset understands and accepts that errors are a vital component of learning and improving.

*Preparation**

Confidence comes from success and success comes from thorough preparation. Every game I umpired was like an examination of my umpiring qualities. With top preparation, I could go into every match feeling as though I'd had done everything possible to prevent situations that might bring about pressure or stress. The right preparation in diet, sleep, and exercise can make you feel physically good. Proper mental preparation in terms of knowing the Laws and having knowledge of the playing conditions, players, and ground facilities will make you feel confident. How you feel has an impact on how you think. If you feel good and positive, you are more likely to think positively – thus begins the most critical vicious cycle.

Be and think positive

Proper preparation and feeling positive begins the process of training the brain to be positive – the more you think positively, the more you literally put your brain onto

---

* Covered fully in another chapter.

auto pilot. Use the positive comments that you receive as feedback to continue to build your self-confidence. It is essential to think about what you are going to do next, not what happened last – file mistakes for later and objectively examine them to use as a learning tool. Every time you talk to yourself, make it positive and when negative thoughts or doubts start to enter your mind, turn them around and focus on the good things.

Keep your head where your body is

We do not have control over the past or the future, so don't let your mind wander into those zones when you are performing. Because you only have control over the present, keep your mind and focus there. This is easier said than done, but can be achieved with constant effort and awareness. When you walk out there to perform, it is important to remember that your performance on the day is all that matters. One good way to keep your head where your body is, is to develop many short-term goals: focus on what is about to happen next; work hard to the next break; get back into your routines and rhythm as quickly as possible.

Visualise

Prior to any task, take some time out to picture yourself in full control of what you are doing to undertake. Visualise yourself arriving at the venue, starting the activity, performing well, and walking away feeling positive with good outcomes. Visualise and expect the unexpected.

Listen to your body

Be aware of how you feel and act on those feelings. When you feel stressed and frustrated, you are more likely to overreact and focus instead on the negative. You need to turn these feelings around quickly and go back to all the positive things. If you are feeling physically sore, stop exercising or whatever is creating the soreness – get some relief and feel good. If you feel down or depressed, do something that will cheer you up – spoil yourself. You deserve it. Remember, when you feel good you will be in a positive frame of mind.

Make positive statements continually

If you can think it, you can achieve it. Whatever you think can be willed into your real world. Think positive outcomes and you will get positive outcomes.

- I am good at what I do.
- I am a good person.
- I make good confident decisions.
- I can easily focus, concentrate, and manage any situation.
- I will do well and succeed.

At the international level of cricket umpiring, we made a conscious choice to use Attitude and Teamwork as our number one in performance assessment. Why? Because the umpire with a top attitude is more likely to be successful over time and be easier to work within a team environment. This umpire will learn faster, recover from setbacks quicker, require less supervision and management, be more self-sufficient, and outperform someone with a poor attitude over time. Some have challenged me by saying that decision-making should be our number one. Yes, decision-making is extremely important. However, all the good umpires are top decision-makers, but the *great* umpires have the best attitude that allows them to be successful over a longer period of time.

Having a positive, accepting, growth mindset, being embracing and inclusive, and having a can-do and supportive attitude are not umpiring skills; these are life skills. We don't use this attitude only on particular days of the week when we go to work, it is something we need to engage in every day, to deal with whatever is thrown at us. Since we are not perfect, we do have our off days, and that's when self-awareness needs to kick in, and we try to recover and respond better. Take control of your thoughts – make the conscious decision to be positive and you will achieve more.

Chapter summary points

- Attitude and thoughts lead to words, words lead to actions, and actions determine the outcomes.
- Attitude is a choice. We can choose to be positive, or not, and let our default thinking take over.
- A negative attitude and self-talk creates self-doubt that affects performance – this will set you up for failure.
- Building a positive attitude and confidence.
  - Leverage off experience:
    - keep a list of good events and comments; and
    - learn from mistakes.
  - Prepare thoroughly.
  - Be and think positive.
  - Keep your head where your body is.
  - Visualise.
  - Listen to your body.
  - Make positive self-talk statements.
- The person with top attitude is going to learn faster, recover from setbacks quicker, require less supervision and management, be more self-sufficient, and outperform someone with a poor attitude over time.

6

COACHABILITY

A QUESTION THAT PEOPLE often ask me is, who do you admire as an umpire and which umpire did you aspire to emulate? For me, it was never about trying to focus on just one successful umpire. Instead, my goal was always to be the best umpire that I could be and see what I could learn and take away from others I was lucky to work with. So, I'd take my favourite attributes from those umpires and apply those strengths to my game. Trying to be the best version of yourself is the most crucial step, and this can be achieved by observing others – what they do better, their strengths, and then applying those learnings to your own game. To be coachable, you must always be looking to learn something new and learn from any resource at any level and see if that new piece of information can improve what you do or the way you do it.

To become world class at anything, you must have an open mind. This is called the attitude of coachability. For me, it is closely linked to the level of humility that you possess and the belief that you don't know it all. I learnt about the importance of this attitude when I began my umpiring career in the early 1990s. Being part of the NSW Cricket Umpires and Scorers Association was an incredible experience, which helped shape me as an individual. Not only was there such a wealth of umpiring talent and expertise in the ranks, but, more importantly, there was a sense of community, sharing, giving back, and camaraderie. While we needed to improve individually, we also needed to be successful as a team. In reality, umpires are the third team of any match, and I feel lucky to have been part of one of the best teams of umpires in the world.

There is so much to be learnt about your chosen trade outside of the battle of competition, be it for a sports person or a business person. The NSW body of umpires is a wealth of knowledge that possessed tremendous walking libraries in the art of umpiring. As an honorary life member of the Association, I continue to have a couple of meetings with them every year. It's important to not ever forget where you came from, nor to forget those who have helped you along your journey. It's an attitude I aimed to keep front and centre. However, just like every successful group or team, the success of the Association in producing 12 Australian Test and 84 First-class umpires over the past 105 years lies not only in the attitude of its members, but also in the sustainable blend of youth and experience mixing together and feeding off each other.

It was once written, 'when the student is ready the teacher will appear'. This puts the emphasis on you, the individual. Being coachable or having a coachable attitude means you must ask questions, search for new information, learn from others, try new things, and work hard.

Having such rich human umpiring resources around me when I started this craft was a blessing. The likes of Dick French, Darrell Hair, Tom Brooks, and Ted Wykes who had officiated Tests, combined with the First-class experience of Alan Marshall, Ian Thomas, Arthur Watson, Paul Dodd, Keith Griffiths, Darren Goodger, and Ian Jackson.

Not long after I started umpiring Sydney grade cricket in the early 1990s, I took up the opportunity to visit the umpires' room at the Sydney Cricket Ground (SCG) after a day of international or state cricket. Several of us keen umpires couldn't wait to soak up the atmosphere in *their* room. The Ted Wykes Umpires' Room is located on the mezzanine floor of the Members' Stand just above the visitors' dressing room. In my early days, the members' toilets were located on the same floor, just behind the dressing room. There was a staircase that ran from the bottom floor of the stand to the top, passing the umpires' room on the way. Looking back, it seemed like a weird thing to do! As a group of us waited outside the room, the passing members must have looked at us with amusement, perhaps wondering who would even want to talk to them!

If you wanted to go into the room after the day, there were a few 'rules' you had to follow, and here they are:
1. Don't enter if the door is closed.
2. Don't bother knocking as the door will be opened when they are finished.
3. Don't sit in the umpires' chairs.
4. Don't take anything from the fridge without asking.
5. Don't overstay your welcome!

These opportunities were like gold as I was able to watch the match, ask some questions, and, more importantly, just soak in the environment, listening and learning how things are done at the next level. I remember listening to the likes of Ian Thomas, Darrell Hair, Steve Randell, Terry Prue, Steve Davis, Peter Parker, and others talk about what went well, and what problems they faced on the field. The experience and access on these occasions, I firmly believe, helped me grow into being a better umpire and help prepare me for the next level if ever I was to be given the opportunity. However, this incredible experience would have been useless if I did not go there with a coachable attitude. Sadly, today, due to security and restricted access, this opportunity no longer exists, but there are other ways to tap into the experience of others if you are prepared to seek and find a way.

I decided to join the training committee with NSW umpires not long after I became part of the Association. I figured that the best way to learn was by teaching, but how could I teach others if I didn't know the subject well enough myself? Needless to say, I made many mistakes as I got up in front of aspiring umpires and attempted to teach them the nuances of the *Laws of Cricket* or various umpiring techniques. Under the guidance of Alan Marshall and the support of the other committee members, these mistakes helped me to learn quickly by accepting and listening to feedback.

In conjunction with the Laws courses on this committee, we were charged with the task of organising and delivering our annual training convention. Like all annual events, our challenge was to make the next convention better than the last. We looked for new material and targeted different methodologies, which added variety and freshness to often similar messages. A different approach could assist us in improving each individual.

In 1998, I was selected to join the Australian Cricket Board National Panel, and immediately started to explore the resources within Cricket Australia. Cricket Australia was already in a period of growing professionalism and success under the captaincy of Mark Taylor, followed by Steve Waugh. Not only were these two fine captains, they were also great strategic thinkers both on and off the field. Together with the coach John Buchanan, Taylor and Waugh took cricket performance to a level not seen before. While I was still very much the new kid on the block, in terms of age and umpiring experience, it didn't hold me back from tapping into these incredible resources.

It was a golden age of performance from the men's Australian cricket team, boasting the likes of Shane Warne, Glenn McGrath, Adam Gilchrist, Brett Lee, Justin Langer, Matthew Hayden, Ricky Ponting, Steve and Mark Waugh, to name a few. However, they didn't just get to number one on their own. They had excellent coaching and support staff around them to assist and support to complement their own coachable attitudes.

It was around this time that I was living in the Sutherland Shire in Sydney, which, by chance, was where some of the Australian team members lived, namely, the Waughs, Ponting, and McGrath. It was also where the Australian team fitness coach, Jock Campbell, lived. One day, I had the courage to call Jock and put the following to him.

'Hi Jock, look I know that you are not tasked or paid to look after umpires with CA, but do you think it might be OK for me to come to some of your fitness sessions and perhaps even have you put together an individual programme for me?'

The coachability aspect saw me approach Jock. He said he'd do it happily as long as I was willing to put in the work and relay my results back to him. Not only was I rapt with his agreement to help and support my fitness development, I was also ecstatic that he was applying his coaching philosophy of accountability. What I loved about his coaching and training style was the variety and challenge. He threw at me things like treadmills, bikes, weights, swimming, sand hills, open runs, strength sessions, and flexibility exercises. He even gave me strength sessions that could be done in my hotel room! Jock understood my drive and attitude here around the fact that if it was good enough for the players, why couldn't it apply for an umpire?

The coachable attitude did not stop with Jock or Cricket Australia or even my fitness. It extended to Simone Austin, the dietician/nutritionist with the men's programme, and she was kind enough to support me to improve my eating habits and explore performance improvements. When she asked me to complete a food diary, I did it. When she provided me with feedback on what to increase and what to decrease, I tried it and had a go. Most of it stuck, and all of it helped me improve my health and well-being along with my on-field performance.

Again, the main attributes of being coachable or having a coachable attitude were in action – listening, looking for new information, seeking to learn from the experts in their field, and trying new things with passion and positivity. However, most importantly, you should be prepared to ask questions and ask for help. The worst thing that can happen is the other person refuses

My search for new information or learning from other successful people did not just restrict itself to cricket. In 2003, Darrell Hair kindly introduced me to some of the key parts of his network. He used to share information with the likes of former rugby league referee's boss, Mick Stone, and the Australian Rugby Union's referee's manager, Russell Trotter. The concept of networking and going places where umpires had not been before is covered in another chapter. Being introduced to Russell Trotter was to have a significant impact on my personal and professional life. Russell was a great resource in my quest to improve. I was inquisitive of what rugby was doing with their training, how they were using technology (particularly audio communication technology), and how they were self-assessing and being coached.

I asked to attend several matches of rugby at different levels, and Russell supported those requests with access to his top referees and matches. I watched what these guys did on and off the field, listened to the match-day communications, observed the post-match debrief, spoke to the coaches, and witnessed how they delivered their feedback and how the referees responded. My thoughts at the time were that these guys and the sport of rugby were well ahead of cricket in the area of match officiating and I wanted to see what processes I could apply to my game that would help me be a better cricket umpire.

My coaching relationship with Russell developed into something more holistic as we explored areas of my life I was unaware of and we seemed to click through a healthy respect for each other. Russell took me under his wing and guided me or kept me accountable where he could, but fundamental to this coaching relationship was my ability and willingness to be coachable. This involved six key behaviour traits.

Clarity (know what you want from your coach)

Russell and I had several chats about what our coaching relationship looked like. We were honest and up front. I made commitments to him that I was prepared to work, be vulnerable and open with reflection and review as well as respond, and he made commitments to ask, support, and offer new things. I was looking for the emotional and soft-skill support from him to help me prepare better for matches, while also help me deal with the setbacks and failures from hard days on the field or away from family. He had a sense of calmness and rational thinking that I was looking for in dealing with the challenges and scrutiny.

Accountability was also something that I wanted from the coaching relationship. He was great (and still is) in responding to everything I sent him, but he would also, when I failed to send him my training spreadsheets or a self-assessment post-match or an update on my annual plan, politely give me a kick up the behind and remind me of what this journey was all about and how it was up to me to do the right thing in the coaching relationship.

I wanted to be challenged, and Russell did that. He had a way of asking me the right question and challenged me to introspect, to find the answer myself, or at least point me in the right direction. Russell also connected me with others who would challenge my current processes, the way of thinking, or the status quo. People like Liz Steet, who looked after the NSW State of Origin rugby league team in the area of rehabilitation and preventative injuries. Russell suggested I do a 'top to toe' with Liz, which I naturally agreed, to see what could be gained. Liz then presented me with several exercises and recommendations to help me improve my back flexibility and posture. All good things to help me with my umpiring travel, match-day performance, and overall health.

Listen (improve your communication skills)

It's often said that men, by nature, are not good at listening, and my wife, Helen, often reminds me how poor my listening skills are! In this area related to coachability, not only do your ears need to be open, but also your mind. Your mind must be alert to the possibilities and potential of getting that small nugget of gold that will help you get that little bit better, as for most of us the difference between hero and zero is often only small.

It all comes back to being coachable. You need to walk around with your eyes and ears wide open as you never know who you are going to meet, what you are going to read, or who is going to cross your path and offer you an opportunity to learn something new. Every person you meet often has at least one skill better than you, or they know something that you don't, and the challenge is to find that out. So, it is with communication that you cannot sit in a team meeting and think that you know it all and close yourself off to the discussion or shoot down an idea just because you did not think of it first.

Improving your communication in the area of coachability really means asking the right question so that you fully understand the issue or potential and walking around with your eyes, ears, and mind open.

Accountability (take responsibility for your performance)

'Your performance today is the only thing that matters.' This was my mantra during the days out in the middle, one of my key self-talk triggers that I used in the pre-delivery process (when a bowler was just about to deliver the ball) to help keep my mind in the present. I really cared about my performance and took pride in everything I put my name to. By that I mean I took responsibility for my own game, and that of my fellow umpires on the day, and did not seek to blame others for an error or poor effort.

It is a massive red flag when I hear someone deny or deflect when presented with a problem or challenge that they should be responsible for. When I hear the likes of 'They made me do it', or 'I didn't do it', or 'That's not my job', I automatically know this person is limiting their ability and potential to be something greater. To be coached and to improve, it is vital to be honest with yourself (and your coach) about your effort, successes, failures, setbacks, fears, and thoughts. They are always your best learning experiences, and if you don't use a coach, you are missing a massive opportunity.

'The search for someone to blame is always successful.' This was a quote which has stuck in my head over the years. It was outlined to me by David Levens who has been an excellent coach for the Australian Football League (AFL) umpires,

Cricket Australia, and now ICC. It simply means if you want to deny and deflect, you can be good at that; however, it is not something that will lead to learning and getting better. With my own coach, Russell, whenever I presented him with a challenge, he normally responded with something like 'So, what do you think you should do about that?' He tried to get me to think 'What is my role in this'. The attitude should be it is my game and I need to take responsibility for what is working and what is not, to look at the options, and take a call on the best action plan going forward.

Ownership (control your actions and focus)

Ensuring you focus on what you can control and leaving other variables aside can be difficult at times, but this is a crucial ingredient to coachability. You can't allow yourself to be distracted by other forces and must stay focused on what is important. In another chapter, I cover the importance of self-discipline, and this is very much related. It's about taking ownership of your thoughts and actions and focusing on the controllables, that is, what you can do. When you make plans with your coach, stick to them – it is just as important as having one in the first place.

Being coachable here means focusing on your own game (whatever that is), doing everything that you can do with what is in front of you, playing your cards, and not finding excuses. While we cannot control the environment that is presented to us, the game situation, or the circumstance we find ourselves in, we can control how we respond and deal with it. With my training, if I was due to go for a run and it started to rain, I would have a Plan B training session. Alternatively, if there were a knowledge part of my game that I needed to improve on, like intimately knowing another set of playing conditions for an upcoming match, I would build a revision and summarising process into my match-preparation routine. It is imperative to take control of what you can to deal with the challenge in front of you and focus on getting past or through it to the best of your ability. Simple as that.

Humility (seek additional help and resources)

The beginning of the end is when we think we know it all. The game of cricket is a great leveller. It keeps you grounded as it continues to offer new challenges and things you have not seen in every match. Experience by definition is the accumulation of learnings from making mistakes and finding out what works. Failure and setbacks are a necessary part of learning and tasting success.

To be coachable, it is necessary to have an attitude where you don't know it all and that others can help you. Sometimes pride and ego can get in the way of asking others for help or support, but what is the cost if you don't?

Whether it's a cricket umpire, a parent, a spouse, or an administrator, we are all a work in progress and come across new situations every day.

One of the best ways to expedite your learning and performance is to tap into the knowledge and experience of those who have been there before you. It's amazing what others will share with you if you ask them respectfully. You see, if you don't ask, you don't get – I'm a big believer of this. Pick up the phone, drop someone an email or text, have a chat with them, and I guarantee if you ask for help with respect, offer reciprocal assistance, and also show gratitude, it is very unlikely you will be turned down. No one can be successful on their own, and it takes the additional help and support of others to make it work. A person is not an island. My wife or I had asked friends or neighbours numerous times to look after the needs of my family while I was away for long periods. I cannot think of a time that they declined our ask for assistance or did not offer an alternative to help us out of a tight spot.

The last part of this coachable component for me involves searching for another source when a coach cannot provide what you need or are looking for. Coaches are like medical general practitioners (GPs), they have an enormous wealth of general health information and can often diagnose the problem, but when they are not, they send you away for tests or refer you to another doctor who specialises in that particular field. In such a situation, I may even go searching for help myself.

I must say that in this particular area I have been lucky to have so many good coaches and people around me during my career. They have all helped in some way, and for that I am truly grateful.

Passionate (be determined to get better)

Don't give up, find a way. When it comes to training or coaching, this is the one time when being self-centred and selfish works. If you are not getting what you need or you feel like you are not making sufficient progress, seek elsewhere or try something new.

Working on the coaching relationship is just as important as working on coaching tasks. It is essential to keep in regular contact with your coach. Be honest, there is no point hiding things from your coach, in sport and life, we don't have time to waste, and if you are doing either of these things, you are costing yourself precious time and most likely wasting the opportunities.

If the coach is the one who is driving the communication touchpoints and the relationship, then that is a red flag. This often means you are not the one who is prepared to work for sustained success. During my career, I'd like to think it was me who drove the coaching, and it was me who pushed the coach to help me. If it had to be, it was up to me. Being passionate and selfish with your training is vital to the coachability aspect as it shows you are prepared to put in the hard work and effort necessary to make progress.

So how coachable are you? Is this an area that is worth improving so that you can reach your potential and be the best version of yourself? My challenge to you is to self-reflect and ask what you could and should be doing better.

Chapter summary points

- Being coachable involves the ability to ask questions, search for new information, learn from others, try new things, and work hard.
- While we need to improve individually, we also need to be successful as a team.
- Be yourself and be the best version of you that you can be through looking at what others do better than you, finding out why that is the case, and then trying to apply those lessons to your game.
- The teacher or coach only appears when the student is ready: are you coachable and ready?
- Learning about your trade or craft mostly happens off the field; seek and find opportunities to engage with experienced people.

- Ask for help, it is rarely declined if done with respect and appreciation.
- Try new things and if they work, adopt and incorporate them into your routines.
- The best learning happens through doing (practise and train).
- The six coachability attribute traits are:
  - What you want from your coach (get clarity)?
  - Improve your communication skills (listen).
  - Take responsibility for your performance (be accountable).
  - Control your actions and focus (take ownership).
  - Seek additional help and resources (be humble).
  - Be selfish and determined to get better (be passionate).

7

WE CANNOT BE PERFECT

Perfectionism is not a human quality – so why do we demand it of ourselves or others?

AS AN UMPIRE, A sports match official, the players, and coaches expect us to be perfect at the start of our career and then get better!

One of the great things about being young is that you can feel indestructible and that nothing is too hard or impossible. You can do no wrong. Starting my umpire experience at the relatively young age of twenty, it was indeed my belief that I would never make a mistake. How could that happen? As a player, you always feel that you are right and the umpire is the one who has got it wrong, especially when there are no television cameras around to provide the necessary proof.

After a few matches at the very lowest level of the game, this opinion did not change. Sure, there might have been the odd player who showed signs of disagreeing with an occasional decision, but certainly there was nothing that could affect my self-belief. The mind, just like a young body, was also indestructible! As my progress moved up in the Sydney Cricket Association, encounters with former and then current state and international players increased. When some of these players would question one of my decisions or approach, perhaps their opinions should be listened to. Or maybe not?

In one of my early first-grade matches between Sutherland and Campbelltown being played at Raby Oval, John Dyson was captain for the visiting team, Sutherland. His team was bowling, and one of the Campbelltown batsmen offered no shot and was hit on the pads. After a very enthusiastic and animated appeal, I declared not out. John, who was standing at first slip was not happy, to say the least, and some might say he threw his toys out of the cot, but his verbal response still sticks with me today. 'Simon, that has got to be the worst decision I've ever seen in first grade.' As a former NSW captain and Australian player, was he right or did I let my perfectionist mindset (back then) let his feedback fall on deaf ears?

One very overriding driver that is evident in nearly all (if not all) cricket umpires that have worked with me, including myself, is that we are driven to perform to high standards by the fear and desire to *not* to make a mistake. This is basically saying that we want to have a perfect game and not make any mistakes so that we can avoid criticism. Well, guess what, cricket umpires and match officials are human, and we make mistakes. It's part of the job. It's just that the umpires at the top end of the sport make fewer mistakes than everyone else.

Being any type of umpire, referee, or match official is good as you get a lot of performance feedback from everyone, even without asking. It's one of those rare vocations where everyone you see expects you to start the season being perfect and then get better as the season progresses towards the finals. A very unrealistic expectation placed upon us.

One of my worst Test matches, if not *the* worst match, was in June 2004 at Trent Bridge with England playing New Zealand. The error count was up to six by the time the match finished on the fourth day, but the damage began at the end the first day. Once the realisation of the first error set in, there was an internal assessment that a perfect game was not achievable. My standards and expectations were so high for myself that anything less than perfect was not acceptable. What was the point of umpiring the rest of the match if a perfect game was not going to happen now? The camera does not lie, and the mistakes made were visible to everyone. The youthful concept of confidence and bravado had been blown away by a very poor performance, and I was left with a feeling of helplessness.

It wasn't until one of my coaches, Russell Trotter, put me through a questionnaire exercise that we realised I too was driven by fear and was not an optimistic thinker. It was a significant discovery of my mental DNA on how I thought and what the default responses were to certain ordinary events. We identified several flaws in my mental strength that needed attention. Russell had me read a couple of books written by Terry Orlick and Bob Rotella.

Reading and researching this area of mental strength was a revelation. It created a real sense of awareness of what was going wrong for me and offered some strategies about what could be done to turn things around and better deal with the issue.

The first big lesson was *acceptance*. We are human, and hence are not perfect. Mistakes are going to happen, and on a higher level of thinking around performance, mistakes are good – provided we can learn from them. This concept is extremely hard to connect with when you are on the field and stuff up a decision. However, wisdom comes later when you review the lead up to that event and how you executed your role in it. Learning to think more objectively about the event, and less emotionally, is the key. It was vital to accept that I was human and there was a likelihood that

I was going to make an error in the next game (despite all the preparation and hard work on the day) and that my response to that error needed to be as rational as possible, not emotional. There is no doubt in my mind, from all the experience on the field, that when you get emotional about an error, you are very likely to make another.

For all of us who have this perfectionist personality trait in us, when we make an error or something less than perfect happens, we get frustrated because we did not get what we wanted. That frustration then leads to anger, and once you get angry, you get emotionally hijacked – you've lost control of your thoughts and now they are controlling you! That anger can continue to build to the point where you are no longer making rational judgements about the next step. I was not managing my own expectations very well here at all and was setting myself up for failure. This was manifested in that 2004 Test match and from a perfectionist's point of view, seemingly created the 'perfect storm' for me to fail.

To survive as a cricket umpire and match official, I had to form a strategy of how to deal with an error, how to deal with not being perfect, and be able to deal with setbacks in a very rational way (covered in detail in another chapter). No umpire goes out there wanting to make a mistake or have a less-than-perfect game, absolutely not, but we have to be prepared when it happens, which leads me to the other big lesson learnt … *we cannot be perfect, but we can be excellent.*

Rather than pushing myself so hard and placing so much importance on being perfect or getting perfection from events and people around me, there is a much more pragmatic and realistic stretch for excellence. If being perfect is not a human quality and there is no such thing as perfect, why do we continually strive for it? Some say that unless you aim for perfection, you are not going to get close to it. From my learnings, trying to attain it is an unrealistic goal. It is a process that is not sustainable because there will never be any sense of accomplishment and positive reinforcement. There is no problem at all in having the highest of high standards, but we rarely see these people achieve any sense of satisfaction with their performances or achievements. 'Never satisfied' is a description I see used for some cricketers and sports people at times, which is a bit sad in a way – it may be a great driver to continue to work harder and improve, but if you never get any satisfaction from what is achieved, where is the reward for yourself? Where is the pat-on-the-back self-talk for doing something well? If you constantly tell yourself that your performance was not good enough or you could do better or you need to try harder and you don't recognise the good things that you did along the way, you are going to burn out mentally. Trust me.

What gets rewarded, gets repeated. We need to enjoy the journey towards excellence and the process of working towards excellence in everything we do and not just judge or assess the outcome. Enjoyment of the process is vital for that sustainability of effort that will see the outcomes take care of themselves.

'We cannot be perfect, but we can be excellent' is not about settling for second best either. My umpiring career has all been about not settling for second best – always looking for ways to get better and improve. Asking myself hard questions – 'What could I have done better?' 'Is this the best way to do it?' 'What can I learn from that person or situation?' 'Did I really prepare and work as hard as possible?' And perhaps the most important question 'If I had the option to go back, would I do anything differently?'

Perfection is an absolute – something is either perfect or it is not. Excellence, on the other hand, has no finish line. Excellence is a journey to get better and deliver more that can also provide growth and self-satisfaction along the way. There is no limit to how excellent you can be – and that is the real driver we should all have.

There is no such thing as the perfect umpire, nor any such thing as the perfect game. However, I believe that an umpire, a match official, or a person can be excellent and the performance or quality of their work can be excellent, and we need to be comfortable with that while continually looking for ways to get better. After spending over twenty-three years on the field, I am not the perfect cricket umpire. After forty-eight years of life I am not the perfect person. But I am a better umpire and a better person because of all the lessons learnt and less than perfect outcomes experienced.

Don't try to be perfect, you'll only disappoint yourself. Don't expect others to be perfect, they'll only fall short of your expectations. Strive for excellence every day and celebrate the little wins and achievements of progress along the way.

> **Chapter summary points**
> - Sometimes our confidence may be questioned with negative feedback – it is essential to reflect on whether that feedback is valid and worthwhile.
> - A lot of us are driven by the fear of making a mistake because we expect everything to go our way.
> - We are all a work in progress.
> - We can set standards for ourselves and others that are way too high and not achievable, but that ultimately leads to disappointment, frustration, and anger.
> - We need to accept that we are human and will make mistakes. Being rational and realistic is important as mistakes are a vital part of development.

- Making mistakes is part of what we do as much as we try to avoid and eliminate them. The best make fewer mistakes than the rest, and they apply the learnings from these mistakes with purpose and gratitude.
- We can't be perfect, but we can be excellent.
- Sustainable excellence means focusing on and enjoying the process of being excellent in everything you do. If all the processes that go into your activity are of an excellent standard, the outcome of excellence will take care of itself.

8
SEVEN TRAITS OF A TOP TEAM

THE INTERNATIONAL GAME OF cricket is played in more than 125 countries. There are now twelve full members of the ICC eligible to play Test cricket with many more who can make it to an ICC World Cup event. Travelling around the world to officiate these matches are twelve full-time contracted umpires, seven full-time match referees, and over fifty part-time umpires and referees. That's a pretty large team that works remotely and may only see each other infrequently.

For a cricket match to take place, or any other match for that matter, there must be three teams – two playing teams and one to officiate the contest. Till today, I've been an advocate for this third team. Not to promote it as being more important than the other two, but to see it given equal consideration when it comes to the provisions of support, structure, training, and development. People don't attend sporting events to watch the third team in action. They go to see their team play (and hopefully win). The last thing they want, and the last thing the sport wants to see, is the focus taken away from the contest or the players through substandard officiating. If the third team delivers what the game expects through its performance, they are rarely noticed, that is how I measure the success of a match-officiating team.

Many process elements need to be focused on to realise the outcome of success. Having been around elite teams for more than two decades, I've seen the top traits of a team to produce world-class results. I'd like to share my top seven traits. While you read, just think about your team and ask yourself if it displays these traits. Maybe there is an area you should discuss with your team?

Inclusivity

One of the challenges, and indeed perhaps one of the strengths, given the size of the international officiating team, is the diverse nature of its members. I could umpire with someone in their twenties, right through to their sixties, that is, with someone young enough to be my child and someone old enough to be my parent. I could be umpiring with a Christian, a Hindu, a Muslim, a Jew, a Sikh, a Buddhist, or an agnostic, to name just a few. I could be officiating with someone from an impoverished socio-economic background or with someone from a very wealthy and educated one, not to mention whether they are male or female.

Our game is global, as is our team. With modernisation in the corporate sector, the world is getting smaller, and you need to think and act more globally. As a result, our teams are also becoming more global. The team trait of inclusivity is, therefore, growing increasingly essential and you need to embrace the diversity within the team.

What does being inclusive look like? Well, one day before each match, we like to visit the ground and do an inspection of facilities. We take part in a net session with the two playing teams, before having a pre-match meeting and team dinner. At the international level, our team is not just the two on-field umpires, but we also have third and fourth umpires, a match referee who typically leads the group, a liaison officer to support us with logistics, a match communications technician, and sometimes an umpire coach – up to eight people for one match.

Our ground inspection will involve *all* members of the team. Every team member has a role to play, but equally important is how you combine and complement each other's performance, and you can only set that up by ensuring all members are included in the preparation phase. When you come together at the ground for the pre-match meeting, it is vital that every member contributes to the plan by providing input and feedback on how the match can be a success. Effective leadership by the match referee plays out by ensuring everyone in the team is given an opportunity to contribute. No one should be excluded as each one can benefit from the collective intelligence of the entire team. It is this collective experience and wisdom that is often one of the real strengths of our team because you need to expose, communicate, and tap into the knowledge of the local members regarding ground, weather, cultural, and unique elements for this match. Then you should use the experience and knowledge of the global visitors regarding what has happened with these teams elsewhere, what interpretations you need to share and be in agreement on and how to be proactive on providing consistent decisions from series to series, especially around acceptable player behaviour.

Being inclusive means taking advantage of the combined experience and knowledge of the team. Although this is not intentional, at times I don't think we make an effort to ensure everyone is invited, included, or actively involved. Yes, there are roadblocks and barriers to inclusivity which you need to overcome, and you also need to be sensitive to the diversity issues within the group. For example, during our pre-match team dinner, not everyone in the group has the same food and drinks preferences based on either their culture or religious framework. As a group, we chose a venue, time, and menu that takes into account and respects diversity so as not to provide an environment where people prefer to opt out or be subliminally excluded. Being inclusive is about setting the expectation of contribution as much as it is about making the environment safe for all to exist within the team.

Egalitarianism

Every member should feel that they are equally important to the focus and objectives of the team. They should feel an equal expectation to contribute, share, inform, advise, create, solve problems, remain alert, provide feedback, work hard, carry the load, and lead when required. A team of champions is not a champion team, but it is how the team members combine that creates a collective and better outcome. To do that, everyone needs to feel and act as a vital member.

Going back to my initial days of travelling to new and different countries, I faced different challenges on this particular aspect of teamwork. In places on the subcontinent, the culture of who makes decisions and how things get done is very different from my country, Australia. One day, I learnt the hard way that I needed to adjust and try to create an environment and understanding quickly amongst my team members, that in and around the match, we were equals.

Let me explain.

As a travelling Emirates Elite Panel umpire, when we arrive in places like India, Pakistan, Sri Lanka, and Bangladesh, we are very much admired and looked up to by the local umpires. While this respect or admiration is flattering, it is also somewhat of a danger sign relating to team performance. Sometimes, local umpires will be third or fourth umpires, and they are very excited to be in the team and working with you. They think you will solve any problem that arises because you are the ICC umpire, the leader. With their culture of enormous respect for 'seniors' or their 'superiors', they will do only what is asked of them without question. They will often see you as their 'senior', while they are the 'junior'. This terminology is too divisive in my view, that is, if anything should be 'less' experienced or 'more' experienced.

With this awareness, at our pre-match meeting, I would go to great lengths, via words and actions, to clearly communicate how being equal is not only expected but also vital for the team to perform well. In my early days with the ICC, this would practically look like giving the fourth umpire one of my spare ICC travel shirts so that we all looked the same when we travelled to and from the ground.

It was always disappointing to see the local umpire not being given the same uniform or tools to do the same job as the rest of us. While this may seem like a small gesture, I think it went a long way to making them feel an equal part of the team. (Several years later we did a similar thing with the communication technicians!) In the meeting, I would look the local umpires in the eye and with, hopefully, a tone of compassion and understanding, outline what we visiting umpires needed from them to have a good game (as a team). I still have those key messages written down on file:

- We are all equal in this match, no 'senior' and no 'junior'. We wear the same logo and represent the same team (the ICC umpiring team).
- If you see something that we should know about, speak up.
- If you think I'm doing something wrong, let me know.
- If we have to lodge a report, we do it together.
- Don't wait for us to tell you what to do, you know your role, and we expect you to get on with it – you don't need our permission to do what is required.

Now, this shift and message of being equal did not change overnight. It was something that required constant work and reinforcement through words and actions – every series, every match. As a footnote to this example, I must say that I have enormous admiration for this cultural trait as it provides many advantages around the family unit in these countries, but often our strengths can be weaknesses in other situations.

Knowing your role

Sport is a great way to explain and connect with this concept to people in business and other pursuits. You are selected to a team, get appointed to a project, or hired for a company to perform a role. It is important for the captain, the team leader, or the manager to clearly explain the role. It's called your 'why': why are you in the team, and this 'why' is your purpose. Just as important as the description of the role is how it fits into the overall team pursuit. If you can understand that, you have a better grip on the 'why' and this completes the picture.

I've talked about having four umpires in the team along with the match referee on match day. Throughout my career, I have sought to better define and communicate the role of each member to each other in the team. It helps focus on what you have to do, why it is important, and to make sure nothing is missed out of significance to the team needs. Like most things, the only constant here is change, and the roles do need to be updated with the new challenges of the game.

Part of that pre-game meeting was to recap and review the roles of the team members. One of our fundamentals is that it is the role of the match referee and third and fourth umpires – the public face of the officiating team – to carry out their functions well so that the on-field umpires focus on their games and have the best match possible. The two on-field umpires do not need to be distracted or have a lack of trust that the other members of the team need to be followed up on to ensure that other support functions are being carried out correctly.

Everyone performing their role well means that you have faith in the ability of others, and you can devote all our focus and effort to what the collective has to do. When you can do that, it leads to better outcomes and higher performance. You see, you cannot look ahead and focus on the target when you are always looking back over your shoulder to see what your teammates are doing.

The third umpire has the most critical role in the team in my view – manage the director, communicate effectively with them as well as the on-field umpires, provide the ball and over counting support to the umpires, keep a check on the over rate progress through accurate recording of delays and stoppages, help with accurate playing condition application, and make the right decisions with DRS and referrals! The fourth umpire has to manage the umpire's needs and dressing room, supervise the maintenance of the pitch and ground, monitor players' time off the field, including injury timeout, and take care of ball selection and replacements.

If any of these functions is not clearly communicated, there is a high likelihood that they will not be done or not done correctly. When this happens, something that might be very small is missed which often manifests itself into a big problem. You might think that looking after the replacement balls is a trivial task for the fourth umpire, but when those balls go missing, or there is not a good variety of replacements, you should see the trouble it causes when a replacement is required and the fielding team complains! It can have a massive impact on what happens next in the game.

Trust

Where would you be without trust? It's the fundamental basis most things are built on – relationships, teams, projects, agreements, deals, success. Trust doesn't just happen. It comes from what you do, what you say, how you act, treat others, and honour commitments. I cannot stress this element or trait of top teams enough.

When you join a team, there is usually an agreed set of values or beliefs with that team, one of them being trust. Trust comes from doing the right thing, doing what is expected and valued within the team. You get trust when you do the right thing without having to be supervised or monitored when performing the role. You earn trust.

It is the foundation of relationships. In my training of match officials and how you might manage conflict, I've often used the metaphor of our relationships with that of a bank account. That is, the relationship will only grow and strengthen to something sizeable and worthwhile over time by making regular and small deposits. The small regular deposits are daily acts of performing your role, doing the right thing for others, and being considerate for their needs. They may not appear significant at the time, but they all add up.

When I'm on the field at the bowler's end and I'm not sure if the ball has come off the bat for a run or a leg bye and I look across at my partner seeking their input, the eye contact and opinion offered from them builds trust. When I've had a tough day, I've made an error, and that has resulted in a player breaching our Code of Conduct, and we need to lodge a report, the fact that the other umpires support the report and help me through this challenging time builds trust. When the other umpires in the team go about their roles, they don't need to be checked up on, and things are ready before we need them, that builds trust. The other team members turning up on time in the hotel lobby to leave for the ground builds trust. Trust means that I can rely upon them to do their job, fulfil their role, and they will allow me to focus on my role.

Team-first attitude

This trait of a top team is very much a paradox for some people. You want and strive for individual development and success, but it should never come at the expense of overall team success. It's been fascinating officiating around some of the best bowlers and batsmen in the world for a long time and seeing their approach in this area. Almost every individual has publicly said that individual performance is not as special if their team has not won the match or the series.

On top of the trait of knowing your role in the team, comes knowing what you need to do to achieve team success. It's in your best interest for your team to be successful. Why? Well, how many winning or successful teams see their team members dropped or replaced compared to losing teams? Quite often you might see individual members act selfishly and be in the spotlight so that you can see how good they are. This self-interest is short-lived and not sustainable as the longevity of success comes only when the whole team benefits. Therefore, what you need to see is every member contributing to the benefit of the entire team and the objectives of that team.

Every team member needs to add value to the overall outcome of the team. I remember once doing a training session with Bo Hansen, a former Olympic rower and part of a very successful rowing team called the 'awesome foursome', in Australia. His session was based around preparation, training, and focus towards doing everything to make the boat go faster. If there was a new idea, a new concept, or a performance discussion, it had to be about meeting this aim because anything else was not in the best interest of the team. The most successful teams in the world are unified and focused on the 'why' – the one big thing that is driving the team forward and providing inspiration and need to pull together to move in the same direction. That's why I love this example of the boat.

Do the people in your team put the interests and needs of the whole team ahead of their own?

When a team member is going through a tough time, not performing to expectation, or potential, what do the other members do? Do some quietly rejoice and seek to elevate their own position at their expense, or do they seek to lift up their spirits and help them get back on track? We know what is desired, but this is the choice and action-based quality that ultimately makes a top team.

I recently had a discussion with a manager of sporting officials who described his team as being 'splintered' – it was his way of saying that there were some divisions and lack of unity within the squad. It was an interesting description to which I replied, 'Well, like all splinters they need to be removed to take away the pain and allow the healing to start.' My advice was that whoever was not putting the team first needed to be removed because they were actually holding the team back from getting better and achieving great things.

Support for your team members

Top teams are like family, they look out for each other. When one is under threat, is hurt, or in danger, the rest of the team members come to their assistance to ensure they survive and get through the challenge safely. When one has excelled in their role, the others join in to celebrate their success. They do this because that is what they would want if the roles were reversed. You want and need comfort in times of trouble and share happiness in times of success. Nothing great was ever achieved as an individual – it takes a team.

In cricket umpiring terms (in non-televised matches), we often describe the third team task as 'two against twenty-two'. That is not to say that we are being disrespectful or combative with the players, but that as a team of two on-field umpires, you have to be united, support each other, and want our partner to have a good match. As umpires we are judged as a team. Observers will group us together with assessments and say that the umpiring today was good or the umpires today were ordinary. Rarely do they distinguish individual performance. You thus owe it to yourself and to the team, to do everything you can to support your team members to perform well.

The top teams in the world have members who continuously look for ways to add value to benefit the whole group and seek to leave the team in a better position than when they joined it. This is about leaving a legacy of support for the next generation of team members that follow you. It's another way of giving back to your team members and supporting the group to move forward and be better placed to tackle new challenges. The reverse of that sees members take too much out of the team environment for their own benefit, and once everything has been taken, what is left? It creates a self-centred, individualistic environment, which is disastrous.

Are you a selfless team supporter or a selfish team supporter?

Agreed team values and norms

The final trait is perhaps one of the most important. It underpins how the team wishes to behave, operate, and conduct themselves when no one is watching. At the international level of cricket umpires, we called it 'The Code.'

It came about in 2008, when the new ICC umpires and referees manager came on board, Mr Vintcent van der Bijl.

At a group conference for international match officials in Dubai, he gave us a challenge, one that was designed to unite us as a team. You had to come up with a set of values in the first instance that you aspired to and wanted to adhere to. It's an interesting process and no doubt many of you have done it in your own teams and organisations.

Coming up with the words is somewhat easy. The real challenge is to discuss and know *why* you end up with these words and really connect with their meaning. Once you come up with that list, is there real ownership of them? That depends on the process, but if you are told what to do, it is very different from wanting to do it. If the core team wants to do this and believe in its importance,

THE PCT CODE

LEADERS**H**IP

ACC**O**UNTABILITY

E**N**JOYMENT

PRID**E**

RE**S**PECT

TRUST

INTEGRIT**Y**

Source: The ICC PCT Code for Umpires

you stand a better chance of making the values stick and mean something. The core team does, however, create an excellent anchoring point for the team to regularly reflect and focus on to keep us on track. Here is The Code as agreed by the ICC match officials created in 2008 that is carried forward to today's team.

We set this up in a way that meant something to our team. As you can see from the list of values, they are held together with a central value of honesty. Our team felt that this was central to all the values. Now there is no right or wrong when it comes to the agreed set of values or team norms. The only 'wrong' occurs when the team members don't buy into the values or are broken, and there is no consequence.

What we did after producing this poster was to have everyone sign a copy. This was a symbolic gesture to show that everyone who signed it took ownership, a form of contract between each member and the team. It always amazes me when I see people hesitate before they sign something like a contract, a cheque, or an agreement. Usually, the thought to make sure it is right and be comfortable before signing it arises. Well, what better process to adopt here?

We also agreed to set about putting a copy of The Code in every umpire dressing room around the world so that we could share our team values with all the umpiring team members and be a constant reminder of what our team stood for.

Following this breakthrough, we followed up the next year by putting some meat on the bones. We took each of the values and identified practical behaviours that we wanted to see consistent with that value and identify the unacceptable ones. These behaviours then became our team norms. Now, these behaviour norms, I think, are best kept in-house within our team, so I'm not going to put them down here. The point is, by identifying and sharing the behaviours we wanted to promote and the ones we wanted to eliminate, we offered more clarity on what we expected of each other and how we were going to conduct ourselves. The specificity is essential to making a positive difference of improvement.

I genuinely hope this example provides you with some good ideas and direction around the process and concept, and why it is on my list of traits of a top team.

> **Chapter summary points**
>
> - The seven traits of a top team are:
>   1. Inclusivity
>   2. Egalitarianism
>   3. Knowing your role
>   4. Trust
>   5. Team first attitude

6. Support for your team members
7. Agreed team values and norms
- Inclusivity:
  - Embrace diversity within your team and ensure everyone is given the opportunity to contribute and provide feedback.
  - Seek to benefit from the collective intelligence of the entire team.
  - Be sensitive to roadblocks that may unintentionally exclude team members from group events or activities.
  - Make the environment safe for everyone to be included and contribute.
- Egalitarianism:
  - Every team member should feel equally important to the outcome.
  - There should be an equal expectation to contribute, share, inform, advise, create, solve problems, be alert, provide feedback, work hard, carry the load, and lead when required.
  - There are no 'juniors' or 'seniors' in a team, only those who are less experienced and more experienced.

- Team members should have equal consideration and tools required to perform their role.
- Knowing your role:
  - The leader or manager of the team needs to articulate the role and expectations of every team member clearly.
  - How the team members combine and complement each other is vital to achieving team success.
  - The team members also need to know the 'why' of the group, that is, the team objective and how they fit into achieving that objective.
  - When everyone knows their role, you have a better ability to focus more on the task and what is expected of it; there is less chance of things being missed or left out.
- Trust:
  - Trust is the foundation on which the team is built.
  - It is earned by doing the right thing without having to be supervised and honouring your commitments.
  - It means you have faith on other members of the team to fulfil their roles to a high standard.
- Team-first attitude:
  - You should strive for individual development and

success, but it should never be at the expense of team success.
- It's in the best interest for the team to be successful.
- Self-interest in a team is not sustainable.
- People who don't put the interests of the team first are holding back the team from success.
- Support your team members:
  - Top teams have members who look out for each other like family.
  - Nothing great was ever achieved by an individual.
  - Celebrate the achievements of each other.
  - Regardless of the individual performance, you are judged as a team – you need to strive to support your other team members to do well also.
  - Leaving the team in a better position should be one of your legacy aims.
- Agreed team values and norms:
  - These underpin how the team wants to behave and operate.
  - The real challenge is to know *why* the words, representing your team values, have been chosen.
  - Real ownership of the values is essential – they have to mean something to the team as well.

- These values are a contract between team members.
- Team values need to be published and promoted for all to see and connect with.
- Behaviours are the key to acting out the team values – which behaviours are acceptable and which ones are not? Being specific leads to better understanding and clarity for all.

9

LEADING WITH INTEGRITY AND VALUES

LEADING WITH INTEGRITY MEANS *doing* the things every day, at every opportunity, that are consistent with your values and beliefs. It means you make a choice in every situation to act out your personal and team values consistently without any exceptions. To break it right down, this involves leading by example.

Everyone is a leader in some way. Leaders can be at home as a parent, in the workplace as an employee, in society as a volunteer serving others, or on the sporting field as part of a team. You don't need to be anointed or given a title to be a leader – it's not about the title, it's about the way you carry yourself, how you act, and how you treat others. True leadership is about serving someone else or something else, a cause bigger than focusing just on yourself. We see far too many examples of our 'leaders' serving their self-interest as the priority. True leaders are selfless and indeed more focused on the success of their people and the task.

Many types of leadership and books around it cover the subject. I want to keep this topic as simple and relevant as possible and focus on the character of an elite leader, their traits, and what styles are more likely to produce meaningful results. Some of these results cannot always be measured.

The *character* of an elite leader

When I think of character, I am reminded of the following quote by the late American basketball player and UCLA head coach, John Wooden:

> Be more concerned with your character than your reputation, because your character is what you really are, while your reputation is merely what others think you are.

To be a leader, you must be your own person. You should be *authentic* and not try to be someone or something else. Being yourself is critical to building *trust* and *respect* because others can often see through your deception. Striving to be the best version of yourself is the mission, because everyone else is already taken.

The best leaders on the field that I have seen have been those who exhibit authenticity. In the heat of competition, when you have to respond and react, your responses need to come naturally. There is no time to think about who you should try to be. The actions need to reflect your character. Character is not something you can switch on and off. From the umpiring world, David Shepherd was a standout. He was able to build trust and respect by simply being a genuine and caring person on the field, but could be tough and direct when the situation demanded it.

On the captaincy front, I've seen Virat Kohli at close quarters for more than ten years at the elite level. He is sometimes a passionate and combative person who can occasionally get emotionally hijacked. Virat now appears to be very much self-aware of who he is and how these character traits can affect his game, and he can adjust when he needs to. He is comfortable in his own skin, and this allows him to be a more authentic leader because he is being the best version of himself. Others who stand by you want your character as a leader to be stable and consistent so that they know what to expect and how you will respond.

When you say one thing and do another, when you are not the person you are, you give others reason not to trust you. If you betray the trust of others, it is highly unlikely that they will forgive you. Think about a television without electricity: it's very similar to a leader, without the trust of their people, it doesn't work.

To be a great leader, you must be *compassionate*. You need to understand that not everything will go as per plan, and mistakes and setbacks will occur from time to time. Compassion is an excellent quality which tells others that you respect they are human, you sympathise and empathise with their situation, and are there to support them. Compassion is *support* – you as a leader are providing some breathing space for their own needs, not yours. I was fortunate to have two very good bosses while working in the printing industry before starting my umpiring career. Both Bob Evans and Mike Webb were very supportive and understanding of my alternative career and time demands. They allowed me to take time off to umpire midweek games without making me feel ashamed or pressured. I returned their compassion and understanding with a higher level of commitment and effort to make up for the time I was absent from work.

The character of an elite leader is not only inclusive of trust, respect, and compassion, but also of *humility*. It's critical that you realise you are not the font of all knowledge and seek out the most talented people, empower them, provide a safe environment for them to contribute, and then listen to them to hear the collective intelligence. The team should give you the best options. A leader's humility allows selection of people who are smarter than them – realising that to serve the objectives of the team, it's not about your ego, but about getting the best performance from the best people, leading to great team outcomes.

Steve Waugh was one such person on the field who was able to offer faith and trust in his bowlers to get their best performance. When he would throw the ball to a Brett Lee or a Shane Warne, it would typically come with a question to the bowler like, 'OK, what's the plan, what field would you like?' He would then back them and offer them full support, and I saw how the bowlers would respond – it was like they grew an extra foot or bowled with an extra yard of pace.

Humility also means you, as the leader, never put yourself above the game. The game owes you nothing, but you owe everything to the game. It's all about leaving the game in a better place. Mark Taylor is a prime example in the way that he served cricket on numerous boards, committees, and voluntary roles. Even when he was playing, he was giving back to the game through his support for his cricket club, Sydney's Northern District Cricket Club. I was fortunate to sit on the ICC Cricket Committee for many years with Mark. He was also a board director of Cricket Australia and NSW during and before that. Even though such roles are voluntary and unpaid, these involve a considerable time, commitment, and effort.

One memorable cricketing example of Mark putting the game and objectives of his team ahead of his own came in 1998 in Pakistan when he declared his team's innings while he amassed 334 runs. He needed only one run to pass the great Sir Donald Bradman's record score and was also in sight of the then held highest Test score (Brian Lara's 375). Here is an excerpt from *Cricinfo*'s report on the event:

> The Australian team held a vote on Friday night and decided that Taylor should bat on. He ignored it, timing the declaration to give the Australians the best opportunity of bowling out Pakistan twice, thus securing a series victory. Australia won the first Test of the three-match series. Taylor said: 'I have equalled Sir Donald Bradman's record and that is more than satisfying for me. The [Brian Lara] record doesn't mean anything. I'd prefer to win this game, that's what I'm here for.'

For Mark, winning the match and the series fell before his personal score. It was not about him, but about the game, the match, his team.

The final ingredient of good character is *accountability*. It's a trait that accepts responsibility for what is not working. As an elite leader, you give credit to your team when goals and objectives are reached. For example, the team wins a match. You then take responsibility for when the team falls short of the mark, that is, during a loss. You do not play the blame game or the victim and accept responsibility for the performance of your team. In doing so, begin the task of addressing what needs to be done. Having umpired many matches and being present at the ground when the broadcasters interview the captains, I always took an interest in what they said. Maybe there was a part of me that wanted to know if they were going to blame the umpires for the loss or criticise one of our decisions!

One captain in particular always stood out in the way that he praised his team when they won and took personal responsibility when they lost. It was Mahela Jayawardene from Sri Lanka. He displayed humility in the way that he invited to and listened to the other experienced members in his side, like Kumar Sangakkara, Tillakaratne Dilshan, and Muttiah Muralitharan. Humility allows a leader to,
- guide but be guidable,
- give instruction, but be able to listen to suggestions,
- be respected but be respectful, and
- be confident but be humble.

Mahela was a leader who set the standards by which the team was guided. If the leader accepts the attitude of 'near enough is good enough', that is where the bar will be set for the team to follow.

Leadership styles

There are many styles and types of leaders. While none of them are necessarily right or wrong, an effective leader can adapt to the situation by strategically adjusting their style to get the best outcome. As the only constant in life is change, an *adaptive* style of leadership allows the leader to remain relevant to the new and different challenges that are presented.

The adaptive leader can read the situation or understand the type of person they are dealing with. It means they look more objectively to what is happening in front of them, without emotion, and think strategically about what leadership style to engage. Some of the best ones I've seen that I will touch on include:

- Visionary
- Servant
- Leading by example
- Supporter

Let us explore each of them with what they have to offer and why they are some of the most important styles.

Visionary leadership style

As a visionary leader, you have an idea of where the team or cause could go. You have an objective to be reached and concept to be explored, and you are not able to just tread water and maintain the status quo. What's more, as a visionary leader you set a pathway for others to follow to be able to reach an objective or destination.

Clearly communicating the vision is also necessary, allowing others to see the benefits of the goal. The vision might be to achieve excellence, to be the best team in the world, or even to put a person on the moon! Everything great though does start with a vision of what could be achieved. Visionary leadership is therefore needed to take the person or the team or the organisation somewhere they haven't been before and inspire greatness – it needs to be worthwhile and meaningful.

Kerry Packer was one such visionary leader, who saw promoting players and the game of cricket in a much more entertaining and professional way through day/night one-day cricket. Where would the game be today without his vision and entrepreneurial skills to take the game to another level – in introducing coloured clothing, the white ball, matches under lights, and advances in the quality of sports broadcasting? He was able to get other key people to see his vision and join him to make it a reality.

The vision does not have to be as big as changing the game, it could on a smaller scale of developing a new product, adding new training programmes to the company, or adopting a better computer system.

Servant leadership style

This leadership style is all about putting the needs of your followers first. It is very rare considering it is one of the most important and valuable in building trust and respect with those who follow you.

Leading in this way makes sure that your people and organisation have the right tools to do the job. They are to be sufficiently educated in the proper processes, and they receive appropriate and meaningful feedback to develop or possibly give a better environment that is safer to operate in.

Everyone is a leader to someone else, and everyone has a customer whether it is an external or internal one. We all have a customer to provide service to, which makes this leadership style an integral part of the leadership options for the elite leader. We need to make sure that the people who are following our leadership are sufficiently provided for and given the tools to get on with their tasks.

The servant leader also serves the organisation and philosophy. For example, those of us who play, umpire, coach, score, or administer cricket also serve the spirit of the game. We should aim to serve the best interests of the game in how we fulfil our role and add value to it as opposed to detracting from it. If we sustain the game and the spirit, it will sustain us. We owe it to the game that has been left to us to promote and protect it and leave it in a better place for the next generation to adopt and take forward.

An example of serving the best interests of the game or your organisation, rather than self-interest, might be the act of praising in public, but criticising in private. In the public domain, criticising merely adds fuel to the fire as people are embarrassed and get angry.

Finally, a servant leadership style makes it better or easier for the people who follow you. I genuinely believe that you should apply this style of leadership regularly so that you leave your game, your business, and your vocation in a better place than when you found it. Not only should you work *in* the business, you should also work *on* the business.

As Tom Rath says, 'Perhaps the ultimate test of a leader is not what you are able to do in the here and now, but instead what continues to grow after you've gone.'

Leading by example style

Leading by example is obviously one of the most self-explanatory and predominant forms of leadership style. It is one of the best ways to show others the pathway to success if done correctly. However, one has to be wary of overusing it. It can be one of the most intimidating for some as you can sometimes set a very high or impractical standard for others. In such case, self-awareness is key here.

I was chatting with Virat Kohli, the current captain of the Indian cricket team, and he reaffirmed the style that I think is worth considering in some situations. He said he doesn't ask his team members to do anything that he is not prepared to do. With this comes the commitment and action of *walking the walk*, not *talking the talk*.

I recall reading something by Mahatma Gandhi, a great servant leader, who was incredibly strong, but also had a massive amount of compassion. 'Be the change that you want to see in the world.' To me, this means that you need to lead by example and do what you want others to do. It sounds pretty simple, but it takes a lot of hard work, self-discipline, and consistent commitment – elements that are covered in more detail elsewhere in this book.

Actions speak louder than words with this form of leadership. The correct actions build credibility, earn respect, and send strong and meaningful messages to others.

Supporter style

This is about leading from behind as opposed to leading from the front. It means your style allows people to be empowered to take the lead and gain new experience and reach their potential. One of the primary roles of every leader is to grow and develop new leaders, and that cannot happen if you don't frequently step out of the way and let others lead. You can still be there, one step behind them, to be the safety net just in case.

This style gives people oxygen in the room to speak up, to provide their input, and to also put their hand up. Being an experienced cricket umpire, you often get appointed with new, inexperienced umpires. We have all been there and were the inexperienced umpire once! You want the experienced one to allow the other to 'be the umpire' when it comes to communicating messages to captains, making team decisions, and taking charge. What usually happens when you work with a new umpire is that the players and captains normally come to you for everything, be it a piece of information, clarification, or decision. I had to try and make a conscious decision to move out of the leading-by-example style and move into the supporter style on these occasions and provide oxygen to my partner. I would direct the question to my partner, ask them to seek out the captain to advise them of the new playing times, or ask them what we should do during an interrupted match.

This is again part of the process of developing new leaders and giving the opportunity to experience new areas. Surely, it was one of the reasons that a new umpire is appointed with a more experienced one – to learn! How can they learn if the more experienced umpire does not shift into a supporter style of leadership when the situation presents itself?

This is a critical leadership style in any team environment because it focuses on being successful through others. We have said that nothing great was ever achieved on your own, so this leadership style should be adopted to achieve team goals.

Being a supportive leader can mean that you give those that follow you your time, the benefit of your experience, or some advice. Giving people time might look like listening to their challenges and being a sounding board for their solutions, followed by asking them some questions. A supporter style listens, ask questions, but rarely tells.

One of the best leaders with this style that I came across was Gary Kirsten. Gary has coached the Indian and South African national cricket teams as well as a couple of IPL franchises with success. In a wonderful chat we had one day in the UAE, we talked about his coaching style and philosophy. What came through was his supporter leadership style. He told me that he and his team simply ask two questions of themselves every day in the quest to get better: 'Are we doing this the right way?' and 'Is there a better way?'

He went on to explain that his role was to help every individual get better at what they did and, in the process, become a resource. Once the player crossed the white rope to enter the field, they were on their own and had to be self-sufficient.

While there are so many other styles of leadership, the ones enumerated in this chapter have been the most important and influential ones over the course of my career at the elite level of cricket. You should practice and implement them wherever you can on the basis that no one style should be adopted all the time. Adaptive style is the best in my view and is more likely to produce sustainable success in many different and changing environments.

> ### Chapter summary points
> - Leading with integrity means *doing* the things every day and at every opportunity that are consistent with your values and beliefs.
> - Everyone is a leader in some way.
> - True leadership is about serving someone else or something else, a cause bigger than focusing on yourself.
> - The *character* of an elite leader include:
>   - Authenticity: being yourself helps gain trust and respect from others.
>   - Compassion: supporting the needs of others.
>   - Humility: you don't know everything and you are not bigger than the purpose you serve.
>   - Accountable: you take responsibility for what is not working and give credit to others when it does work.

- As the only constant in life is change, an adaptive style of leadership allows the leader to remain relevant to the ever new and different challenges.
- Visionary leadership style:
  - You have an idea of where the team or cause could go.
  - You set a pathway for others to follow to be able to reach an objective or destination.
  - Clearly communicating the vision is necessary along with the benefits.
- Servant leadership style:
  - Putting the needs of your followers first.
  - Making sure that your people and organisation have the right tools and resources to do the job.
  - You serve the organisation, philosophy, and purpose of the group. Always adding value, not taking value away.
  - You leave your game, your business, your vocation in a better place than when you found it.
  - Not only should you work *in* the business, you should also work *on* the business.
- Leading by example style:
  - One of the best ways to show others the pathway to success if done correctly.

- Don't ask your team members to do anything that you are not prepared to do. With this comes the commitment and action of *walking the walk*, not *talking the talk*.
- Be the change that you want to see.
- Actions speak louder than words with this form of leadership.
- Supporter leadership style:
  - Lead from behind, give your people breathing space and let them do things for themselves without excessive supervision or instruction.
  - Let others make some mistakes for themselves so that they can learn from them and develop themselves.
  - Focus on being successful through others.
  - Being a supportive leader can mean that you give those who follow you, your time, the benefit of your experience, or advice.
- An adaptive leadership style provides the best opportunity for sustainable success.

10
THE 'C' WORD

CULTURE – THE CURRENT BUZZ word in sport, business, and society right. What is culture? A few of the best definitions that I've come across include:

> 'A set of values and behaviours that outline what we expect and accept.'
>
> 'How people behave when they know they are not being supervised.'
>
> 'It's the way we do things around here.'

It is fair to say that there are a lot of organisations and industries that need much improvement in this space around values and how peoples' behaviours are acted out according to those values. You only have to look at our Parliament and politicians, the finance industry, the banks, our clergy in some of the religious orders, several of the sporting codes, and many sporting stars. And, yes, I was part of those sporting codes with ICC and Cricket Australia.

It is interesting how the 80–20 rule applies here also. Often, the actions of 20 per cent of the organisation can define the culture as being weak or poor when the other 80 per cent is doing pretty well. That can be the case for several reasons, which will be dealt with in this chapter.

Values

This is probably the easiest part of the development of culture. The process most likely looks something like this: we all talk amongst ourselves, maybe even call in a consultant, perhaps survey the staff, and try to come up with an even better list of words that describes more effectively who we are, what we stand for, and how we are supposed to act. After that list is agreed to, circulated, and put up on the wall and the website, we feel pretty good with ourselves. Right? We say, 'OK, that's our values and culture sorted.' Wrong!

We do need to have an agreed set of values that articulate the above. However, we need to correctly understand what they mean and what they look like in terms of actionable behaviours. This is where the hard work starts.

Other factors need to be considered. For example, is the

environment safe enough for people to call out behaviours that fall outside of our agreed values? How do we deal with behaviours and people who don't fit into the culture when they break the rules? Who monitors the culture and who is responsible for its improvement?

The fact is, a culture will exist whether you want it or not. It will define itself by default. Therefore, why not take action to shape it into something that truly represents who you are, what you stand for, and what you are proud to be associated with? Everyone thinks they have a pretty good culture, but it could be better and remains a constant work in progress.

Ask yourself this question, based on your work environment: how would you define your culture? Is everyone around you performing to their potential and making a significant positive difference? Yes? No? So, how can we improve our culture?

This is my take on the 'C word', culture, after having worked in several 'high performance' sporting and business environments and seeing first-hand what has worked and what has not. Hopefully, you will gain insight and learn from what could be done and, perhaps, what to avoid.

A poor culture, like a poor attitude, is like the other 'C' word, cancer – it spreads. If it is not caught and diagnosed early, and treatment administered, it can be terminal. If caught early, the cancer can go into remission, but it requires constant monitoring and checking to make sure it doesn't come back and if it does, to again treat it early. Like dealing with cancer, the decisions involved with culture are often hard, but they need to be made.

Textbooks on this subject would have us believe that there are several types or forms of culture, but I'd like to focus on the one that we should aspire and work towards – a self-regulating culture. This is a type of culture where people do not depend upon one leader or manager to act by example. Everyone in the group takes individual responsibility to ensure the values are acted out, and when they are not – the person who sees it, calls it out, and does something to correct it, before it becomes the new standard. By what we do or don't, when the opportunity arises we set the standard. This principle came to life in 2013 when the former chief of the Australian army, David Morrison, had to deal with the culture of some men in the armed force towards women in service. He focused on everyone's behaviour in his organisation when he said 'the standard you walk past, is the standard you accept'. I'm not sure we want a culture of behaviour that only works when the chief, CEO, or captain is around, and we certainly don't want one which relies on the troops reporting every breach of values or behaviour standards to the leader or manager. The best culture sees its people empowered and encouraged to self-regulate, to deal with matters as they crop up so that breaches don't escalate into significant events. *Every individual has a role to play in creating and shaping an actions-based culture consistent with its agreed values.*

In the March 2018 Cape Town Test, it was unfortunate for three Australian male cricketers to pay a high price for their actions following the ball-tampering saga. Yes, their actions required them to be held accountable, but it should never have got to this level of significance. Enough has been said about the people involved and, on that part, I genuinely feel for them and their welfare.

Let's focus on the issue, and the issue is *not* what happened in Cape Town. The act of deliberate changing of the condition of the ball at Newlands was not the illness; it was merely a symptom. However, it was significant for people inside and outside the sport to stop and review how we are playing. It was big enough for the behaviour (and culture) to be called out and sanctioned in a way that we had not seen before. In my role as chair of the Highlands Cricket Association in Australia, we talk to clubs about player behaviour being a club responsibility. The clubs are encouraged to manage the behaviour of their own people and not pass the buck by saying that the governing body's code of behaviour will deal with it after an umpire has reported it. Clubs are best placed on choosing who plays, who has leadership positions, and how they want to play.

Attitude

Choosing the right attitude is one of the founding elements that underpin the shaping of a self-regulating culture. Some aspects are more important than others, which I'll now list and put into context.

Humility

This attribute plays out through the belief that you don't know everything. Other members of your team have important contributions to make, providing better solutions to problems or ideas and suggestions that require careful consideration. It is the attitude of 'the collective intelligence of the group is greater than the individual'. A red flag should be taken notice of when people stop asking questions, don't seek the input of others, don't collaborate, are not inclusive of others, or think that they have answers on their own.

Humility can also play out by remembering where you came from, why you wanted to be part of the team, and who you represent (those who have gone before you and contributed to helping you be where you are today). As an umpire of this generation, I'm fully supportive of playing the game hard, but to conspire to cheat deliberately and then deny it, is putting yourself and victory ahead of the best interests of your team and the game. The individual is never bigger than the game. The game is where it is because of the efforts of the collective and those that have contributed to it in the past. The game is not owned by an individual or an organisation. It belongs to all of us and is something we pass on to the next generation. It is a collective responsibility to leave it in a better position than we found it.

Team first

This is an essential attitudinal trait because it signifies selflessness. Nothing great was ever achieved by one person acting alone. We all need to improve as individuals and may even compete as individuals for a place in the team. However, when it comes to how we prepare, execute, and review, it should be on the basis of putting the team's objectives ahead of personal ones. If the team does not perform well, where is the value or satisfaction with individual performance? For example, a winning team is unlikely to be changed for the next match, whereas a losing team encounters typically at least one or two changes. Therefore, it is in everyone's best interests to see the team successful.

When I would prepare for my matches to umpire, aside from focusing on my own game, I would plan and strategise around who was umpiring with me and how I could help them have a good game. I would have the attitude of wanting my teammates to have a good game. There is absolutely no value in me having a good game and my colleague having a poor one. We are judged and viewed as a team when others say that the umpires had a good game or their performance was poor.

If we are doing something that is not in the best interests of the team, you would have to ask why are we even doing it. There is no place for a selfish player or attitude on the team – this attitude will see the team go backward and undermine the sustainability of the teams' purpose.

Open feedback and communication

Many organisations these days engage with their people or customers mainly through surveys. While surveys have a place, they only tell part of the story. They are somewhat limited in obtaining qualitative information and are just a one-way form of communication. They are usually an anonymous way of collecting information where people can often say what they want – and they normally do with an agenda. What does it say about the culture of a team or an organisation, when people may be afraid to speak up and have an open conversation about what is working and what is not, only when there is no way of possible retribution? One of the most critical elements of a high-performance culture is to have a safe and trusting environment, to be brutally honest with each other. That brutal honesty is what leads to constructive discussions, which leads to real ongoing progress.

Any disconnect or lack of effective communication between managers and team members can be addressed through one simple action: by employing a 'management by walking around' approach. Those who make the most important decisions should 'walk the shop floor' regularly with their people to see and feel what is working and what is not. The strategy also promotes active direct engagement and communication with those who are tasked to deliver the programmes and implement decisions. This concept is not new, but is extremely effective and far more worthwhile than relying on surveys. Often, the people at the coalface have practical solutions to the challenges. All leaders and managers need to do is to engage, ask the right question, and *listen*.

At Cricket Australia with my match referee team and umpire selection panel, I felt it necessary to be at the ground with the umpires and referees to see where the performance gaps were. People were able to show me their frustrations; I could see first-hand where they were excelling and how I could better support their development. I didn't have to rely on a survey, I had my own eyes and ears. Apart from the benefit to myself, there was a non-measurable benefit to the match officials. On the most part, they welcomed the interaction and opportunity to share, update, and receive feedback. It hopefully provided the non-verbal message that I cared about them, their performance, and their role within our team.

We need to be vigilant with what I call 'bracket creep behaviours', that is, small shifts in behaviours that are not aligned to the agreed values. At the time, the behaviour may not seem like a big deal – it may be being late for a meeting, a comment that undermines a colleague, or not following company credit card policy. Without any intervention, over time, they will continue to shift, with new 'acceptable' standard being set, until a point is reached where the behaviour stands out as being unacceptable. When all those red flags have been missed or neglected, it takes something significant to happen for the group or others outside of it to stop and reassess how the culture got to that point. Sometimes this is called a 'train smash', which could have been avoided had we acted early.

Training and development on character, ethics, and integrity

Imagine this situation: you are presented with an opportunity to do some training to improve your or your staff's skills, and are presented with the quote from the supplier. You present the business case to your boss who says, 'What if we spend all this money on our people and they end up leaving?' My suggested response would be, 'What if we don't and they end up staying?'

Within the culture, it seems there are a couple of initial challenges concerning training. The first is to have a training programme and schedule part of the norm within the organisation or team. The second is to commit a component of the overall training towards improving the character, ethics, and integrity of the individual and/or the team. Let's assume we can get past the initial roadblock of having a suitable and appropriate annual training budget. What do we do with it and how do we improve performance? Part of improving performance involves shifting behaviours that will deliver sustainable results. The most effective approach here consists in dealing with peoples' character, strengths/weaknesses, default behaviours, and derailers, under pressure or stress and how to use discretion in making compassionate decisions.

There must also be some regularity to the touchpoints through regular activity-based training interventions, on an annual basis or more regularly if possible. This helps keep the importance of the right behaviours and culture front and centre of performance.

It is essential for people to understand and be aware of what strengths and weaknesses they have with their default behaviours and what is likely to happen with their behaviour when put under pressure. Many behavioural or psychological programmes can be used to provide feedback and improve self-awareness. Personally, I've participated in several, the best one being the Hogan Profiling model. This model outlined where I was strong and where those strengths would be counterproductive in certain situations or environments. The Hogan reports also gave a better indication of what role within the team I was best suited for and where I could best fit. The feedback also clarified which roles and tasks I was least suited to and helped me make informed decisions of what areas of work I should take on. It saves individuals and organisations time and money and speeds up the process of getting better results.

At the end of the day, people are just that – people. Everyone likes to be treated with respect and dignity. The adage and value of treating others as you would like to be treated rings true. From a training and development perspective, we need to be dealing with the individual holistically and not just sports or occupational skills. Performance and well-being deal with the whole person – mental and physical, personal and professional.

Apart from having an agreed list of values that the organisation or team wants to follow, the key to delivering on those is understanding and actioning the required behaviours. Training is therefore essential to drill down and focus on the specifics. Improvement and development never happen around being general or generic, it only occurs when we get clarity through specifics. The role of training and education concerning culture is to train on practical examples of behaviours that are acceptable and expected and also outline those that are not. This can be done with role plays, scenarios, case studies, holding workshops on previous situations, and highlighting correct behaviours along with those that were inconsistent.

Leadership

There are several leadership styles and types of leaders. I look at this aspect similar to my umpiring – what is likely to give us the best outcomes? What does high percentage umpiring look like here? What is high percentage leadership behaviour to produce what we want to see?

I believe in an adaptive leadership style for the situation. Sometimes it is important to lead from the front, sometimes from behind, and we should always be cognisant that everyone is a leader and we should have role-model behaviours that we want others to adopt. Above all, leadership is about serving others and the purpose of the organisation or team. The role of every leader is to develop new leaders, and this requires dedicated training and mentoring programmes. While leadership will be covered elsewhere in this book, it is important to provide some context here when we are referring to culture.

Managers, captains, leaders, and umpires set the tone and environment for how the culture is shaped. They have a direct influence and communicate what behaviours are expected and accepted.

We are human and we make mistakes. Mistakes are an intrinsic part of growth, development, and improvement, and are necessary for the learning process. What effective leaders need to do is to allow room for making mistakes in the training environment. When mistakes occur outside the training environment, support and additional training should be given to ensure the same mistakes are not made.

A trusting and safe environment where people can share and learn from each other, without fear of being ridiculed, is also a key aspect of having the right culture. One of the best ways to do this is for the boss, the captain, or the leader of the group demonstrate vulnerability by owning up to their shortcomings within the team. They should articulate what they got wrong and why, and make a public commitment to learn from it and deliver better with the next opportunity. By being a role model, in a manner how they want their team to behave, they are more likely to provide a consistent message on what is acceptable and what is not.

What is measured (goals and targets)

As a former Emirates Elite Panel member, my development and performance focus has always been on the process. If the process of preparation, technique, and match management were hitting my goals, quality decision-making accuracy would follow. Yes, I made the odd error, but when I did I had to go back to my process anyway and make an adjustment – usually concentration, positioning, self-talk (focus), or decision cues. If my entire focus was getting my decisions right, the other parts of my game would suffer, and my consistency followed by accuracy would drop away. In other words, if all the inputs and ingredients were being measured and were of a high standard, the outputs were much more likely to be correct and take care of themselves. *Process, process, process.*

Having the outcome goals shifts the short-term focus that is required for the long-term focus, which is not helpful as it's too far away in the future.

Selection of team members and performance reviews

Select people based on their ability to perform, but also select or appraise based on their character. What sort of a person are they? What are their values? Do their values truly align with those of the organisation and will they add value to your team?

I've always said throughout my career that to be a good umpire you need to be a good person, especially for sustainable success and longevity of tenure. No one epitomises this more for me in the field of umpiring than David Shepherd. He was a simple man, who loved the game, and treated others with respect. A humble man who always put the game first, gave his best, and cared about everyone in it. I'd umpire with David any day of the week and would always love to have him in my team.

Performance is important, but not at a win-at-all-cost approach. The ends do not justify the means. We have to play within the Laws, rules, and conventions of the contest. The quality of the contest is long remembered after the scoreline.

People with poor character traits, those that are based around being selfish, are going to be a drain on the team in the long run. They are unlikely to add value to others apart from their own performance and are unlikely to go the extra mile for you or help others during times of struggle. So, where is their overall long-term value? People with poor character are going to be high maintenance and provide more problems than solutions and end up costing the team in other ways.

When we have similar performers or people with potential, the character should always be the difference between who moves up and who moves out. Good people make good teams, and we should always be focusing on improving our character as well as our cricketing skills (or other job skills).

As one of the Cricket Australia umpire selectors, here is what we said about where character (and culture) fitted into our policy and process.

Umpire assessment: Focus areas

Umpires are broadly assessed and selected according to their performance across four core areas:
- Competency: what they can do.
- Capability: what they should be able to do.
- Character: the quality of the person, their values, and behaviour traits.
- Chemistry: the ability to fit in and add value to the team.

1. Assessment areas aligned with the ICC (accreditation competencies)

2. Assessment feedback aligned with what Cricket Australia umpire selectors are looking for:
   - Composure: being able to handle the big moments.
   - Character: being able to be trusted on and off the field; being accountable for performance; and being professional.
   - Humility: having a growth mindset (never knowing it all), sharing knowledge with others, and no sense of entitlement with their role.
   - Credibility: consistent high performance under all conditions and formats, over time.
   - Leadership: setting high standards for themselves and the group, and serving the game.
   - Presence: unobtrusive, but visible when required.
   - Courage and commitment: making the tough decision when required (good umpires know what to do, great umpires execute).

c) Match assessment (match referee assessments)

There are seven meaningful scores produced from a match performance:
   - Match score (a composite of the five performance pillars).
   - Teamwork and attitude.
   - Preparation.
   - Man and match management.

- General decision-making.
- Technique.
- Correct decision percentage (CD%)

It is the preference of the National Umpire Selectors to select umpires who have demonstrated officiating competencies and capabilities, however, the selectors also highly value the character of the person (attitude, honesty, integrity, work ethic, coachability) and their chemistry (how they fit in and add value to the umpiring team) to complete the 'package'. Should two umpires be similar in competencies and capabilities, it is the superior official in areas of character and chemistry who will be selected. For selectors, outstanding people make outstanding Cricket Australia match officials.

As for performance appraisals, what is rewarded is repeated. How a person goes about their tasks, their adherence to the agreed organisational team values, and their attitude must be given equal consideration to fulfilling their objectives (goals).

In this time where executive salaries and bonuses are under scrutiny, the ethics of such high monetary benefits are at the heart of the organisation's culture. What are the ethics behind bonuses being paid to the management in businesses facing significant shortcomings, at the expense of the staff who deliver these programmes?

As was mentioned earlier in this chapter, my personal performance reviews were interesting. They solely focused on my own goals that were agreed with my manager and feedback on my performance against the values. The first part was straightforward, and I did enjoy that process with my manager. We worked hard to identify the right process goals and alignment tasks with the overall unit strategy. The second part was more subjective and a little less clear. How do we measure performance against values? Most businesses like to put a number against it. With my staff, my preference was to offer feedback through examples of behaviour throughout the year (which was always discussed with them either at the time or during the monthly catch up).

Our daily behaviours must be aligned to our values. There is no room for mixed messages of behaviours – we cannot say one thing and do quite the other. When we make mistakes, a behaviour is seen not aligned with our values. It is then action must be taken to realign the behaviour. Our culture requires constant attention and maintenance. Think about it like your car – if we don't get it serviced regularly, if we fail to ignore the warning lights flashing on the dashboard, if we ignore the strange sounds and vibrations of the engine, it is likely to breakdown at a most inopportune moment, causing us inconvenience. The cost to fix the car is going to be far higher than if we had dealt with the warning signs when they first appeared. Similarly, we have an opportunity to work on our culture every day through the behaviours we accept and expect.

> **Chapter summary points**
>
> - Culture can be defined as an agreed set of behaviours that are accepted and expected aligned to the values of the group.
> - Once values are agreed to, you need to drill down and outline examples of desired behaviours and those that are not acceptable.
> - A culture will exist by default. It is worthwhile being proactive to influence and create the right culture you want rather than let it develop on its own.
> - Everyone has a role to play in developing a great culture.
> - A great culture is built upon the foundation of a trusting environment where people can raise difficult matters without the fear of ridicule.
> - The ideal culture is one of self-regulation through:
>   - Attitude:
>   - Humility.
>   - Team-first approach.

- Open feedback and communication:
  - A safe environment for dialogue.
  - Managers or leaders who walk the shop floor.
  - Strong, active listening.
- Commitment to regular training and development:
  - Ethics and integrity.
  - Working on improving character.
  - Awareness of one's strengths and development areas.
- Leadership:
  - Adaptive style of serving others and the group purpose, and leading by example.
  - Being vulnerable.
- What is measured:
  - Short-term focus targets on process.
  - It is not all about the bottom-line profit or money.
- Selection or performance reviews:
  - Value people's character and chemistry as much as their competencies and capabilities (results).
  - Reward and acknowledge ethical behaviour (process) more than hitting a performance goal (outcome).
  - The behaviours that are rewarded are repeated.

- Good people make good teams, which leads to great results. Choose and keep good people of character.
- Your team culture requires regular attention and maintenance to prevent it from breaking down and causing great inconvenience and incurring a huge cost to your purpose.

11

PRESSURE CAN CREATE A DIAMOND OR BURST A PIPE

PRESSURE EXISTS ONLY WHEN we care about what people think. If no one cares about the outcome of the task or the quality of the function, including yourself, where is the pressure to perform? Whether pressure is perceived or real does not matter as perception *is* reality.

Pressure can appear in the form of quality of the task, accuracy of the outcome, being on time, or meeting others' expectations. It can come from either yourself (internal) or from others (external). Often when we are doing something, there is both – we are often trying to live up to our own expectations and/or those of others.

Pressure can be good – it has the ability to create a diamond. The right amount of nerves before an event – an exam, a performance, a game, or a challenge – is good. It gets the adrenalin running through the body and you feel excited. An experienced international umpire that I stood with early on in my career once told me, if you don't feel nervous before the game, it means you don't care about your umpiring. His statement made me stop and think. Perhaps what he was really telling me was that being under some pressure is natural and good. We should accept and make room for the nerves in what we do – accept the pressure and use the heightened senses to be able to lift and perform better.

In some of my matches, it was effortless to get 'up' for the match. The quality of the contest and the players, the context of the match, or the fact that a large crowd was coming to watch – for any TV match, it is easy to have the right amount of arousal for my game, as there is sufficient external pressure to drive me to work hard and focus on getting my decisions correct. Getting up for a Test match, a One Day international, or an international T20 is easier, but the more you do, the higher the risk of not respecting the opportunity and importance of the fixture to your career, the careers of the participants, and the enjoyment of those watching at the ground or on television.

When some or all of those elements are missing, there is less external pressure, and that is when there is a danger of not being 'up' for the match. That's when my internal drivers and self-imposed pressure need to take over. I need to get myself up for the match and place some expectation of my own performance on me. I need to remind myself of my standards and create self-awareness of what the outcomes will be, unless I show a higher care factor for my game. A match with no crowd, no atmosphere, nothing riding on it, in hot and humid conditions is mentally challenging. However, as we say, we are only one ball and decision away from disaster, so we need to remind ourselves of the goals and the importance of the quality of our effort.

The ability of match officials to deal with pressure can frequently be linked to how well they can control their levels of anxiety or stress. Controlling anxiety in the big moments of a match is what can distinguish a good official from a great one. Anxiety may also be associated with the concept of fear, or more specifically, for officials, the fear of incorrect decisions leading to unsafe situations. Any official who manifests anxiety before and during a match can experience an elevated level of arousal and feelings of tension and apprehension.

While pressure can create a diamond, it can also burst a pipe. When we are too nervous, or the feelings of pressure become somewhat overwhelming, we tighten up, forget how to do things, forget what to do, and therefore are not able to perform freely. Our minds are thinking about other the impact of a negative performance. Our emotions completely take over our good senses and this leads to the bursting of the mental pipe.

Pressure can lead to panic, and panic leads to poor decision-making. The most amount of pressure I have felt occurs inside the third umpires' box. It is like being an airline pilot – a lot of hours of observation and monitoring, interspersed with a few minutes of critical decision-making such as during takeoffs and landings. You sit in the chair with a lot of work and things to keep on top of – communication with the director, the on-field umpires, counting balls, managing time stoppages, supporting the match referee. And then a decision is referred to you. The whole world is now watching you and you have to process the decision quickly. Time seems to stand still! Sometimes that panic and pressure can burst the pipe as it did during a one-day match at the Melbourne Cricket Ground in 2003. Australia was fielding against Sri Lanka. A run out appeal was referred up to me. I looked at one replay and saw that Adam Gilchrist had knocked off a bail before he caught the ball and then broke the stumps with the batsman well short of his ground. I made my decision and put on the green light. Not out.

After the next ball, *Channel 9* replayed on a different angle which showed that despite one bail being removed too early, the other bail was still resting on top of the stumps. Adam had still broken the wicket fairly, and the batsman was out. Under pressure I had made an incorrect decision. I should have slowed down, taken a breath, and maintained composure. I remember turning to the match referee Clive Lloyd, acknowledging the error, and apologising. I was feeling low and embarrassed, but learnt a lot from it.

Apart from umpiring, I quite enjoy playing golf. I'm not a bad golfer with my handicap floating between fifteen and nineteen. On a very good day, I could par the course with a handicap of twelve shots, but that is getting rarer. I've always found it interesting with the mental challenge of placing the ball on the tee and trying to put the ball on the fairway, avoiding the trees on the left and the out-of-bounds fence on the right. The more you think and feel the pressure of not going out of bounds on the right, the more you tense up. And, guess what, the ball goes out of bounds on the right! So, you're now playing your third shot from the tee. When this happens to me, I usually think, *What the hell, you might as well just have a good crack and put it down the middle. Nothing to lose.* What typically happens is just that I put the ball down the middle like I should have done on the first attempt. Why is this? Because with the replay stroke, I

Pressure can create a diamond or burst a pipe 167

feel free to play without any pressure of going right or left. I focus on the task and just do it. Our bodies can do what we want if our minds let it.

I find I umpire best when I focus on my game, what I have to do, and keep my routines and processes simple. I try not to get distracted too much about what others are doing, especially outside the boundary. I often think too many people overcomplicate the game. Quite simply, it is just a game. Yes, my work as an umpire is important and means a lot to not only myself, the players, and those watching, but it's just a game. If I'm feeling too nervous or starting to overthink what might happen, I try to remind myself that it's only a game, what could be the worst thing that can happen? This technique creates a better sense of perspective and reality, rather than the one playing out in my mind.

People often ask me about how I handled the pressure of the 2011 ICC Cricket World Cup Final – a match watched and followed by over one billion people. To say it was an important match is probably understating it, but it was how I handled the previous match and took a lot of self-confidence from it – that made the final a lot easier. The semi-final was between India and Pakistan, two traditional rivals and both supported by perhaps the most passionate and enthusiastic fan bases. I knew media hype was going to be extreme and the focus on this match enormous – it was a final in itself. The match was to be held in Mohali, India, a reasonably small town by Indian standards, so escaping pre-match hysteria was going to be next to impossible. My strategy of handling the external pressure was to focus on what I had to do and realise it was just another game of cricket. Landing at the airport and getting to the hotel was hard – so many planes, so many people, so much 'noise' around this match. I started to try and block it all out.

We arrived at the hotel two days ahead of the match, and at the check-in, I asked for the Do Not Disturb (DND) feature to be set on my room phone. I asked for no newspapers to be delivered and put the television control in the top drawer of the desk. I did not want to watch any television. Anyone who has been to India may know that there are a couple of hundred TV channels, most of them dedicated to news and sports. I did not want to know anything about this upcoming match from an outside source. Apart from the ground inspection and a nightly meal, I kept pretty much to myself and away from all the outside noise. I kept telling myself, this is just another game of cricket and everything inside the boundary is just the same.

It turned out to be one of my better matches, and while I had some very tight calls to make, I trusted my instincts and abilities and got them right. I can't remember what the scores were or who made runs or who took wickets. I was focused on respecting each ball and keeping it simple. I blocked out a lot of everything else. Post-match, I remember sitting on the steps of the dressing room with my partner, Ian Gould. We just sat there with a drink in hand. It must have been around forty minutes after the winning run that they began to switch off the stadium lights. The crowd had dispersed and the TV crew was starting to pack up. It finally hit me – this was a big, big match, we survived it, and we did well. I was exhausted from the mental and physical strain and didn't want to go anywhere – I just wanted to soak up the sense of achievement and relief.

How can we better handle the internal and external pressure that comes with the task? Firstly, we should embrace some pressure and accept that it is good and can help deliver your best. Trying to shut all pressure out is like pretending you are invincible or that the colour black is actually white. We need to accept that some pressure is helpful and indeed necessary for you to deliver your best.

If you are suffering from excessive internal pressure, you need to look at moderating your own thoughts. Perhaps you are setting yourself too high a standard to reach or placing too much importance on the outcome. Those levels set could be extreme, irrational, and impractical. I would suggest still having good goals, but perhaps ensure that they are more process driven and not outcome focused. I would also recommend working with your coach on better defining what success looks like for you and placing better context around what is realistic and achievable.

Some other techniques for moderating high internal pressure include writing a list of achievements. This builds self-confidence, that you are deserving and ready for the opportunity in front of you. Also, try to focus on the basic tasks ahead of you. For my work, that meant simply watching the ball and keeping my mind in the present. Slow and measured breathing is also a great way to help relieve pressure, stress, and panic of any situation. This helps you reconnect with your body and the moment by acknowledging self-control at that particular moment. It helps your mind recalibrate and reset just like you would if your home computer programme was failing to respond to a command. Reboot through controlled breathing – simple, but very effective!

When there is excessive external pressure, along with the breathing technique, here are some things that worked for me that might work for you.

- Stretching: a physical movement to release some tension (arms and legs).
- Singing a song: this was a great reliever for me. Stadiums play lots of songs throughout the day. I'd pick one I liked and in between balls or at the end of the over I would sing it to relax a little more, if needed.

- Positive self-talk affirmations: keep reminding yourself of the short-term process goal for the day. Talk to yourself in a supportive way along the lines of I can do this or I'll be fine.

One last technique with regards to external pressure that is really worth exploring comes from something that I learnt from rugby union and referees like Stuart Dickinson. It's the technique of putting the pressure back on the player. Sometimes the pressure comes from those who have created the situation or challenge for us. In umpiring, for example, we feel pressure when we need to make a hard or unpopular decision like applying a penalty for a slow over rate or taking a bowler out of the attack for running on the pitch too many times. In such situations, putting the pressure back on the other person is very powerful and helps us stay on track with our own game.

Here's an example. The fast bowler Jimmy Anderson is a very well-respected, top performer of England. He does have a habit, from time to time, of running on the pitch in his follow through into a protected area, which is to be monitored and managed by the umpire. Effective communication is essential, along with committing to the decision to take action and the strategy of putting the pressure back on the player and captain. As an umpire, if I can stay out of the game and let it flow and not have to penalise people, then that is a good thing. Why should we hand out 'parking tickets' if we can prevent some offences and not become the focus of the game unnecessarily? If I have spoken with Jimmy and told him, 'Jimmy, you're running on the pitch, you need to come off faster', and he doesn't respond with a different behaviour, I could say the following and put the pressure back on him: 'Jimmy, I've asked you to come off, if you don't come off now, you leave me with no choice, but to officially caution you which could lead to suspending you from bowling. Is that what you want?' Through this language and even sharing this with his captain, I'm leaving the decision to Jimmy. I've offered him help, but if he ignores my message, the consequences rest solely with him, not me. The pressure is now only on him to shift his behaviour, not on me.

Other lines I've used with players to put the pressure back on them (and take it off me) include:

> 'There's a match referee up there just ready to lighten your wallet. How about you help us by keeping quiet for the rest of the day?'
>
> 'We've told you now three times your over rate is dropping. We'll apply all the time allowances we can, but if you don't try to pick up the speed of the game now, you leave us with no choice but to penalise you.'

'If you don't want me to call wide, don't bowl the ball down the leg side.'

'Come back with your front foot, otherwise you can expect a No ball call.'

'You are too tight with the front foot, if you take a wicket now, I'm going upstairs to check, and you don't want to take a wicket off a No Ball, do you? Come back now.'

Nerves, butterflies, and pressure are all good if they are at the right level for you and can be leveraged off to help you deliver your best performance. Not enough is equally as detrimental as too much. It would be best if you worked with your coach to find the right amount that works for you and have strategies in place to deal with the extremes.

I'd certainly like to see more diamonds out there in business and sport than burst pipes.

Chapter summary points
- Pressure exists only when you care about what you and or others think. Caring about your game is good, not caring too much (out of a fear of failure) or excessive anxiety.
- Self-belief also plays a role in handling pressure – believing you are good enough, deserve the opportunity

in front of you (selectors and others think you are ready), and you have put the work in and deserve to be successful. We don't get what we want, we get what we deserve.
- Internal and external pressure both may need to be worked on with your coach.
- The right amount of pressure is good. Nerves show that we care about our game. They can elevate our game and help create a 'diamond'.
- Excessive nerves or pressure to the point where it overtakes your thinking or performance will burst the 'pipe'. We need the appropriate amount of nerves to be 'up' for the match or task.
- The ideal is to play or umpire freely. Play like you care but don't care.
- It's just a game. Don't put more pressure than required on yourself than is helpful and try not to overthink the task or the possible outcomes. Stay focused and process simple.
- Put the pressure back on others through using simple key phrases that offer proactive advice, manage expectations, and position any further action at the responsibility of the other person.

- Keeping pressure in check and maintaining composure are essential for clear thinking – slowing things down and considering options.
- Pressure leads to panic and poor decision-making.
- The best get the 'big moments' right through being able to manage internal and external pressure.
- Some techniques to relieve pressure are being self-aware, breathing, stretching, singing a song, positive self-talk affirmations, listing achievements to build self-confidence, focusing on your game, keeping it simple, doing the basic tasks well, and acceptance of the challenge and environment.

12

MANAGING CONFLICT

IT HAS BEEN A real blessing to be involved with cricket umpiring and the sport to learn new skills and become better in dealing with most challenges. Conflict is inevitable in a competitive sporting environment, both on and off the field. The transferrable skill of managing conflict is one of the things that I cover with more match officials across different sports and businesses than most other subjects. It is learnt, and while conflict is inevitable, arguments and fighting are optional. I want to share with you some tips and techniques that I've employed within officiating that will help you manage conflict and get you back to core business faster.

Before we get into the specific tools and techniques, there are some basic things that we need to be aware of that can set the foundation for being able to manage conflict better.

There is no doubt good people who are respected are more likely to manage conflict better, or have less conflicts to manage. Why is this? When a manager, an umpire, or a person in a position of authority is known and respected to the other person, there is often a reduced sense of anxiety and things tend not to escalate. This respect often comes from past performance, but it also comes from having a relationship based on trust and knowing the people involved.

As a former umpire selector for Cricket Australia, when looking for match officials for finals and local derby matches, umpires were appointed according to who players respected through performance and who were well known and trusted by all to perform. These people have the skills of being able to manage anything that comes their way. While the first part is respect of the participants, the second is that of trust. Trust comes about when people know you, understand your motives, and know how you are going to act, especially under pressure.

With this, I'd like to introduce you to the concept of the *relationship bank account*. Like any regular bank account, the relationship version grows through making small, regular deposits that build over time. The relationship account grows when we make regular efforts through touchpoints to show others how we respect or value them. For example, with the players or coaches that I would regularly officiate, that might mean I would see them at breakfast, in the hotel, in the gym, at the airport, at the ground inspection, at training, or at functions. It doesn't take much effort to greet or congratulate other people. To empathise with a player or a coach when they have had some misfortune, injuries, or bad results is also essential here. By using good, common manners, you can often go a long way to making those relationship bank account deposits be worthwhile, but they have to be genuine.

When we have conflict, it's a real advantage in having a healthy balance in the relationship account (respect and trust), as conflict could result in a withdrawal. If there are insufficient funds, the penalty interest makes the experience a more expensive one. Therefore, why not be proactive and build trust and respect with those around you in non-threatening environments, so that when conflict does happen, it is easier and less costly for you.

Here are some tips and techniques that could help reduce and manage conflict better, no matter where it occurs.

Buy time

The destination is the same, the pathways are many. We all want a good outcome, but how do we know the best way to handle a situation? One key thing to do is buy some thinking time. Ask yourself: do I need to respond immediately? As an umpire, my job was to manage the match with my colleague (sometimes I had up to two umpires and a match referee to support me). As an on-field team, we were supposed to be in control. Just to stand there and make eye contact when something was going off the rails with regard to player behaviour is a great way to regain control. It is similar to the powerful technique of a pregnant pause in a conversation or presentation – to make people stop what they are doing or thinking.

Steve Davis and I were umpiring a Test match in Barbados between the West Indies and South Africa in 2010. Sulieman Benn, a lower order batsman for the West Indies, was trying hard to stave off defeat when Morne Morkel bowled him. As he walked back and past the South African fieldsman Dale Steyn, he did or said something that Dale reacted to quite strongly. I caught the reaction from the corner of my eye from the bowler's end, and Sulieman kept on walking while the South African team appeared to get more enraged. What happened there and what should I have done?

To buy time, I walked across to my on-field partner Steve and asked him what he saw. Steve saw nothing of the episode, but had caught Dale's reaction also. It was then several South African players approached us and complained that Sulieman had spat at Dale as he walked past him. We listened to the complaint and told Graeme Smith, the then captain, that we would review the matter at the end of the day. We had no information apart from the complaint to work on. We needed to buy some time to collect the facts and then decide what action, if any, we were going to take. In the meantime, we had to calm the players down and check the situation. We asked Graeme to leave the matter with us and not take any retaliatory action into his own hands, and reassured that we would review the matter after play.

In walking across to Steve, I was attempting to buy some thinking time about what happened and decide the course of action. In responding to Graeme's complaint, we bought time to gather the facts and let the emotion of the incident subside. We did not need to provide them with a commitment to take action against the batsman right then and there, but we did need to de-escalate the situation with a promise to follow it up later.

Don't pour fuel on the fire

This can involve choosing the most appropriate moment to get involved in conflict or situation. Stepping in too soon with a player versus player conflict will add fuel to the fire and quickly turn it into a player versus umpire conflict.

Early in my international career at the SCG, Australia was playing the West Indies in a day/night match. It was a balmy summer evening and the crowd was really into the game. They were responding passionately to every run and

Managing conflict

appeal. The West Indies' Brian Lara was at the crease, and his team was under pressure. The Australian fielders were trying to unsettle him and put him off his game. If they got him out, they were well on the way to winning the match. Michael Bevan was fielding in the covers, someone who was very quick on his feet, but normally quiet when it came to chatting on the field. I had my own things to focus on, having made an early error in the innings. I was standing at the bowler's end when I noticed Brian was having a go at Michael about something. I immediately went over and asked Brian to get back to batting and leave Michael to me. Michael must have said something to him because Brian was pointing to him while complaining to me.

Brian was then just as upset, if not more, with me. I reflected on the incident, what I could have done better. Post-match I spoke with my experienced on-field partner, Darrell Hair. He told me that these two players were very experienced and had been around a long time. It might have been a better strategy to give them a little time initially to see if they were going to sort the matter out themselves before jumping straight into something that had nothing to do with me. A good lesson to learn for the future I thought.

Picking your moment is just as important in not creating conflict, in other words, picking your battles. Glenn McGrath was a bowler who prided himself on accuracy and consistency. No surprises to learn he hated being hit to the boundary. I was umpiring him one day at North Sydney Oval in a state one-day match. He was not bowling particularly well in his early overs and was square cut for four runs. As he walked past me to go back to his bowling mark, I tried to be proactive and ask him to come back with his front foot as he was getting close the front line (and close to bowling a No ball). He responded by taking his aggression and frustration out on me and remarked, 'Don't worry about the front line, just get your decisions right down the other end!' What I should have done is left him alone after getting hit for the boundary and picked the right moment, perhaps at the end of the over or the start of the next one, to offer him that information when he had calmed down.

Manage the person

When conflict happens, it is essential to manage the person *and* to manage the issue. Sometimes we omit to manage one of these critical aspects or have too big a focus on one to the detriment of the other.

One of the most interesting conflict situations I've had to manage occurred in a Pakistan versus India limited overs series held in Peshawar. The then captain of the Pakistan cricket team, Inzamam-ul-Haq, was batting. Inzi, as he was better known to the playing group, was naturally a very popular and prominent player, a prized wicket for the opposition to get. Pakistan playing India is like Australia playing England in the Ashes – it's a contest of the greatest rivalry for spectators and the media alike. I was standing at the bowler's end to a delivery from S. Sreesanth, and Inzi hit the ball back to Suresh Raina at mid-off. Suresh then threw the ball back towards the keeper's end. Inzi was some distance out of his crease at this point and decided to intercept the ball and block it when he could have turned and avoided this (not being in danger of being injured). Upon seeing this, the Indian side appealed for Obstructing the Field. The appeal, a first in the fifteen years of my umpiring career, was under my jurisdiction at the bowler's end.

The first thing I did was to walk very slowly over to Asad Rauf at square leg, to buy some thinking time. I asked Asad a straightforward question, 'Did he deliberately hit the ball away not avoiding injury?' Asad replied, 'Yes.' I then declared Inzi out. Needless to say, Inzi and the Pakistan contingent were not pleased, and Inzi came across to complain. We needed to manage the person and the issue. How did we do this?

We managed the person by calmly listening to his complaint and why he thought he was not out. We also used his name to acknowledge him as an individual. Asad and I stood side by side to send a non-verbal message that we were united in our decision. We stood tall in posture, heads up, and with full eye contact. Our body language communicated that we were committed to the decision and we were not going to back down. Our verbal message was clear, concise, and accurate. We explained why he was out very simply and concisely, which left Inzi nowhere to go, but off the field.

After the match, we then had to manage another person in conflict, the late Pakistan coach, Bob Woolmer. Bob came into our dressing room with Inzi to seek an explanation (his words) or complain (our words). We used a couple of other techniques in managing the person with this example of conflict. We used empathy with Bob, where we told him that we understood why he might be confused about the Law or how it is to be applied – it was a very rare form of dismissal. We appreciated it was an important, high-profile match and a unique decision. We again heard his side of the story and why he thought the decision was wrong. He got a good listening to! We respected his role as coach to seek clarification and understanding and then we explained the Law with the use of the MCC's little blue book and why Inzi was given out. Again, we were clear, concise, and accurate. Despite all of this, Bob and Inzi left our dressing room unconvinced and somewhat unimpressed, but a little calmer.

Manage the issue

With the above example in mind, we also had to manage the issue. We had to manage the appeal and subsequent dismissal. We used some techniques to do this well. Asad and I acted as a team. We used the combined information for me to reach a decision and Asad supported me through the whole process along with the rest of the match officials afterwards in the dressing room. Post-match, we also explained to Inzi and Bob how Inzi left us with no choice given his actions. In deliberately playing the ball away while it was still alive, and given the Indian team's appeal, we had to process the appeal. If Inzi wanted to avoid this outcome in the future, he needed to leave the ball alone when it was being thrown in from the field.

To highlight and describe other techniques available in managing the issue, I'm going to use another example from my career. It happened in a Test match in Sri Lanka, with the home side playing the West Indies in 2005. Shivnarine Chanderpaul was the then captain of the West Indies and the issue involved Tino Best, one of their fast bowlers.

A bowler is not allowed to bowl a full toss above the batsman's waist, also known as a beamer. If they bowl two of these types of deliveries in an innings, they are not allowed to bowl for the rest of that innings. These deliveries from pace bowlers can be very dangerous which is why we have a guideline to call No ball even for the ones that are marginal on height. Full tosses of this nature belong in baseball, not cricket.

Tino bowled his first waist-high full toss, was called for the No ball, and got his first and final warning. This is where another technique of managing the issue comes in. My on-field colleague, Tony Hill, who was umpiring at the bowler's end, explained to Tino why he had been cautioned and also explained him and his captain what would happen should a similar delivery be bowled. In other words, the current and future consequences were clearly covered. Tino was not happy with the decision even though we had explained the guideline in the pre-series meeting with the captains, and now we were merely applying and setting the standard. While the decision and call should not have been a surprise, we were managing the issue through a prior explanation of what was not acceptable (drawing the line) and then setting the standard with applying the penalty.

Tino continued to bowl and soon followed up with a similar delivery, again called out a No ball. But this time he was given his hat back by Tony, while Shivnarine was asked to bring on a different bowler to replace Tino. Shiv and Tino were most displeased, but they could not complain about the process as we had managed the issue very well.

In the second innings, when Tino came on to bowl, I recall I used another technique to manage the issue, by asking for his help. 'Tino, can you do us a favour (and yourself) and not bowl any full tosses around waist height and keep us out of the game?' I was asking him to learn from his earlier mistake and spare us from making such decisions. Unfortunately, this approach did not work. He bowled another dangerous delivery in the second innings and again we had to call it.

In setting the standard and managing the player and the issue, the conflict that arose became less difficult to manage, and we were able to get on with the match faster.

Conflict is inevitable but fighting and arguing are optional. If we can buy some thinking time, refrain from responding immediately to the situation, show some empathy, and engage in active listening skills, we are more likely to de-escalate the conflict quicker and move on faster.

Chapter summary points

- It's unlikely for you to eliminate conflict, but it's important you manage it more effectively and get back on track faster. Conflict is inevitable, but arguments are optional.
- Managing conflict is like maintaining a relationship bank account – make small but regular deposits to

build a decent account balance from which a sizeable withdrawal can be made, without being overdrawn.
- Buy some thinking time to consider options; there is no need to respond immediately.
- Focus on the issue, not the person.
- Pick your moment and battles, don't jump in too early, nor too late.
- Manage the person:
  - Use their name and connect with them.
  - Listen to understand not listen to defend.
  - Appeal to their role and what people expect from them.
  - Be the calmest person in the room – behave in a manner you would expect from the other person.
  - Body language communication needs to match verbal communication. Be side by side if you are working with someone else or just off to the side if you are on your own. Try not to be in their face and in a confrontational position.
  - Use effective communication tips like inclusive verbal language (use 'we' and 'us') and good manners.
  - Be clear, concise, and accurate in expressing your decision.

- Use non-verbal body language to show your importance in decision-making.
- Manage the issue:
  - Ask for help.
  - Put the pressure back on the player.
  - Teamwork with your partner – be united and stick together.
  - Set the standard and boundary for behaviours.
  - Communicate possible consequences if the behaviour continues to avoid surprises later.

13

WHY FOCUS BEATS CONCENTRATION

HOW DO YOU STAND out there and concentrate for up to seven hours?

Without getting too technical, concentration is the ability to apply your undivided attention to the task at hand. Whereas I prefer to use the term 'focus', as it describes the act of applying your undivided attention to the *main* or *central component* of the task. Our concentration does waver, and at any point we are concentrating on something which is perhaps not the main task! This is why focus beats concentration.

Back to the question. There is no possible way someone can focus their attention for seven hours. Lessons at school are limited to fifty minutes for a reason, and in today's world attention spans are getting shorter and shorter, especially with the younger generation. In a four- to five-minute video posted on *YouTube*, for example, research has shown that fewer than 60 per cent of the viewers will still be watching till the end of the video, against 75 per cent for a one- to two-minute video.

Being able to focus is all about the ability to keep your mind where your body is, that is, in the present, and have your attention on the right things at the right moment. This is best done through being composed, having strong routines, positive self-talk, and a high amount of self-awareness. The ability to avoid distractions and remain on task is fundamental as well. For now, let's focus (no pun intended) on the positive ways to stay focused.

Mentally staying in the present is critical. You cannot be thinking about anything else except what you are seeing in front of you at the time. Being fully connected with the events as they unfold and seeing or hearing what you need to is the ultimate in focus. Being relaxed and composed is also vital as this minimises the chance of your thoughts wandering into the past or future. At times in my career I would be able to focus on the 'here and now' by commentating on the events happening in front of me, talking to myself and describing what I was seeing. It worked well and is one of the better techniques.

Having a pre-delivery routine that involved positive self-talk as the bowler was running in was another useful technique. The self-talk trigger did need to change from day to day in order for me to listen and pay attention to myself though! Some examples included, 'this ball', 'watch the ball', 'now', 'want the decision to come to you', 'focus now', 'see the impact', and so on. What is important is that the words used with self-talk should matter to you, they need to have meaning and should be connected to your goals in some way.

In my game, I only needed to have a narrow focus for several seconds at a time, and then I could switch down. What do I mean by narrow? There are two types of focus – narrow and broad. Narrowing your focus means to reduce the elements you are watching and processing – for example, the ball or the play at the time. The other is a broad focus; this is when you are more aware of other things going on around you like the hum of the crowd, someone walking behind you, your partner moving back into position, all at the same time.

Switching between narrow and broad focus is also a skill to be practised. Often I hear about people who switch on and switch off. This pattern of focus was blown away when I was lucky to listen to Ian Healy when he spoke at one of our NSW umpiring conventions in the 1990s. Ian was one of Australia's finest ever wicketkeepers, playing over a hundred Tests for his country. A wicketkeeper, just like an umpire, needs to watch every ball carefully, expecting to be involved in the play, and has to be ready to respond. Ian's messages were simple and are still applicable today. He said, 'I don't switch on and off, I switch up and switch down'. In other words, he goes from a narrow focus when the ball is being delivered to a broad one when the ball is dead. Just like an umpire! However, what he said next also was very interesting. 'I work really hard in the first fifteen minutes of a session to get my routines right for each delivery, and then I can settle in and don't have to try too hard – they just flow after that.' To me, that sounded exactly like a plane taking off – full thrust to get enough speed to get into the air, and when sufficient altitude is reached, pull back on the throttle, level off, and consider engaging the autopilot. Focus and seeing or hearing the important cues are built into routines: get those basics right and your game (whatever that is) becomes a little easier.

What do *you* need to have a narrow and broad focus for in your world and routines? How can *you* have a narrow focus in a conversation with a colleague, or while writing an important letter, or completing a report? How can *you* switch to a broad focus in a presentation to pick up the body language cues of the audience and shift your style appropriately? Do *you* find yourself having too broad a focus and paying too much attention to the wrong cues? Do *you* know what the right cues are in your 'match' to make better decisions?

In cricket, like most sports, most things that happen occur in a similar sequence. American sports call them 'plays'. With ball sports, what I've discovered is that the best players and the best officials don't focus on the ball most of the time, they focus on the play. Please don't think you don't have to watch the ball, you do. When Brett Lee or Shoaib Akhtar are bowling a 160 kilometre per hour thunderbolt from my end, I need to watch the ball, but once it is clear of the batsman and any fielder, I need to watch the play – the bowler's follow through, the batsman running down the pitch, the fielder coming in to the stumps, the batsman touching down for runs, the fielder throwing in, and so on. By watching and reading the play, I'm able to focus on the right things at the right time and capture most of what is needed. At the bowler's end, my focus has to shift from narrow (seeing the striker at the crease) to broad (hearing the bowler running in) to narrow (to see the front foot land) to broad (seeing the ball come in view) to narrow (seeing the ball hit the pitch and then the batsman) to broad (watching the play) to narrow (seeing the ball settle in the keeper's gloves)!

With writing a report, having a long conversation with a colleague, making a presentation, I don't see how you can have a narrow focus for several minutes at a stretch. How

Why focus beats concentration

can you vary your focus from narrow to broad and pick up other vital cues to improve what you are doing at the time?

Back to my game. I cannot focus all day or even two hours at a stretch. I sometimes use the analogy of eating a meal when talking to other people about this subject. How do you eat your evening meal, I ask? Hopefully, they respond by saying, one mouthful at a time. And that's the right answer. We use our knife and fork, or hand, to cut or pick up just enough that we can chew at one time. My job was to umpire one ball at a time, to umpire it to the best of my ability, and then repeat. When I got to six valid balls in an over, I stopped and went to a different position. When we repeated that for sixty minutes, we either had a drinks break or an interval like lunch, tea, or stumps. How could I walk out to officiate a Test match and think, gee I've got thirty hours and five days ahead of me to get through. I had to break it down into manageable, bite-size chunks. I thought about it like this: first ball, first over, first hour, then have a break. When that was done, I just repeated the process ... first ball, first over, first session, then a break. And when we ran out of balls, we called 'Time' and went back to the hotel for a rest. We need to keep big tasks simple by keeping them small and manageable.

The other way I've answered the question above is by asking the person, 'Do you think *you* could umpire one ball of cricket very well?' They normally answer yes or that they think they can. I then respond, 'OK, then all you have to do is be able to repeat that 270 times from one end in a day's play, or 1,350 times across a Test match.' Sounds easier? Well, the best in the world do the basics to an excellent standard, consistently well, all the time.

If by some chance the positive tools to remain in the present have not worked, that is where your self-awareness needs to kick in. If you can be aware that you are thinking about something in the past (like a previous decision) or something in the future (like what the others might say when you walk off the field), you are almost there to getting back to focusing on the present. Whatever you were using to stay in the present has not worked, and when this happens you need to try something different. Apart from mental tools, there are some physical ones you could try. Taking a deep breath is one and releasing it in a controlled way – focusing on the breathing in and the slow exhaling reconnects your mind with your body. Another tool is to look at your hands: this is where my body is, this is where my mental state needs to be. Another is to look at the goal, the objective, the task, and connect with the 'why' again – why are we doing this activity in the first place? These things will help you regain your focus, and in particular your narrow focus ability.

Focusing on the right things at the right time is the goal. It takes mental effort and good routines along with a high level of self-awareness. Your mind needs to be where your body is and both need to be connected for true focus. Reminding yourself why this task is important and what it means to you will help increase the respect you have for the opportunity in front of you. Keep the process simple, break the task down into simple pieces and think about one thing at a time. Then repeat. And don't forget to have a break, refresh, and recharge regularly – no battery lasts forever!

Chapter summary points

- Focus beats concentration because it means the main or central part of what is being done is treated as the most important. Focus also means we have our undivided attention on the right things at the right time.
- Focus means having our mind where our body is – in the present.
- Focus comes through being composed, having strong routines, positive self-talk, and a high amount of self-awareness.
- Techniques to focus and stay in the present include:
  - Commentating on what is happening in front of you.

- Positive self-talk before the event (through meaningful phrases).
- Deep, controlled breathing.
- Looking at your hands.
* There are two types of focus, narrow and broad, and we need to be able to move from one to another to make better decisions.
* We switch our focus up and down, not on and off.
* Work hard to get into your focus routines quickly, and then the rest of the task process becomes a little easier.
* Don't always focus on the ball, focus on the play; don't have a narrow focus all the time.
* Break your focus and task down into bite-sized chunks.
* First ball, first over, first hour, have a break, and then repeat.
* The best in the world do the basics to an excellent standard, consistently well, all the time.
* Self-awareness is vital to know when your focus is not right. Use one of the tools to come back to the present.

14

BOUNCEBACKABILITY

SOME PEOPLE CALL THIS resilience, some call it mental toughness, some call it perseverance. I call it 'bouncebackability'. It's the skill of facing a setback or failure and being able to regroup, refocus, and get back on track to face the next challenge. In this chapter, I'd like to offer you some vulnerability by sharing some of my hardest and most difficult moments, and how I dealt with them. I'll share things that did not work, but more importantly, some techniques and strategies that did, so that you can perhaps try them in your world.

Probably the best definition I can offer of mental toughness is the 'ability to control your thoughts and emotions and not let them control you'. As a cricket umpire, I can almost remember every single mistake I've made on the field or in the third umpire's box. Even today, several years after retiring from representative umpiring, people often compliment me on my performances and standards, telling me how much they admired the accuracy and quality of my umpiring. I'm humbled and often embarrassed, especially when I know and can still recount all of my errors and shortcomings. You see, for me, every mistake is like a mental scar and is attached to the emotion of frustration, anger, despair, sadness, or disappointment.

I believe the majority of any sport is predominantly played out in the space between the ears. Umpiring more so, as nearly all our game is mental. We need to have tremendous knowledge across many Laws, playing conditions, and several policies only to be matched with the ability to stay in the present and think on our feet when something new presents itself. That said, I spent a substantial part of my career, and still do, researching and reading to improve being able to control my thoughts and emotions and be more rational and objective in dealing with events.

Being emotionally hijacked

There are three places your mind can be – past, present, or future. Being a cricket umpire is just like being a pilot. There are hours and hours of observation and only a few seconds or minutes of panic! And when something goes wrong, and we need to switch off the autopilot, you want the best person with their hands on the controls. The fact is you cannot focus or concentrate one hundred percent of the time.

In the previous chapter, I told you how Ian Healy best described his focus routine in his wicketkeeping role as 'switching up and switching down', not on and off. The reason is you need to be aware of what is happening around and remain grounded in the present. If we were to switch off, our mind would be thinking about something in the past or in the future. It was a great insight and piece of advice from Ian as his role was very similar to mine – we needed to expect every ball to involve us in some way and be ready to respond correctly.

When I'm working, I need to be aware of what is going on around me. I need to be reading the game and have an appreciation and understanding of what the players and teams are trying to do and be ready for what might be coming next. Just like a good captain, I need to be in front of the game tactically. It is also important to be still in the present while at square leg, to be able to support your partner and be there for them when they need some help on ball counting, runs off the pad, or even just reassurance. There is also your own role to play around monitoring fielding restrictions, height judgements for deliveries, and line decisions. The key message is you can switch down at times, but you cannot switch off.

Some might think staying in the present is easy, but the reality is different. There is so much time to think that often our mind gets hijacked with other thoughts, and we don't entirely focus on what is happening right in front of us. Staying in the present is a skill and requires hard work and practice, but often we have to learn skills the hard way. On that point, I'd like to share with you a story of how I got emotionally hijacked in a Test match at Trent Bridge, how it affected my performance, and subsequently what I learnt from it.

It was June 2004, and I was appointed to stand with Australia's Daryl Harper – someone whom I had umpired a lot with – in a Test series between England and New Zealand. I was ably supported by the third umpire, Mark Benson, and match referee, Clive Lloyd, for this match. We were also working with two excellent captains and leaders, Stephen Fleming (New Zealand) and Michael Vaughan (England). By the time this series came around, I had umpired international cricket for five years and been on the Emirates Elite Panel of ICC Umpires for over a year so that one would have thought I had sufficient experience under my belt. However, the truth is somewhat different, as I was to discover, and there is always something to be learnt.

There was nothing unusual about the preparation, lead up, or circumstances surrounding this match. I was just as determined and focused on doing well as ever and worked hard accordingly. Everything seemed to be going well, until deep into the last session on day one when I turned down an LBW appeal from Matthew Hoggard. After leaving the field, I received feedback that it was an error; the call should have been Out. That night I tried to analyse why I had made the error. Like most mistakes, I must have replayed the ball and decision in my head thousands of times while failing in my attempts to go to sleep. I spoke to myself harshly and berated myself for stuffing up. *You idiot, how did you get that one wrong? You've just ruined a good game for yourself. You won't be getting an A+ on the match assessment for this game.*

On day two, I declared Graham Thorpe out incorrectly off the pad down the leg side. That was two decisions against England now, and the crowd's response was not kind, but I wasn't worried about the crowd as I gave myself another mental uppercut. My errors on day two and three continued to flow with another caught behind decision on Scott Styris and an LBW error on Andrew Strauss, whom I gave out after the ball pitched outside leg stump. I remember walking in to lunch on day three and trying to have the courage to look at Clive Lloyd in the eye and asking him, 'Is there any chance I might be able to string two sessions together without stuffing something up?' Clive put his hand on my shoulder and said, 'We all have a bad game from time to time, you'll be OK.' *Not me*, I thought, *I don't have bad games, and I've certainly not had a match like this before.*

At the end of day three, I reached out to Darrell Hair who was living in Lincolnshire then and happened to be at the match. Darrell knew my game better than anyone else as I had apprenticed under his watch. I could not figure out where I was going wrong, so I met up with Darrell that night for a drink and a chat. Dinner was off the agenda as I had no appetite whatsoever. I asked, 'Where am I going wrong? Can you see anything in my game that is causing me to make these mistakes?' To my dismay, all Darrell could say was, 'You look fine, everything appears normal to me, your technique looks good.' *Wow*, I thought. *I don't feel normal, and nothing about my game is good right now.*

I didn't sleep much that night as the events replayed in my head and I certainly wasn't looking forward to day four. In fact, the only thing I was looking forward now was the flight out of London. Finally, the match ended on day four with England winning, and I remember standing on the field for the match presentations. It was a place that I did not want to be. I was still looking for a big hole to crawl into and keep out of sight. While these things were running through my head, John Bracewell, the New Zealand coach, came up to me. What he said took me by surprise. 'Look, I know you've had a tough game, but I want you to know that our boys are really impressed with the way that you stuck at it and you didn't take it out on the players.' I wasn't up for compliments and I merely thanked John and apologised for my substandard performance. Looking back on it, it was a genuine gesture from a member of the losing side, one that I respected from a man who was pretty tough and set high standards for himself and his team.

Overall, this Trent Bridge test saw me deliver six clear decision-making errors, the worst match of my career, and it was there for all to see. It was new territory for me, and I didn't know how to handle it. It wasn't something that I had prepared for. Here is the paragraph from the general summary of my match self-assessment that I wrote that night:

> An extremely disappointing performance. The result was completely out of character for me. The result was not proportionate to the amount of preparation and effort put into the match. Was I just unlucky? I have to analyse this performance further to identify how I can improve on the field.
>
> The pitch conditions were testing – slow and seaming with some variable bounce, but nothing out of the ordinary. I lost confidence early in the game and never seemed to be able to recover and compounded things by making more mistakes. Whatever the case, I needed the resource of being

able to talk to someone who knew me and my game during the match to try and pick me up and get me back on track.

I was not happy with my game and the results. I can do better as demonstrated in the past, but need now to focus on future games and ensure better outcomes.

I recall walking out of Trent Bridge hating the feeling I felt and if this was what international cricket was about, then it wasn't for me. Right there and then I questioned whether or not I wanted to continue to umpire at this level. I had a choice to make. Was I going to find a way and continue, or give up and walk away? I think you know what I chose. However, what was the thing that helped and what did I do to turn it around I hear you ask? It was a long flight leaving London, and I had a book with me that I had intended to read, but had not gotten to it yet. As I have expressed in other chapters, I always looked to learn from others and improve my mental skills, so the book I intended to read was called *Winning Ugly* by Brad Gilbert, the former tennis player.

During the test, I could not put my finger on what was going wrong or why I could not execute to my usual standards. The following eight hours and the next couple of days were to provide me with a significant light-bulb moment and several tips to reflect on. I'm not going to summarise the whole book for you here, but a couple of things resonated with my game and my lack of mental toughness at the time.

Changing the self-talk

The way I spoke to myself was all wrong. I should have been talking to myself in a way that encouraged or supported a better outcome and to keep errors in perspective. For example, how do we speak to our kids when they are learning to ride a bike and make a mistake and fall off? I'd like to think we would say, 'It's OK, these things happen, are you alright? Let's get back on and have another try.' Right? And we'd say it in a supportive and soft tone, not one of criticism and harshness. Right? Well, why, when we stuff up as adults, do we talk to ourselves in a way that we would not talk to others? Pretty silly really, but therein lies the tool. We need to show ourselves that we care, but not through language and tone that puts us into a negative spin. Our language and tone need to allow us to acknowledge, accept, and reinforce what we need to do, and will enable us to move forward, not get stuck in the spiral of despair.

Move on: Don't dwell

I continued to beat myself up mentally. I was allowing the negative thoughts and events to continue and did not know how to break the vicious cycle that I was perpetuating. I was showing myself that I cared about my game, but I should have had a trigger or process to move on and to be able to move back into the present because you cannot look ahead when you are looking behind at the same time. You see, controlled anger is a great motivator, a great way to get your attention, but if you don't control it, it will control you. I needed to focus entirely on what I was going to do next.

Focus on the process

I think I gave up on myself and my game. I was assessing my match during the competition and 'watching the scoreboard'. I allowed myself to check out of the match as the ideal match report was gone, and what was the point of continuing with the match for me. I was not staying true to the process of my pre-delivery routines for each ball, nor was I focusing entirely on the ball in front of me. My focus was on the outcomes, the number of errors, and the match assessment report. I was focusing on outcomes, not processes. This realisation reinforced the view that if we created robust and correct processes, committed to them, worked hard, practised, and executed with purpose, the outcomes would take care of themselves.

Maybe I should have read Brad's book on the flight over? Perhaps if I did, the messages, learning, and tools would not have connected so much as doing reading it after the match? Whatever the case, I sat back several days later and was grateful for the match and the book, as I genuinely believe that it made me a better umpire as well as a better person. Remember what I told you about the post-match ceremony, how I felt and what I was thinking as I left Trent Bridge? I was pretty low and ready to give it away. If someone had told me that in three months' time at the inaugural ICC Global Award I was to be presented with the David Shepherd Trophy for being the ICC Umpire of the Year, I would have told them to go see a psychiatrist. And that is precisely what happened.

Acknowledgement

A vital part of moving on from an error, a setback, or a failure is having the honesty to acknowledge it. This is not an umpiring skill, and like all the other skills covered in this book it is a transferrable life skill. Having the courage, internal or external, to be honest, and admit it is one of the first steps to being able to move on and bounce back by focusing on what comes next.

Acknowledgement often takes the heat and anger out of the situation faster. Let me give you an example. I've umpired India a lot in my time, a good side with some great people. They had an exciting opening batsman in their team by the name of Virender Sehwag who had an enormous talent for scoring quick runs and taking the game up to the opposition. One of Viru's normal fielding positions is at square leg, often close by where the striker's end umpire stands. In one match, I made what I thought was a close Not Out call, against an Indian bowler. The Indian team was not happy with the decision and at the time let me know it through their response. After calling 'over' and going to my position at square leg, Viru, who was standing close by, decided to encourage his team by calling out, 'Come on guys, let's get him out a second time'. He then repeated it, even louder, which was not necessary as I'm far from deaf. Now there are several ways I could have handled this, and did so, during my career, but perhaps the best technique I ever used was on this day, when I turned to Viru and simply said, 'OK Viru, I may have got that one wrong, but what can we do about it now? Am I going to listen to this chat all day, or are we going to move on and play cricket?' By acknowledging that I may have got the decision wrong, it took the wind out of Viru's sails and gave him nowhere to go next. It also told him that I got his message and that was that. I wanted him to move on, and I wanted to move on to, so being upfront and confronting the issue (and the person) allowed us both to move on faster. Following that, I think Virender and I grew in respect for each other, and today that continues off the field.

It is vital to acknowledge the error as it allows the door to learning to be opened, because if you don't acknowledge it, is there anything to learn from it in the first place? Denial or dishonesty is, therefore, one of the roadblocks of being open to learning opportunities. Putting your hand up and taking responsibility for falling short of the mark is a scarce commodity these days. The easy road is to say, 'I didn't do it', 'It's not my fault', 'It happened because of someone else', 'It's because of the lack of time given' – all these excuses are just that. While they may have had some impact, at the end of the day it comes down to you.

Ownership of the setback, the error, or the situation comes down to you. Take responsibility for what is working and what is not in your game. If we reflect on the role of setbacks in the learning process, the rational part of our brain should be welcoming these events rather than trying to suppress them or deny that they ever happened.

Release: Let it go

Following acknowledging the setback or negative outcome, it is really important to let it go. From my game example above, it was quite apparent that I held on to my errors and kept thinking about them and what impact that was going to have. Because I was holding on to the setbacks, my brain was stuck in the past, still thinking about the why and what impact it would have for my report or what others were going to think. When things are not going well, we get stuck.

Letting go of negative thoughts and events sounds easy, but it is not. I learnt this the hard way, and it is something that requires constant effort and practice. Here are two of my best tips and tools that worked for me to help move on faster from a setback:

1. *Write it down.* I kept a notebook on the field and would record the number and type of appeals. Now, these notes were brief, but allowed me to record the very basic information. For example, on any day I could tell you how many LBW appeals I had, and how many of those were correct and which ones required review later. The point is, writing it down at the time allowed me to park any issues and deal with them after I left the field.

    Writing things down means that the setback has been noted, you can move on to other more important things, like the next ball in my case, and focus. Writing also provides more clarity and objectivity when it comes to work through the setback. Writing detailed and specific self-assessments from each match provided me with an opportunity to download what worked, what didn't, and ideas for what I needed to work on for the next match. Another example of writing for clarity and moving on faster included a trends analysis file. I would maintain a spreadsheet of my errors (setbacks). Writing down all these events by match type, day, session number, and type of bowler/batsman provided perspective. I was able to look objectively at the issues and see if there were any trends in my setbacks and better identify learnings to be able to focus on how to address the one thing that I needed to do to improve this area.

Without writing all these things down, the emotion of the errors causes too much confusion and anxiety. Writing it down showed me objectively and rationally where I was going wrong, how many times, and where the commonality may have existed. It put the setbacks into perspective and reinforced the thinking that things are never as bad as they seem (mostly, in our head).

2. *Talk about it.* This is something I did better towards the end of my umpiring career. We now have far better people resources and skills in the game to do this than when I started out, but, for me, my style was to keep my errors and setbacks to myself and my coach. So, when I say talk about it, I mean share the setbacks more with the people around you, your team.

What does this look like? We often work in teams. How often does your team sit down and reflect on the days' or weeks' performance like a cricket match? We do a daily debrief on the days' play. Like most good processes, we sit in a group and reflect on what went well, what did not, and what we need to do better going forward. The modern umpires who are going places are very open, honest, and willing to share what did not go well (for them) in a group environment. Why is this important and helpful? It shows a professional approach to learning, a vulnerability that no one is perfect, that we all make mistakes, and offers an opportunity for others to provide input on the setback that may help us to move on faster. Sharing and talking about a setback in a safe environment is an excellent way of being able to let go and put the event behind us quicker.

Imprint: Visualise the right thing to do

See in your mind what you should have done or what you need to do. Visualise this and see yourself getting it right. Being positive and visualising the right outcome is the last step in bouncing back from a setback.

Visualising getting the task right helps building self-belief. It needs to be supported with positive self-talk. An example I used in this area was telling myself, 'I am a good umpire, I will umpire well, I am going to umpire well'. This can be applied to what you need to do next by repeating and imprinting the positive self-talk message:

> I am a good …
> I will …
> I am going to …

Whatever you are striving to do, you need to be able to see yourself there and believe that you can get there through visualisation and positive self-talk. This process will complement the hard work, focused effort, and skills development being done and setbacks encountered through the learning process on your journey to get there.

Acceptance

We all make mistakes and sometimes, like a batsman, the ball is just too good and you can be out for a duck on the very first ball. As an umpire, I really hated every mistake and found it hard to accept making it. The reality is, making mistakes is part of the job and you have to learn to accept this to minimise the impact that errors have on your mental state. This is a tough concept to get comfortable with since players, fans, commentators, coaches, and your own self expect you to get everything right and make no mistakes because that is your job. Whether it was umpiring fifth grade in Sydney or a Test match at Lords, the expectation of all those people was the same. And just on that point, umpiring is a funny pursuit, everyone seems to expect when you start your career or season that you are perfect and then as the season or career moves on, you get better! The reality is, fifth grade gets fifth-grade-standard umpires, and Test-match umpires make fewer mistakes. The way I was trained and taught was to treat every match as someone's Test match, and focus and strive as though it were my Test match too.

There is no doubt that I would get angry at myself for making a mistake – it was a setback for me. Getting angry with yourself is quite a normal emotional reaction for many of us. This shows that you care about something very much, but it is a sign of getting emotionally hijacked and losing control of your thoughts and focus. I needed to accept that these types of setbacks were part of the job and to get more rational in learning from them and moving on faster. This response was very difficult for me, as accepting something less than being accurate was just not acceptable. In my case, it was partly a process of accepting that we cannot be perfect, but we can be excellent.

The next time you suffer a setback, you make a mistake, or you get knocked back, try asking yourself, why? Where is the learning here? What could I do better to improve the outcome next time? Ask this in a way that is not very critical, but in a way that is supportive and constructive. This approach may be hard at first, but I guarantee it will be a step in the right direction for you.

Acceptance of the situation for what it is, or at least acknowledging the event will, at the very minimum, allow you to park the thoughts and move on to what comes next.

Bouncebackability is a skill, something that takes practice and perseverance in itself. It is something to be learnt and improved with trial and error as everyone handles it a little differently. Perhaps I can offer you a quote that might put this concept into perspective: 'The easy road gets harder, and the harder road gets easier.'

Giving up is the easy road. Anyone can do that. It takes no talent or effort. Nothing great was ever achieved without some setbacks along the way. You should never give up on what is important and, most of all, never give up on yourself. The hard road involves picking yourself up, reflecting on the process, learning from the experience, adapting and shifting what you are doing, putting in hard work, and having another try based on your new knowledge. The more you do this with the right attitude of 'failure is part of success' and mental toughness to accept and acknowledge setbacks, the easier the road to excellent outcomes will become.

Chapter summary points

- Bouncebackability is the skill of having a setback or failure and being able to regroup, refocus, and get back on track to face the next challenge.
- High performance requires mental toughness.
- Switching our focus up and down is better than switching off and on. We still need to be aware of what is going on around us at all times.
- To perform at our optimum, we need to be mentally in the present, not in the past or future.
- We need to talk to ourselves in a way that is supportive and positive and not beat ourselves up when things go wrong.
- We need to be self-aware when we start to talk to ourselves with negative thoughts. We need to replace negative thought with a positive one.
- Don't self-assess in competition or during the activity, just focus on what you have to do next.
- The four steps to moving on from a setback faster are:
  - Acknowledgement of the error or situation.
  - To release and let it go.
  - to visualise the right thing that should have happened.
  - Acceptance of the setback and your role in it.

- Bouncing back from setbacks is not easy and is a mental skill that requires practice and development.
- Setbacks are part of the pathway to success – never give up on the task and never give up on yourself.

15

DISCIPLINE IS THE DIFFERENCE

ONE OF THE REAL benefits of working within the field of the game at the highest level has been the ability to tap into some great successful people both on and off the field. Along with that, spending a lot of time on your own in hotel rooms, on airplanes, and waiting in queues can be spent reading and researching why others have been so good at their chosen profession.

From practical experience and from what has been learnt from others, I can offer you my take on the fundamental difference between success and failure, which will be revealed only at the end of this chapter. Before doing that, it is essential to outline the elements of what it takes to be successful in the first place. Success is something we all want, but not too many of us actually know how to get unstuck from our current habits and achieve it. So here is my personal formula or strategy to be successful at something of your choice.

Hard work

Nothing beats hard work! It is fundamental to being successful. What do we mean by hard work? For the job that I chose to take on at a very young age, it meant learning the fundamentals of cricket umpiring very quickly, practising them a lot, and doing them very well, consistently in every game. These fundamentals, that is, the basics that have been constructed by pure hard work are the very things that underpin your whole process, just like the foundations of a house.

When a performance or outcome is not up to mark, and I have a bad day or a bad game, it is the fundamentals or basics that I go back to. There is no substitute for hard work. You have to put in the time and effort to learn your trade and skills.

Hard work does not just apply to learning and developing the basics. It also applies to preparation and I'm very big on it. For me, preparation is king. Over the years this has been a cornerstone of not only my personal success at cricket umpiring, but it is common to successful outcomes and achievements of others as well. Preparation is all about Plan Bs and what ifs, and it takes considerable amount of hard work and time devoted to thinking about your strategy.

If you don't move, nothing happens! Doing nothing and standing still in today's world means going backwards. Hard work means spending less time talking about what you are going to do and actually doing it. You don't have to get it right to start with, you just have to make a start and then keep refining from your learnings. Successful people have a real bias towards action and doing things. They spend less time in front of the TV or sleeping and more time practising and trying new things. You must 'do', have a go, and put in the hard work and effort.

Innovate

One of the first books that I read when performance improvement mattered to me in my umpiring career was written by the successful rugby league coach, Wayne Bennett. One line that has stuck with me all the way through my Test career is, 'If you do what you've always done, you'll get what you've always got.' His words, not mine, but what a powerful thought.

Sure, I was a very young umpire when I started my representative career and there were many things going for me at the time, such as a youthful appearance, slimmer physique, good eyesight, and hearing, et cetera, but one thing that really helped take my umpiring to a higher level was the constant search to try new ways to get better. To innovate.

Throughout my career I have come across umpires from all over the world, who have been officiating particularly at a lower level, but thought they should be umpiring Test cricket. They genuinely believed they had the ability to officiate Test cricket. Some could have, but the real thing that was holding them back was their attitude not to try new things. They already thought they were good enough and so were closing their minds to opportunities to get better. You see, if you continue to do things the same way, day after day, week after week, you are going to get the same results and outcomes. You don't get what you want, you get what you deserve. It's no wonder then that frustration and a negative attitude starts to spiral and thus begins the blame game – you blame others or the system.

Why don't people want to try new ways of doing things? Perhaps because they don't want to make a mistake, fail, or they think they already know what the outcome is going to be. That negative mindset is a self-imposed barrier. The opposite may also be just as possible – you may end up making a breakthrough. One thing we know for sure though is that if you don't try (innovate), you will never know, and that is a worse outcome than making a mistake.

Here's a story to help illustrate the point. It comes from a Test match that I umpired with Billy Bowden in Zimbabwe back in November 2003, my first year on the Emirates Elite Panel of ICC Umpires. We were due to start day three early as we had lost time the previous evening, but that changed when the fourth umpire, 'Justice', came in as we were getting dressed and told us that a practice ball had gone under the roller while the curator was rolling the pitch. Ah well, we thought, and carried on with our preparations until Kevan Barbour, the third umpire, came in and said that we should go and have a look as it was a massive dent in the pitch, just short of a good length to a left-hander. We went to check, and he was right. This would be a huge problem for the West Indies who were batting and had no less than five left-handers in their side, including Brian Lara.

What were we going to do? We chatted with Robin Brown, the groundsman, and he had no ideas. We thought about filling the dent with a quick setting/drying cement or clay mixture, and someone (who shall remain anonymous) even suggested the possibility of abandoning the match. We involved Brian Lara, the batting captain, heavily. We were going to play, but the decision was to either leave this big hole or try and repair it, and if we chose the latter, how? Ray Price, who was playing for Zimbabwe, nephew to golfer Nick Price, came up with the idea of trying to cut the affected area out with a golf putting green device. We consented and off went the ground staff to the golf course behind the Harare Sports Club to get the required material.

We tested the process three times, taking out sods of the pitch, replacing them in other non-critical areas of the pitch, trialing the use of wet clay around the sod and extra grass clippings so that the ultimate 'cut and paste' would not only play well, but look good as well. The groundsman did an excellent job, even Brian Lara was impressed. We managed to get play underway two hours later, but had made Test history. Or so we thought.

During the day's play, the ball did not hit that spot once as the West Indies proceeded to score 6/240. We would not have had such a successful outcome if we did not open our minds to trying something new when faced with a unique problem. Innovation is all about having a positive mindset, a find-a-way approach, and true leadership and success are about taking people and problems to places no one has been before. You see, we don't know what our true performance potential is unless we try new things and push the boundaries of what is possible.

Take personal responsibility for what is not working

It is effortless as a cricket umpire to make excuses for mistakes or blame others for something that has not gone according to plan. It is often said the search for someone to blame is always successful. In today's cricket, four umpires look after an international match. The two on-field umpires have the primary responsibility for managing the game, but in reality every umpire has to do his or her job exceptionally well for the whole team to be successful. There is no team success when one umpire has a poor game. If one team member is not performing their role well, it is vital that the other umpires help them instead of blaming. Umpires are judged as a team and I've often heard comments like, 'The umpires did a good job today' or 'The umpiring in that game was poor'. People don't often single out one umpire for comment, they are seen as a group.

My preparation and performance default is if I see something that isn't right or needs attention, I speak up, take action, or address it. Taking personal responsibility for what is not working in your own game or your team is vital to being successful.

The face of international cricket changed on 3 March 2009 with the terrorist attack on the buses that were carrying the Sri Lankan cricket team members and match officials in Lahore. Going into that tour, the match officials were provided with certain assurances of safety and security provisions and resources. The events of that day have been well documented, and there is a complete chapter devoted to it in this book, but one of the takeaway lessons for me was to accept personal responsibility for what did not work. For subsequent tours, I took an active interest and role in understanding, requesting, and being satisfied with the security plans of those responsible. I have also taken an active role in reporting any failures in the delivery of those plans to appropriate people as it is also my safety and security at stake.

In my game, I take full responsibility for my performance on the day and try not to leave anything to chance. For me, it's about controlling the controllables wherever possible. My pre-game, pre-tour, pre-match preparation is stronger than most others and a lot of work is put into giving myself the best chance of getting the desired outcomes. That's what I call high percentage performance.

Sacrifice

Success comes at a price! One of the worst parts about the job of an international cricket umpire is the amount of time spent away from your family and friends. On average we are touring for 180 to 210 nights per year, often up to a couple of months away at a time. It is a heavy price to pay for what we do, and it is essential to remain focused and successful. It is imperative that you have made a commitment and are comfortable with what you are prepared to sacrifice.

To be good at something or to follow a passion or to serve others involves a commitment of your time. Why is this so important? Because time is your most precious non-renewable resource. Once you spend it, it is gone forever. Having umpired for nearly thirteen years at the international level, based on the averages listed above, I've been away from my family and friends for around the six years out of those thirteen, and that's not counting the training time and umpiring work when I have been in the same country as them. That's a significant time commitment and a considerable sacrifice, one that I was prepared to make at the time, and a topic of much and regular discussion with my wife.

To be successful, you need to commit time, energy, and other resources. It is critical to do the things you love and vice versa if you are going to devote time to it. Once you have made that decision to commit your time, you need to commit fully and ensure that there is a great return on that investment.

The other important thing to remember is that success is never achieved on your own. It involves the contribution and sacrifice of others around you – your family, friends, coaches, mentors, and workmates, to name a few. Most of these people do not charge you for their time and support! Other people often sacrifice a lot to help you get to where you want to be, and for me it is imperative that you acknowledge their contribution and share your successes with them. Success is empty unless you have other people to share it with. I look back with fond memories the first time I was lucky enough to be awarded the ICC Umpire of the Year trophy in London. Now, we don't umpire for awards or trophies, and it is definitely not the reason why I umpire, train, and spend so much time away from my family. That award was for all those around me who helped me get to that level. I wanted them to feel that they were special and deserved to share in the very public success of that recognition, that we were doing something right and worthwhile. So, following that award, we held a very modest celebration at our house where I was able to thank them all and appreciate their company and companionship personally. That night everyone got to hold the trophy and we took individual photos, and I sent them copies of the photographs with a personal note of thanks. Nothing big perhaps, but I hope the thought and effort showed these people how much I appreciated their support and sacrifice and how much they mean to me. Great moments, great memories, and a great feeling.

There is the personal sacrifice to be successful and sacrifice by those around you. Be committed and ensure you put something back into those around you who sacrifice with you. Celebrate success with your support team and reward yourself for great performances. What gets rewarded gets repeated. Time is our most precious non-renewable resource, make it count and do something positive and worthwhile with it.

Integrity

Successful people have integrity. They have a focus on just doing the right thing. In my game, there are a couple of people who stand out as people of integrity. One of those is Ranjan Madugalle, an ICC match referee and a former captain of the Sri Lankan cricket team. When we get tested with difficult situations like ball tampering, suspect bowling actions, breaches to security, and code of conduct, Ranjan has always done just the right thing for the game.

It is important to do the right thing for the right reasons. The right thing means being selfless. What would you expect a leader in a responsible position to do? To do the right thing of course. In my role as a cricket umpire, to be successful, it is vital to know and apply all the playing conditions and policies of the ICC in a fair and unbiased way. I cannot show favouritism and, above all, there must be consistency. This allows people in our game, players, and coaches especially to know where they stand. They know if they try to bend the rules, action will be taken. It is here that integrity means acting out what you say you are going to do, or what the Laws and playing conditions of the game say should be done.

Honesty is closely linked with integrity. You have to be honest with yourself. We would say 'fair dinkum' in Australia and be honest with others. When I go to training, prepare for a match or a series, or even as I walk off the field at the end of the day's play, I need to reflect and be honest with myself about the amount of effort. If I am not honest with myself, I am severely limiting my opportunity for self-improvement. It is important for me to identify what I did not do well, put my hand up and admit my mistakes to myself, and acknowledge that there is room for improvement. That is the right thing to do. Similarly, it is essential to be honest with those around you to be successful, to do the right thing and make responsible decisions in the best interests of the organisation, not yourself. Ranjan is someone who has always followed that. No one, not even I, can influence him to say or do something that is not right. We have a great relationship, I consider him one of my best friends, but when he assesses one of my matches as match referee, our friendship has no bearing on it. He assesses and marks with integrity. Why? Because if he does not, the value of his work and the value of the report becomes meaningless, to me as well as to the ICC. If he does not act with integrity, people will not trust him or his work. The value of his performance thus gets undermined and his role becomes untenable.

Passion

I'm passionate about cricket, umpiring in particular, helping others achieve great things, and my family. It means that I have an emotional investment in all of these things. When I commit, I commit fully and I really, really care about them. I love what I do, and I do what I love.

Those people who know me best know that when it comes to cricket umpiring, I'm almost thinking 24×7 (and working on it); it's part of me and I'm part of it. Cricket umpiring has almost been an obsession of mine for the past thirty years – how can I do this better, what can I do to improve, how can I add more value and help the third team?

Passion involves throwing yourself into the task or pursuit holistically. That meant getting involved within the NSW Cricket Umpires and Scorers Association more fully than just umpiring on a weekend. It meant joining the training committee, attending monthly meetings as a ritual, joining the board, being a vice president, and always looking for ways to help other members and the body itself. Over the past few years, it has meant working on the ICC Cricket Committee to represent the views of international umpires, being a member of the MCC Laws sub-committee to help frame the Laws and help umpires, and being a member of the ICC Elite Umpires' Executive and representing the needs of umpires with MOU negotiations, contracts, and training and support programmes. The passion has extended to making our side of the sport better for the current and future generations.

It's not a job, it's a way of life. Passion helps you go the extra mile. And when you go the extra mile, there is less traffic.

Learning from your mistakes

This is a classic component, but one that is often hard to work through when it happens because we don't often look at the bigger picture. We don't see the learning opportunity at the time and how a mistake or setback may actually be a good thing or an asset going forward.

Let me cite a prime but important example, which I have already discussed earlier. I received the 2004 ICC Umpire of the Year award the same year I had my worst Test match, the one between England and New Zealand at Trent Bridge, where I had made seven errors! By day three, my entire focus was just trying to get through a session without making a mistake. I didn't read any newspapers or watch any highlights (or lowlights), but I'm sure the commentary on my performance was not great. I had sat down with Darrell Hair, who knew my game better than anyone else back then, trying to work out where I was going wrong, but he had merely said I looked normal.

When the game was over – and gee was I glad it was over – John Bracewell's words of encouragement made me rethink what I wanted to do. And that's when Brad Gilbert's *Winning Ugly* came to my rescue. A book that encourages you to not beat yourself up when things didn't go according to plan. A must read for anyone who wants to improve their mindset skills.

I had a choice after that match, to give up or learn something from my mistakes and become better. It's pretty obvious what I chose now, but it was tough then. That match turned out to be one of the best things that could have happened to me personally and professionally. I learnt so much about myself and what it took to umpire test cricket. I learnt how to bounce back, how to think more positively about my performance, how to recover faster after a mistake, how to better prepare for a good game, and what to avoid.

It's alright to make a mistake, but not the same mistake twice. It sounds quite simple, but it is not easy to do. What would you say to a child if they were learning to ride a bike and they fell off? I suspect you would comfort and support them, be compassionate, and encourage to keep trying. What I have learnt from these setbacks is that I need to encourage myself by looking at the situation more rationally and not so emotionally. It is critical to ask yourself about the learning opportunity. This approach is part of something called mental toughness, having a growth mindset. Learning from mistakes takes rational thought, an ability to look at the bigger picture of what you are trying to achieve and not focusing on the emotion of the short term.

The other big key to learning from a mistake is *honesty*. As an umpire or a professional at the highest level in your chosen field, it takes a lot of courage to put your hand up, to look at the person in the mirror, and admit that you have fallen short of the mark, that you have done something wrong and have made a mistake. That level of courage is different depending on what the mistake is and the impact of it, however, it does not prevent you from being brutally honest with yourself. Many journalists have asked me over the years how I feel after making a mistake. I do feel terrible, hurt, and it's a dint to my pride, but the expectation is to get the next decision right and that is my focus. Being honest about what you have done and how to improve is vital. The whole process of improvement starts with honesty, and if you cannot get past first base here, there is no chance for learning and growth.

In our game, video replay doesn't lie. It's there for everyone to see. However, there are occasions where the replay is not conclusive, and we can live in shades of grey if we choose to. Deep down, every umpire knows whether they made the right decision for the right reasons and every umpire knows whether they performed well or otherwise. I suspect you do too about what you do, you just know. There is no value in trying to fool yourself and pretending that something did not happen, or that a mistake was not a mistake. There is no value or learning in blaming others or looking for excuses. The real value in the mistake comes from the learning opportunity, so grab it and use the experience as a positive one. You've paid the price with the mistake, get some return from it. Be brutal about what you do right and where you need to improve and then plan a course of action required to address the weaknesses. Be true to who you are and what you want to achieve. You may be able to mislead others, but you cannot deceive yourself, because you know the truth.

The best umpires and the most successful people are honest about their performance and work ethic. They learn from their mistakes and consider them a stepping stone to greatness. Having umpired nearly 350 international matches, on the field or in the TV hot seat, does not automatically mean that I've been a good umpire. All it means is that I've had an opportunity to make my fair share of mistakes and the longevity of years and matches should indicate that I've learnt from those mistakes and because the selectors have had faith in my ability to officiate them well. Mistakes are good, provided you are honest about them, treat them as a learning opportunity, and work hard to ensure you don't repeat them.

Emotional intelligence

Emotional intelligence (EI) is quite undervalued compared to intellectual intelligence (IQ) when it comes to being successful. One of the best learning experiences I had through my umpiring career was at an ICC match officials' seminar in Johannesburg back in 2007. Our umpires and referees manager, Mr Vintcent van der Bijl, asked a good friend of his, Dr David Crombie, to present his knowledge and expertise in the area of EI. As you can probably understand, when you have the 'best' cricket umpires in the world sitting in one room, and a university professor or scholar comes in to talk to you about peoples' emotions and feelings and how that relates to sport, there is a lot of scepticism for relevance. My training attitude was different from most of the other umpires, I had a thirst for knowledge and was always on the lookout for anything different that could help me get better. It is probably not surprising to find out then that I was the only Emirates Elite Panel umpire that finished David's training course. It was hard work, and it was hard to get your head around the concepts and topics (and I told David this), but it was worthwhile.

Why is EI important here? It was something that kick-started my work on mental toughness. Through his initial assessment, David showed me why I was not as capable in this area and he was able to show a correlation between successful cricket teams and sportspersons and their level of EI. Well, I was on board if having a high level of EI helps you become more successful! Being ranked as ICC's number one umpire, it was also interesting to note that my EI score at the time was the highest among the other umpires tested, but that did not satisfy me. I wanted my EI and the score to be higher and stronger. There was a lot of room for improvement. Thus, I accepted David's challenge. I am so grateful to Vince and David for the opportunity to work on this area, and there is no doubt that I feel I am a better and more successful person than before. Thanks guys. I do concede, though, it is still not the strongest part of who I am, and it is still a work in progress.

I do not plan to extol the nature and concepts of David's work further here – you can do an Internet search just as quickly – but I do want to cover how EI helped in the pursuit of excellence. Nearly all umpiring skills come from between the ears. Yes, there are some physical skills, but the majority of our game is mental. EI helps us to control our thoughts and emotions, not the other way round, so you have a better chance to perform freely, at your optimum, to your potential. For me, this is the best definition of mental toughness that I have come across. Being able to build stronger relationships, understand the emotions of others, be in control of your own emotions, all help you to be able to make better tactical and judgemental decisions.

In my game, we deal with frustrated players, coaches, and administrators from time to time. Frustration leads to anger, and anger reduces the ability to make good decisions. My job as an effective cricket umpire is to listen, empathise, and understand the issue and their point of view, at the same time controlling emotions and thoughts and responding with a good decision with integrity, an outcome that is reasonable and consistent. We cannot meet the aggression of another person with aggression, we cannot meet their frustration and anger with our frustration and anger. We have to remain calm and behave the way we would expect from the other person.

Be a good person

To be successful at no matter what you do, especially for a reasonable length of time, you need to be a good person. Sustained success is not possible unless you are a good person – you are who you are twenty-four hours of the day, seven days a week. Why is this quality so important? Because I believe that change always has to start with the person, not with the job performance or activity. If I want my umpiring performance to improve, I need to improve myself. If I want the outcome of what I do to improve, I first need to improve who I am. There is no finish line here to improving yourself, and it is always a work in progress. Please understand, I'm no expert on this topic, I have had my fair share of personal failings, but the desire and work ethic to be a better person is very strong. Even though my on-field international umpiring career has ceased, my work on being a better person has not. For me it's not about what you do, it's all about who you are.

When we look at the qualities of a great cricket umpire and even if you asked others what makes an excellent cricket umpire, I hope that these would be on the list: communication, teamwork, preparation, managing conflict, handling setbacks, mental toughness, fairness, consistency, confident body language, and decision-making. Apart from the last one (decision-making in the sense of declaring the Outs and the Not Outs), the others are not only umpiring skills, these are life skills. If you can develop and improve these in what you do *all* the time, you will enhance your umpiring at a faster rate as you take all the improvements into your next game. In the many workshops, seminars, and conventions that have been conducted, the focus has been

Discipline is the difference

on improving these qualities and skills, Monday to Friday, so that you can apply them when you umpire cricket on Saturday and Sunday.

One cricket umpire whom I learnt a lot from to become a good person is the late David Shepherd. Shep, as he was affectionately known, had been associated with the game for a very long time, first as a player and then as an umpire. Together with Steve Bucknor, Shep stood in more Cricket World Cup finals (five) than any umpire ever will. Not only was he one of the best umpires that we had the pleasure to work with, he was also one of the finest gentlemen. I first came across Shep when I was appointed as the third umpire in a Sydney Test in the late 1990s. The pinnacle came a few years later when we did a 2003 Cricket World Cup Super 6 match together in Johannesburg. Following that we officiated the first India versus Pakistan Test series in over fifteen years in Pakistan. Both pressure matches and series, but the way Shep carried himself and went about his job was superb. He had the ability to build strong relationships with everyone. He was approachable, empathetic, caring, strong (when he needed to be), funny, and wise, but above all very human. There is no doubt that the ICC appointed guys like Shep to the top games and series because they knew he had the respect of the players and that if anything seemed to be going wrong, he had the people skills and temperament to handle it.

As a cricket umpire, you are expected to get every decision right, that's what the players demand and expect. We all get them wrong from time to time, and Shep was not on his own in this regard. What I did notice was that because he was such a good person and earned respect within the game, when he did make the odd mistake, the propensity of players and others to forgive and forget was so much greater. Being a good person gave him some breathing space in his performance and allowed him to be more successful at what he chose to do. I happened to read an excellent quote the other day by Jonny Wilkinson, the former English rugby player, in his autobiography, a fax he received from his friend and guru, Steve Black: 'I've learned that people will forget what you said, people will forget what you did, but people will never forget how you made them feel. Make us all feel wonderful. We'll never forget.'

I don't know how many games Shep umpired, and I don't remember all the pieces of advice he gave me, but I do remember the way he made me feel and the confidence he gave me when I, the new kid on the block, umpired with him. A great umpire, but more importantly a great bloke and a special friend. I miss him greatly.

Look after your health

You cannot function if you are unwell and your performance will suffer. I often ask people how much time each week do they devote to looking after themselves and their health? The response from most is disheartening. We all have a tendency to not eat well or exercise to save time for other things that are 'supposedly' more important. What could be more important than looking after your health? Even during safety briefing on a plane they instruct us to first put on our own mask before helping others. Simple really, for us to be able to help others, *we* need to be in good shape first!

We all lead busy lives and it feels we just get busier. We all have the same twenty-four hours, the same seven days in a week, to get things done. Why are some people healthier than others? Pretty simple. The healthier ones have the courage and strength to make better choices and decisions with their time.

Life as an international cricket umpire is no different. We travel extensively, work, prepare, and have other family responsibilities. While I lived in the Sutherland Shire, Jock Campbell, the Cricket Australia team fitness coach, helped me with my fitness regime. He developed my cardio, strength, and flexibility programme and monitored my performance in these areas almost monthly. As the improvement followed, it became Cricket Australia and then ICC policy for umpires to do an annual fitness test, and some benchmarks were set. However, as I have mentioned repeatedly, fitness is not an umpiring skill, it's a life skill. Yes, I wanted to be a better umpire, but Jock helped me be a fitter, healthier person and the benefits flowed through to all aspects of my life.

Before cricket, I worked in the corporate industry as a production manager for a printing company that operated all through the day, six days a week. My working day started there around 5 a.m. and ended around 5 p.m. Where was I going to find the time to look after my health? One solution was to meet some workmates at 12.30 p.m. every day to jog around a local park, come back, shower, change, and have lunch. All in 30 minutes. There is time if you make time and make decisions consistent with what is important to you.

As travelling umpires, we are lucky to have gym facilities in most of the hotels we stay at now. The facilities are usually very good, but the gym is a useless room unless you go there and do something physical. The food choices are exactly the same. I have been lucky enough to tap into the resources of Cricket Australia and their dietician during my career, Simone Austin (now with the Hawthorn AFL club). She told me about all the bad things I was eating after I did a seven-day food diary for her. I'm a confessed chocoholic and love dairy and sweets. Following her advise, I had to make some tough decisions. I have stuck to some, also fallen off the wagon from time to time, but I gave up butter in sandwiches, stopped drinking soft drinks, and reduced my saturated fat intake. My health has improved and I feel better. Feeling better and putting in the extra work helps me to umpire and perform better in all areas of my life.

What about rest and recovery? When it comes to looking after your health, who thinks about this? Well, I do from the point of view of planning my rest periods and knowing how much sleep to get before a game. How do I know this? With the amount of time zone travel we do, I started to research how much recovery time was recommended and discovered that there is no right answer. Jock suggested a few things, but the one I liked the most was maintaining a performance diary. In that, one of the things I would do is keep a record of what time I would go to bed every night and what time I would wake up during a series. I could then track my on-field performance and the way it felt against how much sleep I got the night before. The outcome of this task was that I umpired at my best when I slept from 10 p.m. till 6 a.m. I was thus able to plan my sleeping patterns for better performance.

That worked for me, but everyone is different. Your health, eating well, exercising, rest, and recovery are important for the mind and body. We all know that. The real benefit comes when you do something about it and make it a priority in your life, and develop good daily habits around these areas. To be successful in anything you want to do, you need to be in good health and good shape – just ask anyone who is sick!

The difference between success and failure is discipline

Having given you my thoughts on what qualities and elements are required to be successful, I'm very sure that you could come up with some of your own that are equally or more important. Those elements we can happily debate on and discuss their merits. However, one thing that I firmly believe is critical to being successful and is always the difference between success and failure is *discipline*.

Without strong self-discipline to stick to your plans, to make decisions consistent with your goals, to do the right things all the time, to say 'no' to people and requests that distract you from your objectives, without that self-discipline, you will not be successful and be a leader in your chosen field. Nobody can make you do what you need to improve. Yes, we can use the 'stick' or the 'carrot' to provide either pain or pleasure to motivate you to do certain things, but it is you who has the power of choice.

If you are still unconvinced that that difference between success and failure is your self-discipline, then I offer you the following quote to reflect on: 'The price of discipline is always less than the pain of regret.'

In my role as a cricket umpire, we are judged primarily by the decisions, what we make or don't make. Some are more obvious than others. However, in each day's cricket we make hundreds, if not thousands, of decisions. Not just is the player Out or Not Out, but where did the foot land, where did the ball pitch, was that behaviour acceptable, which side should I move to, was that a wide, what did the ball hit, have we got time to bowl another over, is that six balls bowled, how should I handle this complaint … the list goes on. Off the cricket field, we make lots of decisions as well. Am I going to get up early and exercise, what will I eat for breakfast, what will I say to the kids before they go to school, what time will I get home, how will I deal with that problem, should I have a meeting after work … the list goes on. The fundamental point is if you make the right decisions every day that are consistent to what is important to your goals and objectives and apply the ten qualities that I have mentioned ahead, I guarantee you will be a successful leader in what you have chosen to do.

In summary:

> HarDwork
> Innovate
> Take responSibility for what is not working
> SaCrifice
> Integrity
> Passion
> Learn from mistakes
> Emotional Intelligence
> Good persoN
> Look after your hEalth

DISCIPLINE is the difference between success and failure.

16
USE BY DATE

MANY PEOPLE HAVE ASKED why I quit so young and so early. In this chapter, I'd like to cover the reasons why, but, more importantly, stress that everyone has a use-by date and should do things for the right reasons. Given that I left international cricket in 2012 at the age of forty-one, I can appreciate the question, an age when most umpires today are still aspiring to reach that level. Most people forget that I started umpiring at nineteen and had been officiating competitive cricket for over twenty-two years, thirteen of those in the international environment!

Life as an international umpire is challenging, demanding, and somewhat unique but similar to that of the international players. However, we do not have a 'home' season. All of the work is away from your country of birth, and you are forever following the summer of cricket, no matter where that is. Anywhere between 180 and 210 days on average are spent on the road, and as more T20 leagues establish the number continues to grow. World Cup years provide additional opportunities, meaning an extra seven weeks away, while the T20 world cup every two years or so requires a three-week commitment.

My decision to leave the Emirates Elite Panel of ICC Umpires did not happen overnight. The thought began as early as in 2009 when I was officiating the ICC T20 World Cup in England. That year I had many serious discussions with the then manager of umpires of ICC, Vince van der Bijl. Vince was a champion on the field as a fine bowler for South Africa and Middlesex, but, more importantly, a champion person and manager. We also had post-umpiring chats with him every year as part of my regular annual planning session with my coach, Russell Trotter. Russell and I planned goals pertinent to umpiring as well as those necessary to develop for life after umpiring, to remain in control of the future. Just like the corporate world, sport is a funny industry when it comes to job security. You never know what series or year might be your last, and I think it is essential to always have an exit strategy to deal with life thereafter.

Before becoming a State, Australian and ICC umpire, I was a production manager in the printing industry, where

I worked my way up from costing and estimating through production to then manage the day-to-day operations of the plant. I was lucky to have two very supportive managers who backed my umpiring career with personal encouragement and flexible annual leave. They also tried to impart many management and administration skills. There is no doubt administration, attention to detail, planning, and being organised are part of my default behavioural traits.

And so, given the work I did every year with my coach and the extracurricular work with the ICC in helping to prepare and present training material at officiating workshops, I was always thinking of life after, rather than when. My reasons for moving from umpiring can be basically put into two buckets, personal and professional.

My personal reasons were based around my wife Helen and our three children, Harry, our firstborn, our middle child, Jack, and Sophie, the youngest. Harry was born the year before I did my first Test, in 1999. Jack was born in 2001, and we were blessed with a girl in 2006. Having joined the ICC panel in 2003, by 2012, I had missed being with my children during their growing-up years. If you do the simple math, being on the road for over six months per year and ten years on the Emirates Elite Panel, I have easily spent five years away. By 2012, I felt I had missed the growing-up phase of my boys and I had a choice to keep going or stop and try not to miss all of Sophie's childhood years. I am fortunate to have such a supportive and understanding partner in Helen, and I felt it was important to move back home and be equal in the parental stakes and start to repay her for all my time away. Bringing up three kids and managing a house and daily life on your own is not easy, and I really take my hat off to her for what she did and how she sacrificed for the sake of my career.

Then there is the issue of a 'normal' life. I cannot remember how many birthdays, marriages, funerals, kids' sporting events, and special school moments I have missed. How do you put a price on these? The number of times that my schedule would be consulted before trying to set a date for a family event was unbelievable and somewhat uncomfortable as many others were always looking to plan their lives around mine. It just didn't seem right or fair to keep this pattern going.

There were then professional reasons and considerations. After spending over twenty-two years umpiring, I felt it was time to do something new, different, and exciting – a new challenge for my personal and professional development. Not that umpiring at the international level was not challenging or exciting, but I needed a change and a different focus from living out of a suitcase, watching a cricket ball with intense focus, dealing with performance scrutiny, often uneducated feedback, and putting your finger up at the right time. From a numbers perspective, I'd officiated 74 Test matches, 174 One Day internationals, 3 ICC World Cups, including one final, and several other ICC finals in other tournaments. If you included third and fourth umpire roles and T20 appointments, my career international matches would tally over 350 matches, but as I say to many, it's just a number. What is more important is the quality of the performance than the number of matches.

I have been lucky to officiate in every ICC full member country by the time I decided to pull stumps, and have seen the best and worst cricket grounds around the globe. I have seen the hottest and coldest places, met prime ministers, been shot at, seen great wonders of the world, all the while just umpiring the game of cricket. Very fortunate indeed.

Professionally, I had always been a hard, committed, and diligent trainer. My effort in physical and mental training was always very high, and I prided myself in searching for that extra edge. Each day not umpiring or travelling was all about consolidating the strengths and improving on the weaknesses. I remember watching a video that Brad Haddin did for one of his sponsors, Asics, around the importance of training and where it fitted into being able to perform at your best. I agreed with Brad when he said once he felt that training was a chore, a burden, and when he stopped enjoying it to become a better cricketer, it was time to give the game away.

In early 2012, I noticed my training and work rate was not what it used to be, and I could feel it. I'd seen other international umpires like Steve Bucknor and Rudi Koertzen achieve fantastic stats and milestones by umpiring over a hundred Test matches, and there is no doubt if I had hung around for a few more years, I too could have reached that number, if not more. Elite sport is not about numbers for me, it is about your pride, your game, and the standard of your performance. You have to want it, earn it, deliver it. Hanging around for a number was a selfish thing to do because the game of cricket owes me nothing. I owe it everything. I did not want to see the standard of my performance drop. There was no way I was going to offer the players, my colleagues, the fans, the game anything less than my best. We've all seen sportspeople and officials stay for that one extra season, that one extra year, and deliver well below the standards we had been accustomed to. On this front, I agree with what Shane Warne had said post retirement: 'I'd rather people ask me why did you, rather than make the comment why don't you.'

When I noticed a drop in my drive for training and search for improvement, I realised my best umpiring was behind me. If I felt I had become the best umpire that I possibly could, which is the ultimate goal, then isn't it mission accomplished?

So, with that I spoke to my family and coach and made the call. Following that, I made a few other phone calls, one to Darren Goodger, the executive officer of the NSW Umpires and Scorers Association, one to James Sutherland at Cricket Australia, and another to Vince van der Bijl at the ICC. All calls related the same messages, thanking them for the opportunities and support, and the appreciation the game had afforded me.

This personal story leads me to the critical message that we all have a use-by date within a workspace or field of endeavour, depending on the person or task. Whatever the case, the cause or work is more important than the individual doing it. If the person serving the cause is not performing at their best or at least striving to improve themselves as well as the result, the relationship is not sustainable.

I firmly believe in the philosophy of changing before you need to change, as when individual performance has slumped consistently, or the results make everyone take notice, it's too late and the time taken to implement action to return is too long. Knowing the right time to make the call and change before you need to change only happens when the person, their manager, or the coach knows their game very well. I believe that the best judge of someone's game or performance is themselves, with the caveat that they can be brutally honest with themselves along with being self-aware.

Given these, the first step is to ask the question of how it felt, what they thought, or what they think they should do next. From an outsider's perspective, you don't know what is going on in someone's mind and we need to ask the right question to allow the person who knows their game best to self-diagnose and discover the most appropriate solution.

At the start of my umpiring career I got involved with the training committee of the NSW Umpires and Scorers Association. I soon developed a passion for training and helping other umpires, and this continued to blossom with my on-field officiating career. I enjoy the challenge of going places where no one has been before and in the domain of cricket, officiating is somewhat the poor cousin, in terms of budget. It has got better in recent years, but over the first half of my career, management support and training resources for umpiring was not where it needed to be, and just like umpiring itself, there is always room for improvement in this space.

Given that there were no trainers, very few coaches, and minimal training resources, I always accepted the challenge to create my own. Often along with a few colleagues we would create videos, presentations, training activities, and assessment tasks to try and create a better learning environment. The more I did this work, particularly with Cricket Australia, the ICC, and the Board of Control for Cricket in India (BCCI), the better I became, the more it began to be received well, and the more I liked it. It started to give me more enjoyment than umpiring itself, and it became my natural progression and focus which helped me make the call on my retirement.

Do what you love and love what you do – it is more than just a nice platitude. It's about who you are, what you want to get up in the morning for, and how you want to make a difference. For me, I began to love something more than umpiring and felt I could make more of a difference and serve the game better off the field than on it. And so it was. In August 2012 that I called 'time' on my international umpiring career and accepted a new role with the ICC as the umpire performance and training manager. A role that I cherished with the support of Vince as my manager. Together we went about setting up and investing in a global structure of umpire coaching for existing and future international umpires.

I didn't stop umpiring entirely after that and went on to fulfil a role with the BCCI at the 2013 IPL tournament where I participated as an umpire, coach, and mentor to the Indian umpires for the event. It was one of my biggest challenges, given the reasons I left the international game, to officiate to a high standard and 'walk the talk' from the coaching and training room, and lead by example for one more high-profile series. The opportunity offered more lessons on what I needed to do to improve in the area of training. For example, I learnt we needed to change the way we provided training and experimented with learning-by-doing style. We got out of the classroom-type environment and constructed simulation examples for on-field decisions like bouncers, full tosses, and ball pitching outside leg stump for LBWs. We also developed more third umpire simulation-based training and recorded the sessions so that umpires could self-assess their development. It was a big step in the right direction and would not have happened without the commitment of people and support of the BCCI and the ICC. While it may seem insignificant to others, it was massive for us and our world.

Life is full of choices, some we make and some we don't, and some that are made for us. I could have hung around for another milestone, but that would have been selfish and something that ultimately would not have made me or my family happy. I was very fortunate to be in a position where I could make a choice and execute it. While some people thought I was leaving umpiring too early, I felt that I was not walking away from umpiring, rather I was offering it a more important and valuable contribution that I enjoyed more. The time was right for me to leave while I still had fuel in the tank and with my reputation intact.

There is no point staying on past your use-by date of being able to deliver your best and add value better than anyone else could. In my case, there was a very good umpire in Bruce Oxenford from Australia, who was knocking on the ICC Elite Panel door and had been for a couple of years. There was just no point in me blocking his elevation, especially when I could see that he wanted it more than I did.

From all of this, I hope you can see that there is never only one thing that determines your use-by date, it is a combination of factors that only you can take into consideration. While it has been an absolute honour to represent my country and the ICC on the international stage, I never took for granted the humility of being selected and the sense of responsibility for taking control of when I thought I had reached my use-by date.

Chapter summary points

- Everyone has a use-by date in their role or function.
- It's important to know who you are, what you want to do, and review your direction/purpose regularly. This is best done with your coach or mentor.
- It is best to consider both your personal and professional goals when deciding what to commit to and when to walk away.
- If you are not totally committed to the role or task, it is better to move on.

- If your commitment to training or preparation starts to drop off or not where it needs to be, it is a sign your use-by date is fast approaching.
- If the person serving the cause is not performing at their best or at least striving to improve themselves as well as the result, the relationship is not sustainable.
- Do what you love and love what you do.
- You have to want it, earn it, and deliver it. Be very clear about why you are doing what you are doing and be comfortable to pay the price for that commitment.
- It's about who you are, what you want to get up in the morning for, and how you want to make a difference.
- Leave with fuel in the tank and your reputation intact.
- There is no point staying on past your use-by date of being able to deliver your best and add value better than anyone else could.
- There is never only one thing that determines your use-by date, it is a combination of factors that only you can take into consideration.
- Never take for granted the humility of being selected and the sense of responsibility for taking control of when you think you have reached your use-by date.

17

ENJOY THE JOURNEY

IN THE MODERN PROFESSIONAL era, we are so focused on achieving the goals, hitting the key performance indicators, and getting the desired results that we don't pause to enjoy the moment and celebrate the small wins. I've seen this manifest over my career from having the time at the end of the game to share a drink and a chat with the opposition to changing flight timings if the match looks like finishing early to get home as soon as possible.

At times, I've been just as guilty and have often learnt the hard way that what gets rewarded gets repeated. It is the value of enjoyment that we need to keep consciously promoting and acting out. We need to acknowledge and celebrate every small performance to encourage enjoyment and sustainability of effort. We need to have some downtime with our team to enjoy each other's company and reconnect with what we are all about.

I suppose following the Lahore terrorist attack my mortality was brought back into sharper focus and I did slow down a little bit. I have always been very committed to my work and mission, I still am. However, some of the decisions – both career and life – that I've taken after 2009 have been to rebalance work, play, and family aspects. There is no doubt there is still room for improvement!

There is little point getting to the end of a work assignment, a job role, or a career and having only a piece of paper or bank balance to speak for it. Good memories and friendships, that cannot be measured, are equally important in justifying why we do what we do. Time is our most precious non-renewable resource, and you need to spend it wisely because once it is spent, you cannot get more. I would very strongly advocate combine the enjoyment and satisfaction of your role with how you spend the majority of our time. If you don't know it by now, I love the game of cricket, I love the third team (the match officials), and would serve both every day in some way, regardless of which organisation is putting money into my bank account, or not. Money is not the driver for me, it is essential, but the enjoyment of making a difference and improving the game or helping others get better is priceless.

Enjoy the journey

Happiness is not a destination either – it is a state of mind, a sense of being. We need to be happy in the present, in the moment, and not just at the finish line.

An important lesson learnt over my career is that it is not about the destination. High performance and excellence have no finish line. We are all a work in progress – we all do things very well at times, make mistakes, and continuously learn and grow. However, we all tend to put off opportunities around enjoying the journey. All work and no play is not a sustainable formula for high performance. It is a value and action we need to address at all times.

While I could probably recall and tell you about all of my mistakes and stuff-ups in and around umpiring, I can also share with you some of the most enjoyable moments, and they have all occurred with some special people around me. For instance, all the firsts stand out – my first One Day international, my first Test match, my first Sheffield Shield match. Most of those had my family, a few close friends, and colleagues around. Those who could be there sent messages of support and congratulations which I still have in my scrapbook today.

I fondly remember my first Cricket Australia national carnival in Melbourne, standing with some outstanding people from around the country. The experiences and friendships made at the NSW Umpires and Scorers annual conventions and listening to the 'wise owls' relate their war stories from years gone past. Umpiring every Saturday (and most Sundays) Sydney grade cricket and developing good friendships with the volunteers out at Bankstown Oval (Brian Freedman and his late wife, Rosie), the tremendous afternoon teas at Balmain (now the Sydney Cricket Club), the wonderful scorers, and friendly faces seen at the end of day's play. The camaraderie of all the fellow umpires, scorers, club volunteers, groundsman, and administrators has been and continues to be a real joy. It is my second family and for that I'm very grateful.

I've had dogs, worm infestations, cats, chickens, and streakers interrupt my matches. One such funny moment occurred in a One Day international match in Brisbane between Australia and India. I was at the bowler's end with Sreesanth running into bowl to Matthew Hayden when Matthew suddenly pulled away. I heard the crowd start to roar for no apparent reason. I turned around to see a male streaker running towards me. I guessed he was heading for the stumps, so I thought I'd give him plenty of room as he was being chased by several security personnel. As he ducked and weaved, leaving his chasers more and more embarrassed, the crowd grew more excited and the Indian fielders watched on. As he approached the bowler's end stumps, he didn't factor in Andrew Symonds's dim view of having his innings

Enjoy the journey

interrupted. Symmo wanted to teach this pitch invader a lesson. As the streaker tried to get around Symmo for the stumps, Symmo dropped the shoulder and put the young man flat on his back with an effortless and stern shoulder block. The crowd, the players, and the commentary box couldn't contain their laughter. I went up to Andrew after the hit and reminded him that probably wasn't the right thing to do, but I also told him it was one of the best hits I'd seen on the Gabba (also known as an Australian Football ground – AFL). Check out the clip on *YouTube* if you can! I still remember the sound of the bodies colliding. Just brilliant to be so close to this event.

Many people think that travelling around the world umpiring is glamorous and exciting. Parts of it are, but there are many aspects, like catching flights at 3 a.m., living out of a suitcase, and spending Christmas away from your family, that are not. This is why we need to focus on enjoying the journey and either creating or accepting opportunities to share a few laughs, experience something new, or build a friendship. Seeing other countries is great. There is no point going to another country and only seeing the airport, hotel, and ground. I value the enjoyment of seeing the game parks in South Africa, the natural beauty of New Zealand, the tea country of Sri Lanka, the Taj Mahal and bazaars of India, the hills of Murree in Pakistan, the beaches and lifestyle of the Caribbean, walking with the lions in Zimbabwe, and the many famous tourist spots in the UK.

What made some of those places even more special was sharing them with my colleagues or my family. Taking my wife and kids to Dubai, England, the Caribbean, and Sri Lanka was very special and rewarding, and I hope they benefited from experiencing things that others may not have a chance to. When I was asked to deliver the thirteenth MCC Spirit of Cricket Lecture, in memory of Lord Cowdrey, I was particularly pleased to be able to share it with Helen. It was an honour and a proud moment for me, my family, the local umpiring association, and the umpiring world.

Success and special moments are not that enjoyable if you don't have anyone to share that moment with. The ICC awards in 2005 was even more special because it was held in Sydney, and Helen was able to attend. Having both families represented there on the night made the journey so much more cherished.

Enjoying the journey also means taking time regularly to sit back and reflect on how lucky you are and being grateful for the opportunities you have had. While on field, I don't get emotionally involved in what the players are doing – whether they are winning, losing, or creating records. However, occasionally I reflect on the sense of privilege of having being part of the history of the game. Yuvraj Singh hitting six sixes in an over in the ICC World T20 at Kingsmead, Durban in 2007. Batsman like Virender Sehwag, Chris Gayle, and Younis Khan scoring triple centuries in front of me. Irfan Pathan taking a test match hat-trick in the first over of match in Karachi. Witnessing M. S. Dhoni score the winning runs for India at the 2011 ICC World Cup final and fighting our way through the crowds to get back to the hotel.

One such tour and event that I really could mix business with pleasure was the 2015 Warne/Tendulkar Cricket All-Stars exhibition T20 cricket series in the USA. Marais Erasmus and Steve Davis joined me to umpire three T20s in New York, Houston, and Los Angeles with thirty living legends of the game. The greats included Sachin Tendulkar, Shane Warne, Ricky Ponting, Brian Lara, Kumar Sangakkara, Mahela Jayawardene, Curtly Ambrose, Courtney Walsh, Shaun Pollock, Matthew Hayden, Daniel Vettori, and the list goes on. Being able to officiate in a more relaxed exhibition style environment and connect with these greats of the game on the bus or at the functions was most enjoyable.

I really enjoyed working and touring with the ICC match referees and some of the more light-hearted moments we would have in the third umpires' box. Having to spend over thirty hours in a week sitting next to someone, you need to find a way to have some fun through all the pressure and work. I'm not at liberty to share some examples here, respecting the confidentiality of the room, but we would find a way during the match and in between games to laugh at ourselves or our golf game or over a meal. Jeff Crowe, Ranjan Madugalle, David Boon, Andy Pycroft, Javagal Srinath, Chris Broad, Alan Hurst, Clive Lloyd, Gundappa Viswanath, and Mike Procter, all had a humorous side to them and provided many enjoyable moments on tour as leaders of the team.

The chapter 'Seven Traits of a Top Team' lists the values of the code of the ICC match officials' team. One of those is enjoyment. We value enjoyment as something that needs to be lived through action. When I was part of that team each year we would pick one value to focus on, and it is was one of the first to be selected by the team. While I'm not advocating a party every week or to increase the entertainment budget exponentially, one thing I want you to think more carefully about with your career and work is to ensure you are looking for and accepting more opportunities to enjoy the journey. Life is short.

Chapter summary points
- Enjoyment should be more of a focus when it comes to performance.

- We must pause to enjoy the moment and celebrate the small wins.
- We need to acknowledge and celebrate even the small but significant performances, achievements, and milestones to encourage enjoyment and sustainability of effort.
- We need to look for ways to enjoy each other's company.
- Time is our most precious non-renewable resource, and you need to spend it wisely because once spent, you cannot get more. Do what you love and love what you do.
- Happiness is not a destination, it is a state of mind.
- We are all a work in progress, enjoy the journey.
- All work and no play is not a sustainable formula for high performance.
- Success and special moments are not that enjoyable if you don't have anyone to share that it with.
- Enjoying the journey also means taking the time regularly to sit back and reflect on how lucky you are and being grateful for the opportunities you have. Gratefulness is the pathway to happiness.
- Life is short, enjoy the journey.

ACKNOWLEDGEMENTS

THIS JOURNEY WOULD NOT have been possible without so many others. Every person I've come in contact with has helped me in some way. Some have told me what to do, some have shown me what to do, while some have shown me what not to do.

This book is a compilation of learnings and experiences made with and for other people.

I am grateful to all my family, in particular my wife Helen and my children Harry, Jack, and Sophie for their support and sacrifice of having me away from home so much. I dearly hope that you are proud of the achievements and this book. To my immediate family members, my mother Ella, brother Chris, his wife Mamiko, auntie Yolanda, and

Acknowledgements

uncle John – you have been there for me and the kids more than you know.

Thanks to every member of the third team I have ever officiated with. Every scorer and umpire has had an impact on my game and my journey. There are too many to single out, but I became a better umpire because of your support and feedback.

Thanks to the volunteers, staff, umpires, and scorers at the NSW Cricket Umpires and Scorers Association – your camaraderie, generosity, opportunities, and knowledge have given me such a wonderful insight into myself and the great game of cricket. May the Association continue to grow and serve future generations of cricket umpires and scorers.

To the staff at Cricket Australia and the ICC, this book was not possible without all your tireless work behind the scenes. Everyone in these organisations has put in so many hours so that we can be on the field and enjoy the journey. Thank you one and all.

To my bosses, mentors, and coaches – Bob Evans, Mike Webb, Vince van der Bijl, David Richardson, Sean Cary, Sean Easey, Geoff Allardice, Chris Kelly, Doug Cowie, Alan Marshall, Ted Wykes, Dick French, Darrell Hair, Arthur Watson, Ian Thomas, Peter Hughes, Darren Goodger, Simone Austin, Jock Campbell, Rob Pedersen, and Russell

Trotter – the career and achievements were not possible without your guidance and wise counsel. Russell has been an anchor for me in the rough seas of life and every one of you has given me more than you will ever realise.

Thank you to the many people who helped me write this book. My friends and colleagues – Owen Zupp, Ben Holmer, Rik Rushton, Arthur and Ruth Kelleher, Peter Hughes, Arthur Watson, David Budge, John Warn, Darren Goodger, and Russell Trotter.

To my fast bowling partner and mate David Budge, who dragged me along to that first umpires' course all those years ago and gave me such a hard time at Barry Knight's Indoor Cricket Centre – you are a legend.

To everyone whom I have worked with so far, on and off the field, you have all played a part in my development in some way.

Thank you sincerely and God bless.

www.ingramcontent.com/pod-product-compliance
Ingram Content Group UK Ltd.
Pitfield, Milton Keynes, MK11 3LW, UK
UKHW041300180426
11947UKWH00009B/582